DIVINE ANIMAL

DIVINE ANIMAL

A Novel

Scott Russell Sanders

[signature: Scott R. Sanders]

Earth Works Publishing
Bloomington & Indiana
2014

Divine Animal
copyright © 2014 by Scott Russell Sanders
All rights reserved.

Printed and bound in the United States of America.
First edition

EARTH WORKS PUBLISHING
1113 East Wylie Street
Bloomington, Indiana & 47401-5083
www.scottrussellsanders.com

ISBN: 978-0-9913102-2-7

Library of Congress Cataloging-in-Publication Data

Sanders, Scott R. (Scott Russell), 1945 –
    Divine animal : a novel / Scott Russell Sanders. -- First edition.
        pages   cm
ISBN 978-0-9913102-2-7 (alk. paper)
I. Title.
PS3569.A5137D57   2014
813'.54--dc23

                                        2013049518

Book design by David Wiesenberg: *www.woosterbook.com*
Cover design by Ruth Sanders
Cover photograph by Peter Forbes: *www.peterforbes.org*

A story of healing, for the grandchildren:

Elizabeth Rachel Allen
Margaret Lys Allen
Anna Katharine Sanders
Claire Ruth Sanders
Benjamin Russell Sanders

As the traveller who has lost his way throws his reins on his horse's neck and trusts to the instinct of the animal to find his road, so must we do with the divine animal who carries us through this world.

—Ralph Waldo Emerson

DIVINE ANIMAL

Chapter One • August 2007

HARLAN

A S HARLAN EMERGED FROM THE WOODS, where he had searched all afternoon for a black bear that might have existed only in his dreams, he paused in the high pasture and gazed into the airy gulf of the Mad River Valley. In all that expanse of drifting clouds, blowing grasses, grazing sheep, circling hawks, and green mountains receding away ridge beyond ridge, his eye caught on a moving speck down between the farmhouse and barn, a speck he recognized, even from this distance, as the Swedish girl rising from the pond in a long white shirt. He watched her intently, wishing he possessed the hawk's acute vision. The girl bent over to wring out the tail of her shirt, shook out her tumble of damp hair, and then crossed the lawn toward the farmhouse with the languid, upright gait that reminded him of a browsing deer. Only when she disappeared into the house did he realize that he had been holding his breath.

Her name was Katarina, and Harlan thought of her as a girl in the same way he still thought of himself as a boy, even though both of them were nineteen, old enough to vote or fight in a war. With the sun dipping toward Black Bear Mountain, she would be going inside to heat water on the woodstove for soaking the widow's feet. Mrs. Winfield, the widow, complained that she never could get warm here in Vermont, not even now in the dog days of August.

Remembering that he had not filled the wood box before going in search of the bear, Harlan hustled down the mountainside along the mowed path, at the loping, headlong pace that used to make Mr. Winfield laugh.

The old man had once compared Harlan to a spring lamb, leaping about, and himself to a three-legged ram, gimping along. "Kick up your heels while you can, my boy," Mr. Winfield liked to say, "before gravity catches up with you."

Recalling this raspy voice, silent now for half a year, Harlan missed the old man keenly. If Mr. Winfield were alive, he would have chided Harlan for neglecting to fill the wood box until Sunday. All chores except milking were to be avoided on the Sabbath. Although Mr. Winfield had refused to attend church since feuding with the Lutheran pastor, he believed in keeping the Sabbath holy, which meant resting both man and beast. Even if rain threatened to ruin a crop of hay, which lay cut and windrowed in the field, he would not bale it on a Sunday. In spite of Mr. Winfield's death, Harlan still felt free only on the Sabbath to lay down his tools and explore the countryside beyond the four hundred acres of the farm.

Nearing the farmstead, he noticed the white shirt fluttering on the clothesline. It was a man's dress shirt, long enough to reach midway down Katarina's thighs. He knew she wore it to sleep in, for several times at night, glancing from his room above the workshop, he had seen her as she passed a lit window in the farmhouse on some errand. Had she bought the shirt, or had some man given it to her? If he pressed it to his face, would it smell of Katarina, or of the murky pond? Trembling there in the wind, it was as lovely to Harlan, and as mysterious, as the Queen Anne's lace swaying on long stems in the ditch.

At the woodshed he filled his arms with split maple, which would make a good hot fire and leave scant ashes. He carried this load inside, inhaling the syrupy smell of the wood, and laid each stick quietly into the box beside the kitchen stove where the tub of water was beginning to steam. Then he went outside for another load. When he returned, and knelt to stir up the fire, he could hear from the parlor the widow's quavery lament: "It was never so chilly in the old country." This was a recurring complaint, although Harlan found it hard to believe that Vermont was any colder than Finland, where Mrs. Winfield had been born. Then he heard Katarina responding in her musical voice, which had a bounce to it that he supposed must have come from her native tongue. She had told Harlan that English was her fourth language, after Swedish and Finnish and German, yet what came out of her mouth sounded better to him than anything that ever came out of his own.

He was kneeling on the kitchen's worn linoleum when Katarina came in to fetch the tub of water. "Here," he said, rising, "I'll carry it for you."

"You think I cannot lift it?" she asked.

"No," he said, baffled as usual. "I just thought I'd spare your back."

"You forget I am not soft like your American girls." She dipped a hand into the water to judge the temperature, her slender arm as graceful as a heron's neck.

"Sorry."

"Ah, well, to save you from sorrow, I will accept your help." She gave him a wry smile that he had seen many times before but could never decipher.

Bearing the washtub, careful to keep the water from sloshing over the rim, Harlan followed Katarina into the parlor, where the widow sat in a lamp-lit recliner with a tabby cat draped across her shoulders and a snarl of knitting in her lap. The needles had been put away, lest she hurt herself, but the tangle of yarn seemed to comfort her.

"Oh, Mr. Winfield," she said, beaming up at Harlan, "I've missed you so."

Katarina smoothed a palm over the old woman's thinning white hair. "It's Harlan, mum, bringing the bath to warm your feet."

A stricken look came over the widow's face. "Is Mr. Winfield ill?"

"No, mum. Not at all. He's only out milking the cows."

The widow accepted the lie, for she kept forgetting that her husband had died. "Oh, yes," she said, "he never neglects the cows." Frowning, she pointed a tremulous finger. "And who do you say this is?"

"It's Harlan. You remember Harlan. He minds the farm."

Mrs. Winfield whispered hoarsely to Katarina, "Is he honest?"

"Honest as the day is long, mum."

Harlan set the washtub in front of the recliner and backed away. He watched as Katarina removed the slippers and socks and rubbed the old woman's gnarled feet, placing each in turn into the steaming tub. No matter how many times he had witnessed this nightly ritual, it still made his throat draw tight.

"Is it evening?" Mrs. Winfield asked.

"It is indeed," said Katarina. "Time for your supper."

Without being asked, Harlan fetched a plate of food from the warming oven above the stove, along with a napkin, bib, and spoon, and he set them out on the pie-crust table beside the old woman's chair. He could see in her milky, unfocused eyes that she had already lost his name, but she smiled at him and said, "Ah, here's that sweet man again. Isn't he a sweet man?"

Without answering, Katarina tied the bib around Mrs. Winfield's neck, then mashed up the beans and potatoes and stewed mutton with the spoon, and began feeding her tiny bites.

Harlan lingered outside the parlor door, listening, as the widow gabbled nonsense, half of it in Finnish, and Katarina patiently answered. After a spell, as if having pondered the question, Katarina said, "Yes, mum, he is a sweet man."

★

Mr. Winfield had told Harlan of seeing bears on the farm in years past, before the forested slopes of nearby mountains had been gouged to make way for ski runs and condominiums. "Usually at dawn or dusk," the old man said, "slouching away with a bellyful of our apples or blueberries." In the spring, a sow bear and her cubs; in high summer, the yearlings foraging on their own; in the fall, burly males that broke limbs in the orchard while pawing for fruit. During his three years on the farm, Harlan had found apple seeds in piles of scat, claw marks on the smooth, gray bark of beech trees, and tufts of midnight hair on barbed-wire fences, but had never glimpsed the animals that left these signs.

The name of Black Bear Mountain, discovered on a map in the Cleveland Public Library, had given Harlan a destination to aim for. He had set out the day after finishing his junior year in high school, near the end of June, and it took him a week to reach that spot on the map, for few drivers even glanced at him as they roared past. Maybe they figured he was a homeless vet, with his Army duffel bag, his mane of coarse black hair, and whiskery jaw. Maybe he looked too hungry. His money had run out after five days, so he was indeed hungry, but for more than grub. He couldn't have said what else he wanted, except to get away, to go somewhere green, to start over. The last of his rides, a truck hauling piney saw logs, dropped him in front of a grocery store at the base of the mountain. He asked in the store if they needed help; the manager said no, they weren't hiring, but gave him two pears. Harlan accepted them with thanks and walked back outside.

Sitting on his duffel bag, he slowly ate the pears, every morsel except stems and seeds, while he studied the mountain. Instead of the soaring peak he had imagined, it was a humpbacked ridge, covered in trees as dense as fur, except for some cleared fields and a cluster of buildings midway up the slope. Climbing it would require no scrambling over scree, no inching along cliffs, no gasping for breath in thin air. Had he come all this way only to stroll up a hill? He almost decided to stick out his thumb and keep traveling until he came to a place that was truly wild. Instead, he peered at that clearing on the mountainside, with its huddle of barn and house and sheds, their metal roofs glinting in the sun. The farm looked so hidden away, so peaceful and safe, as different as could be from the place he had left. With the taste of pears on his tongue, hungrier than ever, he stood, shouldered his bag, and started up the winding mountain road.

He was just breaking a sweat when he rounded a curve and saw a wooden sign announcing Black Bear Farm. Smaller signs dangled below the large one, advertising fresh eggs and cream, blueberries, honey, and lamb. The list made his belly grumble. He turned up the rutted gravel drive, passed the open bay of a workshop, and came to a weathered house whose white clapboard siding badly needed paint. A giant cottonwood shaded the front yard, the largest tree of any sort he had ever seen; from a lower branch hung a rope swing with a plank for a seat. On the porch, which ran the length of the house, a pair of rocking chairs rested side by side, each with a turned-up length of log for a footstool.

A man, bent over and limping slightly, was just emerging from a doorway onto the porch as Harlan neared the steps. When the man stepped into the sunlight, Harlan could see he was well up in years, and he looked as though he had lost a lot of weight, the way the straps of his overalls drooped over bony shoulders, the way shadows hollowed his cheeks. The old man asked Harlan in a crisp Yankee accent if he was looking for eggs, and Harlan answered that he was looking for work. The man sized him up slowly, then said he could use a hand, all right, but couldn't afford to pay for help. Couldn't hardly pay the light bill, the way prices kept going up for everything except what a farmer raised. Harlan said he would work for room and board.

"You aren't from around here?" the man asked.

"No, sir."

"How old are you?"

Harlan considered adding a couple of years, but he told the truth. "Sixteen."

"You a runaway?"

"I'm on my own," Harlan answered carefully.

The old man looked him over once again, head to heels, then gave a sharp nod of his chin, pointed to a window on the second floor of the workshop, told him to put his bag up there, wash off the dust of the road with a dip in the pond, and then come inside where Mrs. Winfield could start easing the hunger out of his face.

*

Had Katarina been living at Black Bear Farm when Harlan arrived, he might not have stayed. For girls were among the confusions he had sought to leave behind. He was afraid of the desire they stirred in him, afraid of the damage he might do. He could not imagine sex without imagining babies. Although his grandparents had never said a word to him on the subject, he knew from health class, and from the misadventures of several high school friends, that the only sure way of preventing babies was to keep your prick in your pants. And the only sure way of doing that, he realized after a few close calls, was to keep his hands off those tempting curves. So the stronger his desire, the warier he became.

But there was no Swedish au pair girl on the farm when he arrived, only Mr. and Mrs. Winfield. The elderly couple asked him where he was from, who his people were, whether he had finished school, whether he was in some kind of trouble. He answered without lying, but also without revealing much. He had come from Cleveland, where his only relatives were his grandparents, who would be relieved to have him out of their hair. He had one year of high school to go, which he could finish through the mail. As for trouble, he assured the Winfields he wasn't running from the law, but he didn't say—couldn't have said—what he was fleeing, or what he was seeking. Eventually, with what he took to be New England politeness, they quit probing.

The hunger soon vanished from Harlan's face, for Mrs. Winfield fixed hearty meals, as if still cooking for the two sons who had long since grown up and left the Mad River Valley. The older son, Harlan would learn, had gone to Middlebury on a scholarship, then to business school in Philadelphia, then to a job high in a Boston office tower, where he bought and sold millions of dollars worth of stock every day. The younger son had studied agriculture at the University of Vermont, leading Mr. and Mrs. Winfield to hope that he might eventually come back home and take over the farm, but instead he had moved to Arizona, where he ran a golf cart franchise. The two sons sent photos and checks, but rarely visited. Once, and once only, Mr. and Mrs. Winfield had flown to Phoenix, and several times they had driven to Boston for holidays, but they didn't know what to do with themselves in their sons' big houses, where all the work was done by servants or machines, and where the grandchildren locked themselves away in bedrooms to stare at screens or fiddle with electronic gizmos.

"You'd think our boys had been raised on a space ship instead of a farm," Mr. Winfield remarked.

*

Within a month of Harlan's arrival, Mr. Winfield began paying him a wage, with money sent by those absent sons. Harlan worked from daylight until dark, doing what the old man no longer had the strength to do. His own strength now seemed to have a purpose. He was clumsy at first, needing to be taught everything—how to swing a hammer from the shoulder rather than the elbow, how to chop weeds in the garden without uprooting the corn or beans, how to start a balky motor, how to bush hog a field, how to dig a posthole in rocky soil, how to milk a cow.

The ponderous, black-and-white Holsteins were impatient with him, stomping their hooves and withholding their milk as he pulled at their teats. But Mr. Winfield merely observed, "Nobody gets it right the first few tries."

That became the old man's refrain, often delivered from a seat on an upturned bucket, as he taught Harlan one skill after another. The only other man who had ever tried teaching Harlan how to do something physical—as opposed to the mental feats in school—was his grandfather, whose quick temper, especially after a few drinks, usually put a bitter end to the lesson.

Mr. Winfield did grow sharp with him once in those early weeks. Harlan was mowing the high pasture one afternoon as thunderclouds rolled in from the west. Pushing to finish before the rain let loose, he gunned the motor while crossing a steep grade, and suddenly the front wheels jounced over a stone outcrop hidden in the grass, making the tractor swerve and tip sideways, and he leapt from the seat, landing inches beyond where one of the huge cleated tires slammed into the ground. He lay there panting, with a metallic taste in his mouth that he would ever after associate with death.

From down in the farmyard, Mr. Winfield had seen the leap, heard the engine clatter to a stop. He hobbled up the slope to find Harlan sitting in the clover, shamefaced but unharmed.

"You think you're driving a hotrod?" the old man scolded. "There's folks been killed in this valley doing things not half so stupid. If you ever rush like that again, on the tractor or anywhere else on this farm, I'll send you packing."

That near disaster aside, Mr. Winfield seemed more amused than upset when Harlan acted like the greenhorn he was—letting the chickens out of their coop, spilling a can of paint, breaking the handle on a shovel, or making other foolish mistakes. The incident with the shovel prompted Mr. Winfield to say, "Son, there's nothing wrong with feeling your oats, but don't ruin your back. It's got to last you a long while. And next time you move a boulder, use a pry bar."

Harlan rarely made the same mistake twice. He had never wanted to learn anything as much as he wanted to learn how to build things, fix things, grow food, and care for animals. Surely his brain and hands ought to be good for something besides adding numbers or tapping a keyboard, which seemed to be all that school was preparing him to do.

Eventually, the cows accepted his touch and let down their milk, the llama guarding the sheep let him approach the herd without challenge, and Mr. Winfield let him use the chain saw to cut up fallen trees. Guided by the old man, he learned how to set fence posts and pull wire, how to roof with shingles and steel, how to hold a squirming sheep and shear the fleece without drawing blood, how to tune the engine on the thirty-year-old John Deere, how to bale hay and stack it in the barn, how to shore up a crumbling stone wall, how to butcher a lamb or a hog.

When not tending the fields or livestock, Harlan painted every building on the place, beginning with a coat of red oxide on the barn and a coat of white on the farmhouse. He plugged a leak in the dam that held the pond, strung an electric fence around the blueberry patch, transplanted ferns from the woods into Mrs. Winfield's flowerbeds, and repainted the signs out by the road that had lured him up the rutted drive. He smoothed out those ruts by spreading a fresh load of gravel with the scraper blade on the tractor. As the months passed, his palms callused over and his lanky frame filled out.

He considered it a blessing to work so much outside. Even on the shore of Lake Erie, he had never been so aware of the sky. Mountains encircled the farm like the rim of a green bowl, meeting everywhere the blue bowl of sky arching overhead. Clouds fluffed and streamed across this immensity day and night, lit up by sun or moon. Occasionally the sky would be swept clear for hours at a stretch. More often, clouds would clamp down a lid stretching from horizon to horizon, yet even on such days the sky seethed, rippling with mottled grays and purples and every shade of white, as if the air were the surface of the sea. He did not see how a person could ever grow bored in the presence of such a show.

All of these grand weathers were mirrored in the pond—sun and clouds by day, moon and stars by night. The coming of Katarina would eventually make the pond a holy place in Harlan's mind, but he had found it exhilarating from his first plunge, when he'd washed off the grime from seven days of hitchhiking. Now, when he went to bathe at the end of a day's work, he dropped his sweaty clothes on the bank and paused there long enough to reassure the frogs and to watch dragonflies dart and swallows glide over the water. After the frogs resumed their croaking, he quieted them again by diving into the shimmering pool. On nights when the sky was clear and the wind calm, stars glittered on the surface, and ripples from his dive churned the pinpricks of light into a sheen of quicksilver. Regardless of time or weather, the cattails and ferns and muck gave off a swampy odor that he drew in hungrily, as if it were the breath of the earth.

He ended his swim by climbing onto a rock ledge that jutted from the bank where a pipe fed water into the pond. He would sit there and rub the mud from between his toes and let the air dry his skin. Now and again he bent down to take a drink from the pipe, which tapped a spring farther up the mountainside. Harlan had read somewhere that a person's body is sixty percent water, all of which gets replaced every seven days, so he figured that the muscle he'd added since hiring on with the Winfields was made up mostly of rain filtered through Black Bear Mountain.

*

Thanks to Mrs. Winfield, he always had a clean change of clothes to put on after bathing in the pond. He had only brought one change with him in the duffel bag. But Mrs. Winfield soon enlarged his wardrobe. She had saved some of her younger son's clothes, in hopes that he might return to the farm. The trousers were six inches too short for Harlan, but the long-sleeved shirts she made over into short-sleeved ones that fit him well enough. At the Goodwill she bought two pairs of jeans, hardly used and in just the right size for Harlan, and she sewed patches on the knees of the pair he had worn from Cleveland. Socks and underwear she bought new at Sears, where she made him accompany her in order to get fitted for a pair of steel-toed work boots. She wouldn't let him pay for any of this, nor would she let him wash his own clothes, insisting that it wasn't a bother at all to add his things to the laundry.

When he came indoors with his forearms scratched up from

pitching hay bales, she rubbed salve into the cuts. She tweezed out splinters from his hands, pushing the glasses onto her forehead to see better close-up. She lanced his blisters, daubed them with alcohol, and covered them with bandages. If he came down with a fever, as he did once or twice each winter, she made him stay in bed and fed him chicken soup. After such attentions, he could not avoid thinking of his grandmother, who had tried, within the limits of her hectic life, to look after him. A desire to relieve her of that burden had been one of his reasons for running away.

After Mrs. Winfield offered several times to cut his hair, Harlan realized she didn't like the looks of a ponytail on a boy, so he agreed to let her have a go. When she asked how short he wanted it, he answered, "Whatever suits you," and she cropped it to within an inch of his skull. She caught the pitch-black clippings in a section of the *Burlington Free Press* and scattered them on the barn ramp, where birds could collect them to use in their nests. He knew by the way she eyed his jaw that she also didn't approve of his scraggly beard, so he took to shaving once a week.

Sometimes after supper, when he sat reading at the kitchen table, she would come up behind him, lay her hands on his shoulders, and give a timid squeeze. Now and again she called him "Honey," then caught herself and apologized with a little laugh. She often urged him to go down to the village, where he could meet other young people in the coffee shop or computer café. But he insisted he would rather spend the evening here, with one of the books he pulled from the parlor shelves—books mainly about nature or farming or tools, some by people whose names he knew, like Henry Thoreau and Rachel Carson, and others by people he'd never heard of, like Aldo Leopold and Scott Nearing and Wendell Berry. The notes that Mr. Winfield had scribbled on nearly every page were an education in themselves.

Finding in Harlan a willing student, Mr. Winfield explained that the settlers who'd cleared trees from this flank of Black Bear Mountain around 1800 had been foolish to plow the thin soil, most of which promptly washed away into the Mad River. "The forest built up that fertility over thousands of years," he lamented, "and in a decade it was gone." Good farmers would have kept the slopes in pasture, as he did. "When folks compliment me on my sheep, I tell them all the credit goes to the sheep. What I grow is grass." When he did bare the ground—to plant orchard trees or berry bushes, or to plow Mrs. Winfield's garden terrace—he would occasionally turn up an arrow head or a spear point. But there were no other traces of the Indians, who'd had the good sense to live down along the river, where deer and other game were plentiful.

Harlan was just as intent on learning from Mrs. Winfield, who taught him the arts of gardening, canning, composting, and beekeeping. Still clear-minded back then, before the stroke that would bring Katarina to the farm, the old woman chattered away any time Harlan was within earshot, telling stories about her sons, the neighbors, merchants in the village, the quilting ladies she met with once a month, and the congregation at the Lutheran church where, in spite of Mr. Winfield's quarrel with the pastor, she attended worship every Sunday. She often sang hymns as she kneaded bread dough or hung out clothes on the line, and in the evenings, before retiring to bed, she would read aloud a chapter of the Bible, usually from the Psalms or Gospels. If she hoped to stir religious yearnings in Harlan, or to draw him into recounting stories of his own, she was disappointed, for he kept his inner turmoil well hidden.

Soon Mrs. Winfield was teaching him to keep the ledgers, and eventually she trusted him to do it on his own. He recorded every expense, totaled up how much fleece and lamb had been sold, how many eggs and chickens, how many bales of hay, gallons of milk, and pints of blueberries. Despite the old couple's thrift, Harlan discovered, their expenses nearly matched their income. The discovery made him work all the harder, as if his muscle and will could make up for the hard winters and thin soil.

★

When snow lay too deep for outside work, Harlan mended gear in the barn or glued rickety chairs in the shop or churned butter in the kitchen. Each place, each chore, had its own smell— from oil and leather in the barn, sawdust in the shop, yeast and peppery sausage in the kitchen. He imagined if he were set down blindfolded anywhere on Black Bear Farm he could have guessed where he was after drawing in a few deep breaths—he would have known the woodshed by its wine-like air, the orchard by the vinegary odor of fallen fruit, the beehives by their honeyed aroma, the cellar by its dank vapors, the chicken coop by its ammonia stench, the hayloft by its dusty sweetness, the woods by the must of moldering leaves.

Whether indoors or out, no matter how tiring, the work was satisfying, unlike the sweeping and dishwashing he had done for his grandparents. In all that while, Harlan never telephoned them, because he was afraid the sound of his grandfather's voice would make him angry, or the sound of his grandmother's voice would make him homesick. Instead, he wrote letters, usually on Sunday afternoons, telling about the farm, the woods, the river and mountains. He told of night skies dusted with more stars than he had ever imagined in Cleveland. He described the animals he'd seen—foxes prancing along the borders of the pasture, swallows cruising in and out of the barn, monarch butterflies feeding on red clover. No bears yet, he wrote, but from the woods he heard the tinkling call of hermit thrushes and the gritty cry of barred owls. He assured his grandparents that he was healthy, that he was finishing his high school degree by correspondence, that they needn't worry their heads about him. Now and again his grandmother wrote a few lines in reply, telling him of quarrels, money worries, aches and pains, and gloomy weather, and inviting him to come on back home if his string of luck ran out.

★

For almost three years, Harlan's luck held. Month by month, the farm came back into trim, and the neighbors who stopped to buy eggs, cream, blueberries, or lamb said as much. But Mr. Winfield, who was approaching eighty, kept losing flesh, and Mrs. Winfield fretted over him. To thicken his blood, she prepared him liver in every way she knew how, disguising it in stew and soup and casseroles, but he was never fooled, and pushed the dishes away. Harlan tried to spare him whenever he could, but the old man would not be coddled. "The day I can't work," he declared irritably, "is the day you can put me in the ground and feed me to the worms."

He did allow Harlan to begin accompanying him on his Sunday morning walks, up through the high pasture and into the woods, to a grove of ancient sugar maples near the peak of Black Bear Mountain, a place Mr. Winfield called church. They sat there quietly on the moss-covered trunk of a fallen yellow birch. For a while, all was still, except for the music of wind in the trees. Then the animals gradually resumed their motions, the squirrels hunting for nuts, woodpeckers hammering, porcupines gnawing on bark, jays flitting from branch to branch, crows cavorting overhead. Occasionally, deer pranced by, skunks rustled through the leaves, raccoons waddled past, but never a bear. After half an hour or so of silent watchfulness, the old man slapped his thighs, as if something had been settled, and they shuffled back down the slope.

Whether going up or coming down, he stopped several times. "To admire the view," he would say. And indeed the view of the Mad River Valley was well worth admiring, but Harlan could hear the old man wheezing, could see his legs trembling. Each Sabbath, the stops became more frequent and lasted longer. Finally one Sunday Mr. Winfield only went as far as the lower pasture, turned slowly to take in the sweep of the valley, shook his head, and limped back downhill. "If a man is going to farm," he muttered to Harlan, "he ought to do it on flat ground."

For a while longer, he still did half the milking, and carried the foaming pails to the cooler. He still collected eggs, still doctored ailing sheep, even split kindling with a hatchet.

Then one bitter cold night in March, during the heaviest snowfall of his third winter on the farm, Harlan was lying in bed under a pile of quilts reading *The Journals of Lewis and Clark* when a movement outside the window caught his eye. Looking out, he saw Mr. Winfield laboring through drifts toward the barn, no doubt to check on the pregnant ewes, to see if any of them were close to lambing. Harlan threw on his clothes, pulled on his boots, and hurried into the night, following the old man's path. Even through broken snow, the going was hard, and he puffed as he waded forward.

By the time Harlan reached the barn, Mr. Winfield lay curled on his side in the straw between two ewes, arms tightly crossed over his chest, eyes closed, face white in the feeble glow of a dangling electric bulb.

"Mr. Winfield?" Harlan said, laying his hand on a bony shoulder.

When no answer came, he gently rocked the gaunt body. It gave no more resistance to his touch than a bundle of rope. His fingers understood this utter slackness before his mind accepted the truth. He knelt there, while the ewes turned their dark eyes on him and their moist breath filled the stall. After a moment, he wrapped the old man in a horse blanket, took him into his arms, a weight as light as a shock of cornstalks, and waded back toward the house, where he would lay the body on the parlor table and go upstairs to wake Mrs. Winfield.

§ § §

Chapter Two • April 1988

DOE

IN THE COSMIC CAFÉ, A FUNKY DIVE where mice and cockroaches vied for fallen crumbs, Doe sat in her favorite spot, a booth upholstered in torn green leatherette mended with silver duct tape, next to a window overlooking State Street. From there, she could survey the students, cabbies, strung-out vets, bag ladies, and bums who patronized the place, or she could watch the strollers and gawkers on the sidewalk, and either indoors or out, she could almost always find a face worth drawing. But not today. Lots of angst and ennui, flickers of romance, but no mystery in any of these faces. Nothing to justify closing her art history tome and taking up sketchpad and pencil.

Due to graduate in a month with a B.F.A. in art, she was suffering from a bad case of senioritis. It was all she could do to keep attending classes and plowing through books. However, she had already disappointed her parents on so many counts—her impractical choice of major, her butch haircut with purple highlights, her sexual predilections, her nose ring and tattoos—that she wanted to gain their approval this once, and also justify the whopping tuition checks they had sent to Ithaca College over the past four years, by finishing her degree with honors. So she slogged on. At the moment, she was reading about abstract expressionism, with as little appetite as she felt for the veggie pizza cooling on her plate. She coaxed herself along by imagining that the pizza, with its dribbles of red pepper and dabs of mushroom, was an action painting by de Kooning or Pollock.

Then the snort of a diesel drew her gaze across the street to the Greyhound station, where the 2:00 P.M. bus rolled to a stop with a hiss of airbrakes. Here was an excuse to quit cramming for exams. She scrutinized the passengers as they alighted, the elderly ones with a helping hand from the driver, the spry ones climbing down on their own, but no face made her fingers itch until a teenage girl emerged from the bus with the wary look of a prey animal sneaking out of its hole. Tall and slim, the girl wore a peacock blue jacket, denim jeans, and black sneakers. Unruly hair of a color midway between cinnamon and ginger stood out in a nimbus about her head. A pink backpack, like one a child might use for school, hung from her thin shoulders. Apparently that was her only baggage, for she did not join the other passengers who waited while the driver retrieved suitcases and rucksacks from compartments in the belly of the bus.

She might be fifteen, Doe guessed, or sixteen at most. Ought to be in high school somewhere, either back where she came from or here in Ithaca. Aside from being too young, she was not Doe's type—too skinny and elongated, like an El Greco martyr, whereas Doe favored the buxom honeys of Rubens or Renoir— but the girl's haggard, hunted expression intrigued her. Pushing the textbook aside, Doe grabbed the pencil. With a few strokes, she caught the tight set of the mouth, the sharp angle of the jaw, the disheveled red hair, as the girl stood there at the curb, glancing nervously up the street and down. Clearly not a local. Nor had anybody come to meet her. The shiny blue jacket was zipped all the way up, which seemed odd on such a mild April day; the narrow stem of her throat emerged from the collar like the neck of a turtle from a shell.

When the light changed, the girl crossed the street, still darting glances here and there, then she seemed to find a direction, and made for the Cosmic Café. The bell over the door clanged as she entered and approached the cashier's desk, where Bertha, the hefty, prickly tyrant who owned the café, was swearing at the credit card machine. The girl waited without speaking until Bertha acknowledged her existence by growling, "You can seat yourself."

"Please," the girl said, and then her tongue seemed to freeze in her mouth.

"Please, what?"

The girl stared at the floor. "I'm looking for the manager."

"You're talking to her. So?"

"I saw the 'Help Wanted' sign in the window."

Bertha gave her the once-over. "What I need is grownup help."

"I'm older than I look," the girl said, although her voice broke, undercutting the claim.

Bertha's eyes, nearly lost in the expanse of her ham-colored face, narrowed with calculation. "You ever waited tables?"

"Lots."

"Tell you what. Where I'm shorthanded is breakfast. You be here at 5:30 tomorrow morning and work your butt off, and I'll let you know at the end of the shift whether you've got a job or not."

Doe watched this exchange from her booth a few feet away, absorbed in studying the girl's profile, tracing its contours on the sketchpad. Viewed up close, the face was oddly familiar, but she could not imagine where she might have seen it before. She hurried to finish the drawing before her subject disappeared.

Instead of leaving, however, the girl merely stood there, teetering back and forth on her black sneakers, while Bertha refocused her ire on the credit card machine. Finally Bertha glowered at her. "Now what?"

"Are there any cheap places to stay around here?"

"Do I look like a travel agent?"

"I was just wondering—"

"Go wonder somewhere else. Can't you see I'm busy?"

Now the girl did turn away, shoulders slumped, face glum, with that sharply-carved profile Doe felt certain she had seen somewhere before. But where? On an impulse, she called out as the girl trudged past the booth, "You need a place to stay?"

Startled, the girl paused, without meeting Doe's eyes. "Yes. But it's got to be cheap."

"My housemate and I have a couch you can use for free."

The slender body twisted with the motion of her refusal. "I couldn't do that."

"Why not?"

"I don't want to impose."

"Hey, no big deal. The couch is just sitting there."

The girl stared out the window. "You know if they let you sleep in the bus station?"

"That would be a thoroughly bad idea," Doe said firmly. "Too many creeps hang out down here. No, listen, come crash with us until you get your first paycheck."

The figure swayed like a sapling in a breeze. "You sure it won't be too much trouble?"

"I'm sure. Now sit down and help me finish this pizza, and then I'll walk you to our place. It's just a few blocks."

With a mutter of thanks, the girl shrugged free of the pink backpack and eased onto the bench across the booth from Doe. Her forehead and cheeks were lightly freckled. How could one ever draw that? "I'm not hungry," she said, in that unconvincing child's voice.

"Here." Doe pushed a slice of pizza over the scarred table. "You'd be doing me a favor."

After a few seconds, the girl lifted the pizza to her mouth and began taking small bites, chewing slowly. Meanwhile, Doe completed the sketch, adjusting the shape of the nose and lips, and in doing so, she realized why the face was familiar. It might have belonged to one of those beaten-down children of sharecroppers or migrant fieldworkers in the 1930's photographs by Walker Evans or Dorothea Lange. A lean face drained of humor or hope, a child's face with the childhood wrung out of it.

"You an artist?" The girl jutted her chin at the drawing, revealing a glimpse of her eyes, which were the minty color of new maple leaves.

"Not yet. Maybe one day, if I keep working at it."

"Can I see?"

With some misgiving, worrying that the portrait might seem too grim, Doe turned the sketchpad around to give her a better view.

The girl's faint reddish eyebrows pinched together in concentration as she studied the drawing. "It's me, isn't it? Makes me look like death warmed over."

"It's only a quick sketch."

"No, no. It's good. I'd give anything to draw like that. Look at the way you got my crazy hair." She raked fingers through her red curls, which sprang back into fiery disorder as soon as she let them go. "The only way to tame it is with hedge clippers."

Doe was about to say she thought the hair was gorgeous, like a burning bush—a flame in which she was tempted to plunge her fingers—but no, she would not start down that path. "Would you like to have it?"

"The picture, you mean? Really?"

"Sure." Doe tore off the page and handed it to the girl, who folded it carefully and placed it inside the cover of a book she fished from the backpack. It was a thick hardcover, visible long enough for Doe to make out the title—*The World's Greatest Poetry*—a surprising object for such a waif to be lugging around. "You like poetry?"

Quickly stashing the book, the girl said, "Some of it."

When Doe offered her the final slice of pizza, she accepted without repeating her fib about not being hungry. Clearly, she was ravenous. To avoid watching the secretive, rabbity nibbling, Doe leafed through the chapter on abstract expressionism, studying the illustrations, searching for ones that did not remind her of finger painting from kindergarten. Finding none, she closed the textbook, gathered her drawing materials, and stuffed everything into her portfolio, careful not to stretch the zipper too far. The portfolio had been a birthday gift from her first lover, a voluptuous beauty who could have posed for one of Rubens's lounging nudes. The lover had long since departed, but the big, square pouch, made of the tough fabric used in bulletproof vests, still protected whatever Doe carried in it, and still identified her, on campus and on the streets of Ithaca, as an art student. Whether she would ever deserve to be considered an artist and not merely a student remained to be seen.

When she felt it was safe to look back at the girl without embarrassing her, Doe asked, "So, what brings you to our fair city?"

The girl swallowed a bite and wiped her lips with a napkin before answering. "Looking for a job."

"Sounds like you've landed one here at the Cosmic."

"If the manager doesn't can me."

"Oh, don't mind Bertha."

The girl shot a furtive glance toward the cashier's desk. "Bertha, huh?"

"Yes. And by the way, I'm Doe."

Again the flash of green eyes. "Is that like in bread, or like a deer?"

"Neither. It's a nickname for Meadow." Doe could have stopped there, but to allow the girl time to finish eating, she elaborated on the story, which had often served to charm new acquaintances. Of course she had no intention of charming this girl, only of helping her, so the abbreviated version would do: "I came along when my mother was in her hippie phase, living in a tipi on a commune called Mellow Meadow, entertaining a string of horny males. Only a blood test could determine which of them was my father. A midwife delivered me right in the tipi, where I took in pot smoke and the smell of burning sweetgrass with my first breath. So my mother tells me. It could have been worse. She could have called me Mellow. Later on, she cleaned herself up and joined the bourgeoisie, earned a Ph.D. in anthropology, wrote books on Indians, married my stepdad, and had three more daughters, all born in hospitals and all given regular names. And how about you?"

"Me?"

"What's your name?

"Oh, yeah. It's Aurora. Kind of hippie too, I guess."

Doe repeated the name, which felt good in her mouth. It brought to mind bare-breasted paintings of Aurora, the Roman goddess of dawn, driving a chariot across the sky, pouring dew upon the earth and bringing light.

★

Aurora balked at the doorway, refusing to enter the apartment, and Doe could not blame her. Any one of three assaults on the senses might have been enough to stop the leery girl—the rush of hot air from the living room, where Pablo cranked up the space heater whenever he worked out, even now, in balmy April; the blast of heavy metal music, which Doe would not abide when she was home; and the sight of Pablo himself, streaming with sweat, clad only in running shorts, at work on his five hundred daily pushups. There was no interrupting him until he had finished, not only the pushups but also chin-ups, stomach crunches, jumping jacks, and several other exercises, for he pursued his calisthenic regime as devoutly as any priest performing the mass.

Waggling her fingers at him as she crossed the room, Doe turned down the stereo, popped out the cassette—a band called Neutron Misery—and put in some vintage Led Zeppelin, which she could tolerate and Pablo would not entirely loathe. She adjusted the volume until it just muffled his rhythmic grunts. Then she retrieved Aurora, still parked in the doorway looking stunned, and led her around Pablo to the couch, which was buried under its usual drift of pillows, blankets, magazines, and catalogs. Doe cleared a space by piling things on the floor, then patted the cushion and invited Aurora to sit.

But Aurora remained standing, with her jacket still zipped up to the chin, the pink backpack on her shoulders, and her legs flexed as if she might bolt. She cast her gaze everywhere except at the center of the room, where the glistening, sculpted body pumped up and down on piston arms.

"That's Pablo," Doe explained. "My housemate. Don't worry about him. He only goes for guys."

The girl seemed to relax a bit as she absorbed this information, even risking a momentary stare at him, before ducking her chin and asking, "Could I use the bathroom?"

"Of course. Down the hall, first door on your left. Want me to take your jacket?"

Aurora pressed a hand to her throat and shook her head no, before slinking away. Doe watched her go, puzzled by this extreme wariness—like that of a stray dog that flinches when you reach out to pet it.

When Pablo finished the aerobic portion of his workout and

began his stretches, he found breath enough to ask, "Where did you pick her up?"

"Shhhh," Doe whispered, pressing a finger to her lips. "I *didn't* 'pick her up.' I met her at the Cosmic, and I could see she was in trouble."

"Ah, another of your rescue projects."

"It'll only be for a few days. Until she gets on her feet."

"I've heard that before."

"Do you want me to kick her out?" Doe hissed.

"No, Saint Meadow. I just like to needle you. So what's her story?"

While Pablo ran through his cool-down routine, his shaved torso gleaming like alabaster, Doe recounted her impressions from the moment when Aurora stepped cautiously out of the bus to the moment when she balked at the apartment door.

"Sounds like a runaway to me," Pablo observed.

"Of course she's a runaway. The question is—from where and from what?"

The creak of floorboards in the hallway alerted them to the return of Aurora, who crept into the room. She had tied her riotous sandy hair into the semblance of a ponytail, and had evidently washed up, for she smelled of lavender soap. She still wore her jacket, but now it was open a few inches, revealing prominent collar bones and a shadowy hollow at the base of her throat. The backpack was cradled in her arms, with a little heap of clothing balanced on top.

Pablo stood up, swabbing himself with a towel as Doe introduced them, the muscles of his shoulders and chest flexing rather more than necessary. This was one of the flirty moves Doe had seen him pull to raise false hopes in straight females. She had witnessed such moves for the first time in figure drawing class, where Pablo worked as a model, paying his way through law school by exhibiting a physique that Michelangelo could have used for Adam on the Sistine Chapel ceiling.

Doe interrupted his game by saying, "I told Aurora she could stay with us until she finds a place of her own."

"Cool with me," Pablo said, "if you don't mind a little mess."

"I don't mind."

"Then make yourself at home." He flashed her one of his hundred-watt smiles, draped the towel around his neck, and swaggered off to take a shower, pausing en route to switch off the space heater, with another rippling display of muscle.

Aurora blinked at his retreating figure. Doe was about to assure her that Pablo really went exclusively for guys, all appearances to the contrary. But Aurora spoke first: "Is it okay if I wash out a few things in the sink?" She nodded toward the kitchen alcove.

"Sure. But there's a laundry in the basement, if you want to run a load."

"The sink's fine."

"If you're short of change, I've got plenty." Even as she made the offer, Doe realized that Aurora might wish to save whatever money she had, and would surely refuse a handout. "But, hey, with just those few things," she added quickly, "why feed quarters to a machine? Help yourself. There's soap in the cabinet under the sink."

Aurora thanked her and headed for the kitchen. As she did so, a sock slithered from the laundry piled atop the backpack, and when she reached to grab it, the whole pile tumbled to the floor, mainly pastel underwear, a couple of white T-shirts, and a gray sweatshirt. She let out a whimper, of weariness or exasperation, set the pack on the couch, and knelt to gather up the fallen garments. Kneeling beside her to help, Doe picked up the sweatshirt and shook it out, preparing to fold it. But Aurora snatched it away, explaining hastily, "I spilled pop on it," as she wadded the sweatshirt into a ball.

Doe pulled back then, rattled, wondering if she had taken on more than she could handle. For in lifting the sweatshirt, she had seen a pair of dark round stains where the gray fabric would have swelled over the girl's breasts.

★

As each of her sisters was born, Doe had watched jealously when her mother began nursing the new baby. She remembered how her mother's milk would leak if too much time passed between feedings, or even if someone else's baby cried nearby. When the bra pads soaked through, her mother would have to change her blouse or suit, because of dark wet blotches like those on Aurora's sweatshirt. Was that the reason for the zipped-up jacket? Because the stains weren't from soda but from milk? Then if Aurora was nursing, where was the baby? And why had she gone so long without feeding it?

Even if Doe could have imagined how to ask these questions without driving the flighty girl away, there was no opportunity to do so that evening. By the time Aurora had spread her laundry to dry on the rack near the water heater in the kitchen, Pablo had returned from his shower, in khaki trousers that were tight across his buns and a topaz polo shirt that was tight everywhere, and now he was regaling her with law school anecdotes while he cut up vegetables and sautéed them with tofu in the wok. He continued his monologue through supper, ignoring Doe's efforts to draw Aurora into the conversation. For her part, the girl seemed content to let him talk, as she ate two helpings of stir-fry, all but the chunks of tofu, which she pushed around on her plate with the fork. Pablo finally hushed at nine o'clock, when he retreated to the living room, settled onto his end of the couch, and turned on the TV, which soon burbled with the canned laughter and inane dialogue of his favorite show.

"Hope he didn't bend your ear too much," Doe said to Aurora as the two of them cleaned up from the meal. "He can't resist a fresh audience."

"Law is interesting. Especially trials and juries."

"Well, I expect Pablo won't ever get near a courtroom. More likely he'll work in a plush office, advising corporations on how to avoid taxes."

"Beats waiting tables."

"Not looking forward to working for Bertha?"

"It's not managers that get my goat. It's customers."

"Oh, the clientele at the Cosmic are pretty laid-back. Also lousy tippers, I'd guess."

They continued in silence for a while, Doe washing and Aurora drying. The racket from the TV, already loud, swelled each time a commercial broke in. During a lull, Aurora said, "Those books on Indians your mother wrote, did any of them talk about the Ojibwa?"

"I can't say." Doe rinsed the last of the plates and handed it to Aurora, who swabbed it with a towel. "Truth is, I haven't read any of her books. Another blot on my record as a daughter. Maybe I was jealous of all the hours she spent locked away in her study, grinding out page after page. Why do you ask?"

Aurora shrugged. "Oh, I did a report on the Ojibwa in school."

Such tiny revelations encouraged Doe to hope that the girl might eventually be coaxed out of her shell. Maybe after a good night's sleep. For now, Doe thought it wise not to pry. She squeezed the sponge and used it to wipe out the wok, leaving a patina of olive oil. "All right," she said, surveying the kitchen, "we're done."

Aurora draped the dish towel over the stove handle, and went to check on her laundry, fingering each garment in turn.

Searching for a way to ask about the sweatshirt, which was

now an even gunmetal gray as it hung from the drying rack, Doe
said, "Looks like you got rid of those stains."

"I told you, it was only pop."

"That's right," Doe said, still unsure whether to believe her.
"You told me and I forgot. I guess my brain's fried from studying.
You must be worn out, too, after your trip. How about if I kick
Pablo off the couch so you can hit the sack?"

"I'm not tired. Let him watch his show."

Not tired? That was the El Greco martyr talking, Doe thought.
She led the way into the living room, where she settled down beside Pablo, whose rapt face was suffused with the glow from the
TV. Aurora followed her without making a sound, as if entering
a church where the service was in progress; she sat on the end of
the couch away from Pablo, and soon fell asleep. Bursts of phony
laughter from the screen did not wake her, nor did Pablo's occasional guffaws. Gradually, the anxiety drained from her face, eras-
ing the frown, smoothing the pallid skin, softening the lines of
her jaw and lips. Doe would have liked to sketch her again, in this
less haunted condition, but she would have to do so from memory. For now she sat very still, breathing in the mixed aroma of
lavender and laundry soap, as Aurora leaned against her in sleep.

After the program ended, Doe shooed Pablo away. Rolling his
eyes, he blew a kiss and made a show of tiptoeing down the hall
to his bedroom. When she heard his door close, she slipped out
from under Aurora's weight and lowered her onto the cushions,
remembering how she used to help tuck her sisters in bed when
they were little. Gazing down on the slender figure, still in those
grubby sneakers, washed-out jeans, and garish jacket, Doe felt
a rush of tenderness. It seemed a shame to rouse her, but she
might not want to sleep another night in those clothes.

"Hey," Doe said gently, reaching down to squeeze one of the
thin shoulders.

The slim body convulsed, eyes flicking open. "What?"

"Sorry, sorry. I didn't mean to scare you." Unthinking, Doe ran a hand over the wild red hair.

Aurora jerked away from her touch and sat up, looking around anxiously. "Where's Pablo?"

"Gone off to his lair." Doe stepped back from the couch, fearing she had made a mistake. "Probably studying torts or wills or some such thing."

"Whew," the girl said. The lines of her face drew taut once more. "Guess I dozed off."

"All you missed was America's dumbest sitcom. I would have let you sleep, but I thought you might want to brush your teeth or something. Maybe take a shower, change clothes. I've got extra nightgowns and pajamas, if you don't have anything dry."

Aurora glanced down at the front of her jacket, and then, seemingly relieved, she slapped her jean-clad thighs. "I'll just wear what I've got on. That'll make it easier for me to get out the door in the morning."

"What time should I wake you?"

"No need. I'll set my watch."

"It's going to be pitch-dark at 5:30. How about I drive you to the café?"

"I can find my way."

"That's a dicey hour for walking downtown."

"I can look after myself," Aurora said, with a forcefulness that warned Doe not to persist.

*

Doe slept fitfully that night, waking every hour or so to check the bedside clock, afraid she might not hear the alarm. She wanted at least to see Aurora off. When a thunderstorm rattled the windows a few minutes before 5:00, she took this as an excuse to insist on driving Aurora to the café. She was less concerned that the jittery girl might get soaked on her way to work than that she might not come back to the apartment at the end of the morning shift, scared off by Pablo's flirting, or by Doe's own sisterly caress.

Wanting to reassure her, Doe got up, slipped into a robe, and went quietly to the living room, expecting to find the lights on and Aurora stirring about. But the room was dark, and when she turned on a lamp she could see that the couch was empty. The blankets were neatly folded and stacked on the coffee table. In the kitchen, the drying rack was also empty, even though the sweatshirt, at least, must still have been damp. On the table there was a scrap of paper, weighted down with a coffee mug, bearing a single word in block letters: THANKS!!! There was no sign of the pink backpack, or of anything else that might suggest Aurora was planning to return.

Dressing quickly and hurrying to the car through slants of rain, Doe imagined that if she reached the café early enough, before the breakfast stampede, she could steal a few minutes with Aurora and woo her back. She might even overtake the girl on the way, stop and open the car door, and the drenched waif would slide in, effusively grateful. While the windshield wipers clacked and rain thrummed on the roof, the two of them, cozy in the darkness, would cast aside all caution and begin sharing secrets.

Doe laughed at her fantasy. She did keep a lookout through the blurry windows, but the sidewalks were deserted. Puddles on the concrete rippled from gusts of wind. Signs shimmied on their posts. Stopping for a red light at the intersection of Buffalo and State, she suddenly had a terrible thought. If those blotches on the sweatshirt really were from milk, maybe the reason Aurora quit nursing was because the baby had died. Maybe that was why she had fled from her home—to escape reminders of her loss—

and why she had arrived in Ithaca so distraught.

A chill ran up Doe's spine. Only the bellow of a horn made her notice that the light had turned green. She let up on the brake, pushed down on the gas pedal, and drove the last couple of blocks to the café.

Never serene, Bertha was in an even more tempestuous mood than usual as she peered up from the cash register when Doe entered, her slicker and umbrella dripping.

"Don't leave a lake," Bertha grumbled. "Somebody'll slip and break a bone and sue my ass. What are you doing here so early? Stay up all night?"

"Actually, I just wanted to have a word with Aurora, if I could."

"Aurora? Never heard of her."

"You know, the tall, skinny girl with red hair who's starting work this morning."

"Oh, that bitch." Bertha's jowls quaked. "She never showed. What can you expect? Kids these days don't want to work. That's all it is, pure laziness. They want stuff but won't lift a finger to earn it. Make you promises, then leave you in the lurch..."

Bertha was still sputtering as Doe backed away, opened the umbrella, and stepped onto the sidewalk, now thoroughly frightened. If Aurora hadn't come to the café, where did she go? Had she gotten lost? Had she taken shelter in a doorway? God forbid, had some lowlife jumped her? Such things happened. Just a few blocks from here, a woman had vanished after wandering out of a bar in the wee hours. No trace of her was ever found. Doe shivered. The umbrella shook from the downpour. The tires of cabs and delivery trucks made a ripping sound as they rolled along the wet pavement. The streetlamps were gauzy yellow blobs, hardly penetrating the rain. Aside from the Cosmic Café, the only business open this early was the Greyhound station, an island of fluorescent light across the street. Ah, Doe thought, waiting for a gap in the traffic, maybe that's where she went.

But Aurora was not to be found among the figures huddled in dark corners of the station, or wrapped in tattered blankets on benches, or staggering about with glazed eyes. Doe even searched the women's restroom, going stall by stall. Then she approached the stationmaster, who had just come on duty. He had not seen anyone matching Aurora's description, but he pointed out that several buses had already left this morning. As Doe looked out through the plate-glass window at the slashing rain, she allowed herself to imagine—because it was all she could bear to imagine—that Aurora had saved enough money to buy a ticket, and was even now riding back to wherever she had come from, regretting this mad flight to Ithaca, her breasts filling with milk as she neared her child, a healthy child eager to suck.

§§§

Chapter Three • August 2007

HARLAN

WHEN KATARINA ARRIVED ON BLACK BEAR FARM in early April, a month after Mr. Winfield's death and three weeks after Mrs. Winfield's stroke, Harlan was greatly relieved. He had not known how to speak with the addled widow, let alone how to care for her while doing all the work of the farm on his own, especially in lambing season. Ladies from the quilting club and the Lutheran church had pitched in to help, bringing food, taking turns sitting with Mrs. Winfield, bathing and dressing her. But they had households of their own to look after and other mouths to feed, so they were only filling in until the widow's sons could make other arrangements.

The older of the two sons, the stockbroker from Boston, hired Katarina through an agency that recruited Scandinavian students who wished to perfect their English in America. She rode by limousine from the Burlington airport, a luxury also arranged by the older son, but there was nothing fancy about the jeans, boots, and sweater she wore as she climbed from the sleek black car that April morning. She insisted on carrying her own suitcases as Harlan showed her to a corner bedroom upstairs in the farmhouse. She appeared tired from the journey, and her blond hair, coiled atop her head in a shining braid, had begun to unravel. Nervous on meeting her, Harlan could not think what to say. Katarina was silent as well, leading him to worry that she might not speak much English, in spite of the stockbroker's assurance. But after she set down her suitcases, inspected the sunlit room, and took in the view of the valley and mountains, she said to him in perfectly formed English, "It is beautiful."

"It is," he agreed.

"Now I should go to Mrs. Winfield."

"Don't you want to rest up first?"

"I come to work, not rest."

Usually when he met a girl his own age, some unreasoning part of him swiftly decided whether she was pretty or not, sexy or not, but this girl confused him, her body was so muffled by the bulky sweater, her face was so frank and unadorned. The pink of her lips and the blush of her cheeks appeared to be their own true color, not something out of a tube. Realizing that he hadn't introduced himself, he said, "I'm Harlan Blake. I look after the farm."

"I am Katarina Swanson." She extended a small hand that gripped his large one with surprising strength. "I spent summers on my grandparents' farm, so I can help you with chores." She gazed at him with unsettling gray eyes. "I was told you live here."

"I've got a room over in the workshop. You can see it there beyond the cottonwood," he said, pointing out the window.

She cocked her head, with a quizzical expression that would soon become familiar to him. "What is cotton wood?"

"That big tree there."

"Why is it named cotton?"

"Because of the fluffy seeds it lets loose in the spring."

"I see." Her lips curled slightly. "So after you work all day you sleep in the workshop?"

Unable to tell if this was meant as a joke, Harlan replied, "Until lately. Since Mrs. Winfield's stroke I've been sleeping on a pallet outside her door, in case she needs me in the night."

"That will no longer be necessary."

It occurred to him that they were standing in the room where this girl would undress at night, near the bed where she would sleep. So he hastened to add, "The house is all yours, if that's what you're wondering. I'll only come in for meals."

Katarina studied him with a directness the Cleveland girls had never shown. "It is an unusual name, Harlan."

"My mother named me after a man she'd read about who lived on a shantyboat on the Ohio River."

"What is a shantyboat?

"It's like a hut on a raft."

"Ah, yes. We have the same in Sweden. I have often thought how lovely to ride along a river and tie up at night and cook your meal on a little stove and sleep with the waves rocking you."

Harlan had imagined such a life, ever since learning from his grandmother the source of his name, but he had never said as much to anyone. And now here was a stranger voicing the same desire within minutes of meeting him. He could only think to say, "Well, make yourself at home. Mrs. Winfield will be glad you're here. I've tried to keep her company in the evenings, after the quilters and church ladies go home, but I'm not much good at talking with her."

"She is forgetful?"

He nodded. "She calls me by her husband's name, or she takes me for one of her sons. The doctor says she might get back some of her wits, but not all of them, and maybe not any."

Katarina took this in with a slight nod. "Her sons come to see her?"

"They both came last month for Mr. Winfield's funeral. Only the one from Massachusetts showed up after her stroke. He wanted to move her into a place for old people in Boston, but

I persuaded him the ladies and I could take care of her until he found somebody to do a proper job."

"I will do this proper job. I know old people, for always I lived close to my grandparents. I left home only when the last of them died."

Harlan wished to say something about his own grandparents, about his own reasons for leaving home, but Katarina's self-assurance made him feel tongue-tied. So he stood there watching her move from the east window to the south window, where she pulled aside the curtain and looked out. Sunlight caught the hair straying from her braid, hair so nearly white as to seem transparent. He wondered how it would feel to run his fingers through the gossamer strands. Without turning to him, she said, "Here is a good place for dying."

★

By the Sunday in August when Harlan emerged from the woods after another fruitless search for a bear and spied Katarina rising from the pond, her bare legs glistening below the white shirt, he could no longer tell which of the two stirred the deepest longing in him, bear or girl. All that summer, he had lost sleep thinking about her, and sometimes he lost track of his work, leaning his forehead against the flank of a cow and forgetting to pull on the teats, or standing with an injured lamb in his arms and remembering to call the vet only when the lamb began to bleat, or halting the tractor in the midst of mowing to gaze down at scarves of fog on the river.

Still, he kept up the farm, although he missed Mr. Winfield's company. A dozen times a day he thought of questions he wanted to ask. What was killing the maples in the sugarbush? Could he use hardwood chips to mulch the blueberries, or should he use pine? How many of the ewe lambs born that spring should he keep to build the flock and how many should he butcher? Should he add lime to the upper pasture? Where could he get the broken cutter bar welded? For all he had learned about farming during three years of the old man's instruction, he was reminded of his ignorance at every turn.

He could seek advice from the few neighbors in the valley who still farmed, but they, too, were mostly well up in years, sometimes foggy of mind, and often suspicious of outsiders. He was likely to remain a newcomer in their eyes, no matter how long he stayed on Black Bear Farm. How long he could stay would depend on the Winfield sons. Would they allow their mother to live out her days here, now that Katarina was on hand to look after her? Since Mr. Winfield's death, the sons had continued sending two monthly checks, one for Harlan's wages, the other for groceries and parts and supplies. To ease his conscience, he sent half the wages to his grandmother, who had begun to speak in her notes of moving out of Cleveland into the country, away from smog and sirens and fights. The allowance he handed over to Katarina, who bought what they needed from the village, including Mrs. Winfield's medicines.

While in the village, she used her cell phone—which found no signal up on the mountain—to call her mother in Grozny and her two brothers, one in London and the other in Bangkok, both of them much older than Katarina. She told Harlan about each of them. The London brother was a mathematician who worked for an insurance company, projecting the cost of damage caused by global warming; the Bangkok brother was an engineer overseeing the construction of a hotel; the mother was a nurse for Doctors Without Borders, currently serving in the midst of a low-grade war in Chechnya. All of these places and professions lay far beyond Harlan's ken, but Katarina spoke of them as nothing unusual. She never mentioned having called her father, and disclosed little about him, except that he lived in the city of Göteborg and worked in the Volvo plant.

On her trips to the village, Katarina also used a computer in the branch library to exchange email with her friends in Sweden. During his early months in Vermont, Harlan had done the same with his own friends back in Ohio, but gradually he had lost touch with all but a couple of them, as their gossip about school seemed increasingly remote, and as the farm claimed his full attention.

Over the course of that summer, however, there was less and less farm to keep up, for within weeks of Katarina's arrival the Winfield sons began selling off the livestock. The hogs were the first to go, squealing, their pink snouts pressed between slats in the back of the truck. Next, the cows were hauled off, their glassy eyes rolling, the calves bawling. Then a pickup carried the chickens away in crates, leaving a trail of feathers. The llama was shipped to breeders in the Green Mountains. Last of all, and hardest to let go, were the sheep, which balked and bleated as they were forced up a chute into a trailer. Harlan dutifully helped with the herding and loading, but he refused to banter with the men sent to fetch the animals, and he watched with clenched jaw as each truck pulled away.

To keep neighbors from stopping by for produce that was no longer available, he unhooked two of the smaller signs—one offering fresh eggs and cream, the other offering lamb—from beneath the large wooden sign announcing Black Bear Farm. The sons neglected to sell off the bees, but a bear put an end to the honey business, for one morning in July Harlan found the white hive boxes smashed and the door ripped from the shed where he kept the beekeeping gear. Perhaps the watchful llama had made it shy away until now. Proof of a bear's presence on the mountain was some compensation for the other losses, but not enough to quench Harlan's anger.

*

At first, the coming and going of trucks, animals, and strangers frightened Mrs. Winfield, who often witnessed the commotion from a rocking chair on the farmhouse porch, her legs propped on a log stool, swaddled in a blanket in spite of the heat. To soothe her, Katarina would sit nearby cutting up beans for canning or packing blueberries into bags for the freezer or braiding garlic. As she worked, she sang hymns in Swedish or Broadway show tunes in English. More than once, Harlan had come into the front yard to find Katarina gliding back and forth on the rope swing, bellowing out a song, while Mrs. Winfield sat on the porch clapping her hands.

After the last of the livestock had been hauled away, a survey crew arrived, dragged their tripods and laser levels and GPS devices around the four hundred acres, and drove orange-flagged steel posts into the stony ground. The surveyors were followed by men in suits who stepped gingerly along the mowed paths in shiny shoes, clicking photos on their phones. A used implement dealer cleared out everything salvageable from the milking parlor, equipment shed, and workshop, and a scrap dealer carried away the rest. A father and son team brought a trenching machine, like a giant chainsaw on wheels, to cut ditches across the hillside for the laying of pipes and cables, slashing indifferently through grass, goldenrod, Queen Ann's lace, woodland sunflowers, and purple asters. The upheaval put Harlan in mind of battlefield photos from World War I.

Next came two nurses wearing powder blue smocks covered in cartoons. They tried speaking with Mrs. Winfield, but failed to penetrate her bewilderment, so they interviewed Katarina about the old woman's habits and needs, one nurse asking questions, the other taking notes on a clipboard. Could Mrs. Winfield control her bowels? No. Could she feed herself? No. Did she know what year it was? Again the answer was no. For the widow had faded month by month, day by day, losing control of her body, losing memory, losing words, until she was reduced to a husk that stared out the window or tapped a foot in rhythm with singing or basked in the sun. Song and sun could still make her smile, as could the sight of cloud shadows dappling the mountains, the taste of spring water, or the touch of Katarina's hands.

★

By summer's end, Mrs. Winfield seemed no longer to notice the coming and going of men and machines. According to Katarina, the widow showed no alarm even when a flatbed truck delivered a bulldozer with much loud clattering right beneath her window. Yellow and massive, with metal treads and a blade as wide as the driveway, the bulldozer squatted in the barnyard for several days before a driver showed up to crank the engine and begin reshaping the farm into whatever the Winfield sons had decided to make of it.

Harlan was in the garden digging potatoes when he heard the engine roar. He watched the bulldozer grind its way out of the barnyard and across the lower pasture, the heavy treads leaving twin ruts behind. When he saw where it was headed, he rushed in pursuit, the spading fork in one fist, and overtook the machine just as it reached the apple orchard.

"Hold on!" he shouted, waving the fork.

The driver, a stout man of about fifty, dressed in camouflage gear from hat to boots, idled the motor and shouted back, "Yeah?"

"Start somewhere else."

"I've got a work order says I start right here."

"But some of these trees are a hundred years old."

"Good for them."

"And the fruit's just coming ripe."

"I can't help that."

"Yes you can." Harlan drew up beside the bulldozer and lifted the spading fork, pointing the tines at the man's chest. "You can back away and go wreck some other place."

Eyeing the sharp tines, which were still clotted with dirt, the driver said, "Listen, kid. Don't do anything stupid. I got nothing against your orchard. I'm just doing my job."

"And I'm doing mine."

"But both of us are working for the owners, and one of them told me you might cause trouble, and if you did, I was to call him and he'd kick you out pronto."

Scared by his own rage, which triggered memories of his grandfather's drunken rants, Harlan lowered the fork and turned away, realizing he was powerless to save the orchard or any other part of the farm. It was not his to save. It was not even a farm any more, but only so many acres of real estate. As he strode back toward the garden, he could hear the bulldozer blade smack the ground, hear the engine rev, hear the apple trees, veterans of many Vermont winters, go crashing down. By the time he finished digging the last of the potatoes, the orchard had been reduced to a heap of twisted roots and trunks and branches. Early apples might have ripened on some of the topmost branches, but he did not have the heart to go look.

A backhoe and dump truck joined the bulldozer the following day, and within a week they erased decades of labor, including most of what Harlan had done under the tutelage of Mr. Winfield. The fences were ripped out. Except for the farmhouse and barn, all the buildings were demolished—the chicken coop, pigsty, corn crib, woodshed, beekeeping hut, smoke shack—and the debris was carted away.

When the workshop was next in line for demolition, Harlan moved his things into the house and made up a pallet on the parlor floor. From there, he could hear Mrs. Winfield call out in the night, followed by quiet footsteps along the hallway upstairs, and then the murmur of Katarina's voice. As he lay drowsing, he would sympathize with the old woman, whose world had been turned upside down, and then his thoughts would drift to the girl, padding about on bare feet, wearing only a loose white shirt.

★

The shirt fluttered on the clothesline that August evening as Harlan sat on the porch steps replaying in his mind Katarina's quiet remark: "Yes, mum, he is a sweet man." By this hour she would have put Mrs. Winfield to bed, and soon would call him to supper. The leaves of the great cottonwood rustled above him. The air smelled of pine resin. In the gathering darkness a barred owl repeated its scratchy cry.

The door opened behind him and Katarina came out, pausing beside him on the steps. "The owl is the rooster of the night," she said.

"I suppose it is," Harlan answered. "I never thought of it that way."

Without mentioning supper, she walked into the twilight, her trim figure vivid in his imagination from a thousand glances he'd cast at her since she had climbed from the limousine in April. All that summer he had studied her whenever he could do so without her noticing. There was hunger in his looking, for sure, but also curiosity. He had never known a girl to move as she did, surefooted, gliding, without any come-on waggle of her hips. Now she made her way to the clothesline, where the shirt hovered like a pale moth, and then she unpinned the garment and turned back toward the house. When she drew up beside him on the porch, the shirt folded over her arm, she touched him lightly on the shoulder. "You are not hungry?"

Harlan slapped his legs and stood up. "Hungry enough to eat skunk."

She forced a smile. "If I had known, I would have cooked a skunk. Instead I have cooked a chicken."

"I'll make do with chicken."

He knew she was trying to lighten her own mood as well as his, but he could not shake off the weight of sadness, and her face revealed that neither could she. He followed her indoors, the sensation from her fingers burning on his shoulder. Their plates were set on the kitchen table, along with a pitcher of sun tea and a vase filled with oxeye daisies and ferns. When it was Katarina's turn to say grace, she recited prayers in one or another of her four languages, but tonight it was Harlan's turn, so he mumbled his usual thanks for the gift of food, and then, without forethought, he found himself apologizing to the land for its ravaging.

When he opened his eyes, Katarina was staring at him, her lips slightly parted as if she were about to speak. But she said nothing.

Only as they began eating did he notice the envelope beside his plate, with the familiar return address from the stockbroker's firm in Boston. He set down his fork and picked up the envelope, turning it over.

"It arrived yesterday," Katarina said. She raised her eyebrows, which were lighter than her sun-bronzed face. "I was afraid to open it."

Harlan frowned. "We're not due any checks."

"No."

He slit the envelope with his table knife, drew out the letter, and read the brief text. When he looked up, once again he found Katarina studying him with those mist-gray eyes.

"They will send her away?" she demanded.

He swallowed before answering. "Next week. To a nursing home in Boston."

Katarina shook her head angrily. "It is wrong. She will be miserable there. Here, she can be happy."

"That's not all." He refolded the letter and pushed it away. "We have to clear out by the end of August. They'll pay us an extra month's wages to help us move. The builders arrive September first."

"She belongs here," Katarina insisted.

The pastures arose in Harlan's mind as they used to be, lush with grass and dotted with sheep, and likewise the burgeoning garden, the sturdy buildings, the lilacs and lilies, the clear-running spring. That image faded into a vision of the mountainside as it was now, crisscrossed by trenches, pockmarked with scars where buildings once stood, littered with piles of bulldozed trees, a mire of raw dirt and trash. By the time the condos were finished, with their clubhouse and curving streets, every bit of care the Winfields had put into this place would be erased, and so would his own work and Katarina's.

As if sharing his thoughts, she turned to look out the window toward the pond and barn and sweep of valley, all in shadow now. Harlan's gaze followed hers. When she turned back to him, her eyes were wet. "Where will you go?"

"I don't know. Maybe Cleveland."

"To see your parents? They must miss you."

"To see my grandparents. They're the ones that raised me."

A question formed on Katarina's face, most likely about why he never spoke of his mother or father. But she said only, "Are there bears in Cleveland?"

"Only at the zoo, and they're lazy and fat."

She tried to laugh, but sobbed instead, letting the tears run down her cheeks. "In the nursing home she will shrivel up. Why can she not die in her own house?"

Harlan reached across the table and grasped Katarina's hands, the first time he had ever touched her except when they brushed against one another in their work. She did not pull away, as he had feared she would. "Did your grandmother lose her wits before she died?" he asked.

"Both grandmothers. They lost memory and speech and every pleasure except music and flowers and caresses. When I rubbed their joints, they purred like cats."

Katarina's hands felt small in his, but firm, work-hardened. "Will you go back to Sweden?"

"For college, yes, but not until next summer. I must learn your crazy language well enough to become an interpreter."

"Then you need better teachers than Mrs. Winfield and me."

"You are not a bad teacher, only you work too much and speak too little."

"Well, there's not much work left to do here, so maybe I'll have more breath for talking."

She ran a finger over the petals of an oxeye daisy. "When will you leave?"

"As soon as Mrs. Winfield gets moved. If I stick around, I'm liable to pour sand in the gas tanks of their big machines. Or maybe toss in lit matches."

Feeling Katarina's hands clench, he let go of them and leaned back in his chair. She stood and carried her untouched plate to the refrigerator. He cleared the rest of the table. In silence, he washed the dishes while she put away the food. Questions for her pressed on his tongue, but he could not let them out.

Their silence was broken by a plaintive call from Mrs. Winfield, who rarely slept through the night. Katarina quickly dried her hands on a towel and hurried down the hall.

Harlan could think of nothing to do but retreat to his makeshift bed in the parlor and read until his jangled nerves let him sleep. But when he walked outside for a breath of air, and passed beyond the vast canopy of the cottonwood, he saw that the night sky was cloudless and moonless and bedazzled with stars. So he decided to take a blanket from the barn and walk up the slope toward the high pasture. As he passed the blueberry patch, he turned off the electric fence, thinking he might as well let wild critters eat up the crop before bulldozers scoured the bushes away. He wanted to pull out the surveyor's stakes along the path, but knew they would soon be put back in.

Only when he spread the blanket on the ground did he realize, from the faint whiff of horses, that it was the one he had used to wrap Mr. Winfield's body. He paused, missing the old man with a sharp pang. Then he lay down and faced northeast, where Perseus would rise just before midnight and give him the best chance of seeing meteors.

From the valley floor came the grinding of truck gears on the highway. He couldn't hate the sound, because he might be snagging a ride on one of those rigs a week from now. But he preferred listening to the crickets, which rang in the grass like ten thousand tiny bells, and to the barred owl, which rasped out its guttural call from the woods beyond the pasture. He stayed awake long enough to see dozens of meteors tracing white streaks across the black sky.

*

Shortly before dawn, Harlan awoke to the rustle of steps approaching over dew-damp grass. Bear, he thought, untangling himself from the blanket and sitting up in a flurry of excitement and fear. But the shape he saw coming, outlined against the brightening rim of the eastern mountains, was Katarina's—a shape as enticing and alarming as a bear's might have been. He wanted her, and he wanted to flee.

She drew up to him slowly, at her browsing-deer gait. "I came to watch the sunrise," she said. "When I climbed the path, I saw you already here. May I sit?"

He smoothed a spot on the blanket next to him. "Sure."

When she lowered herself beside him, he could see that her jeans were soaked to the knee from the wet grass. Her feet were bare, the toes like shining pebbles. "I cannot stay long," she said.

"You want me to go listen for Mrs. Winfield?"

He made as if to rise, but Katarina hooked a hand under his arm and held him down. "No," she said, leaning her head against his chest. "Please stay."

He kept still, as when a fox or a perching hawk showed itself to him. He could feel the pulse in his throat, the cramping in his legs. Fog blanketed the river. Crickets chirred. As the sun poured light into the valley, the air warmed and the soil released its summery fragrance. Soon goldfinches were nibbling seeds from black-eyed Susans, the stems bending under their weight, and swallows were cruising for insects over the tall grass.

Out of the silence, Katarina asked, "Why is your Lake Erie called a great lake?"

"Because it's big, I guess. Too big to see across."

"Like the sea," she murmured. "Except without salt or gulls."

"Oh, we have scads of gulls."

"What does it mean, 'scads'?"

"Lots and lots."

She tilted her face up at him. "Will you show it to me, your great lake?"

After months of glancing into her gray eyes, he found them no less unsettling. He shivered. "It's a long way to Ohio."

"Not so far as Sweden."

"Won't your parents want you to go back home, now that your work here has fallen through?"

"I have no home there. My parents got divorced soon after I left for America."

"Ah, I'm sorry."

"No need to be. It is good for my mother. She stayed in the marriage only until I could stand on my own. Now she does not have to put up with my father, and she can travel anywhere in the world to nurse people who are suffering from wars or earthquakes or plagues. My father lives in the house where I grew up, but so does his latest mistress, and she does not want me underfoot." Before Harlan could absorb all of this, Katarina added, "So if you will take me along, I wish to see your lake and your grandparents and your city. But I am afraid of hitchhiking. American drivers all carry guns."

As he thought this over, his desire won out over his fear. "The train goes right through Cleveland, a few blocks from my grandparents' place. Or we could take the bus."

"Then we will go? And also see the shantyboats?"

"There's some on the Cuyahoga River."

"The river that caught fire?"

"That's the one. My hometown stream."

Katarina was about to say something else when Harlan heard thrashing nearby and pressed a finger to her lips. She hushed. They both turned toward the noise, which came from downhill in the blueberry patch. In the early light he could see that a section of electric fence had been flattened, and just inside the patch, a bear, smaller than the ones he had imagined, was squatting on its haunches and stripping berries from a bush with its teeth. Beyond that bear he saw a second one, also small, round-eared, plump, and then he spied a third, much larger, as large as any he had ever imagined, and he realized the trio must be a sow and her two cubs. The sunrise licked silver highlights onto their black fur. Their obsidian eyes glistened. Their teeth clicked, mashing the berries, and they grunted with what Harlan took to be pure delight. Katarina tightened her grip on his arm, letting out surprised little gasps as the bears uprooted bushes with their exuberant eating.

§ § §

Chapter Four • September 1993

AURORA

FROM THE BREAKFAST BUFFET, AURORA SLIPPED an apple and a banana into the pockets of her apron before opening the doors of the Seneca Hotel café. She looked around for the two spindly, towheaded schoolboys who often sidled up to accept her secret handouts. She never gave them donuts or sugary drinks, but always fruit or yogurt or whole wheat muffins, foods that a real mother might give them. They were brothers, she had learned, the older one eight and in third grade, the younger one five, just beginning kindergarten. They lived in a trailer park in the hills outside of Ithaca and rode into town each morning with their mother, who cleaned rooms in the hotel. Although they sometimes appeared hungry, the boys were always neatly dressed in the white shirts and navy blue shorts of Immaculate Conception School, a uniform not so different from Aurora's own waitress togs of white shirt and black slacks.

But on this Monday morning, the only person waiting outside the café when she opened the doors was a blind man. She could tell he was blind not merely from his white walking stick and wraparound dark glasses, but also from the way his face betrayed no expression until she wished him good morning, and then he gave a cautious smile. His teeth gleamed in contrast with skin nearly as dark as the lenses in his sunglasses, making Aurora feel, by comparison, washed out and anemic.

"A table for one," the man said, in a voice that sounded rusty from sleep, or maybe from solitude. "And a little guidance, if you'd be so kind."

He bent an arm and held it out from his side. After a moment's hesitation, Aurora grasped the arm above the elbow, where the bicep swelled. She was surprised at how thick it felt through the sleek blue fabric of his shirt. He was about her height, 5'9" or so, but much broader, with plenty of meat on his bones. From his burgundy tie to shined cordovan wing-tip shoes, he was more sharply dressed than the usual businessmen and professors who passed through the hotel. As she led him to a table, with his other arm he swung the walking stick from side to side before him, the tip whispering over the carpet.

"Here we are," she said, pulling out a chair.

The man eased himself down and sat there expectantly.

"Coffee?" Aurora asked.

"Hot tea, please. Chamomile, if you have it. Otherwise, anything herbal."

"Chamomile it is. And to eat?" She drew a menu folder from her apron, but caught herself before offering it to him. "Would you like me to read the menu? Actually, I could recite it in my sleep."

His smile brightened. "I trust you have oatmeal?"

"You bet. Made from oats organically grown by bachelor farmers in the hills of upstate New York." Despite long practice in such patter, aimed at increasing tips, it did not come naturally to her. She would rather have waited on customers in silence.

He laughed obligingly, a warm rumble. "Oatmeal, then, with brown sugar, raisins, and a dash of cream. And an English muffin with orange marmalade."

Now that his voice had limbered up, he sounded like a broadcaster on NPR, not like any black man she'd ever met. Close your eyes, and you'd never guess his color. "Coming right up," she said.

When she returned with his order, he was hunched over the table, murmuring into a little silvery gadget, as she set the food and tea before him. Straightening up, he said, "Ah, wonderful."

"I hope you enjoy it, sir. Anything else for the moment?"

"There is one thing." His sunglasses reflected her face, as wan as skim milk. "It's so quiet in here, I'm wondering, if you're not too busy, would you mind saying a few words into my recorder?" He lifted the silvery gadget, which was about the size and shape of a deck of cards.

In nearly a dozen years of waitressing, counting from when she'd begun clearing tables in her parents' tavern at age ten, this was a first. "Is it for the radio?"

"No, no. For research. I'm the only one who'll hear it."

Uneasy to think of a blind man listening to her voice inside his unlit cavern, she asked, "What would you like me to say?"

"These few words, if you please." He pulled a card from his pocket.

Taking the card, she skimmed the list: *creek, route, house, tomato, aunt, roof, neighbor,* and ten or fifteen more. Still hesitant, she licked her lips and read the words aloud, bending close to the recorder, close enough to smell his aftershave, like vanilla mixed with rum.

When she had finished, and he had thanked her, she backed away, studying him, free for once to stare at a customer. He set the recorder aside, tucked his necktie into the pocket of his sky-blue shirt, and ran his fingers over the bowl, cup, teapot, cream pitcher, and silverware, before he began to eat. She couldn't help noticing his wedding band; the noticing was an old habit, and a pointless one. She wasn't in the market for a man, least of all a blind man. The handle of the walking stick jutted above his head; except for the white shaft, it resembled the staffs used by hikers in the Ithaca gorges. His hair, barbered close to the skull and tightly curled, was jet black, without a thread of gray. Probably in his late twenties or early thirties—it was hard to tell, since the wrap-around glasses hid his eyes, but the skin around his mouth was as smooth as chocolate.

With a familiar ache in the pit of her stomach she thought of Tommy, who wasn't so dark but had the same stocky build. She thrust her chapped hands into the pockets of her apron and hurried away. Wishing to think of something else, anything else, she remembered the schoolboys, with their knobby knees and stick legs. She checked once more outside the door of the café to see if they had come for their secret snack, but there was no sign of them, and she felt let down. It was silly to put so much stock in those kids, who would have ignored her entirely if she hadn't baited them with food.

As the flow of morning customers picked up—a flight crew, salesmen shuffling papers, rumpled professors going over lecture notes—Aurora had to quit watching the blind man. Yet she managed to see when he raised an index finger, as though testing the wind, and she brought him the bowl of fruit he requested; later, unasked, she brought a fresh teabag and a refill of hot water. Each time she paused to run her gaze over him. His muscular bulk made her feel scrawny. Her landlady and co-workers sometimes asked if she was ill. She assured them she felt fine; she simply couldn't put on flesh.

When she approached the blind man with the check, unsure how to present it, he relieved her uncertainty by asking her to add a five dollar tip, insert his room number, print his name—James Trevor—and then to loan him a pen and guide his hand to the spot where he should sign. Under her thin fingers his felt massive, like the limbs of a slow but powerful animal, a starfish maybe. She let go, touched her throat, and watched him scrawl a jerky signature.

"Can I show you out?" she offered.

"No, thanks." He pushed back from the table and stood. "Once I've walked somewhere, I can usually find my way again."

"Well, then, enjoy your time in Ithaca, Mr. Trevor."

"I hope to, Miss." He paused, standing there with a fist gripping the handle of his walking stick. "If I'm going to eat breakfast here the next few days, I can't keep calling you Miss. Since you know my name, isn't it fair that I should know yours?"

She was flustered, so used to being anonymous in her white shirt and black slacks, with her flyaway red hair lassoed into a ponytail—a plain, skinny woman of twenty-two whom nobody looked at twice. "It's Aurora," she answered. "Aurora Eliza Blake."

He repeated her name, as if it were the first line of a song he was trying to recall. Then he asked, "You're not from upstate New York, are you?"

"No, sir."

"From Ohio, I'd say."

"That's right," she admitted. "A buckeye, born and bred."

"More precisely, northern Ohio. Urban. Cleveland, perhaps?"

It disturbed her, that he could detect her origins so easily. "How can you tell?"

He smiled broadly. "I'm a student of American dialects."

"Well, that's scary." She would have said more, but was aware of unattended desires building up across the dining room, customers wanting more coffee or pats of butter or checks. And so she muttered, "I'd better go earn my big bucks."

"Of course, of course." Wearing that confident smile, James Trevor turned and began skittering the stick across the carpet ahead of him as he walked away.

*

Although Aurora had always been scrawny, she had not always been plain. For a spell when she was thirteen and fourteen, the men at the Iron Ore Tavern began following her movements with their eyes or patting her as she lugged trays among the tables. Some even tried slipping their hands under her skirt when she leaned over to set down pitchers of beer. She batted their hands away, but did so with a laugh, to keep from losing tips. So long as she didn't cut school, she could work at that age because her parents owned the tavern, and she could dress like a tramp—her mother's description—because her father knew what was good for business. When her tight blouse began to show the nubbins of breasts and her short skirt began to reveal a curving rump, the men took an interest. Neither rump nor breasts ever got much bigger, however, and what had seemed cute in a girl became disappointing in a woman, so that now, well beyond puberty, Aurora snared no man's eyes. Most of the time this neglect was fine with her, because the early, fleeting rush of male attention had led only to grief.

When she was a girl, the men who frequented the Iron Ore Tavern, just off Euclid Avenue in an area of Cleveland that had fallen on hard times, worked, if they worked at all, on Great Lakes freighters, in warehouses, tire shops, and rusty mills; they drove squad cars and taxis; they tarred roofs, bagged groceries, laid brick. They often showed up straight from work, in sweat-stained shirts bearing the names of their employers across the back and their own names stitched over the breast pockets. Pete, Sammy, Carlos, Tony, Will. White, black, red, and brown, all buddies in booze, or at least willing to ignore the colors of skin while drinking. Some of them, Aurora knew, were drinking up the rent money. Some were hiding out from bill-collectors or nagging wives. When they fought, as they occasionally did, her father charged

out from behind the bar and collared the one who'd started it and
threw him onto the sidewalk. After a few wallops from her father
when she was little, Aurora had never dared to make him mad,
especially when he was liquored up—which meant just about any
time the bar was closed. She read his moods with the life-or-death
vigilance a Great Lakes sailor gave to the weather.

Sugar, the men called her, or Sweet Cheeks, Princess, Doll.
When they traced her new curves with bloodshot eyes and callused hands, she never took them seriously, for they were mostly
older, graying and balding, smelling of grease and sweat and ciga-
rette smoke, wearing sideburns or scrubby moustaches, their bel-
lies sagging. The leering and fondling irked her but also flattered
her, as if, after years of invisibility, she had become a solid presence, with her own gravity and radiance. Merely by crossing the
room, she could stir these gruff men, and this newfound power
thrilled as well as frightened her. Their voices assured her it was
all in good fun. As they made over her they often winked at her
father, who winked back from his post at the bar. Yet she sensed,
behind their teasing and laughing, a danger that made her wary,
and so she played along just far enough to gather tips.

Then one Saturday night in March when Aurora was fifteen,
and she felt her allure beginning to fade, a guy came into the
tavern off a freighter with a driver's license showing him to be
twenty-one, but she guessed he was younger. Later she would
find out he was only eighteen. Her father didn't bother checking
IDs too closely, because several cops from the local precinct were
regulars at the bar when off-duty, and they appreciated the free
drinks he set before them now and again. "Nightcaps for cops,"
he called these wet bribes.

The boy who claimed to be twenty-one settled on a stool at
the bar, where her father served him a glass of beer and a plate of
onion rings, one of her mother's specialties. As Aurora delivered

orders and cleared tables, the boy swiveled on his stool to give
her the eye. She looked his way often enough to notice his broad
shoulders filling out a yellow slicker and his thighs stretching the
fabric of his jeans. Even without his straight black hair drawn into
a braid, his high cheekbones and nut-brown skin would have told
her he was part Indian. After a few minutes, he took his glass and
plate to an empty table and sat down, watching her steadily. Even
when she was turned away from him, Aurora could feel the pressure of his gaze. Soon he crooked a finger at her, and she ignored
several other beckoning customers to approach his table.

"Another beer?" she asked.

"One's my limit," he answered, his voice low and soft, like water sliding over stone. "But I could use a hamburger with fries."

"Sure you don't want quiche?"

"What's that?"

She laughed. "Just kidding. It's egg pie. You won't find it here.
But my mom makes a killer meatloaf sandwich."

"Your mom?"

"She's the cook. My dad's the bartender. A family enterprise."

His eyes were two black pools. "A meatloaf sandwich, then."

"Good choice. And I'd go with potato salad instead of fries.
Less grease."

He nodded gravely. "Whatever you say."

His freighter, it turned out, was docked in Cleveland for a
week. He spent all seven nights in the Iron Ore Tavern, always
choosing a corner table, where he and Aurora could exchange a
few words beyond earshot of her father. Soon he was calling her
by name and asking her to call him Raven. It pleased her that he
never drank more than one beer, a restraint the other boozers
rarely showed; that he smelled of shampoo instead of oil and
sweat; that he sat upright instead of slouching; that he stacked
his plates and silverware when he finished eating. It pleased her

above all that whenever she glanced at him, his black eyes were fixed on her.

During the lulls, when nobody was demanding more drinks or grub, the two of them began swapping life stories. Aurora didn't have much to tell, never having traveled far from Cleveland or done much outside of school and tavern. But Raven, it seemed, had gone everywhere and done everything, thanks to money from his father, a Detroit banker, and from his mother, an heiress in one of the automobile families. He was half Ojibwa on his mother's side, from a long line of chiefs. He knew the ancient medicine of the tribe. In high school he was a champion wrestler, winning the Michigan state heavyweight title. Lots of colleges tried recruiting him, but he wanted to see more of the world before he took up any of those offers. That explained why, in spite of his wealth, he worked on a freighter.

Later, she would discover that most of Raven's story, like his ID and his name, was phony, made up to intrigue her. If she hadn't been such an ignoramus, she would have realized that no Ojibwa woman could have inherited an automobile fortune, and no son of an heiress would have been working as a deckhand. But at the time Raven's boastful talk drew her to his table each night for longer and longer spells, until her father grumped from behind the bar that there were other customers to serve.

*

Six years later and two states away, Aurora was still serving customers, and still, she had to admit, pretty much of an ignoramus. She borrowed books from the library, on travel and history and spirituality, not the romances or mysteries other women favored, but she found only a few minutes to read each day, mainly during breaks at the hotel and before falling asleep at the rooming house. Until she rode the bus to Ithaca as an utterly panicked sixteen-year-old, she had never crossed the Ohio border. Even the trip to Ithaca was mostly a blank, as were her first few days in the new city. On the bus, a man stinking of booze had pestered her. She remembered that much, and she remembered arriving broke and hungry, without knowing a soul in Ithaca, without a job or a place to stay. Across the street from the bus station there was a skuzzy diner, with a "Help Wanted" sign in the window, so she got up her nerve and went in to ask about work. The manager almost bit off her head, but a customer there, an art student, offered to put her up. What option did she have except to go along? Then the student and her roommate freaked her out so much she snuck away in the night and wandered the streets until she found a church shelter, just before a rainstorm broke.

She couldn't recall what had spooked her about the art student or the roommate. It wouldn't have taken much, she was such a raw-nerved wreck at the time. In the following days and weeks, she kept imagining she would run into them; but they must have graduated and left town, for she never laid eyes on them again. The bullying manager at the diner—a place called the Cosmic Café, long since torn down to make way for a bicycle shop—reminded her too much of her father, so she found a waitressing job somewhere else, and year by year she worked her way up the ladder until she reached the Seneca Hotel. The customers here were far better heeled than the men she'd served in her parents' bar. The tips were larger, the clothes fancier, the voices more refined. Nobody traced her scant curves with hands or eyes—nobody paid her much mind at all, in fact, and this was fine with her. Since that week of basking in Raven's attention, a week that began in joy and ended in sorrow, she had come to appreciate the safety, if not the loneliness, in being invisible.

★

When James Trevor showed up for breakfast again on Tuesday, it occurred to Aurora that she was literally invisible to him, only a disembodied voice. He arrived just as she was giving cups of yogurt to the two schoolboys. She put a finger to her lips and raised her eyebrows at the boys, who tiptoed away, keeping their handouts secret from the blind man. A few steps down the hall, the younger one glanced back with a grin, two front teeth missing; it was all she could do to keep from rushing after him and squeezing him to her chest.

"Good morning, Mr. Trevor," she said.

"And to you, Ms. Aurora Eliza Blake," he said with a little bow.

The sound of her name in his radio voice made her shiver. After delivering him an order of waffles to go with his chamomile tea, she checked on him occasionally as the dining room filled. Once when she brought extra syrup, he asked her to describe the view through the café windows. She told him the only windows opened onto the hallway, where you could see a woman vacuuming. Then he wanted to know if there was art on the walls. There were photographs, she told him, the size of bath towels. They'd been put up a few days earlier, to advertise an exhibit at the History Center.

"Photographs of what?"

"Old timey Ithaca, it looks like. One shows boys lugging cartons of empty pop bottles—Canada Dry—to a corner store. Another shows a pile of boys in a schoolyard, some wearing baseball mitts, all of them mugging for the camera. There's one of a little boy in shorts squatting down to watch an egg fry on a sidewalk. And there's one of boys ice skating on Cayuga Lake."

"Nothing but boys?"

"Well, there's a photo of a girl in a frilly dress, with a necklace and square bangs, opening a purse to buy a cupcake at a bake sale. But even that one's got a small boy—maybe her brother—

crowding up to point out the cookie he wants."

Aurora excused herself to wait on other customers, but really she wanted to quit thinking about those little boys, with their broomstick arms and crooked grins and their skulls so exposed beneath burr haircuts. Not just the photographs, but the streets of Ithaca seemed to be tilted toward boys. From the loading dock behind the hotel, where she went during breaks to catch a breath of fresh air and read a few pages, she could see toddlers playing across the street in DeWitt Park, and nearly always she counted more boys than girls. Most days, when she walked home to her attic room in a house a few blocks west on Buffalo Street, she passed by Immaculate Conception as school was letting out, and of the children scampering to hug parents or nannies, or climbing into the backseats of cars, or taking a last few swings in the playground, way more than half, she estimated, were boys. Once or twice a week she saw the two brothers whom she secretly fed, the kindergartener and third-grader, trudging from school to the hotel to meet up with their mother. Aurora didn't dare speak with any of these children, for fear the crossing guard would think she was trying to kidnap them.

She often wondered what the children made of their school's name. If they were instructed in the meaning of *immaculate* and *conception*, would they imagine that their own births, unlike the birth of Jesus, were tainted? Would they imagine that every mother except the Virgin Mary was corrupted by having consorted with a mortal man rather than with God?

Today, the press of customers kept her from pondering such matters. The blind man made no surprising requests this time when she brought his check. He went through the same routine as he had the day before, leading up to her guiding his hand to the spot for the signature, a hand nearly as big, she imagined, as a baseball mitt.

★

During that week of basking in Raven's attention, back when she was fifteen, Aurora played along farther than she ever had before with any boy at school, let alone with any of the rough men at the Iron Ore Tavern. Night by night, in the alleyway behind the bar or in the stairway leading up to her family's apartment, she let his hands roam over her body, first on top of her clothes and then beneath them. Her father must have noticed the two of them slipping out, but so long as she returned in time to clear tables and refill pitchers, he didn't bark at her. Her mother, trapped in the kitchen, knew nothing.

While they kissed, Raven's fingers rubbed and probed her insistently, unerringly, as if he already knew the map of her skin. Between kisses, he murmured promises. He would talk with her parents before he shipped out. Tell them he wanted to marry her. Not right away, of course. Not until she graduated. When he returned from his next tour on the freighter, he'd take her to meet his folks in Detroit, show her all the sights up there. Show her their country house, too, on a lake in the Upper Peninsula. Teach her to waterski. It was a private lake, so they could go skinny dipping. No end of things they could do. Listening to him, Aurora envisioned herself in those far places, freed from the gossipy school and smoky bar, no longer a gawky girl but a woman, utterly desired.

On Raven's last night in port, convinced that he loved her, afraid nobody else ever would, she let him into her room above the bar, let him undress her, let him inside her. Intent on giving him pleasure, she acknowledged her own pain only after he withdrew and stood up to retrieve his clothes from a chair. Streetlight through the window outlined his muscular body. Older girls had warned her there would be pain, but she hadn't imagined it would be so sharp. They had also warned her to make sure the boy used a condom—a rubber, they called it—but in the rush toward bed she had been afraid to ask Raven if he had one, and she had none to offer.

As he turned to pull on his jeans, she could dimly see on his left shoulder blade, next to his braid, a jagged black shape as large as a spread hand. A swastika?

"What's that?" she asked, startled.

"What's what?"

"On your back."

He jerked around to face her. "A tattoo."

"Yes, but what's it of?"

"It's for good luck. A spiritual thing."

"It looks like—"

"It's holy, not for talking about." He quickly buttoned his shirt, stepped into his boots.

Aurora lay there aching, filling herself with the sight of him, fending off the sense that he was lying. "Can't you stay awhile?"

"I've got to board the ship or they'll sack me."

"How long 'til you come back?"

"Oh, six weeks, two months." He zipped the yellow slicker. "Depends on what we're hauling and where it's bound. No later than June, for sure."

"Then we'll go visit your folks?"

"We'll see. Depends on when I get vacation."

"Raven—"

He waited with a hand on the doorknob. "What now?"

She wanted to ask if he loved her, if he found her beautiful, but his hard cheekbones and taut lips, licked by streetlight, made her say instead, "Be quiet, so you don't wake my folks."

"Sure thing." He blew her a kiss, and that was the last she ever saw of him.

★

The last she ever heard of Raven came the following February, two months after the birth of her son, who entered the world with a swatch of hair as black as his father's and skin almost as brown. The baby was sleeping behind the bar and Aurora was waiting tables one night when in rolled a beefy, gray-bearded man whom she remembered as a shipmate of Raven's. For a while she was too nervous to approach the man, talking instead with a few of the regulars who asked about the baby. Her standard answer was that all he did was eat, sleep, cry, and fill his diapers. None of them seemed to think it strange that she was a mother at sixteen, with no husband in sight, that she had dropped out of school and had zero prospects for any job paying more than minimum wage. She gathered they had sisters, daughters, or nieces who'd been in the same fix.

When she could no longer ignore the bearded man, she approached his table warily, took his order, and was just turning away when he said, "Shame about Tommy."

"Tommy who?"

"Tommy Two Bears," the man said. "Maybe you knew him as Raven. That's what he called himself when he was in port. Part of his Indian rigmarole the ladies went for. He was awful sweet on you, I remember."

"What about him?"

"You didn't hear?"

"Hear what, for Pete's sake?"

He raked fingers through his whiskers, avoiding her eyes. She waited, hands on hips, head cocked. At last, with an air of reluctance, the man told her that a pilot from their ship had spent an evening in the tavern last summer, figured out from looking at her that she was in a family way, found out from asking around who the father was, and then went back and told Tommy he'd better go to Cleveland and do right by her. But instead Tommy had joined the Navy, sailed aboard an aircraft carrier into the Persian Gulf, and died there when a jet overshot the flight deck and spun out of control. "Only nineteen," the man concluded. "He's buried in Arlington Cemetery. You could go see."

Aurora swayed and would have fallen, had the man not lurched from his chair to catch her. She came to in the kitchen, stretched out on the counter next to the grill. Her mother was flipping hamburgers with one hand, pressing an icepack to Aurora's forehead with the other.

Raven's shipmate stood there looking on anxiously. "You okay?"

"I'm just tired, is all," Aurora said. She took the icepack from her mother and sat up, still woozy. "I haven't slept three hours at a stretch since the baby was born."

"I just wanted to say I was sorry about Tommy." The man rocked heavily from foot to foot. "I didn't mean to bring bad news."

"Tell me, was he really the son of a banker in Detroit?"

The man snorted. "Not hardly. He was from Marquette, in the U.P. Never mentioned any dad. I met his mom once when we docked there, a real quiet Indian woman, from one of them northern tribes. She had diabetes so bad she couldn't work. Lived off the checks Tommy sent her. Now maybe she'll get a veteran's payout."

"One more thing," Aurora said. "Did you ever see him with his shirt off?"

"Plenty of times. It gets hot as blazes below deck."

"You saw the tattoo on his back?"

"The swastika?"

"He told me it was a good luck charm. A spiritual sign."

"That's the kind of thing he'd say. More Indian malarkey. It was a swastika, all right. If anybody asked him about it, he'd glare back with his jaw set. So we let it go. A ship is a snug place. If a man has a secret, you let him keep it."

Just then her father stuck his head through the kitchen doorway. "Hey, when you get finished with your little drama, we've got a bar to run."

Her mother snapped back, "Luther, you leave her alone."

"Don't tell me what to do."

"I will if you're being cruel."

"Who got herself knocked up by a half breed?

"For God's sake, can't you see she's hurting?"

Over their voices and the hubbub of drinkers, Aurora could hear the baby's piercing cry.

*

No sign of the schoolboys on Wednesday, but James Trevor showed up early in another pricey shirt and tie, eyes concealed behind those opaque shades, his face wearing that expectant smile, as if he counted on kindness. Aurora knew better than to count on kindness, although every once in a while someone, like this blind man, surprised her.

When he was settled at his table with tea and omelet and toast, he asked again if he could record her voice, and then asked her to describe Ithaca and its waterfalls. She didn't know what to say, nor did she have time to say it amid the breakfast rush, so she proposed that during her morning break they could ride the elevator to a lounge on top of the hotel and she could describe the view from there.

"Ah, marvelous," he said, as if her offer were another serving of food.

At 10:30 they met in the lobby and rode alone in the elevator, which filled with the spicy aroma of his aftershave. For this morning's outing, he told her, he had postponed his daily trip to

Cornell, where he was helping to develop software that would enable visually impaired students to hear class notes and books read aloud by computers, instead of having to decipher everything through Braille. Aurora wondered if he thought of himself as "visually impaired." Did a fancy name make it less of a loss?

In the tenth-floor lounge—where the mother of the schoolboys, a bedraggled woman with pockmarked cheeks and bowed legs, was emptying wastebaskets—Aurora led this inquisitive, dapper man from window to window, telling him what could be seen in each direction. Speaking into the recorder, she explained that Ithaca lay in a sort of bowl, with hills on every side except the north, which opened onto the long blue finger of Cayuga Lake. The towers of Cornell rose above trees on a ridge to the northeast, and the towers of Ithaca College loomed from a ridge to the southwest. Now, in September, with maples beginning to flame red, the town seemed to be cradled by the encircling hills and lake, but in winter, frozen beneath layer upon layer of snow, the place could feel cut off from all promise of warmth or growth. The houses in town were mainly wood, the stores and banks mainly brick, the churches mainly stone. She counted seven steeples within a few blocks of the hotel, the tallest of them narrow and sharp with crosses at the top, like rockets aiming at heaven.

"You'd think we'd be holy and smart," Aurora said, "surrounded by colleges and churches. But you couldn't prove it by me."

"You don't attend church?"

"Sometimes I go and sit with the Quakers, because they don't make you sign on to any creed. They let you find your own way in the silence. My folks were allergic to religion, so I never went to church when I was growing up." She told him then about her parents sleeping in on Sundays, their only mornings free of toiling in the Iron Ore Tavern, and about how she waited tables beginning in fifth grade. Once the words started flowing, they kept coming. So she told about the sailors and railroaders and cops, the fights, the puke on the floor, the struggle to do schoolwork at the bar during slow times, her father's boozy temper, her mother's perpetual weariness, the lonely sound of freighters bleating in fog on Lake Erie. She even told about falling for a liar who called himself Raven—told everything that mattered about her growing up except the one thing that mattered most, the one unspeakable thing.

By the end of her headlong tale they had arrived back in the lobby, where she handed him the recorder and apologized for rattling on.

"Nonsense," he replied. "You've been quite generous." His lenses gave back two tiny images of her face, like dollops of cream floating in cups of coffee.

Hesitantly, she said, "Do you mind if I ask you a question? It's kind of personal."

"Not at all. Go right ahead."

"Well, I've been wondering why you wear those glasses. Is it to protect your eyes from light?"

"No, it's to hide them. I learned early on that their appearance is disturbing. People are used to reading emotions in eyes, and I gather that mine are unreadable."

"I was just curious, that's all. I didn't mean to pry."

"Not to worry." His fingers brushed her elbow, and then ran down her arm until they squeezed her hand.

★

On Thursday morning the younger of the two schoolboys was standing in the hallway alone when Aurora opened the café doors. "Where's your brother?" she asked.

The boy shrugged, but said nothing. Whenever she had spoken to the boys, only the older one had answered, and even he would never tell their names.

"Is he sick?" she asked. "Did he stay home?" The boy nodded. "But your mommy's at work?" Another nod. "Is somebody at home with him? Your daddy?" The boy shook his head so hard his entire body twisted. "Your grandma?" Now he nodded again, lower lip thrust out.

Aurora wanted to hear his voice, so she kept asking questions. "How do you like kindergarten? Do you have a nice teacher? Are you learning to read?" The boy stared at his brown leather shoes, which were run over at the heels but polished so the scuffs barely showed. She wanted to kiss his bare, bony knees. Only hunger kept him standing there, she realized, so she drew two muffins from her apron and he took them and darted away, a Superman backpack thumping against his frail shoulders.

When she turned from the scampering boy, she found James Trevor standing behind her at the entrance of the café. "Who's your friend?" he asked.

"Oh," she said, "it's the son of a woman who works in the hotel. Sometimes I give him a treat from the breakfast bar. Don't tell my boss."

"I can keep a secret." His face broke into that trusting smile.

Mr. Trevor's smile was the last one she saw that morning, as the other diners seemed to be in a foul mood, perhaps because the weather was dreary. Today's background music didn't help, as one song after another moaned about a lover who'd done the singer wrong. Blues, blues, and more blues. In one song, which played every hour or so as the CD repeated, a man kept wailing, "I want my baby back." Aurora knew that the "baby" here was the man's two-timing girlfriend, but she kept imagining a real baby, an infant, too young even to crawl. If you'd lost a baby, wouldn't you want it back more than you'd want any sexy gal or guy?

As he signed his tab for breakfast, Mr. Trevor asked if she would be working today after 4:00 or so. When she told him no, she'd be in class, he asked what she was studying, and she told him court reporting.

"How interesting." He rose from the chair and gripped his white stick. "What led you to choose that unusual profession?"

Disarmed by his curiosity, she explained: "I used to wait for the bus to school out front of a place called the Academy of Court Reporting. They had signs in the windows telling how much you could earn. Way more than a waitress makes. I'm hoping once I finish my training I can get a job with the court and move out of my landlady's attic and buy a trailer in the hills. Maybe even a house one day. Who knows?"

He nodded, as if he had dreams of his own. "Have you observed many trials?"

"Only on TV. When I'd come into the bar after school, my dad would be watching this old lawyer show. Perry Mason was the guy's name. He won every case. I liked the way there was always a clear verdict, guilty or innocent, nothing in between."

"Why not study law?"

She let loose a scoffing breath. "Fat chance. It took me four years after moving here to get my GED. There's no way I'll ever go to college."

"I see," Mr. Trevor said, which sounded odd coming from a blind man.

"If I can sit in a courtroom tapping keys, taking down what lawyers and witnesses and judges say, that'll be about my speed."

"Do you have classes tomorrow afternoon as well?" He rested both hands on top of the walking stick and leaned toward her.

"Not on Fridays."

"Then I wonder if you'd consider doing me a great favor."

Aurora studied the smooth skin of his cheek, which was like

brown silk, shot through with light. "What sort of favor?"

"Would you take me to one of the famous Ithaca gorges? I leave early Saturday, so tomorrow will be my last chance."

"I don't have a car," she said, and then quickly added, "but there's a waterfall we can walk to." Just as quickly a pang of fear prompted her to say, "I'm sure folks from Cornell could tell you a whole lot more than me, about geology and stuff."

"I'd prefer you as a guide. No recorder this time. Just a pleasant outing. What do you say?"

His confident voice and smile, his thick shoulders squared back, everything about him announced that he expected her to say yes. And that is what she said.

*

They set off from the hotel the next afternoon as children from Immaculate Conception were streaming down the sidewalk, the younger ones clutching the hands of big brothers or sisters or grownups. But one tyke waited alone at the corner of Buffalo and Tioga for the light to change, his white shirt untucked from the blue shorts, his backpack dangling from a single strap, and Aurora, waiting on the opposite side of the street with Mr. Trevor, saw that it was the kindergartener, still without his brother. He looked tired. She would have waved at him, but she imagined him dashing into traffic, a thought that made her shudder.

When the light changed, she guided Mr. Trevor down from the curb while gripping his elbow. As the boy passed them she called out, "Hey there, kiddo," and patted his blond mop of hair, the first time she had ever touched him. He glanced up at her, blurted out, "Hey, Muffin Lady," and scurried on toward the hotel.

"Ah, your ravenous young friend," Mr. Trevor said.

"You know that because he called me Muffin Lady?"

"I know because I heard the same flutter in your voice when you spoke with him yesterday morning."

No one had ever listened to her so closely before. Of course there was nothing personal about the blind man's listening, she reminded herself. His keen ears merely compensated for his ruined eyes. He kept registering sounds as they headed north along Tioga Street. Tapping his stick, he could tell when they moved from sections of sidewalk made of concrete to sections made of slate. He heard the trickle of Cascadilla Creek a block before they crossed over it. He identified the clatter of children riding scooters, the singing of robins and wrens, the scrape of a spade against stone, the whining fan belt in a truck, the crunch of leaves underfoot. When he asked if the shade trees were maples, she told him yes, they were lighting up like torches all along the street.

Then he asked her what flowers were blooming in the yards. She didn't know their names, but from her descriptions, and from bending down to smell or touch the blossoms, he identified impatiens, chrysanthemums, geraniums, petunias, sunflowers, marigolds, red cannas, zinnias, and roses.

"There weren't any flowers in my part of Cleveland," she said, "so I never learned what they were called. But I could name you thirty kinds of beer."

"So what's the best beer in Cleveland?"

"I hate them all. I hate every drink my daddy ever sold or swallowed."

"Your parents don't run the tavern any more?"

"Oh, probably. It's all they know how to do."

"You never get back home?"

"Home is here," she insisted.

"You don't talk with them on the phone? Don't write letters?"

"Not since I left."

"And how long is that?"

"Five years."

They walked on a few paces in silence. Aurora sensed he was waiting for her, giving her a chance to explain. She felt an overwhelming need to confide in him, this man who had treated her so kindly and who would board a plane tomorrow and fly away.

"I cut myself off from them," she said, and then bit her lip.

"You cut yourself off from them?"

"Because I did something terrible." Trying to decide how much to confess, she paused before adding, "Something unforgivable."

He stopped. She thought he was going to ask what she had done, but instead he pointed off to the right and murmured, "The falls."

She couldn't hear them yet, but she could lead him there. North on Lake Street to the bridge, then down the footpath into the Fall Creek gorge, her hand tightening on his arm lest he stumble on the loose stones. She described for him the deep, layered walls of the gorge—slabs of old seafloor, she'd heard, although it was hard to imagine the sea ever reaching upstate New York—and she described the trees high above tilting over the rim, the vines hanging down, the stream flowing over a flat stony bed, and along the path a swirl of white butterflies alighting on flowers.

Again he stopped, his arm flexing where she grasped it. A smile stole over his face. "A violin," he whispered. "Playing Vivaldi."

Although she could hear nothing except the purr of water, Aurora trusted the blind man's ears. Such a thing could happen in Ithaca. And sure enough, as they rounded a bend she could see, well back from the waterfall, a woman sitting in a blue lawn chair, wearing a straw hat, and playing a violin. Now that Aurora saw the instrument, the bow moving over the strings, she could hear it, but just barely.

She guided Mr. Trevor past the violin player to a mossy ledge near the base of the falls, and there they sat, enveloped in the roar and mist.

"It's like milk pouring down a giant staircase," she told him, her lips close to his ear, "all white and frothy. It's like the train on a bridal gown. It's like—I don't know. It's beautiful. It gives me goose bumps."

He turned toward her, his sunglasses damp from the spray, his face gleaming. "Nothing is unforgivable," he said.

She let go of his arm and squeezed her hands between her thighs. "You wouldn't say that if you knew what I did."

"Do you want to tell me?"

She looked down at her legs, so narrow in the black slacks. She had thought of changing from her waitress outfit into a dress before their walk, but it didn't matter how she looked. She existed for him only as a voice and as a touch on his arm. "I ran away from my parents," she began, and then her throat clenched.

"Lots of kids do that."

"I didn't just leave my parents." Aurora glanced toward the violinist, who was still fingering the strings and sliding the bow, but she could hear no music over the thrum of water. Before her nerve failed, she told him the rest of it, or nearly all the rest, leaving out the part for which she still had no words. "The first man I'd ever trusted got me pregnant and sailed away and died. I sank into a black fog. I was a terrible mother, the worst ever. It was my mother who kept the baby alive. I knew if I stayed I'd hurt him. So I left him for her to raise and I took off. He was too little even to sit up, and I left him in that stinking tavern. Then I rode the bus to Ithaca and I've stayed here ever since, too ashamed to call and see how my boy's doing, let alone go back and look him in the eye."

"Five years," James Trevor said. "He'd be starting kindergarten."

"Yes. If he's healthy. If he's been looked after." Aurora wiped her cheeks with the back of a wrist. "I've never told anybody before."

"That's a heavy load to carry," he said. "But you can lay it down."

"I don't see how."

"You can lay it down because you're forgiven."

"Says who?" When he did not answer, she turned to him, trembling. "I trusted you with something. Now trust me with something."

"What do you want?"

"Let me see your eyes."

His lips tightened into a solemn line. Slowly he removed the dark glasses and presented his face to her, his eyes like chalky moons, like planets wrapped in clouds, like twin knots of foam in the milky tumble of Ithaca Falls.

§ § §

Chapter Five • August 2007

HARLAN

NOW THAT THE FENCES WERE DOWN, the bears shambled out of the forest each day at dawn and dusk to raid the blueberry patch and the orchard, and to lick the last drops of honey from the smashed hives. Katarina wanted to steal up the slope and spy on the bears from close by, but Harlan persuaded her to stay down at the farmhouse and watch through binoculars from the porch. She asked him what his heroes Lewis and Clark would have said about a man afraid of bears, and he replied that Lewis and Clark had kept their crew alive by knowing the difference between fear and respect.

Katarina didn't fear much, so far as Harlan could tell, but she did fear hitchhiking. The Hollywood films she had watched while growing up in Sweden had convinced her that lunatics cruised America's roads, on the lookout for victims. Although Harlan had met a few wackos on his travels, he figured they weren't any more common here than in other countries. Besides, at nineteen, muscled up from work on Black Bear Farm, he believed he could handle whatever danger came his way. He wouldn't seek it out, but he wouldn't shy away from it, either. Without that confidence, he could not have imagined going back to face his grandfather.

When he told Katarina they could ride the train to Cleveland, where his grandparents were expecting them, he hadn't counted on spending a month's pay for the tickets—money he'd rather save toward buying land. The bus wasn't much cheaper, and the airplane would cost even more. So as they were preparing to leave the farm, packing up their things and getting Mrs. Winfield ready for her move to the nursing home, Harlan kept reassuring Katarina about the sanity of American drivers.

"Mostly the ones who pick up hitchhikers are just lonely or bored. They hope you'll be more interesting than whatever is on the radio."

"You call it riding your thumb?" she asked, curious as always about American lingo. She was folding Mrs. Winfield's faded nightgowns.

"That's one way to say it. Then if you don't get a lift and you have to walk, that's called riding shank's mare."

"Who is Shank?"

"Your leg," he said. "The shank of your leg." And with that he reached down to squeeze her knee through the denim of her jeans.

She pulled her leg free of his grip, but not brusquely, and not without a slim smile, like a crescent moon. "Here," she said, handing him the stack of nightgowns, their lace frayed from many washings. "Pack these in her small suitcase. They will be familiar to her, when everything else has become strange."

*

The Winfield sons had made their plans clear to Harlan, who clamped his jaw to keep from swearing as he listened to their voices over the phone. After Mrs. Winfield was moved to what the sons called a rest home in Boston, antique dealers would arrive to pick through the furnishings in the farmhouse. Whatever

was left would be auctioned off on August 31st. Since that would
leave Harlan and Katarina without beds on the last night of their
employment, they would be welcome to stay in a motel, at the
sons' expense, and they were also welcome to take a small keepsake or two if they wished. "Although we'll trust you not to claim
anything valuable," the stockbroker added.

After the place had been picked clean, the barn would be
turned into a recreation hall and the house would become a sales
office for Mad River Meadows, as the development was to be
called, and then condos would rise from the sloping pastures and
hayfields. Refugees from the cities would visit in summer for the
cool breezes, in fall for the fiery maples, in winter for the snow, in
spring for the flush of new leaves, and in all seasons for views of
the Mad River Valley.

Instead of development, what Harlan saw was desecration,
yet he couldn't blame those who wished to feast on the sight of
this land, as he had done for the past three years, since journeying
here from the flat pavements of Cleveland in search of a dot on
the map named Black Bear Mountain. What galled him was that
the land, which had been farmed for two hundred years, would
never again grow anything but decorative flowers and poison-
perfect grass, and the people who came to enjoy the view would
stay for only a week or a weekend and then go back to wherever they made their money. For them, the valley would never be
home; it would be scenery.

"Scenery is all well and good," Mr. Winfield used to say, "but
you can't eat beauty." No, you can't eat beauty, Harlan thought,
nor can you live without it.

★

"Found your keepsake yet?" Harlan asked Katarina on a day
when antique dealers were combing through the farmhouse,

opening dressers and closets, inspecting linens and paintings, reading the makers' marks on the bottoms of dishes, searching every nook and cranny. "If so, you'd better tuck it away before the vultures find it."

"I have put a memento in my suitcase," Katarina replied.

"What did you pick?"

"A shawl, the lavender one. So I can picture her in the chair with knitting in her lap and the shawl around her shoulders." Katarina grimaced, as if the image was too bitter to contemplate. "And you—what is your keepsake?"

"A claw hammer with a beat-up head and a hickory handle. It wouldn't fetch two dollars at the auction, so the Winfield boys won't be out much cash."

Although Harlan mistrusted money, he could not help thinking about it during those final days at the farm. What he had saved from his wages would buy maybe five acres, at the price land was going for back in Ohio, but that would do for a start. On that much ground he could build a cabin, put in a garden and pond, plant berry bushes and fruit trees. What cash he needed he could earn by doing carpentry, painting, woodcutting, and other jobs. Five acres would support him just fine—would even support two people, if Katarina decided to stay here in America among the crazies. He kept wanting to ask her, but he always held back, afraid she would say no.

His grandmother often fretted about money in her letters. She complained of his grandfather's temper, her long hours of cooking for drunks, the aches in her joints, the ceaseless racket of traffic, the smoke. They were getting too old to run a tavern, she wrote, but they couldn't afford to quit. They couldn't even buy health insurance; Papa had veterans' coverage, but if she suffered a bad illness it would wipe them out. She was counting the months until they could go on Medicare and Social Security.

That, plus Papa's Army pension and the money Harlan had been
sending them—every penny of which they had saved—might allow them to move out of the city. But she didn't know if they
could handle such a move by themselves, especially with Papa's
cranky back. Although she never wrote in so many words that it
was high time for Harlan to come home and help, that is what he
read between the lines.

★

The last week of August, on a day as hot as any that summer,
Harlan eased Mrs. Winfield down from the porch in her wheelchair, across the bumpy lawn, into the shade of the cottonwood.
Katarina stayed indoors, refusing to take part in handing over the
old woman. A telephone call had alerted them that the limousine
would arrive soon to carry Mrs. Winfield to the nursing home.
Harlan had offered to borrow a car and drive her to Boston, but
the son who lived there insisted on hiring a chauffeur and a nurse.

Long, black, and polished to a high gloss, the car that rolled up
the lane might have carried gangsters or movie stars. The driver
who climbed out wore a visored hat with a flat crown and a suit
as black as the limousine, and the nurse who climbed out after
him wore a blue smock spangled with pictures of rabbits. Mrs.
Winfield waved at them, as if imagining they must be friends
whose faces she had forgotten, as she had forgotten nearly everyone else. These days, although church ladies and quilters still
visited occasionally, the only person she appeared to know was
Katarina, if not by name then by voice and touch.

Harlan bent over the wheelchair and lifted Mrs. Winfield, who
weighed no more than a yearling ewe, but unlike a sheep's wriggling body, hers was altogether limp, and smelled of camphor
rather than lanolin. He carried her to the limousine and settled
her gently into the backseat. As he straightened up, the porch

door banged and Katarina came rushing down the steps and over the grass. She squeezed past him and leaned in to lay a kiss on the old woman's brow.

"Sweet!" Mrs. Winfield cried, reaching for her. "Stay!"

But Katarina drew back. "I can't go with you, mum."

A stab of fear twisted the widow's face. The nurse slid in beside her and shut the door, the driver climbed behind the wheel, and the glossy car crunched over the gravel.

Harlan turned to see if Katarina had caught that terrified look, but she was hurrying away, her braids jouncing, and she disappeared around the corner of the house. He followed hesitantly, unsure how to comfort her. He, too, ached to think of Mrs. Winfield exiled from this farm where she had lived more than sixty years. But he had been numbed to loss early on—or at least he had learned not to let his heartache show.

Katarina was sitting on a stone bench beside the pond, unbraiding her hair, tugging impatiently when the strands tangled, sobbing. He sat beside her and snared her hands in his own and held them firmly until she stopped yanking. She leaned forward then, still weeping, and let him unsnarl the braids.

"Rest home!" she cried. "She can rest *here*. Why make her die among strangers, in a place that means nothing to her? In Sweden, we do not put our grandparents out."

"She's not our grandmother," he said, trying to calm her. "We don't have any say in where she goes."

Katarina gave a shake of her head, and the spill of hair—as light in color as corn silk, but heavy, luxuriant—spread over her back like a shawl. She rose abruptly and began unbuttoning her shirt.

"I feel dirty," she muttered.

Harlan watched, then turned away, then watched again as she took off her clothes and waded into the pond, the shimmery film of water rising up her calves and thighs and swallowing her entirely when she dove.

Presently her head broke the surface, haloed by that wealth of hair. She glared up at him on the bank. "Don't you feel dirty?"

He was going to protest that he felt grief, not guilt, and grief could not be rinsed away in a pond. But the set of her mouth and the ache in her eyes warned him this was no time for arguing. So he stood up from the bench, turned away from her stare, and slipped out of his clothes. He paused before turning back toward her.

"No need to hide," she said. "I know how boys are made. Come in. Come."

Before shyness could seize him he leapt in, and it was like leaping into the sky, for the pond reflected gauzy white clouds against a background of blue. When he swam within reach of Katarina, she wrapped her arms around his neck and drew him close, pressing her slippery length against him. "Hold me," she whispered.

Treading water to keep them both afloat, Harlan eased her toward shore, until he could stand with his feet wedged into the muck at the bottom of the pond. There he balanced, every inch of skin tingling where his body touched hers. She trembled as he stroked her hair, her throat, her breasts. Then gripping his shoulders and buoyed by the water, she opened her thighs and thrust against him and before he could think he slid inside her like a key into a lock. The surprise of it overcame his panic. As they clung together, rocking in a rhythm that Harlan was astonished to find he already knew, they sent ripples toward the edges of the pond, where cattails swayed and bullfrogs hunkered down in silence.

*

His awkwardness must have been obvious, for afterward, as they lay naked on the grass beside the pond, allowing the sun and wind to dry their skin, Katarina asked, "You have done this before?"

Afraid to look at her, Harlan studied the sky. "In a pond, you mean?"

"Anywhere."

"Not often," he said. But a lie seemed ungrateful, and so he admitted, "Actually, never."

"Never?" She rolled onto her side and studied him, her corn-silk hair tumbling over her breasts, one pink nipple showing between the strands. "How can this be, a handsome galoot like you? Is that how you say, 'galoot'?"

"That's how you say it. Where'd you learn a word like that?"

"From westerns. Cowboys are either galoots or hombres or long drinks of water."

"When I watched westerns, I always rooted for the Indians."

"Why so?"

Harlan was about to joke the remark away by saying he meant the Cleveland baseball team. But that would have been another lie. So he told her, "My father was Indian."

"Was?"

"He died at sea a couple months after I was born."

"How terrible. It is why you never speak of him?"

"I don't know much about him except he was Ojibwa, from up in Michigan. Tommy Two Bears. How's that for a name? He worked on freighters before joining the Navy."

"Tommy Two Bears," Katarina murmured, turning the words into a little song. She touched a finger to Harlan's chest. "So that is why you are tan everywhere, and your hair is as black as a crow?"

"I always figured I took after him, but I can't say for sure."

"Your mother kept no pictures?"

"My mother . . . " Harlan began, and he meant to go on, he wanted to go on, but his throat tightened up. He thought of those bullfrogs, hiding in the cattails, panicked into silence.

"Your mother?" Katarina prompted, waiting for him to continue. When he only shook his head, she began slowly tracing figure-eights on his chest. After a while, she asked, "Why have you never had sex?"

He watched the clouds, which were hustling from the west. "Scared, I guess."

"Of what? Sin? God hurling thunderbolts?"

"Of getting a girl pregnant." He closed his eyes and concentrated on the movement of Katarina's finger over his skin. "Right now I'm scared we started a child."

"Don't worry. We haven't started a child."

His eyes snapped open. "How can you be sure?"

"Because I take the pill. My mother got me a prescription when I enrolled in gymnasium —what you call high school. It is common in Sweden."

Relief washed over Harlan. Now he could recall their lovemaking without alarm—the sureness of her moves, the delicious fit of their bodies. His elation might have been no more than a rainbow slick on a well of sorrow, but he would savor it. "So," he ventured, "you must be pretty experienced by now."

"I have tried sex with a few boys," she said, in the direct way she had of saying everything. "Once or twice with each of them. But this is the first time it has meant anything except curiosity or pleasure."

"What does it mean this time?"

Her finger paused on his chest as she considered. At length she said, "You are not a boy. With you it is no longer play."

Katarina stood up then and began putting on her clothes. Now Harlan gazed at her openly, instead of glancing away, as he had done these past five months whenever he thought she might catch him looking. She had a compact body, every curve and limb and joint in lovely proportion. Her arms and legs were sun-browned, as dark as he was all over, but her torso was a luminous white, as if she had been molded of light. Maybe every bit of her, from her gossamer hair to the small pebbles of her toes, was made of light. Maybe his own body, dark as it was, and the river, the mountains, the circling hawks, the bears and blueberries, the sheep and grasses—maybe everything was made of light.

*

Hitchhiking from Ohio to Vermont had taken Harlan seven days; the return trip, with Katarina along to catch the eyes of drivers, took only three. Most of the drivers were men, long-haul truckers or sales reps, but a few were women, who may have glimpsed in Katarina a flashback to their younger selves. Men or women, she kept them talking by asking questions, teasing out their life stories. People told her about their woes, their bullying bosses or doddering parents, showed her photographs of children or dogs, turned up the radio for her to hear their favorite songs. When drivers used a bit of slang or an odd word that Katarina didn't know, she would ask them to repeat it, and Harlan could see her filing the terms away in that multilingual brain of hers. Mainly he watched the roadside, aching for Black Bear Farm and the Mad River Valley, worrying about his grandparents, wondering how he could persuade Katarina to stay with him.

A man who picked them up near Syracuse slid a hand onto Katarina's knee; before Harlan could react she lifted the hand away and set it on the gear shift, without missing a beat in the conversation. Later on, near Buffalo, a driver showed them how he could watch DVDs on a screen mounted above the dashboard, playing a movie clip that featured a robot firing a flamethrower into a crowd of people, a scene that made him chuckle. The woman who delivered them to Erie warned that she didn't think it wise

for young people to go hitchhiking these days, and to empha-
size the point she drew from under her seat a shiny pistol, which
made Katarina's eyes go wide and Harlan's heart skip a beat before the gun was tucked away. Their last ride into Cleveland was
with a retired professor, who chatted with Katarina in German,
the language he had taught at Oberlin.

Not wanting the professor to see the Iron Ore Tavern, which
likely had become even shabbier in the past three years, Harlan
asked him to let them out a few blocks away, on Euclid Avenue.
They emerged from the car into the muggy air of a late August
afternoon, and into the din of jackhammers and dump trucks.
The street had been undergoing repairs of one sort or another as
long as Harlan could remember, and here it was torn up again.
He shouldered his duffel bag and let Katarina heft her two suitcases, for she remained stubborn about carrying her own load.
As they picked their way among the machines and barricades, he
told her this stretch of Euclid used to be called Millionaire's Row,
back when the Rockefellers and other fat cats lived here. Now,
the mansions were gone, half the shops were shuttered, and the
grand churches, built by folks with deep pockets, advertised free
hot lunches and tax advice and services in Spanish. Passing the
Academy of Court Reporting, which he was pleased to see still in
business, he pointed out to Katarina the bus stop in front where
he used to catch his ride to school.

As they entered Harlan's old neighborhood, he showed Katarina the steam grates in the sidewalk where he used to warm
his feet in winter, the cracks he used to jump over to keep from
breaking his grandmother's back, the kiosk where he bought
cigarettes for his grandfather, the doorknobs he rattled to pester
shopkeepers. He was stalling, afraid the dingy tavern would re-
pulse Katarina, so he stopped every few paces to offer her a story
from his childhood. But when they turned north from Euclid and

came to his home block, where memories crowded too close for telling, he couldn't delay any longer and hurried the rest of the way, only to halt, perplexed, at the tavern door, where a sign announced:

CLOSED FOR RENOVATION

SAMMY'S SUSHI BAR

OPENING DECEMBER 1

UNDER NEW MANAGEMENT

Harlan was still planted there, at a loss, when Katarina caught up with him. She scanned the sign and then tried the door, which swung open, and she barged on in, as if she were the one who'd grown up here, as if she felt his eagerness but not his dread. Harlan followed, stepping into the familiar room, which was dark except for a shaded lamp over the bar, where his grandfather was watching a ballgame on TV.

Katarina had stopped abruptly just inside the door, in the shadows. Pausing beside her, Harlan set down his duffel and called, "Papa?"

His grandfather flinched, gave a grunt, and pivoted slowly, as if afraid of tipping. The gaze he turned on them was bloodshot and flinty.

A chill shot through Harlan. His grandfather used to drink only in the wee hours, after the last customer had left, or on Sundays when the saloon was closed. Never on a weekday afternoon. Yet here were those red-rimmed, watery, menacing eyes. More than anything else, it was those eyes Harlan had run away from, those eyes and the quarrels they set off between his grandparents, the shouts and pleas, the slamming of doors and whimpering.

"Well, look who's turned up," Papa said, pronouncing the words deliberately, as he did when he wished to keep from slurring. "Don't stand there in the dark, boy." He shut off the TV and came out from behind the bar, thick arms spread wide.

Harlan stepped forward and embraced him warily, smelling the whiskey, the sweat, and he realized Papa was an old man, still bulky but gone soft, shoulders drooping, bald head splotched with sores, breath ragged.

"Easy, you bruiser," Papa muttered, pushing Harlan away to arm's length and looking him over. "What did they feed you in Vermont?"

"Spring water and hard work."

"Cheese and lamb, more like it." He slapped Harlan's belly, then hitched up his pants, as if to rein in his own ponderous gut. "You made it back early."

"Thanks to my traveling partner here." Harlan gestured toward Katarina.

As she emerged from the shadows, Papa loosed a phlegmy laugh. His eyebrows shot up. "My, my, my."

"Papa," Harlan said, "meet Katarina Swanson."

The old man grasped her hand and seemed reluctant to let it go. "So you're the gal he's always going on about in his letters."

"Does he?" Katarina replied.

"Every page has got your name on it. And here we thought he was exaggerating. My wife said you sounded too good to be true."

"Where is Nana?" Harlan asked.

"Upstairs packing knickknacks."

The darkness of the saloon had kept Harlan from noticing until now that the shelves behind the bar were empty and the walls were bare. His grandmother's landscape paintings had been taken down. Sports banners no longer dangled from the ceiling and the glass cases once filled with Cleveland Indians memorabilia were now empty. "What's with the sign on the door?" Harlan asked.

"We're moving out of this dump," Papa said. "We talked for

years about selling, even before you took off. Nana was sick of frying hamburgers and mopping up puke. All she wanted was to sit down somewhere pretty and paint. All I wanted was to get off my feet and never listen to another sob story or jukebox song. Then a guy came in last week offering to swap his place in the country for the tavern. Thinks he can make a living here serving raw fish. So we took him up on it. Signed the papers three days ago."

"What sort of place?" Harlan asked.

"An old farm that's been whittled down to forty-some acres, along the Red Hawk River, about an hour east of here, over toward Warren. There's a house and barns and a tractor and whatnot. Even an old pickup. Nobody's lived there for quite a while, so it needs work." He gave another of his phlegmy laughs. "What it needs is an overhaul. But Nana's got her heart set on moving there. Calls it a painter's paradise."

Harlan shouted "Nana!" as he raced up the stairs, through the layered smells of booze, then Lysol, then his grandmother's lily-of-the-valley perfume.

She met him at the top landing, flung her arms wide, and hugged him tightly, rocking side to side, crying, "Oh, Harlan, you're home, you're home! I heard voices, and I thought it's too soon for them to arrive, they're still out there beside some highway waiting for a ride. But here you are! And where is your precious Katarina?"

"Talking with Papa," he said, resting his cheek on Nana's gray permed hair.

She twisted away to look down the stairs. "Is he—"

"Yes, but not bad. Not sloppy or mean."

Returning her gaze to Harlan, Nana reached up to lay her hands on his shoulders. "Just look at you! I swear you've grown three inches. You've filled out so. How will I ever feed you? And you're brown as a berry. I'm sorry you're coming home to such a mess." She waved at the stacks of boxes lining the hallway. "But we'll get a new home soon. We're moving to the country!"

"Papa told me."

Her face glowed with a look of jubilation. "It's run-down, I'll admit. Maybe more than we should take on. But, oh, Harlan, there are woods and fields all green as glory and a river winding by and the air smells of growing things instead of diesel fumes and you can see stars at night and there's plenty of room in the house for you and a wife and children."

"Whoa," Harlan said, laughing, "let's not marry me off so fast."

"I just thought, from the way you've written about Katarina . . . ." Nana angled her shining face up at him. "But there's no rush," she added, squeezing him tight again. "Oh, sweetheart, I just know you'll love the farm. You won't ever want to leave."

★

That afternoon, Harlan led Katarina on a saunter past his old haunts—Jacobs Field where he used to watch Indians games with Papa, Playhouse Square where he used to attend Sunday matinees with Mama, the Cleveland State campus where he listened to science lectures while playing hooky from high school, the soaring and shadowy nave of Trinity Cathedral where he often sat in a pool of light tinted by stained glass windows reading books of exploration, the public library on Superior where he borrowed those books and studied maps, the pocket parks here and there among the gleaming towers where he daydreamed of wilderness. There were a few shantyboats tethered along the river, and Katarina studied each one, assessing its virtues and flaws, spinning out visions of living aboard such a cozy craft and plying the waters of America.

This ramble eventually took them past the Rock and Roll Hall of Fame, where Harlan noted that the building always reminded him of the hodgepodge structures he used to make with Lego blocks. They followed East Ninth until the pavement gave out at the end of a pier, with boat slips on either side and the vast lake spread before them. An onshore breeze lifted waves into white-caps, and gulls patrolled the wrack line. A freighter slid along the horizon. The cries of children rose from a nearby beach. He kept silent, watching Katarina take it in.

At length she turned to him. "Even without the smell of salt, it reminds me of the sea."

He drew in a deep breath, trying to imagine salt spray, and remembering. "When I was fourteen, one night I snuck down to the port and stowed away on a tanker. I took along a knapsack of food and drink and hid out for three days before they caught me."

"You daredevil! Were they very mad?"

"Not so mad. The captain had done the same when he was a boy. He let me stay on board until the ship returned from its run and then he delivered me to my grandparents."

"Poor Nana and Papa, they must have been so worried."

"Fit to be tied."

She flashed him a quizzical look. "Fit to be tied?"

"You know—furious, hopping mad, steamed up, spitting nails."

"Oh, your language is impossible! How will I ever learn it?"

"You sure won't learn it back in Sweden."

She pursed her lips and said nothing.

★

Run-down seemed a rosy description of the farm, Harlan decided, when he and Katarina rode with his grandparents to see it the following day. The lane leading in from the county road

was more dirt than gravel, rutted in the low spots, where Papa
gunned the engine to keep the old Pontiac from foundering.
On either side of the lane, rusted equipment hulked in scrubby
woods that had once been cultivated fields. The fences were all
down, the posts tilting. The pastures had grown up in burdock,
sumac, brambles, violet ironweed and Joe-Pye weed, white-head-
ed boneset, black-eyed Susans, and milkweed spilling cottony
seeds.

"It's a bit rough," Papa conceded, as he steered them into the
farmyard.

At first glance the house looked sound enough, a sizeable
red-brick box with two full stories, a dormered third story, front
and back porches, and a slate roof. A pair of towering pin oaks
flanked the entrance, their limbs trimmed up high enough to admit winter sunlight into the south-facing windows while providing summer shade. Once Harlan was out of the car, however, he
could see that a number of roofing slates were missing, the chim-
ney listed precariously, maple saplings sprouted from the sagging
gutters, and plywood covered several windows. The front steps,
where his grandparents went to sit, were cobbled together from
swaybacked planks.

He was calculating what needed fixing first when Katarina sidled up to him, looped a hand around his waist, and said,
"Doesn't it have lovely bones?"

The house did appeal to Harlan, with its pyramid roof, deep
eaves, foursquare shape, and welcoming porches. "Could you
imagine living here?" he asked.

She seemed to have considered this, for she answered firmly,
"If you stay, I will stay. Until next summer, when I must go home.
But first ask your grandparents."

"There's no need to ask. Nana already has your room picked
out—at the top of the stairs, with a view of the river—and Papa

wants me to paint that room first, whatever color you choose. Look at them, perched there on the steps, watching us and wondering how their bashful grandson wound up with a girl like you."

"Yes, it is a deep mystery." Katarina gave him a sidelong smile. Then she drifted away in search of flowers, leaving him to size up the outbuildings and walk the property boundaries.

The dome-capped silo appeared sturdy, and so did the corncrib and chicken coop. The hog pen had collapsed, but he could salvage lumber from it to repair the springhouse, where he was pleased to find water burbling into a sandstone trough. At present there was only a trickle, but once the corroded outlet pipe was replaced, there might be a reliable flow. The main barn needed a new metal roof and a coat of paint, but it stood plumb on its foundation. When he stepped inside, into the fragrance of hay and dust and ancient manure, slivers of light showed through gaps in the plank siding. A grain shovel, hayfork, wood-toothed rake, and other tools dangled from pegs, all of them still usable. There was even some dry tack and harness of the sort Mr. Winfield had kept from his days of farming with draft horses. Rubbed with neatsfoot oil, the old leather might become supple again.

Everywhere Harlan looked he saw the need for work—years of work—but also possibilities. There was a ragged orchard that might be coaxed, with pruning and manure, to bear apples, cherries, and pears again. The garden plot, long-untilled, was still fertile enough to grow head-high weeds. The pond had silted in, but could be dug out, and the dam could be patched with clay. Fresh pilings could mend the dock on the Red Hawk River, which marked the western boundary of the farm. Seventy or eighty feet wide where it flowed through an aisle of sycamores and maples, the river should run deep enough in spring and fall to bear a canoe. Under a shed roof attached to one side of the barn Harlan found an ancient Farmall tractor that had once been red, and a vintage Ford pickup that was green or gray, too encrusted with dirt and bird droppings for him to determine which. Maybe he could get them running again. Maybe he could get the whole place running again, he thought, gazing back toward the house, where Katarina was offering Nana an armful of flowers.

§ § §

Chapter Six • April–July 1995

NAOMI

Naomi Rosenthal didn't see how she could move skinflints in Congress to vote for a universal healthcare bill, short of injecting large doses of compassion into their wizened hearts. Still, she made the long trip from Michigan's Upper Peninsula to join several hundred other physicians in Washington for two days of reasoning, arguing, and pleading with any elected official who would listen. Ironically, in order to clear the time on her schedule, she had to cancel the free Saturday clinic she offered for uninsured patients, who crowded into her office from near and far, bearing their ailments with resignation, resentment, or shame.

Her last appointment was with a congressman who listened impassively to her reports of diabetics losing limbs, elders suffering strokes, workers hobbling on crookedly knit bones, children going blind, street people dying from infections, all for lack of simple treatments they couldn't afford. The legislator, a jowly man who seemed a likely candidate for cardiac arrest—and who would enjoy free healthcare for the rest of his life at taxpayers' expense—gave her five minutes or so, made a few notes, thanked her for sharing these concerns, and then rose to shake her hand. Naomi recognized the gesture as one she herself commonly used to inform a patient that a session was over.

Dismissed, with two hours before her flight home, she had just enough time to fulfill the other purpose of her trip, which was to visit her brother's grave in Arlington National Cemetery. Although she had hunted up Ozzie's grave on previous trips to Washington, she still had to consult a map before she could locate his headstone, for it was indistinguishable, except for the inscription, from tens of thousands of other white stone markers that stretched away in every direction, row upon row. It was as though all these dead soldiers and sailors were still wearing uniforms and marching in ranks. Naomi kept her eyes lowered, to avoid being reminded of so much loss. The April beauty of this place—the grass burnished by sunlight, the cherry trees in snowy bloom, the venerable oaks and maples glimmering with newly-minted leaves—could not dull the ache she still felt for her brother, over twenty years after he'd stepped on a landmine in Vietnam. But she had not come here to mourn, she had come to remember, to keep Ozzie alive in her mind.

The inscription on Ozzie's headstone showed his full name, his rank and military unit, his dates of birth and death, and, near the top, a Star of David. Her parents had insisted on the symbol, against her advice, for they saw it as an affirmation of Jewish identity whereas Naomi saw it as a target for vandals. And sure enough, on two earlier visits she had found traces of graffiti still legible on the marker after cleansing by groundskeepers. One time she could detect the ghostly scrawl of *Christ killer*, the other time, *Fire up the ovens*. Today, thank goodness, the white marble was unblemished.

From her shoulder bag she retrieved one of Ozzie's matchbox cars, which she had rescued along with some of his other childhood toys when her parents moved from their grand house in Evanston to a condo. She also drew out a pebble of milky quartz she'd collected on the shore of Lake Superior near Marquette, a place Ozzie had come to love, as she had, during childhood summers spent in a cottage there. She balanced the pebble on top of the marker, and beside it the miniature car, a roadster with much of its red paint worn away. As a boy, Ozzie had imagined the water-polished beads of quartz were jewels, and she, the big sister, two years older and wiser, had played along. To humor him, to rouse his crooked grin, she had also played with his matchbox toys, rolling the tiny rubber tires in the dirt of backyards and the sand of beaches, across floors of oak and terrazzo and tile in the progressively larger houses the family moved into as their father's musical career prospered. Their mother had given up her own singing career to stay home with Ozzie and Naomi while their father flew to concert halls around the world bearing two first-class tickets, one for him and one for his cello.

Songs their mother had sung to them as children came to Naomi now, and she quietly sang three of them, all in German, before Ozzie's marble slab. When he was little, he would ask what the strange words meant, for he never learned the language their parents had brought with them from Vienna during Hitler's war. What is *Leben*? What is *Licht*? Ozzie, Ozzie, so full of questions, so earnest. He often had a pinched look, such a worrier, but their mother's singing would smooth the wrinkles from his forehead, the crimp from his mouth, and under the spell of music he would become a carefree boy.

Looking up after her own singing, Naomi blinked at the beneficent wash of spring light and at the scattering of other visitors strolling among the graves. There, Ozzie was alive again, if only in her mind, and she could return home. For a change, she had remembered to bring a camera, and now she remembered to use it, snapping two pictures of the headstone with its pebble and car, one picture for her parents, who rarely traveled here from Chicago, and one for herself.

As she headed back toward her rental car she could see to the east, rising above tree-line, the chalky obelisk of the Washington Monument. Braggart men, she thought, with their spears and missiles and phalluses aimed at the sky. Only a woman could have designed the Vietnam Veterans Memorial, with its trench leading down into the earth.

After passing a sign urging "Silence & Respect," Naomi noticed beside the path a young woman lying facedown before a grave marker, propped on her elbows, head bowed, sobbing. Was she a sister, a daughter, a lover, a wife? Exposed above the woman's blue sundress, her shoulder blades hunched up in a way painful to see. The sobs sent tremors through her body. She had taken off her sandals, which lay in the grass nearby. Her feet were pointed and her legs clenched together like a diver's, as if she were plunging into the stone. The scene brought back to Naomi with the force of a blow how it had felt when Ozzie's death was fresh. She was not close enough to read the dates on the stone, but the marble appeared to be newly cut. Not wishing to intrude on the young woman, and not wishing to forget her, Naomi clicked a photograph and hurried on by.

*

Naomi's decision to open a practice in Marquette after finishing medical school had displeased her parents, who wanted her to settle in Chicago. With Ozzie dead, who was going to provide grandchildren for weekend visits? Who was going to look after them in their old age? When Naomi and Ozzie were growing up, and the family vacationed August after August in a cottage on Lake Superior, alongside other exiles from Vienna who rented cottages nearby, Naomi's parents had never imagined she would become so enamored of the place. For the parents, Simeon and Ingrid Rosenthal, these sojourns in Marquette had been merely an escape from the sweltering city, a chance to see childhood friends who'd also fled from Hitler, and a break for Simeon from his grueling round of concerts.

But the North Country had seeped into Naomi's imagination. She loved the sand dunes at Grand Sable, the rouge bluffs of Presque Isle, the panoramic view from atop Sugarloaf Mountain, the breakers at Laughing Fish Point. She loved the forests of maple, aspen, paper birch, white cedar, and pine, where she and Ozzie took field trips from summer camp, coming across beaver lodges and stumps aglow with foxfire. She loved the rocky streams where camp counselors taught them how to fly-fish, and where she managed to catch and briefly hold and then release a few iridescent trout. She loved the blue distances over the lake, the gulls cruising, the buoys gonging, the ships bleating in the fog or lit up at night beside the ore dock like constellations. She loved the cloudless nights when real constellations glittered with a hundred times as many stars as ever appeared in Chicago, and especially the rare nights that shimmered with the billowing veils of the northern lights.

While the stars were abundant up north, the people were scarce, and their works seemed ephemeral, mere scratches on the stony lip of the lake. Marquette's low buildings and gabled houses huddled between forest and shore as though held in place by the burden of sky. Even the Landmark Inn—pride of the town, host over the years to Amelia Earhart and Louis Armstrong and The Rolling Stones—was only six stories high. And the Peter White Library, which had appeared so grand to Naomi when she and Ozzie used to enter between the stone pillars to collect their weekly supply of books, was only half as high as the hotel. Paint was no sooner applied to the wooden houses than it began to peel, and the gutters, no matter how scrupulously cleaned, soon sagged again under the weight of leaves. Even the buildings of sandstone and brick seemed in constant need of repair, just as the town's many boats needed overhauling in dry dock to undo the ravages of water and weather. Despite the web of roads, the pox of dumps, and the smear of ore-stained lagoons, the hold of people on the place felt tenuous, as if one more hard winter might force everyone to pack up and head south.

Still today, fourteen years after beginning her practice in Marquette, when Naomi visited her parents they pestered her about moving back to Chicago, as they pestered her about finding another husband. They had given up hope of grandchildren, in light of her age, forty-three this June. But they had not given up hope that she would marry again. Her parents must have scoured the city to find the Jewish widowers whom they invited for suppers during her visits—doctors and lawyers, an architect, two bankers, a professor, a pianist, even a rabbi, all carefully vetted and briefed, all angling for a new wife.

The widowers seemed to Naomi like decent men, but so had her former husband, whom she'd met in medical school. On their fifth wedding anniversary, a date when they had agreed to begin trying to conceive a child, while she was preparing a celebratory dinner and her husband was supposedly finishing his rounds at the hospital, he called from the airport to say he was moving to Atlanta with one of his patients. "It's nothing against you," he told Naomi, "I just need a fresh start." What he actually needed, Naomi suspected, was a mate who wasn't longing to have a baby, for he had resisted becoming a father—not wanting, as he said, to crowd his weekends.

Simeon and Ingrid Rosenthal could not understand why Naomi didn't just forget the lout who'd dumped her. Let him stew in his own juices, him and his floozy. Why didn't she marry one of these prosperous widowers, give up her practice, abandon the wilds, move into the condo next door to theirs and ease their twi-

light years? In his seventies, Simeon still flew around the world
for performances, one seat for him, one for his cello, but now the
tickets were economy class and the concert halls were humbler,
for arthritis had stiffened his fingers. Decades after her last vacation in the cottage on Lake Superior, Ingrid spoke about Marquette as if it were a frontier town, a hangout for lumberjacks
and sailors and Indians. She recalled the mosquitoes, the rude
drivers of pickup trucks, the sand in every bite of food. Ingrid and
Simeon would not consider flying up north to see Naomi, for all
they had ever liked about those Augusts in Marquette were the
Viennese friends and the cool breeze off the lake and the sight of
their children romping outdoors. Now, Ingrid pointed out, with
one child buried and the other married to work, there would be
no more romping; air-conditioning made Chicago bearable, even
in August; and most of those Viennese friends were homebound
or dead.

So Naomi saw her parents only in Chicago, three or four times
a year, as often as her nerves and schedule would bear. In between visits, she consulted by phone with their accountant, at-
torney, financial advisor, cleaning woman, mechanic, her father's
booking agent, and their various doctors, to make sure that her
parents and their affairs were being properly looked after. She
kept gamely meeting and then discouraging the widowers, a few
of whom proposed marriage but none of whom, not even the
retired ones, proposed joining her in Marquette. Had a smart and
lively and tender suitor shown enthusiasm for moving north, she
might have thought twice before declining his offer.

*

On the Saturday following her return from Washington, the
stream of patients at the free clinic kept Naomi at her office, as
usual, well into the evening. Around seven, Colleen Fitzgerald,

the nurse practitioner, brought in a plate of fettuccine from the
Casa Calabria, and she refused to usher any more patients into
the examining room until Naomi ate a few bites.

"You're thin as a rail," Colleen said. "What kind of example is
that for these anorexic girls you're always treating?"

"I don't starve myself," Naomi said. "I just burn up everything
I eat."

"You miss too many meals, and you don't sleep enough."

Colleen herself was a buxom woman, who set a formidable
example for the emaciated girls. Naomi lifted a forkful of noo-
dles. "Well, I promise to reform, doctor."

Colleen laughed. "Don't you pawn off your M.D. on me. I've
more than enough to do with my N.P."

When Naomi finished the last of the paperwork, most of the
fettuccine lay congealed on the plate. She scraped the food into
the toilet and flushed it down and rinsed the dish, so Colleen
wouldn't have reason to chide her.

Walking home, Naomi reflected on her nurse's warning. It was
true, she didn't take good care of herself. From hospital rounds
beginning at 6:00 in the morning, through an unbroken day of
appointments, to an evening of answering phone messages and
checking lab reports, and then a few minutes of reading medical journals before tumbling into fitful sleep, she rarely let up. It
had not always been so. During the five years of her marriage,
she and her husband had found time to see movies and dine out,
to attend concerts and host parties, to canoe and camp and ski;
but after the divorce, although she still walked along the moody
lake and bicycled to the woods and went out occasionally with
friends, she gave herself more and more completely to work.

Arriving at the house, she found in the day's mail a packet
from the photo lab, which puzzled her for a moment, until she
realized it was the film from her Washington trip. She tore open

the envelope and riffled through the prints until she came upon the two shots of Ozzie's grave. She set aside one of these for her parents, and then she turned to the photo of the grieving young woman. From bare feet to bowed head, the woman's body stretched out on the grass like an arrow pointed at the headstone. The weight of the image pressed Naomi into a chair at the kitchen table, where she examined the picture more closely through reading glasses. Next to the stone were a small American flag on a stick and a bouquet of white peonies. The inscription identified the year of death as 1988. So the woman's grief was seven years old. And whom had she lost? Tilting the photo to catch the light, Naomi read the name: Tommy Two Bears.

Startled, she set the photo down and looked out her kitchen window at the twilit waters of Marquette Bay. She had known Tommy Two Bears, or at least she had treated a boy with that name. And how many others could there be? She still treated the boy's mother, Teresa Two Bears, and still winced at remembering the last time she had allowed him in her office. She had begun seeing him early in her practice, when he was a shy boy with chronic ear infections, and she had continued seeing him over the years for the usual things, rashes and gashes, a broken bone or two, no doubt other ailments or injuries which his file could remind her of. But she needed no reminding of the last time he had come to see her, on the eve of his joining the Navy.

Tommy must have been eighteen or nineteen that day when he showed up with a fever and a hacking cough. When she entered the room he was seated on the exam table with his shirt off, and the muscles of his upper body were as sharply defined as those in the anatomical chart on the wall. She seemed to recall he was a celebrated athlete of some sort, perhaps a wrestler, before he dropped out of high school to work on freighters. As a teenager, he had worn his dense black hair in a braid, but this day it was cut short, suggesting he had already visited the Navy barber.

As she closed the door behind her, he broke into a coughing fit that brought the blood to his angular face. Bronchitis, most likely. She asked him the usual questions and he replied in a grudging voice, for he had only come to the office because his mother had insisted. Naomi warmed the head of her stethoscope by rubbing it against the lapel of her white coat, but still he shivered when she pressed the metal ring against his chest. She listened to his lungs as he took deep breaths, and then she moved to the other side of the exam table to listen through his ribcage from the back. As she came around the table, however, she stopped short, glimpsing on his left shoulder blade the pitch-black tattoo of a swastika.

She jerked away, as if the tattoo were a giant spider, and then with a muttered excuse she hurried from the room and down the hall to her office, trembling. Colleen Fitzgerald followed her there to ask what was the matter, and Naomi explained. They both whispered, glancing in the direction of the boy whose coughs echoed through the walls. What to do? Naomi was so frightened by the swastika, so repulsed by it, that she thought of sending Tommy away. Colleen balled up her fists and offered to run him off. No, no, Naomi replied, regaining her composure. She couldn't send a sick boy away without treating him. Then I'll come along with you in case he tries anything, said Colleen. But again Naomi said no. She would gather herself, finish the exam, give him a prescription, and then tell him he must find a new doctor, for she would not continue treating anyone who bore such a symbol of hate on his body. And that is what she did.

"It's not a symbol of hate," Tommy grumbled when she told him.

Naomi ignored him as she wrote out a prescription.

"It's not," he repeated. He dipped his bare shoulder and turned it to her. "Here, let me show you."

She looked away. "I've seen enough."

"Just let me explain."

"There's nothing to explain. Now please put on your shirt."

Still grumbling, he shoved his arms into the sleeves of his blue work shirt. "Tell me one thing. Are you a Jew?"

In spite of her fear, Naomi glared at him. "I am."

"What is it with Jews? You think you invented suffering."

"I think nothing of the sort."

"Read up on what's happened to Indians, and then we can talk about suffering."

"I don't wish to argue." Shaking with fury, she held out the prescription. "Now take this and leave or I will call for help."

He snatched the paper and stalked out, shirt still unbuttoned. She could hear him coughing all the way down the hall.

And that was the last Naomi ever saw of Tommy Two Bears, except for the photograph of him in his Navy uniform that showed up in the newspaper when he died in the Persian Gulf, in some sort of accident on an aircraft carrier. That was seven years ago, according to the headstone, yet she could still see the swastika vividly, the black ink fresh, the surrounding skin inflamed, as if the needles had only just finished their work. Whether Tommy had ever told his mother about the incident, Naomi didn't know. She had never brought it up with Teresa Two Bears, whom she continued to see regularly for treatment of diabetes, and Teresa had never mentioned it to her.

Now, seated at her kitchen table, gazing out at the lights of ships gliding over the darkened lake, Naomi felt certain this Tommy Two Bears must have been the one whom the young woman was grieving for in Arlington Cemetery. She looked down at the image of the prostrate body, the bowed head, hunched shoulder blades, clenched legs, and bare feet. The woman could not have been Tommy's sister, for she was too fair-skinned, nor was she his daughter, for she looked to be nearly as old as Tommy would have been, had he lived. So she must have been his widow or lover. What did she think of his tattoo? Did it make her cringe? Did it give her a thrill? Was it anything more to her than an inky design she casually touched while rubbing his shoulders or making love?

★

When Teresa Two Bears came for an appointment a few weeks later, Naomi waited until the exam was completed before asking where Tommy was buried.

As if searching for a name, Teresa peered into the willow basket she held in her lap, one of the traditional Ojibwa designs she made. She wore beaded moccasins, another of her crafts, and a flower-print dress the color of mustard. "He's buried in that big cemetery they've got in Washington," she answered.

"Arlington?"

"Yes, that one," Teresa replied, with a nod that set her long gray braids swaying. She was a large woman, her body swollen by diabetes and, Naomi felt certain, by a poor diet. A bag of peppermints and a box of cookies jutted from the basket. "Why do you ask about Tommy?"

Seated on a stool at the counter, Naomi spoke while jotting notes in Teresa's file, as if she were only making polite conversation. "Oh, I came across a headstone with his name on it when I was in Washington not long ago."

"I went there one time to see," Teresa recalled. "So many white stones lined up, like teeth. There is a flame where President Kennedy lies, but not for my son. Tommy said to bury him there if he died in the Navy. He worked all over the Great Lakes, and was never afraid, but he had a dream of drowning in the ocean. Then stay home, I told him. But he would not listen. He was headstrong, even as a baby."

"So he drowned?"

"No. An airplane landed cockeyed on his ship and crushed him."

"How awful." Naomi gave up the pretense of jotting notes.

Teresa curled her thick fingers around the handle of the basket. "It is done."

When Naomi was a little girl, her father used to say she had midnight eyes, because they were so dark, as were her stubborn curls. But Teresa's eyes were darker, nearly black, and they were hard to read. Or perhaps it was Teresa's face that was hard to read, the creases seemed so fixed in place.

"I took a picture of his grave," Naomi said. She drew from the pocket of her coat the photograph she had brought from home to show Teresa.

Setting her basket on the floor, Teresa laid the photograph in her lap and stared at it for a long time without speaking. Her face did not lose its customary stolid expression, but her eyes soon brimmed with tears.

Realizing she had caused pain when she had only meant to satisfy her curiosity, Naomi regretted having asked about Tommy. "I didn't mean to upset you."

Teresa ran a blunt forefinger over the figure of the woman in the picture. "That is how it feels. You want to crawl into the earth after him."

That is how it feels, Naomi thought, her own eyes watering. Ozzie, Ozzie. She knew it was improper to have such a conversation with a patient in her office, but she couldn't resist asking, "Do you know who she is?"

"Some girl who loved him."

There was a tap at the door, which would be Colleen signaling that the afternoon appointments were backing up. "Another minute," Naomi called out. Then to Teresa she said quietly, "He wasn't married?"

"He asked a girl once. She was willing but her parents said no. Too Indian, they said. I'm only half, he told them. That is half too much, they said."

"Could it be a friend from Marquette?"

Teresa shook her head. "I knew all his friends here. She is a stranger."

"Then could it be someone he met when his ship was in port?"

"He knew many girls in ports." Teresa kept stroking the photograph. "Whenever he came home, I asked him did you find a sweetheart. And he said, oh, the pretty ones aren't rich, and the rich ones aren't pretty." Her hand grew still, covering the picture. "I only heard the love ache in his voice once, for a girl he got in trouble."

Now Naomi knew she was being unprofessional, prying into a patient's life. But again she could not hold back. "What kind of trouble?"

"Knocked up, you know. Her parents had a bar in Cleveland and she worked there. He met her while his ship was docked. He cried when he told me about her. Marry her, I said, and the two of you live with me, and I will care for the baby. But she was too young and too white and he was afraid her parents would say no and shame him again. So he joined the Navy to get away."

"What became of the baby?"

Teresa let the tears run down her face without wiping them. "I do not know. Maybe she got rid of it. Maybe she gave it birth. Maybe she is a good mother or a bad mother. I only know the child is lost to me."

"You can't remember the girl's name or the name of the bar?"

"No, Tommy would never say."

Again came the tapping at the door, and this time Colleen opened it a crack to inquire, "Is anything the matter, doctor?"

"We're just finishing." Naomi rose from her stool, brushing her cheeks with the back of a hand. Teresa rose as well. She laid the photograph on the counter, picked up her basket, and tucked the braids back over her shoulders.

"Well, then," Naomi said. "See me in three months. Remember, if you're ever too sick to come in, I can stop by your house. I pass it every night on my way home. And watch your sugar."

"I will, doctor." Teresa glanced at the sweets in her basket.

"Would you like to keep the photo?"

"No. I remember without a picture."

"Of course." At the door, Naomi squeezed Teresa's plump shoulder, and felt compelled to say, "My brother is buried not far from Tommy. He died in Vietnam."

The creases around Teresa's black eyes softened. "So you know how it is. War steals our men."

*

Naomi framed the photograph and mounted it above her desk at the office, alongside other pictures that spoke to her affections—Ozzie seated at a grand piano for his senior recital, her parents dancing at the Jewish Community Center, her mother as a girl in Vienna singing in a satin gown, her father bent over his cello at Carnegie Hall, she and the man she would marry donning their white coats for the first time in medical school, the campsite where they honeymooned on Isle Royale, holiday cards showing the grinning children of friends, scenes from the forests and rivers and shores of the Upper Peninsula. When she sat at the desk doing paperwork after a day of seeing patients, worn ragged by their many needs, she would often glance at these photographs to regain a sense of who she was.

The photograph of the woman at Tommy's grave was chastening to Naomi, as was her conversation with Teresa, for if they loved this menacing boy so keenly, how could she despise him? How could she imagine him as just an aimless, muscular youth like the thugs whom Hitler enlisted to carry out his poisonous plans? Perhaps the swastika meant no more to Tommy than a sign that he was a tough guy. In an anthropology textbook Naomi had read in college, Margaret Mead argued that every society must figure out how to harness the aggression of teenage boys and men in their early twenties, or they would wreak havoc. The most common solution to this problem, and also the worst, according to Mead, was to make these young males into warriors, give them weapons, and turn their aggression against the "enemy"—whoever the political or religious authorities deemed the enemy to be.

Ozzie had never been a tough guy, preferring to read books or draw pictures or make up scenarios with his matchbox cars rather than engage in rough-and-tumble play. While other boys went out for sports, he devoted himself to the piano. After studying music at Interlochen during the summers of high school, he decided, at their parents' urging, to spend a year working in Chicago with a private instructor, one of the Viennese exiles, before enrolling at Juilliard. He had not realized that by interrupting his schooling he would lose his student deferment. He wept when the draft notice arrived.

And yet, when Ozzie returned home on leave after basic training, bronzed and lean, something had gone hard in him. He spoke of the men in his platoon as if they were brothers he would die for. True, one guy made a crack about Jews being pussies, but the sergeant let them work it out with their fists, and Ozzie broke the guy's nose. He proudly displayed for Naomi his bruised knuckles. He couldn't wait to land in Vietnam and show what he was made of. After he did land, and started going on patrol from the base at Danang, his letters home took on a cocky tone that didn't sound like her brother. He spoke of calling in ordnance, humping a load, torching the bush, smoking tunnels, and other harsh matters Naomi didn't always understand. In his last letter home, he bragged that he hadn't touched a piano for over a year and he didn't miss music one bit, now that he had tasted what it meant to be a man.

★

Two months after that troubling conversation with Teresa Two Bears, on the last Saturday in July, Naomi stepped from the clinic at dusk into a wind so stiff it made her stagger on her way down the front steps. Coming from the northwest, off the lake, it should blow up some lusty waves by tomorrow. She had always loved big weather, so she walked home slowly, east along Magnetic Street to Spruce, then south on Spruce to Ridge, catching glimpses of the lake through the trees. By the time she reached the house, her hair, a confusion of curls at the best of times, was a rat's nest. She tugged at it with a brush and pinned it back with barrettes. There was nobody here to care how she looked, and had not been since her husband walked out, yet she still couldn't allow herself to look a fright.

Sitting at the kitchen table over a cup of Earl Grey tea, she recalled what it had felt like to have someone welcome her home, or to welcome that someone, his chin raspy against her cheek at the end of the day, his arms encircling her, his eyes giving back the tiny reflections of her face.

Naomi shook herself to banish the memory. She gazed out the kitchen window at red oaks thrashing in the wind. Beyond the oaks, far out in the darkening bay, great swells would be gathering. She could imagine how the combers would break against the bluffs at Presque Isle. Thinking of the spray shooting up and mist on her face, she grew too excited to stay at the table, so she got up and paced around the house. Instead of sitting at home tomorrow to catch up on bills, as she had planned, why didn't she bicycle out to Presque Isle and sit on the rocks and watch the waves? With a book to read, a bag lunch, and a bottle of water, she could stay there until sunset. When had she last spent a whole day outdoors?

Before going to bed, she went into the garage to pump up the tires and oil the chain on her bicycle. The energy that sent her pacing through the house made her itch to climb on right then and wheel out into the darkness. But she resisted, and went to bed, and was a long time in falling asleep.

Soon after daybreak she packed a rucksack and set off. The wind had dropped, but there was still enough of a breeze to make her legs burn as she pedaled north along Lakeshore Boulevard, from the lower harbor and Coast Guard station, past the twin smokestacks of the power plant and the gigantic ore dock, on through the rustic gateway of logs that marked the entrance to the park. Here she was surprised to find a swarm of vans and pickups and trailers converging so early on a Sunday. Then she noticed the booths and banners, and realized this was the weekend for the annual fair at Presque Isle called "Art on the Rocks." She and her husband used to come every year, chatting with the craftspeople, admiring the handiwork, buying a bowl or a weaving or a basket to mark their anniversary, which also fell in late July. After the divorce, Naomi gave away all of those items, including a birchbark basket they had purchased from Teresa Two Bears. She meant to replace them with purchases of her own, untainted by memories of her husband, but as the years went by she lost track of the fair, as she lost track of nearly everything outside of work.

Dismounting, she rolled her bicycle through the avenue of booths as vendors tightened guy ropes on canopies that shuddered in the wind. On tables weighted with stones they uncovered their wares—jewelry, paintings, photographs, woodcarvings, pottery, stained glass, leather goods, clothing—so much careful and skillful work. Naomi scanned the booths to see if Teresa might be here, and sure enough, off to one side of the pavement, there was the big woman in the familiar mustard yellow dress, unloading boxes onto a blanket in the shade of a maple.

Naomi called to her, "Oh, Teresa, I must have one of your baskets!"

Kneeling on the blanket, Teresa lifted her placid face. "You look happy, doctor."

"I'm going to watch the waves. I haven't done that in ages."

"It is a good day for waves. The breakers are loud."

Naomi listened, but heard only the rustle of leaves and the squawks of gulls. She laid the bike in the grass and drew closer. It was a Hudson Bay blanket Teresa knelt on, scarlet with wide black stripes near the edges, and it was covered with an array of beaded moccasins and woven baskets. There were coiled baskets made from sweetgrass, square ones made from split ash or oak, round ones made from pine needles and willow, but none of birch. "Do you still make baskets from birchbark?" Naomi asked.

Teresa lowered herself into a folding chair with a sigh. "No more. Tommy collected the bark for me, and I have used it all."

Naomi had not thought of mentioning Tommy, but the surge of energy from the night before still buzzed in her this morning, and the question she had long wanted to ask suddenly burst out: "Speaking of Tommy—did you ever see his tattoo? The one on his shoulder?"

Teresa nodded gravely. "He was my boy. I saw every inch of him."

"I don't mean to pry. But this has bothered me for years. Do you know why he got it?"

"For good luck, to protect him when he went on the water."

The hideous shape rose in Naomi's memory. "How could it protect him?"

"By wrapping him in the arms of the four winds," said Teresa, crossing her own arms over her ample bosom.

"I don't understand."

"The tattoo, it shows the four winds."

"I'm sorry," Naomi said, baffled. "We must be thinking of different tattoos."

"No, he had only one. Here, look." Teresa picked up a round willow basket and turned it upside down. With her thick forefinger she traced on the bottom of the basket the intersecting strands that formed a broken cross. "See, the weaving begins with the sign of the four winds. This is because when the willow grew, the wind swirled it around, feeding it with the world's power. It is also the sign of the four seasons and the four directions, a holy sign. That is what Tommy wore on his back. But the medicine was not strong enough to keep him alive."

Naomi stared at the pattern in the basket. It formed a swastika, but with the bent arms at the tips of the cross pointing counterclockwise, not clockwise as in the Nazi symbol. She had been too repulsed by her glimpse of the tattoo to look at it closely, and she had not allowed Tommy to explain. She had banished him from her care, and all these years she had thought of him as hateful, as if he were in league with the brutes who drove her parents from Vienna and the vandals who painted taunts on Ozzie's gravestone. How appalling, to condemn a boy in haste and loathe him forever after. "I see it now," she said quietly. "Whirling winds. I had imagined something else."

"The Creator gave this sign to the Ojibwa in the beginning, to remind us how the world moves." Teresa drew a circle in the air with her finger. "Like the sun and moon. Like the year."

"Like the wheel of life," Naomi said, "turning from birth to death to birth."

Teresa gazed at her intently, as if puzzling something out, before saying, "You lost your brother to war. I lost my son. Is that why you ask about Tommy?"

Naomi considered a moment. "That's one reason, I suppose."

"It is good of you to carry Tommy in your mind. But you have many others to carry, all the sick people who need you. Tommy is mine to carry. You can let him go."

"You're right. You're absolutely right. I'll try. I promise."

Teresa rose from the chair and held out the basket. "This is for you."

Naomi shrugged off the rucksack and fumbled for her wallet.

Teresa shook her head. "I do not want money."

"No, really, you must let me pay," Naomi insisted.

"The people you treat on Saturdays, you do not let them pay. You make a gift of what you know how to do. And so I make a gift to you." Teresa wrapped the willow basket, as small and round as a bird's nest, in tissue paper. "To hold your happiness," she said, bowing her head.

Naomi bowed in return as she accepted the basket. She stowed it carefully in the rucksack, retrieved her bicycle, gave a parting wave to Teresa, and went pedaling uphill toward the stony tip of Presque Isle. She could hear the breakers well before she reached the rocks. She clambered up through a scattering of weather-beaten white pines, birches, and maples to her favorite spot, on a glacier-scoured outcrop that was as cracked and furrowed as the hide of an ancient elephant. The stone, she knew, was older than the whole tribe of elephants, older than any life on land, nearly half as old as Earth. Up here she caught the full force of the wind, which tousled her hair and whistled in her ears. Whitecaps broke far out in the bay and came rolling in as giant waves to pound the shore, lofting a mist that licked her face.

Opening the rucksack, she took out the basket, unwrapped it from the tissue paper, and set it on the rock before her. Except for the hoop handle, it might really have been a nest, for it had been woven of willow shoots as slender and brown as dried grass. To keep the basket from blowing away, she dug from a crevice a handful of pebbles. "For Ozzie," she whispered, laying a pearl of milky white quartz in the basket. She added a stone for her mother, one for her father, and then the rest of the handful for her patients and friends, until the basket was weighted down by these mountain shards that had been buffed to the smoothness of eggs. Deeper in the crevice Naomi found a few pinches of grit, which she scooped up and cradled in her palm. After thinking of all she wished to let go, she uncurled her fingers and gave the dust to the wind.

§ § §

Chapter Seven • September–December 2007

JENNY

WHEN THE COUGH AND ROAR OF A BIG ENGINE rattled windows in the upstairs bedroom where Jenny and Katarina were unpacking the last of the boxes, Jenny thought some delivery truck must have made its way down the lane, braving the washouts and mud. Maybe the UPS man was bringing some part or tool that Harlan had ordered. But when she glanced out the window she saw a tractor the color of burnt umber stuttering across the barnyard, with Luther in the driver's seat and Harlan perched behind him gesturing at the controls. The engine drowned out their voices, but Jenny could read their mood from the flush of blood in their faces and the taut tendons in their necks.

Katarina glided up beside her and peered out. "They rub each other the wrong way," she said. "Is that the correct expression?"

"I'm afraid it is," Jenny replied.

"They are tired. Harlan pushes too hard."

"There's certainly more work than any of us bargained for." Jenny dragged a palm across her forehead and began hanging clothes in the closet. She meant to stop there, but Katarina's expectant silence, so welcoming, so free of judgment, prompted her to add: "But it goes deeper. Luther's always picked at Harlan, yelling at him, sometimes giving him a swat. Early on, Harlan just clamped his mouth shut and ran out the door. Every time they had a fight, he ran farther. Once he stowed away on a ship."

"Yes, he told me," Katarina said, opening a box of linens.

"Did he tell you about hopping trains? About hitchhiking to Canada? About stealing a canoe and paddling to the Ohio River?"

"No."

"Each time he ran off, I feared he was gone for good. But he always turned up again after a few days. By the time he was fifteen or sixteen, he started yelling back, and that was even worse. I thought Luther would break his neck. Harlan must have thought so, too. They had a furious shouting match, the worst ever, the night before he took off for Vermont."

Stacking sheets and pillowcases on the bed, Katarina looked at her with a sympathetic smile, but said nothing.

"Naturally, I was worried sick," Jenny went on. "Then he began writing letters, and I felt relief, not just that he was safe but that he and Luther wouldn't fight any more."

Coming upon her one good dress, a simple A-line she had sewn from midnight blue satin, Jenny held it to her chest and looked down, guessing she might still fit into it, although she hadn't worn it in ten years. She felt as though she had gone almost that long without speaking this openly to another person. The girl's patient listening drew out more than Jenny had meant to say. She was going to take some of her words back—try to sweeten the history—when a loud bang from the barnyard made them both jump.

After a moment, Jenny said, "Backfire!" and laughed.

"Ah, backfire." Katarina laughed with her. "Harlan told me he would get the tractor going. He loves to tinker. He fixed all of Mr. and Mrs. Winfield's machines."

"He didn't get the knack from his grandfather, let me tell you. Whenever anything in the tavern broke, I had to fiddle with it myself, or else hire some repairman who charged an arm and a leg. Luther couldn't even wire a burnt-out lamp. If he did tackle a job, he was liable to wind up swearing and throwing things."

Fearing she might have been unfair, Jenny went on to say that Luther had many good points. When they were courting, and she was away at art school, he wrote her the sweetest postcards, which she still kept in her underwear drawer. Early in their marriage, while he was in the Army, he showed her distant parts of the world, places she had never dreamed of seeing. Germany, Egypt, even Japan. They danced in recreation halls on four continents. He used to sing when he was happy, in a wonderful baritone. True, he didn't sing much any more, but he still praised her paintings, even though she was a rank amateur, having dropped out of art school to care for her parents. Luther's parents had died when he was young, but he helped look after her mother and father in their old age as if they were his own. After he injured his back lifting ammunition crates, the Army discharged him, which stymied him for a while, because he had counted on a military career. But pretty soon he set them up running the tavern. It wasn't the sort of life either of them had imagined. Yet all these years he had stood behind the bar, wearing a brace on his back, listening to malarkey from customers, just to keep a roof over their heads.

"It's no wonder he's got a temper," Jenny concluded, "with pain gnawing at him night and day."

"It is also why he drinks?" Katarina suggested.

Jenny was taken aback. After a month in the girl's company, she still could not get used to her bluntness. The day the young people arrived from Vermont, when Jenny began to make up the living room couch as a bed for Harlan, Katarina had said not to bother, for the two of them would sleep in Harlan's bed, and not to worry, because she was on the pill. And now this, about Luther's drinking.

"The pain must be part of it," Jenny conceded. "But he never used to drink except when the bar was closed."

"My father is the same. He drinks only after he comes home from the factory, and then he drinks until he falls asleep. In Sweden many men do this. Women, too. They work sober, and give all the misery to their families."

"That's how it is," Jenny agreed, although she found it disconcerting that Katarina could declare the truth in such a matter-of-fact way. As she arranged Luther's clothes along the closet rod, she stole glances at this candid young woman, whose face was as fresh and transparent as a pool of rainwater, and as revealing of every disturbance. Jenny couldn't help imagining what Aurora might have been like at this age. More guarded, for sure, less eager to share chores or trade stories, less comfortable in her body, less open to delight. Long practiced in dodging thoughts of her daughter, Jenny busied herself with sorting out which of Luther's shirts needed ironing.

"Where should this go?" Katarina asked.

"What, my dear?" Turning from the closet to find the girl holding a shoebox, Jenny said abruptly, "Here, I'll take that."

"It contains photographs," Katarina said, handing her the box.

"Yes. I've meant to put them in albums, but I never found the time."

"Do you mind that I peeked in? There are pictures of Harlan as a boy. But who is the girl?"

Jenny clutched the shoebox against her chest, debating how to answer. Clearly Harlan had not explained. But sooner or later Katarina would have to know. Better I should tell her, Jenny decided, before she overhears some rant from Luther and imagines an even darker story. "The girl is our daughter, Aurora," she began. "Harlan's mother."

"Ah, yes. I have wondered why he never speaks of her."

"He has no memory of her. He was only a few months old when she left."

"Left?" Katarina sucked in a short breath, a mark of surprise by now familiar to Jenny. "And she has not come back?"

"Not yet."

"She writes to him, then? She calls?"

Jenny dipped her chin and shook her head. "Come, let's sit down."

She and Katarina settled onto cane-bottomed chairs that were drawn up beside a round cherry table at the window. The tractor grumbled somewhere in the distance. In the radiance of afternoon light that fell on the tabletop, Jenny laid out the photographs, one after another, from earliest to latest, and spoke briefly about each one. Here were the wedding pictures, with Luther and his groomsmen in their Army uniforms, Jenny in her borrowed gown, the brothers and sisters, aunts and uncles, parents and grandparents, all looking ill-at-ease in their dress-up clothes. Jenny pointed out how trim Luther was, and how thick his wavy red hair. Her own hair was auburn in those days, look there, and she hoped for a houseful of red-haired children. Only one child ever came, Aurora Eliza, whose hair at birth had scarcely any color at all, as if it were spun from moonbeams, but gradually it turned ginger and then red, as the later pictures showed. Here she was starting school, her legs so thin under the baggy shorts, and here she was turning cartwheels on the beach, and here playing softball in the park. She was good at sports, could run faster than any other child in her class, could throw a ball overhand like a boy. But she never brought her friends home, because she was ashamed of living above a bar. And she hardly ever went out, except to the library, where she borrowed piles of books. At night, when she wasn't doing homework or helping in the tavern, she was curled up reading. If you went to pick her up at school, you would find her standing apart from the other children, her nose in a novel.

"She is pretty," Katarina said.

"She never thought so," Jenny replied, realizing she had been holding the same photograph for several minutes while rattling on about Aurora. "Too skinny, she said. Too plain. Her hair wasn't blond, like the popular girls, and her sandy eyebrows hardly showed. She had freckles, even on her shoulders, so she always wore a T-shirt over her bathing suit at the beach. She claimed the boys never looked at her twice. Then one boy did look twice, and she fell for him all the way."

"They had sex?"

Jenny blinked, again taken aback, and then she nodded. "Once, but that's all it took."

"This was Tommy Two Bears?"

"Harlan told you about him?"

"A little. Please, you tell me."

Staring out the window, Jenny recalled that long-ago customer. "I could see what attracted Aurora. He was a broad-shouldered boy, with coal-black hair, a sly smile, and dark eyes that followed her as she waited on tables. Plenty of our regulars gawked at her once she became a teenager, and some of them pinched or grabbed her as she passed within reach. Mind you, these guys would have groped a manikin so long as there were curves in the right places. It infuriated me, but Luther said it would toughen her up, and it was good for business. Tommy was different. She told me he was tender and kind, which was why she snuck him upstairs to her room. She swore he loved her, even though after that night she never heard from him again."

"Harlan says he died at sea."

"Yes. In the Middle East, where they've been killing one another for thousands of years. Why we send our boys over there to die I'll never know."

"You have no pictures of Tommy?"

"I wish we did, so Harlan could see what his dad looked like. But Tommy only came to the tavern six or seven nights, while his freighter was in port, and we didn't know how much he mattered to Aurora until months later, when she told me who'd gotten her pregnant. She never let me take pictures of her while she carried the baby," Jenny said, flipping through the photographs, "but here she is with Harlan the day he was born."

Katarina bent close to look. "He has so much hair."

"Indian hair, Luther called it. And I suppose it is. The ruddy skin, too. Tommy belonged to one of those northern tribes."

Jenny watched for a reaction, but Katarina seemed unfazed by the news, if it was news. Maybe in Sweden people didn't hold prejudices against Indians.

A few photographs later, they came to a shot of Aurora nursing Harlan. She had one hand cupping the baby's head, and a faraway look on her face. "See those eyes?" Jenny said. "It's like her mind is already on the road."

Katarina laid a hand on Jenny's arm, and their heads tilted together as they thumbed slowly through the rest of the pictures, tracing Harlan's childhood up until the end of his junior year in high school, when he, too, hit the road.

"I was afraid he'd disappear," Jenny said, "just like Aurora. You should have heard me shout when we got his first letter from Vermont. He hadn't forgotten us!"

"Certainly not," Katarina put in. "When something on Black Bear Farm pleased him, he would say, 'I wish Nana could see this.'"

"He always wanted to live in the woods. That's why Luther and I took on this ramshackle place, which is a crazy thing to do at our age. We don't know the first thing about living in the country, as you can see. We're hoping the land will hold him."

"And Aurora," Katarina asked delicately, "she is still alive?"

Jenny stared at the picture of her daughter nursing baby Harlan. "If you ask Luther, he'll say no. Maybe he's right. Every time I see on the news about some girl murdered, I think: that could be my daughter. But I can't believe she's dead. I tell myself the reason she hasn't come home or written or called is because she's ashamed."

"It could be so," Katarina said, again with that little sip of breath. "Shame has sharp claws, my grandmother used to say."

The rising growl of the tractor drew Jenny's gaze out the window, and there were Luther and Harlan, rolling back into the farmyard on their loud machine, looking calmer. She savored the sight only a moment before noting that the sun was dipping low, and here she hadn't done a lick toward supper. "Time to stir," she said. "Our boys are going to be hungry." Leaning over, she kissed Katarina on the cheek, which tasted of salt.

★

Most days that fall, Harlan and Luther worked together in a surly kind of truce; at any moment they could begin snarling, like two dogs circling one another, hackles raised. The quarrel might be set off by Harlan saying Luther had no business climbing a ladder—which was true enough, Jenny thought—or by Luther wanting to quit in midafternoon on a job that Harlan wanted to pursue until dark. Jenny sympathized with both of them, two headstrong men, one too young to imagine the bone-weariness of a grandfather, one too old to accept orders from a grandson.

Aggravating all their differences, of course, was Luther's drinking, which usually began after supper and reduced him to a grouchy heap by bedtime. But one or two afternoons a week, he would invent reasons to head off in the Buick, and a few hours later he would come back soused. Harlan, who had worked alone in the meantime with furious determination, would have nothing to do with him then, turning away, refusing all offers of help, and Luther would retreat somewhere to sulk. Jenny tried hiding the car keys, but that did no good, for Luther had made extra copies at the hardware store, copies he tucked here and there, as he tucked bottles away in the workshop and barn.

On their peaceful days, Luther and Harlan made slow headway in restoring the derelict place. They reglazed broken windows on the farmhouse. They tore out the rickety front steps and laid up new ones of sandstone, levering the massive blocks into place with pry bars. Luther held the ladder while Harlan climbed onto the roof to replace the missing slates. Before the weather grew too cold for painting, they put a fresh coat of white on the house and two coats of red oxide on the barn. They ordered loads of gravel for the driveway, which Harlan leveled with a scraper dragged behind the tractor. Luther showed he could handle the tractor by bush hogging the weed-grown yard, then he moved on to the orchard, hay field, and pastures. Harlan reset fence posts and stretched hog wire around the garden plot and orchard, to discourage deer, and barbed wire around the barnyard, to keep in the livestock he planned to put there.

In the evenings, Harlan overhauled the old Ford pickup, which proved to be forest green, a color that pleased him no end. Soon he had it running, if raggedly, and then instead of ordering lumber or shingles or paint, he and Luther could go fetch what they needed from Ravenna, Warren, or Youngstown. They traveled up to Geauga County to buy a used woodstove from an Amish family. They drove all the way to Cleveland to find a stainless steel pipe for the springhouse. Once they had the pipe installed, the water poured out cool and clear, with a restful sound that could be heard from the back porch.

As Jenny checked on them now and again, she could see Harlan trying to spare Luther's back—grabbing the heavy end of whatever they were lifting, digging postholes, mixing concrete.

He may have imagined that his grandfather wouldn't notice, but of course his grandfather did notice, for Luther bristled at any challenge to his manhood. Jenny thought of all the Sundays when she had begged him to have a look at something broken in the tavern or apartment, and he stormed out the door shouting that a man deserved a rest, or he settled deeper into his La-Z-Boy with an open bottle in his fist, drinking himself into a stupor. To see him now on his sober days, working alongside Harlan, made her wonder if during all those years of scowling behind the bar he had simply been depressed.

Depression was a malady often spoken of on the talk shows Jenny used to listen to while frying hamburgers and hash browns and onion rings. At first she had imagined it was only a highbrow name for the blues that everybody felt once in a while. But as she heard experts talk about brain chemicals gone awry and heard victims talk about their paralyzing sense of worthlessness, she began to imagine what it might be like to dwell in perpetual twilight, your limbs too heavy for lifting, your heart an echoing shell. All these years, she had failed to draw Luther out of his gloom; now Harlan was succeeding, if only for a few hours at a time.

The sole relaxation Harlan allowed himself was an occasional expedition into the woods or down to the river with Katarina. But even on these walks he kept thinking about work, for he would return with plans for healing gullies or thinning the sugarbush or reseeding the pastures. No matter how many tasks he accomplished, the list always grew longer.

Meanwhile, Jenny and Katarina peeled wallpaper, mended plaster, and painted the interior of the house room by room; they even stenciled a band of cornflowers near the ceiling in the parlor. All of these jobs were new to Jenny, for she had grown up in apartments, where nobody was allowed to mend or paint except the landlords, and the landlords rarely bothered. After

Harlan tilled the garden plot, Katarina showed her how to plant onion sets and cloves of garlic in the rich loam. She also taught Jenny how to prune the apple trees, as well as the grapevines they found twining around a half-rotted trellis behind the chicken coop. Toward suppertime each afternoon, Jenny hauled out her old recipes, which she had rarely used during years of cooking bar food, and taught Katarina how to make each dish. The girl also wished to learn how to make quilts, another art that Jenny had long neglected. So when the pace of work slowed down in winter, they would dig up some patterns, buy some fabric, oil the Singer machine, and sew up a storm.

Jenny marveled at how many skills Harlan and Katarina possessed, and how much energy. After supper they often sallied out into the twilight, their breath pluming in the autumn air; when they returned an hour or so later, they would look as fresh as when they had left. Jenny waited up for them, fighting off sleep, just to see the glow in their faces.

She was working even longer hours on the farm than she had at the tavern, yet she didn't mind, for here the work added up to something. But she worried about Luther. At sixty-eight, after years of smoking, he might keel over from a heart attack. He yelped with pain as he undressed at night. When he came to bed after his shower, she rubbed liniment into his back and shoulders. Her fingers knew every knot in his muscles, every lump on his spine. As she massaged his body, so changed from the young man she had married and yet so familiar, he quickly fell asleep if he had been drinking; but on his sober nights, he stayed awake long enough for them to talk—about money or weather or errands, but mainly about Harlan and Katarina. Would their boy settle down on the farm and keep them company in their old age? Was it selfish of them to hope so? How would he earn a living on forty acres of abused land? Should he go to college? And how would they pay for that? Was Katarina a good match for him? What if he followed her back to Sweden?

The questions looped round and round until Luther began snoring, sometimes in the middle of a sentence. Then Jenny would kiss his slack cheek, and try to fall asleep before he began writhing from the ache in his back.

★

One night in December, Jenny was reading in bed when Luther stumbled into the room, white-faced and trembling. "What is it?" she asked.

He didn't answer. He seemed not even to see her as he shrugged out of his clothes, groaning when an arm caught in a sleeve, kicking his overalls across the floor.

"Luther, what's wrong?"

He pawed the air with one of his big hands, still without speaking, turned away, and staggered naked into the hall. Jenny threw off the covers and followed him. By the time she reached the bathroom, the door was shut. Leaning close, she listened for the hiss of the shower, but all she heard was a dull thumping, like the pounding of a fist, or a heart. Where was Harlan? She glanced across the landing at the bedroom he and Katarina shared. No light showed under the door. It was too early for them to be asleep. Most likely out walking, or in bed making love.

The thumping continued. Frantic with worry, Jenny turned the knob and eased the door open just far enough to peep in. Luther stood in the tub, hands braced against the wall, banging his head on the tiles. She rushed to him then and pulled at his shoulders to make him stop, but he was too heavy, too strong, and he went on pounding his face against the tiles. She looked around desperately for some way to restrain him, and just then Katarina appeared in the doorway, dressed in pajamas, hair unbraided and dangling to her waist.

"Where's Harlan?" Jenny gasped.

"He has not come in."

"Well, grab an arm. Maybe the two of us can make him stop."

After a struggle, they did make Luther stop, tugging him away from the wall and sitting him down on the edge of the tub. Blood ran from cuts in his forehead. His eyes were squeezed shut and his body shook. Jenny fretted momentarily about Katarina seeing Luther naked, his sagging belly, his limp cock, and then she chided herself for caring about such a thing right now. Katarina seemed unruffled, gathering cotton swabs, alcohol, and antiseptic cream from the medicine cabinet; she handed each in turn to Jenny, who cleaned and anointed Luther's battered face. Under her touch, he gradually stopped shaking, and the tears quit leaking from beneath his closed lids.

"Should I find Harlan?" Katarina whispered.

"I can manage," Jenny replied.

"Not Harlan," Luther muttered, slumping forward until his elbows rested on his knees. Again he said, "Not Harlan."

Jenny spread a towel over his shoulders to keep him from catching a chill. She turned on the faucets, and the pipes began to clatter. She would undress and shower with her husband, as she had not done for years, would soap his back and chest, would lean against him under the warm spray, and maybe then he would explain why he was so upset. She turned to let Katarina know she could leave, but the girl, with her usual sense of tact, was already backing out of the room. Only then did Jenny register that the pink flannel pajamas Katarina wore had been Aurora's favorites at age thirteen or fourteen. Right then Jenny felt a stab of yearning fierce enough to buckle her legs, as if her daughter had vanished not nineteen years ago but yesterday.

★

Luther did not offer an explanation that night, or any time the following week, as the bruises on his face darkened like storm clouds. He brooded in his La-Z-Boy, flipping through old copies of *Sports Illustrated* and *Baseball Weekly*, or he made himself snacks in the kitchen, or he rummaged in the attic, or he played solitaire in the dining room. The only part of the house he avoided was the basement, where Harlan was installing a sump pump and insulating the heating ducts. As far as Jenny could tell, Luther and Harlan never spoke a word to one another—certainly not at meals, where she and Katarina tried in vain to break their silence.

That Luther remained silent all week was more bearable to Jenny because he also remained sober, his longest dry spell since closing the tavern. It was not for lack of booze; she felt certain he had bottles stashed away. Besides, if he had exhausted his supply, he could have driven to town and restocked. She knew better than to get her hopes up, for however often he climbed onto the wagon, sooner or later—and mostly sooner—he always tumbled off. Still, while it lasted, the change was a blessed relief. She would not remark on it to Luther, for she had learned early in their marriage not to bring up his drinking, even when he was sober; nothing sent him into a rage more swiftly. Several times in those early years, having provoked his fury, she had run to neighbors for shelter, carrying baby Aurora. So now she held her tongue.

Then toward the end of that booze-free week, Jenny and Katarina were cleaning up after supper when Luther came into the kitchen and offered to help with the dishes, a rarity for him.

"Go along, now," Jenny said briskly to Katarina. "You're off duty."

"But—"

"Shoo! There's a full moon. Why don't you and Harlan go see if the river is frozen solid enough for skating?"

A sharp look from Jenny prompted Katarina to hand the dishtowel to Luther and slip out of the kitchen. Soon, voices sounded

from the mud room, where Harlan and Katarina were bundling
up against the cold. Jenny washed plates and Luther dried, neither speaking until they heard the back door close.

Then Luther said, "I'm staying off the bottle."

"I've noticed," Jenny replied, in as neutral a voice as she could
manage.

He stood there by the sink, wiping and wiping a plate, which
looked like a saucer in his huge fingers. Jenny waited, sensing
the words rising in his chest. Finally he cleared his throat and the
story poured out. The night when he came back to the room in
such a frenzy, he had sipped his way through a fifth of scotch, taking nips now and then, pretending he was going outside to look
at the stars, while he and Harlan worked in the shed on the tractor. They were taking off the cylinder head to replace the gasket,
but when they came to the last bolt Harlan couldn't get it loose,
so he sprayed it with penetrating oil, to cut the rust, and said to
let it soak awhile for the juice to work. But Luther felt juiced up
himself, wanted to show the boy a man's strength. He grabbed
the socket wrench and stuck a pipe on the end for leverage and
went at the bolt, while Harlan kept telling him to let it alone, let it
alone, and that made Luther push all the harder, until the head of
that damn bolt twisted right off. Harlan yelled at him, said only
a fool works drunk. Things went black then for a while and the
next thing Luther knew he had the pipe raised up over his head
and Harlan was backing away from him into a corner. The look
on the boy's face made Luther drop the pipe and go stumbling
away.

"I could have killed him," Luther ended in a whisper. "I *wanted*
to kill him. And he knew it."

Again Jenny waited, watching this man she loved and feared,
loved more than feared, as he grimaced from the memory. He
set down the plate, took up another one, and began wiping it
round and round with the towel. The plate had been one of her

mother's, a flow-blue pattern of flowers and leaves, on English ironstone, brought over from London by a great aunt before the First World War. Jenny was afraid Luther might drop it, he was trembling so, but she said nothing, for what he was telling her was more important than even that treasured plate.

"I came that close." He snapped his fingers. "I keep seeing that look on his face. It scared me good. Scared the taste for liquor right out of me. I swore I'd never touch a drop again." Lifting the hand that held the towel, he ran the back of a wrist across his lips. "But the thirst came back again the next day. I've been fighting it ever since."

Jenny took the plate from him and set it on the counter, took the towel and hung it on the stove handle, wrapped her arms around his waist and pressed her cheek against his chest, feeling tremors pass through him. They were standing there when Harlan and Katarina returned from their walk, entering through the back door and stamping their boots in the mudroom.

"It's glorious out there," Katarina sang out.

"And cold!" Harlan added. "The river ice would hold a truck."

"We heard owls calling, like the ones at Black Bear Farm."

"Barred owls, a pair of them, down in the cedars."

"The moon cast shadows on the snow."

"There was so much light you could read a newspaper."

It cheered Jenny to see them so happy, even as she nestled against her troubled husband. She could feel him growing calm while the lovebirds rhapsodized about all they had seen in the moonlight.

Suddenly, Luther said to Harlan, "You need a hand with anything tomorrow?"

Harlan studied his bruised face for a moment before answering. "Sure. If you're feeling up to it."

"I'm up to it. I may look like something the cat dragged in, but I feel fine."

Jenny could almost see sparks flying through the air between her two men. But it was a reconciliation of sorts, however temporary.

★

Maybe it came from having young lovebirds in the house, or
from going without drink, or from breathing country air. Whatever the reason, Luther became friskier in bed than he had been
for years. Jenny was embarrassed by the pleasure this gave her,
long after she had ceased to think of herself as desirable, but not
sufficiently embarrassed to hold back when Luther stroked her
breast or slid a hand under her nightgown. She had almost forgotten what it felt like to be touched in that caressing way.

Once or twice a week now, Jenny and Katarina exchanged
conspiratorial smiles across the breakfast table, reading the same
tranquility in the other's face, while Harlan and Luther made a
list of the day's chores. Harlan set aside the list only on Sundays,
following the example of the elderly farmer in Vermont who
had taught him so many country skills. This habit of honoring
the Sabbath was all the more striking to Jenny since Harlan had
never shown any interest in religion while he was growing up,
nor had she and Luther ever taken him to church or sent him
to Bible camp—a reaction against their own pious parents, who
were Dutch Calvinists on Luther's side and Southern Baptists on
Jenny's.

His church was outdoors, Harlan liked to say, so on Sunday
mornings, regardless of the weather, he took long walks, usually alone, since Katarina preferred to muse beside the woodstove with a book and a cup of tea, and neither Jenny nor Luther could keep up with him. On his return, he would give an
excited report of the birds he had seen in the woods, the animal
tracks he had found in the mud or snow, the stage of the river,
the look of the sky.

On Sunday afternoons, Harlan and Katarina drove to Ravenna, the county seat, where she could use her cell phone and both of them could use the library computers. Every other week or so Jenny would tag along, to replenish the pile of whodunits for her bedtime reading. Katarina would sit at one machine, writing to her family and a raft of friends she kept in touch with through this technology that mystified Jenny, and Harlan would sit at another machine, zipping off messages to a couple of his buddies from high school and friends he had made in Vermont. Even more mystifying to Jenny was the way the youngsters searched the nebulous thing called the Web to find answers to the most obscure questions. Katarina printed out quilt patterns and recipes for Swedish cookies and plans for a sauna she thought Harlan should build near the springhouse. With a few clicks of the keys, Harlan found sources for truck parts and a watershed map of the Red Hawk River. He discovered the phone number of the nursing home in Boston where Mrs. Winfield stayed, so he could call to check on her using Katarina's little folding phone. He looked up hardware and tools. Once he summoned onto the screen the picture of a tractor, which he told Jenny was a 1963 Farmall, the same model as the one he and Luther had fixed up, only this one looked brand new, everything shiny, even the tires. The tractor out at the farm, which she had thought of as burnt umber in color, was only rusty, Harlan declared. He aimed to buff it up and repaint it the original fire engine red, like the one on the computer.

★

The Sunday before Christmas, Harlan relaxed his Sabbath rule to help Jenny put up curtains, while Luther drove Katarina to the library. When Jenny had asked for help, Harlan remarked that he didn't see the point of covering windows unless you were worried about scandalizing the birds, since the nearest neighbors were a quarter mile away. But he agreed readily enough when she explained that the curtains were not for privacy but for color.

They began upstairs in the east-facing bedroom that Jenny had claimed for Luther and herself. She and Katarina had sewn the curtains for this room from lemon-colored, filmy cotton that would let morning sunlight filter through. Jenny had always wanted to wake up to sunshine, but the apartment above the tavern faced west and it was shaded all day by taller buildings. Here, she could bask in the glow from two big windows that caught the dawn.

Working from a stepladder, Harlan fastened the brackets into plaster above the windows because he said it would be sacrilegious to drill holes in the walnut trim, which he and Luther had painstakingly refinished. As Jenny threaded the lemony curtains onto rods, she admired the precise way Harlan measured for the brackets, the way he seated plastic anchors into the wall with taps of his hammer, the way the muscles in his forearm flexed as he tightened the screws. She couldn't get enough of watching him. Nor could she get over how swiftly Aurora's baby, once tiny enough to sleep under a bar towel, had become this strapping young man, who would turn twenty in a few days.

After tugging on the brackets to make sure they were firm, Harlan announced he was ready for the curtains. She handed them up to him and he fitted them in place and the room turned a diaphanous yellow.

"Isn't it gorgeous?" she said. "I've adored this color since I was a child, staring into the throat of a daffodil."

Harlan nodded, but he seemed to be thinking of something other than the light in the room. As he climbed down from the ladder and packed away his tools, Jenny could sense that his mind was churning. She began folding a pile of laundry on the bed, to give him time.

At last he said, "Katarina tells me you showed her pictures of my mother."

"I didn't think you'd mind. She came across them while we were unpacking."

"I thought you'd burned them."

Jenny shuddered. "Certainly not. She was my daughter long before she was your mother."

"Could I see them?"

"Of course. They're on the top shelf in my closet, in that box your basketball shoes came in."

Harlan fetched the box and sat down with it on the floor, just as he had done as a child, and peered at the photographs one after another. Glancing over his shoulder while she folded clothes, Jenny could see that he paused longest over the images of Aurora. As a young boy, he would ask every now and then to see the photographs, and he would pore over them, as he was doing now, with a solemn look on his face, never crying, rarely asking questions. Jenny could only guess what triggered the requests—maybe the sight of a classmate's mother showing up at school, maybe something he'd read in a book. Then one summer day when Harlan was ten or so, after sorting through the box while she was downstairs cooking in the tavern, he pulled out the pictures of Aurora and bound them with a rubber band and left them on Jenny's dresser with a note saying, *PLEASE BURN THESE. They make me mad.* She wouldn't think of burning the photographs, but she did hide them away, and he never again asked to see them—until today.

She was matching up socks and balling them into pairs when Harlan twisted around to look up at her, with an expression as sober as any he had shown her in childhood. "You'd tell me if she was dead, wouldn't you?"

"She isn't dead," Jenny shot back.

"How can you be sure?"

"I just am. It may sound silly, but there's a thread binding me to her, and I'd know if it broke."

Harlan shifted his gaze to the luminous windows. "You think she loved Tommy, even after he ditched her?"

"She was only fifteen when they met. What did she know about love? A handsome sailor sweet-talked her for a week and she gave him what he wanted." Aware of the dismissive note in her voice, Jenny recalled being a high school girl herself, pausing in the hallway between trigonometry class and social studies, when Luther touched her for the first time, a brush of fingers along her forearm that set her body vibrating like a plucked string. So she felt bound to add, "Yes, I suppose she loved him."

"Did Tommy love her?"

"There's no way to know. He didn't act like it. But he was a year or two younger than you are now, too young to fancy becoming a father."

Harlan's voice dropped so she had to strain to hear him say, "Well, I've been imagining it."

"You have?"

"I thought it might keep Katarina from going back to Sweden," he admitted. "But she just scoffs and tells me she's not planning to have babies for another ten years."

"Is that why you're curious about your parents all of a sudden?"

"It isn't sudden. I've always been curious. It just hurts too much to ask about them when there's no chance of getting answers."

"We've told you all we know, sweetheart."

The sound of the front door opening alerted them to the return of Katarina and Luther from the library. Jenny called gaily down to them, but instead of returning her greeting they kept talking, in a hard-edged tone she found disquieting. Harlan gave her an apprehensive look, and then began hastily putting the photographs away.

There was a quick patter on the stairs and Katarina came rushing in, her cheeks rouged from the cold or perhaps from excitement. "Harlan, I searched the Michigan directory and found five people named Two Bears. One of them lives in Marquette. That is the place you said, yes? Teresa Two Bears. I wrote down her number. We'll call her. Maybe she knew Tommy."

Luther slouched in, puffing from the stairs, his face tight with what Jenny recognized as barely contained anger. "I keep telling her he was scum, Harlan, not anybody you need to know about. He ruined your mother's life. He's dead, and that's how you ought to leave him."

§ § §

Chapter Eight • April 2000

JACK

JACK HAYMAKER COULD TELL HE'D BEEN ON THE ROAD too long, away from his wife, when the undulating land began to resemble the contours of reclining women. That was how the snowy terrain of Michigan's Upper Peninsula was looking to him as he neared Marquette at dawn on the fifteenth of April. Two thousand miles, twelve days, and six concerts separated him from his wife and twin daughters back in the Skagit Valley of Washington. Tonight he would give the seventh concert of this tour in a library on the main drag in Marquette, a town he had never set foot in but one the promoter assured him was teeming with Jack Haymaker fans.

What such a claim usually meant was that enough tickets had been sold to cover the cost of gas and food, but not enough for a motel, if Jack wanted to have any cash left over to take back home. So he had driven all night instead of paying for a room on the road from Green Bay. Because he refused to set foot in airplanes, which seemed to him like group coffins with windows, he roamed from gig to gig on wheels. The current wheels belonged to a turquoise Volkswagen van whose most conspicuous bumper sticker announced FOLK SINGER & PACK ANIMAL, and whose odometer had rolled up 212,119 miles before surrendering to entropy.

At thirty-nine, Jack had rolled up enough years to realize that entropy was gaining on him, as well, but not enough to make him quit carrying his songs across the country, still hopeful that some day one of his albums would win raves in *Billboard* or one of his lyrics would wind up in a television ad for some not entirely malevolent corporation and he would begin drawing audiences of thousands instead of hundreds or dozens. Such lightning good luck had struck a couple of his friends in the music business, so he knew it was possible, if unlikely. He needed a breakthrough song, one that would crack open the hearts and haunt the memories of listeners coast to coast. Was that too much to ask of the Muses? Yet for the past two years, since his parents drowned in the Skagit River, Jack had been unable to write anything at all. He just kept singing his old standbys, hoping the creative juices would begin flowing again. But he saw little promise of a thaw in the snowy flanks of northern Michigan.

All he knew about Marquette was that it was a port on Lake Superior where freighters loaded up with iron ore. He was curious to see the big ships, but he wasn't seeing anything too clearly as he cruised into town, partly because the sun was just breaking the horizon, mainly because of an eye infection he'd picked up on one of his stops in Wisconsin. So his first order of business this morning, after brewing coffee on the propane stove in the back of the van, was to find a doctor who would take pity on an uninsured troubadour and squeeze him in on a Saturday and prescribe some antibiotic drops without charging him more than this gig was likely to pay.

★

By 7:30 that morning, Jack was standing with a gaggle of other people, most of them looking as scruffy as he did, outside the office of one Naomi Rosenthal, M.D., whom he had chosen from the Yellow Pages because of her address, on West Magnetic Street, and because of her name, which brought to mind a winsome Naomi from his high school days. That earlier Naomi had once told him he reminded her of an actor who played thuggish parts in B movies, a comparison Jack chose to find encouraging. This Naomi Rosenthal's prime attraction, sight unseen, was her sex, for when he felt poorly he always sought comfort from a female, first his mother and then a sequence of girlfriends and then his wife, so the prospect of having a woman doctor lay even a latex-covered hand on his inflamed eyes soothed him.

Although puzzled by the number of patients waiting on the icy sidewalk half an hour before the office was scheduled to open, he felt at home among their lined faces, gap-toothed smiles, frayed coats, and scuffed boots. These were the sorts of people he knew from the Cascade Mountains of Washington—loggers and waitresses, mechanics and mill workers, farmers and checkout clerks. And these were the sorts of folks who made him want to throw his whole soul into the music when they showed up at his concerts, for he knew they might have to shake the piggy bank or hunt for lost coins under the couch cushions to pay for even his low-priced tickets and bargain CDs.

More than a dozen people had gathered outside by 8:00, when a nurse unlocked the door. Why so many? As they filed in, Jack put the question to a grizzled old gent who was missing the forefinger on one hand. "Because," the man explained, "Dr. Rosenthal don't charge nothing for treating you on Saturday if you're hard up." When Jack asked how the doctor could tell you were hard up, and not just some cheapskate trying to rip her off, the man answered, "She ain't a lady you can lie to."

An hour later, when Dr. Rosenthal swept into the examining room where Jack waited, he could see what the old fellow meant. She was a lean woman, the long white coat masking whatever curves she might have had, with an open, expressive face rather like his mother's, disorderly black curls threaded with gray, and gleaming chestnut eyes that made him feel transparent. She took one look at him and said, "Those must hurt."

Blinking his swollen lids, Jack replied, "Like two balls of fire."

"A Jerry Lee Lewis fan, eh? 'Goodness, gracious, great balls of fire!'" She crooned the last words, making Jack laugh. He guessed she must have been in her forties, but it was hard to tell, she was so trim and vigorous. She kept her gaze on him as she washed her hands at the sink and pulled on gloves, all the while asking him questions that brought out where he was from and how his daughters had just turned twelve and what fine pottery his wife made and why he had come to Marquette.

"So you play your own songs?" the doctor asked, tilting his head back with a finger under his chin and studying his eyes with a penlight.

"Mostly," Jack answered. "But sometimes I throw in a few by my heroes."

"Such as?"

"Oh, Lead Belly, Woody Guthrie, Pete Seeger, Bob Dylan, Phil Ochs, Willie Nelson—dissidents and bluesmen and balladeers."

She leaned close with the light. "Where do you get your ideas for songs?"

"All over. People I meet, newspapers, books, photos, memories."

"I envy you. I've been steeped in music all my life, but I couldn't write a line," she said. "Now close." Shutting his eyes, Jack could feel her wiping the crust from his lids with a cool swab. "My mother is a singer," the doctor went on, "or she *was* a singer, until my brother and I came along, and then she stayed home while my father played concerts around the world. Perhaps you've heard of him—Simeon Rosenthal?"

"The cellist? I own a bunch of his recordings. He's a master."

"Indeed. So you can imagine how disappointed he was when I quit piano at twelve and voice lessons at fifteen. I had absolutely no gift."

"I don't claim any gifts," Jack said. "I just love singing."

"Do your girls miss you when you're traveling? I always missed my father."

"It eats at me, being away so much. But touring is how I get my music out there. I produce my own albums, so if I don't tour, nobody knows I exist."

"And when my father did come home," the doctor mused, probing delicately with her fingers around Jack's puffy eyes, "it seemed he was never fully there. He was always practicing. Sometimes I wanted to hide his cello, or smash it."

Jack flinched, not at her touch but at the image of a shattered cello.

"You can open up now," the doctor said, and her fingers left his face. He cracked his lids to see her stripping away the gloves. He noticed she wore no rings. "What you've got," she said, jotting on a prescription pad, "is bacterial conjunctivitis, commonly known as pink eye. These drops should clear it up within a few days, but in the meantime you're contagious, so keep your hands washed and don't share towels with anybody."

Since he would share nothing as intimate as a towel until he returned home in another ten days, Jack felt a pang of loneliness. As he accepted the prescription, he said, "You set the record for the most talk I ever heard out of a doctor in my whole life."

"It does slow things down," she conceded, "but I went into medicine to treat persons, not bodies. Besides, so far as I know, you're the first songwriter I've ever had in my office. Now put in those drops and keep your hands clean."

"Yes ma'am." He stood up and shrugged into his coat. "Where do I go to pay?"

"We don't charge on Saturday," she said firmly.

"Why not?"

"Because I earn enough the other days of the week."

"But you could always earn more. That's the American way, isn't it?"

The corners of her chestnut eyes softened with amusement. "Do you ever give benefit concerts, Mr. Haymaker?"

"All the time. Too many, according to my wife. She balances the checkbook."

"Well, think of my Saturday clinic as a benefit concert."

He nodded. "Fair enough. But if you won't take money, could I put you on the guest list for tonight's show? Of course, my music won't sound anything like what your dad plays."

"You think I'm a classical snob? I love folk and blues, too."

"Then you'll come? Eight o'clock at the library. I'll put you down for half a dozen tickets. Bring your family, bring your friends. Bring everybody you can lasso."

The doctor smiled, considering. "Maybe I will, if I finish here early enough. I haven't heard live music in the longest time." With that, as if having said more than she intended, she hurried out to look after those other hard up patients.

*

Jack wasn't sure he qualified as hard up, since he owed nobody a cent. He and Megan, his wife, had built their house, room by room, as they could afford the materials, after the fashion of a nautilus adding chambers to its shell, and in the same way they had built a pottery studio for Megan and a barn where the twins kept a pair of Palominos, gifts from his parents. All three buildings were mortgage free. They paid cash for everything, from the Volkswagen van to the midwife's fee for delivering the twins. Still, they lived from gig to gig, album to album, never able to sock much away. They had a college savings account for the girls, but kept having to raid it when the refrigerator conked out or the property tax doubled or somebody came down with the flu. Unable to afford health insurance, Jack and Megan drew up a ranked list of what they would sell to pay the bills if one of them fell seriously ill.

Megan earned a little from peddling her pots at galleries and fairs, but she couldn't go far afield since Jack was so often away. The money Jack brought home from his tours was the only compensation he could offer for leaving her alone to care for the girls, the horses, and the house. For the first dozen years of their marriage, she could always call on Jack's parents, who had lived just down the road and had pitched in to cook, clean, run errands, or look after kids whenever Megan needed help. But that help ceased abruptly two years ago, when a rockslide shoved his parents' car through a guardrail into the glacial meltwaters of the Skagit River.

Because she believed in his music, Megan still put up with his itinerant ways. Since his parents' death, however, when he called home from the road, Jack could hear the strain in her voice. What troubled him even more was that the twins, Annie and Sophie, had less and less to say to him over the phone, as if they didn't trust him to understand what was happening in their lives. And when he returned home, instead of finding three adoring females, as in the old days, he found two sullen girls who gave him cursory kisses before retreating to their room, and a frazzled wife who presented him with a list of things needing immediate attention.

Recently, Megan had also begun leaving on his dresser notices of job listings, especially from the Forest Service, North Cascades National Park, and Seattle City Light, the only outfits in the area sure to provide health benefits and unlikely to ship jobs overseas. In the early years of their marriage, before he took the gamble of making music fulltime, Jack had worked in the park as a ranger, and occasionally he still worked there on short-term contracts, as a firefighter or trail-builder. On the eve of this latest trip, Megan had shown him a posting for a new facilities manager at the park, to replace the backwoods genius who had trained Jack in trail-building, and who would be retiring in May. Working with dirt, wood, stone, a puny budget, and makeshift crews, this man had created shelters and paths throughout the park that were entirely worthy of their spectacular mountain setting. Jack had loved that work. If he was ever forced to give up touring in order to earn a steady paycheck, he could imagine spending his days outdoors, overseeing crews, climbing the slopes.

Because he showed some interest in the facilities manager's job, Megan taped the listing inside the lid of his guitar case, where he allowed it to stay, and where he saw it once again the afternoon of his arrival in Marquette as he took out the guitar for a sound check in the library auditorium. By then he had napped and had dosed himself with the drops three times, and the fire in his eyes had begun to cool. His vision was still blurred, but he would be able to see the audience well enough when the show began this evening.

*

By 8:00 there was a good turnout, well over a hundred, Jack estimated, as he surveyed the crowd. On entering, people stomped snow from their boots and peeled away coats, scarves, and hats; as they settled into their seats they kept up a buzz of conversation—not about the concert, most likely, but about their overlapping lives. It was the sound of friends and neighbors glad to be together, a sound as welcome to Jack as the murmur of riffles in a creek. He also welcomed the mix of ages, from toddlers to elders, and the range of incomes reflected in their outfits, from glad rags to work shirts emblazoned with car-care logos and jeans patched at the knees.

Scanning the rows, he was disappointed not to see Dr. Rosenthal. Then, at five past the hour, just as the sponsor, a slight man with gray goatee and rainbow suspenders, was approaching the mike to introduce him, Jack saw her coming down the aisle with a bevy of five other women, two of whom he recognized as nurses from the office. There was no husband or boyfriend in the bunch, which might have meant only that any man in the doctor's life was busy tonight, or else no fan of folk music. Noting the absence of a man, as he had earlier noted the absence of a wedding ring, Jack was reminded yet again that he had been away from his wife too long. The doctor and her friends sat in the fourth row and turned expectantly toward the stage.

"And now," the sponsor concluded, "please welcome Jack Haymaker!"

Wearing his usual black jeans, white shirt, brown leather vest, and clodhopper boots, Jack strolled on with the guitar slung over his shoulder, leaned close to the mike, and launched into the opening song, about workers who'd died while building dams on the Skagit. The stage boomed as he stomped it, a reminder that he was packing a few too many pounds on his frame. Because of his sore eyes, he had trouble reading the audience, but they sounded lively. By midway through his first set, they were cheering and whistling, and the aisles were filling with dancers on the fast tunes, so he tried to keep the pizzazz going by avoiding too much patter between songs.

One person he could make out fairly well was the doctor, because she sat within the spill of light from the stage. As he worked through his repertoire of songs about farmers and loggers, broken soldiers and corporate crooks, daughters and wives, he kept glancing at her face, which revealed her shifting emotions the way the surface of a pond reveals every breeze, just as his mother's face used to do.

During intermission he went to mingle with folks at the table where the promoter's teenage daughter, who reminded Jack achingly of his own two girls, was selling albums. Most musicians he knew would have gone backstage to chill, but he needed to push Haymaker merchandise. The doctor and several of her women friends were already there, reading the liner notes on his CDs and opening their wallets. As he approached, the doctor beamed at him and cried, "Bravo!"

"Liking it so far?" he asked.

"Loving it." She held up a stack of CDs. "Enough to buy all five albums."

"Here, let me make a gift of them."

"Nonsense. The workman deserves his pay."

"My mama used to say that. It's in the Bible somewhere."

"Possibly. I learned it from my father, whose recordings put me through college."

"Then how about if I sign them? To Dr. Rosenthal?"

"To Naomi," she said. "I'm a doctor only when I wear a white coat."

Tonight she was wearing a pantsuit the color of moss. She carried a beaded shoulder bag and her lush curls were pulled back with a silver clasp that glinted when she turned her head to share a laugh with her friends. As Jack signed the CDs, her name summoned up the bewitching Naomi from his high school days, giving him cause yet again to wonder, as a man faithfully married to Megan, what he should do with the yearning aroused in him by the beauty he kept meeting in other women. His solution, so far, had been to pour his yearning into songs.

Love songs were mostly what he offered in the second set—love not only for people but also for mountains, rivers, and trees, for salmon and sandhill cranes, for clouds and rain and rocks and the whole glorious planet. He ended the show, as he often did, with a song about Annie and Sophie riding their Palominos at dusk while he and Megan sat watching from the back stoop. When he reached the last line of the chorus—*So now I'll be a father as long as I live*—his voice cracked, which surprised him, and he had to play through the chord progression twice before he regained control.

Never one to retreat backstage after a concert, Jack set down his guitar and waded into the audience, accepting congratulations and hugs. He could see Naomi Rosenthal hanging back until the last of the crowd had scattered, and then she approached him with a look on her face he might have called rapture if he had been a churchgoing man. Instead of flinging her arms around him, as so many others had done, she gripped his chin and tilted his head toward the light and studied his eyes.

"They're looking better," she said, "but still it's a wonder you can sing with so much gusto while your eyes are burning."

"I couldn't see too well," Jack admitted, "so I just threw myself into the music."

"Well, it filled me with the mixture of elation and sorrow I always feel when I'm listening to Bach. Light and shadow. Why does that feel so true? Because whatever we love we're going to lose?" She gave a self-deprecating laugh. "Sorry. I'm babbling."

Always embarrassed by praise, Jack said lightly, "That's the first time anybody's compared me to Bach, and I expect it'll be the last."

"Here," she said, reaching into the beaded shoulder bag. "I brought something for you." She handed him a framed snapshot, which he glanced at only long enough to see that it was of a woman lying facedown in the grass before a gravestone. When he looked up quizzically, the doctor explained, "You said sometimes you get inspiration from photos. I thought you might get a song out of this one."

Squinting, he perceived that the woman in the picture was young, maybe early twenties, her body long and willowy. She wore a blue sundress that left her shoulders bare; her legs and feet, also bare, looked strikingly pale against the grass. She was propped on her elbows before the gravestone, face buried in her hands, and her hair was wound into a bun. Jack couldn't read the name on the stone, but he could see that hundreds of identical white markers stretched away behind it, row upon row, toward the horizon.

"Who is she?" he asked.

"I don't know for sure," the doctor said. "The stone is for a local boy who was killed on a Navy ship, maybe a dozen years ago. I took the photo about five years ago, when I was visiting the grave of my brother, who died in Vietnam. When I saw this girl, it was as though I were seeing myself at the moment I learned of his death."

"It's hard to look at her and hard to look away," Jack said. "She's so miserable, and yet beautiful."

"I keep her picture on my desk, to remind me."

"Then you oughtn't to give it away."

"I've got the negative. I can make another print."

"You have no idea who she is?"

"I have a hunch. The boy's mother told me he joined the Navy because he got a girl pregnant, a teenager who worked in her parents' bar near the docks in Cleveland."

"And this could be the girl?"

"That's my guess." The doctor gave Jack a searching look. "What do you say? Will you make a song for her? I want something good to come out of all this grief."

Music wouldn't undo the losses, he knew, but it might preserve a trace of the beauty. Four nights from now he was due to play in Cleveland, where he might track down this sorrowful woman. So he accepted the photograph from Naomi Rosenthal,

accepted her quick embrace, and accepted the view of her retreating figure as the last he would ever see of her.

★

Tired as he was, Jack wanted to put some distance between
himself and the latest focus of his unacceptable longings, so he
loaded the Volkswagen and drove south and east from Marquette
toward the Straits of Mackinac. Although his eyes still burned,
his vision had cleared. The moon, nearly full, shone down from
a black sky onto the snowy countryside. Mile after mile, the road
was flanked by forests, interrupted now and again by frozen lakes.
Twice he saw owls gliding across the headlight beam. Once he
spied a fox squatting on its haunches along the berm, as if waiting
for a ride, its eyes glinting like green gems. Even without mountains, Jack imagined, this landscape might claim a man's heart.
      When his head began to nod he started looking for a place to
park for the night, finally stopping at a pull-off along the north
shore of Lake Michigan near the Cut River Bridge, where he
could wake in the morning to a view of water.
      When he did wake, and wriggled out of the sleeping bag, at
first he could see nothing through the frosted windows, and then
gradually he could make out the boxy silhouette of a portable toilet, on which three crows perched like gargoyles. Uninspired by
the exterior view, he concentrated on the interior. He fired up the
stove, the blue flame sputtering momentarily before it steadied.
While coffee perked and eggs boiled, he took out the photograph
Dr. Rosenthal had given him. The wan daylight filtering in was
too faint, so he put on his headlamp, then his reading glasses, and
finally he could decipher the name on the gravestone: Tommy
Two Bears. The woman who lay in mourning across the grave
called up Jack's own grief. Unlike her, and unlike Naomi Rosenthal, he had lost no loved ones in war, but he had lost his parents to even vaster forces. He loved mountains no less because a

rockslide had hurled his parents into the river, and he loved rivers no less because of the drowning. His passion for the wilds was tempered only by the knowledge that nature doesn't return one's love, doesn't love or hate or feel anything at all but simply rolls on according to its own merciless ways.

War, on the contrary, was always the result of human choices. It seemed to him the greatest folly of his species. Nature dished up plenty of suffering, so people damn well ought to avoid heaping on more pain by fighting one another over territory, ideology, or loot. As he jotted these thoughts in the notebook where he worked out his songs, he began to imagine what the dead sailor might say about war to the woman left behind to grieve, and what she might answer. Sipping coffee and eating bread slathered with butter and eggs, Jack gazed out through the clearing windows at pewter waves scouted by gulls, wondering who she was, this woman in the blue sundress sprawled with such heartrending beauty on the grass. Was she the barmaid in Cleveland whom Tommy got pregnant? If so, did she bear the child? And if she bore the child, what had become of it, and of her?

The questions kept bubbling up all that day as he drove toward his next gig in Lansing. He propped the photograph on the dashboard and opened the notebook in his lap, where he could scrawl notions while keeping one hand on the wheel. Megan didn't approve of this stratagem, preferring that he keep both hands on the wheel and eyes on the road. She was right, as usual. Yet he persisted in scribbling as he drove, because good ideas tended to be flighty unless he wrote them down, and also because, as his mother used to say, he ignored the common sense God gave him.

The highway hugged the shore of Lake Michigan as far as the strait, where he crossed over the long Mackinac Bridge, one of those marvels that occasionally revived his faith in human skill. From there he followed the interstate south, through forests and farmland; eventually the snow thinned, until patches of mud began to show, and then stretches of brown grass. Sensing that the word *child* needed to be in the song, he began thinking of rhymes, from full ones like *wild* or *mild* to slant ones like *stilled* or *died*. Other rhymes welled up, such as *graves* and *waves*, then phrases, then a few rough lines. He scribbled everything down, switching his gaze between paper and road. For the first time since the death of his parents, he was feeling the tingle of excitement that preceded all his best songs.

After his concert in Lansing, he phoned home to share his exhilaration with Megan, but she was upset because the girls had left a pasture gate unlatched and the Palominos had run off and she'd spent half a day retrieving the horses and meanwhile she'd neglected a batch of pottery in the kiln and spoiled the glazes and the pilot light had gone out on the water heater and right now the girls were fighting over whose turn it was to do the dishes. So could he call back another time? He could, Jack said, and he was sorry, and he loved her. From Megan's end came only a sigh and a sharp click.

Even this discouraging call did not staunch the flow of words, which began to suggest melodies. On the following days, around the edges of shows in Ann Arbor and Toledo, he noodled away at tunes on his guitar, searching for one that would convey the blend of elation and sorrow he had spoken of with Dr. Rosenthal. In Toledo he bought a two-CD set of Simeon Rosenthal performing Bach's *Suites for Solo Cello*, a duplicate of a recording he often listened to at home but had not thought to bring along on this trip. Musing on his own tunes while listening to Bach was like piling up a sand castle next to a real castle, yet these were the sounds Jack craved just now, these weavings of light and shadow, so he listened to the album nonstop all the way to Cleveland.

*

If the woman at the grave was Tommy's barmaid, and if her parents still owned the bar, it shouldn't be hard to find her. But

Jack hadn't reckoned on the number of drinking establishments within walking distance of the docks. He went around to eight or ten on the afternoon of his arrival in Cleveland, showing the photograph to the owners, if they were on the premises, and otherwise to bartenders, but nobody recognized her.

Fortunately, after an evening concert at a club on the Old River Road and a night's hospitality in the home of his promoter, Jack had a layover day before he would need to roll on toward Columbus for his next engagement. So in the late morning he resumed the search, his footsteps beating a rhythm on the sidewalks and the new song taking shape in his head. By midafternoon, still with no leads, deciding he'd wandered as far from the docks as he should go, he turned from Euclid Avenue onto a side street that ran north toward the lake. Within a few blocks he came upon a tired looking place called the Iron Ore Tavern, with neon signs for Pabst Blue Ribbon and Carling Black Label glowing in the window. The door stood open to the spring air, and a sports announcer's drawl sounded from inside.

When Jack entered, a bald man in a stained white apron greeted him from behind the bar, while keeping an eye on a television screen that showed a coach arguing with an umpire. The man looked to be around sixty, hunched but heavily built, with biceps as big as hams and massive hands that were splayed on the counter. He had the florid face and bulging gut of a devoted drinker, but he appeared to be sober at present. Three other men, sitting well apart from one another along the bar, bent over their glasses.

"Baseball season already?" Jack offered, as he straddled a stool.

"At last," the bartender said. "I didn't think spring would ever come. The Indians are playing the Orioles tonight in Baltimore. Nagy's on the mound for the tribe."

As his eyes adjusted to the gloom, Jack noticed Indians memorabilia everywhere—pennants, posters, jerseys, score sheets, scuffed bats, mug shots of players, autographed baseballs in glass cases—as if the bar were a shrine. The only stretches of wall not devoted to the Indians were filled with paintings that appeared, from a distance, to be landscapes rendered in colors vibrant enough for Eden.

"What'll you have?" the bartender asked.

After nipping into so many bars without a swallow, Jack figured he was due for a drink. "What's your best local beer? Let's say a lager."

"I'd pick Dortmunder Gold, from Great Lakes Brewing."

"Then that's what I'll have."

As the bartender filled a mug, Jack mentioned he was looking for someone.

"What's the name?"

"All I've got is a picture." Jack laid the photograph on the counter.

The bartender set the beer in front of Jack and leaned down, studying the photo. Then he grunted and picked it up, carefully pinching the frame in his thick fingers. He let out a breath or a curse, and then bellowed through the serving window into the kitchen: "Jenny! Jenny, come out here!"

Presently a small woman with gray permed hair emerged through a louvered door, looking as tired as the tavern. The lenses of her spectacles caught orange reflections from the neon beers signs. "You sound like you're calling a dog," she scolded.

"Look at this." The bartender thrust the photograph at her.

Before accepting it, the woman dried her hands on her apron and pushed the spectacles onto her forehead. As she peered at the image, drawing it closer and closer, the creases around her eyes deepened and her jaw sagged open. "Oh, God in heaven."

"Are you sure?" the bartender asked. "You can't see much of her face."

"It's our girl," the woman said, choking out her words. "She's older, filled out some. But those are her feet. There's the birthmark on her right calf. That's her red hair. And Tommy's name is on the stone."

Now the bartender let out a groan, as if he'd been punched in the belly. He rested a meaty arm across the woman's shoulders, and the two of them bent over the picture.

Their names, Jack learned, were Luther and Jenny Blake, and the woman at the grave was their daughter, Aurora, whom they hadn't seen since she'd run away, twelve years ago this month. In all those years, this was the first evidence they'd seen that she was even alive—or at least that she had survived into her twenties. Jack explained to them where and when the snapshot had been taken and how he had come to possess it. Over the next half hour, as the television jabbered on with its litany of balls and strikes, as customers ordered drinks from Luther or food from Jenny, the story of Aurora's seduction and disappearance emerged in snatches.

When Luther came to the part about the sailor's death at sea, he growled, "Served him right, the son of a bitch."

"You don't need to swear," Jenny said.

"I'll swear if I want to. He was a half-breed son of a bitch."

"Maybe he would have come back for her, if he'd lived."

"That's bullshit and you know it."

Husband and wife scowled at one another, then returned their gaze to the photo and resumed the story. They had helped Aurora with the baby as much as they could, but it was hard, with the tavern to mind every waking hour. When they went downstairs one morning and found four-month-old Harlan sound asleep in his basket on the bar, and a note beside him saying, "Sorry, so afraid, I've got to go," they kept hoping she would return. But months went by, and then years. Eventually they gave up hope. All this while they'd been raising Harlan, who was in sixth grade now, a moody boy with a hankering to wander, still full of hurt about his mother.

"The police couldn't find her," Jenny said.

"They didn't hardly try," Luther said. "She was just another runaway to them."

"They made us feel it was our fault, somehow. And maybe it was."

"It wasn't our goddamned fault!" Luther slammed his fist on the bar. Jack flinched and the other patrons looked up from their drinks. They looked down again as Luther wiped his mitts on the front of his apron.

"We even hired a detective," Jenny said.

"Cost us a fortune," Luther put in, "and didn't turn up a thing."

Dismayed that he had stirred up such anguish, Jack offered to let them keep the photograph. But Jenny insisted on returning it, saying she couldn't bear to look at it. Though her perm was gray, her hazel eyes, brimming now, suggested where Aurora might have come by her red hair. "A picture is only paper," she said, her lip quivering. "It's my girl I want. I want my girl! My girl!"

Her cries startled the patrons again. Luther hooked a hand under her arm and led her back into the kitchen, where his growls mixed with her wails.

Jack rose from his stool, feeling he should leave them to their grief, but also feeling he should apologize for upsetting them. If he had known they'd lost their daughter, he would never have shown them the photograph. What loss could be worse? After hesitating for a moment, without touching the beer, he decided to go.

As he emerged, blinking, into the sunlight, his eyes still mildly inflamed, he almost ran into a gangly boy who came bounding along the sidewalk toward the doorway of the tavern. The boy muttered a pardon me and darted past him into the dim interior. Jack swung around quickly enough to see the mop of black hair, the lanky frame weaving among tables, the arms too long for their sleeves thumping a backpack onto the bar, and the boy disappearing through the louvered door into the kitchen. It must be Harlan, home from school, Jack realized. When the boy came upon his grandparents, would Luther and Jenny tell him why they were distraught? Or would they keep silent about the visit from the man with a photograph, the man who couldn't bring Aurora back, who could only renew the pain of her vanishing?

*

If there were Muses, they blessed Jack on the following days, for the new song grew line by line as he rolled on south through Ohio, then west through college towns in Indiana and Illinois, and on back across the Great Plains into Idaho and eastern Washington. He heard the opening stanza in Tommy's voice:

> *I left you with child, my love, in that room above the bar,*
> *then rode a killer ship across the sea to war.*

In the following stanza he heard Aurora's reply:

> *You promised to leave the water and stay with me on land*
> *if I agreed to lie with you, no ring upon my hand.*

Like a pair of owls calling one another, the two voices played back and forth throughout the song, right up to the closing exchange. First Tommy:

> *War hasn't made a man of me but it has made me wild*
> *to hold you again, Aurora, and dandle our growing child.*

And finally Aurora:

> *Round your headstone grass is greening, as if you had not died,*
> *while I am left alone to nurse a fatherless child.*

The song would need work before it was ready for the stage. Still, after the show in Spokane, the last of this tour, Jack couldn't resist singing the duet to Megan over the phone. For the first time since he'd left home she responded tenderly, perhaps because she recognized the longing in his voice was for her and the girls. Would Aurora's ballad crack open the hearts of listeners coast to coast? Probably not—but it had cracked open his own heart, allowing him to let go of his drowned parents.

Driving west from Spokane through the Colville Indian Reservation, Jack recalled his glimpse of Harlan, a long-limbed boy with raven-black hair, coming home from school to a tavern. Although loved by grandparents, the boy would always carry scars where a mother and father should be. Jack thought of Annie and Sophie, only a year older than Harlan, girls poised to become women soon. Too soon, too swiftly, their bodies were swelling like rivers in spring. How much would they have changed in his absence, as each day sculpted their faces and tuned their voices? He thought of Megan, the woman who shimmered behind Aurora, behind Naomi Rosenthal, behind every alluring female he met, the woman he looked for even in the contours of a snowy landscape.

The van chugged on the climb above the snowline into the Cascades, rumbled through the passes, and purred on the downgrades as he tilted toward home. When the Skagit Valley opened before him, greening with spring, and he passed the raw gash from the rockslide on Sourdough Mountain, he thought maybe he would put in for that job at the park. Maybe he'd give up the road for a few years, until the twins went off to college. He could write songs while Megan and the girls slept, and on weekends he could perform in Bellingham, down in Seattle, out on Whidbey and Bainbridge and the other islands, any place within half a day's travel where an audience would gather to listen. He didn't need to sing to thousands, or even hundreds. Dozens would do, if they welcomed what he had to offer.

§ § §

Chapter Nine • January–May 2008

HARLAN

PAPA SIMMERED DOWN AFTER A FEW DAYS and quit trying to bully Harlan into giving up the plan of driving north to meet Teresa Two Bears. The old man huffed and puffed, but when Harlan wouldn't back down he let it go. Papa seemed to have been spooked by his own temper, ever since the night back in October when he'd stripped a bolt on the tractor and had come within a nerve twitch of smashing Harlan's skull with a length of pipe. Drink had fueled that clash, as it had fueled a string of violent quarrels before Harlan took off for Vermont. But even when drunk, Papa had never threatened him before with anything more than a swipe of his big paw or a lash of his belt. Whatever the reason, Papa hadn't touched a drop of liquor since that night, so far as Harlan could tell. No predicting how long he'd stay dry, but every sober hour was a blessing.

Harlan's only concession to his grandparents' misgivings was to postpone the trip until May, by which time the snow should have melted even in far northern Michigan. While waiting, he could mull over questions to ask Teresa Two Bears when he met her in person. He had felt awkward speaking with her by phone, and she must have felt the same about speaking with him, for their brief conversation had consisted of more silence than talk. When he finally worked up the gumption to call, a child answered, and when he asked to speak with Mrs. Two Bears the child said let me go fetch her and don't hang up because she moves real slow. Several minutes passed. In the background he could hear the high-pitched laughter of children and the nattering of a TV.

The voice that finally came on the line was soft and lilting, as if for Teresa Two Bears, as for Katarina, English was a language closer to music than to speech. After giving his name, which would have meant nothing to her, Harlan asked if she knew anything about Tommy Two Bears. The first of the long silences followed. Then Teresa asked him by turns if he was from the government, the Navy, or Social Security. No, he assured her.

"You are a friend who knew Tommy?"

"No, ma'am."

"Then why do you ask about him?"

Harlan took a breath to steady himself before saying, "Because I'm his son."

Teresa kept quiet for so long that Harlan would have thought she'd hung up, except for the ruckus of squealing children and yammering TV. At length she said, "How do you know this?"

He recounted the story of his birth, the few scraps he knew. She didn't interrupt. When he finished, again there was a long pause. Finally she said, "I must see you to know if what you say is true." She would tell him nothing more over the phone, would answer none of his questions, only kept repeating that she must see him in the flesh before she could decide whether to believe him.

*

Calculating that a trip to Marquette and back would cover thirteen hundred miles, Papa urged Harlan to take the Pontiac, which dated from the era when Detroit built cars to last, but

Harlan insisted on taking the old Ford pickup, which could be
fitted with a camper top, saving the cost of motels. "You're not
going to make Katarina sleep in the back of a truck, are you?"
Nana scolded. To which Katarina replied that it would be a lark,
like sleeping in a shantyboat, only on land instead of water.

Harlan found a used camper shell at a junkyard in Akron,
scoured off the rust, hammered out the dents, repainted it forest
green to match the Ford, and mounted it on the truck. He furnished the interior with the necessary gear and stowed everything
neatly as if it truly were a boat. Katarina climbed in to try out the
air mattress, the fold-down table, the lantern and stove. Charmed
by the setup, she cajoled Harlan into spending one clear, cold January night in the truck, while it was parked in the snowy pasture
under the stars. Even with their sleeping bags zipped together to
form a single pouch, they shivered for a long while before they
warmed enough to make love. They woke off and on throughout
the night, when a foot or an elbow brushed against a cool stretch
of fabric or when a gap at the top of the sleeping bag let in icy air.
In the morning, Harlan found Katarina hunched into a ball beside
him, dressed in all the clothes she'd taken off the night before,
from wool socks to knit cap embroidered with reindeer. They
decided not to repeat the experiment until after the last frost.

When to expect the last frost was a question Harlan asked the
old-timers whom he ran into at the hardware store and lumberyard. The garden seeds had arrived, and by the middle of February they were sprouting in peat pots on every south-facing win-
dowsill in the farmhouse. Harlan would have known when he
could safely set plants into the ground back in northern Vermont,
but he had no notion when to do so here in northern Ohio. All
the old-timers could agree on was that you never knew these days
when the last frost might come. Could be March, could be June,
the weather in recent years had turned so weird. Seventy degrees
in January and freezing in May, downpours in the dry season and

drought in the wet season, bugs and weeds never seen before in these parts cropping up everywhere, record blizzards one winter and bare ground the next, hundred-year floods coming every little while.

Harlan talked over these observations with Papa as they worked in the barn, with Nana as they sat by the woodstove in the evenings, with Katarina as they lay in bed at night. Papa scoffed, saying gaffers always complain about the way things are going nowadays. Nana confessed that she tuned out news about the environment, it sounded so grim. But Katarina, as usual, addressed the matter head on: "It is simple physics. We are heating the atmosphere with our greenhouse gases, and that disturbs the climate. Everybody in Europe knows this. In South America, China, and Japan also. Only in the United States do people blame liberals and God."

During his years in school, Harlan had never heard a teacher mention global warming or acid rain or ozone depletion or habitat destruction or the collapse of ocean fisheries or the extinction of species or the toxins in polar bear fat and mother's milk—all subjects that Katarina had studied in her own science classes. As a boy, he had been drawn to books of exploration from the nineteenth century, when much of America was still wild, before people had become numerous enough or technology powerful enough to spoil the continent. The early naturalists couldn't imagine this great abundance yielding before the assault of guns and axes. Not until reading Mr. Winfield's collection of books at Black Bear Farm did Harlan begin to realize that humans were capable of damaging not only a continent but the entire planet.

*

In March, the sky was briefly redeemed from contrails and smoke by flights of sandhill cranes heading north. If Harlan was indoors when he heard their jangly calls, he would rush outside and search the heavens until he spied them.

Work kept him mostly indoors that month, while he and Papa ran three-strand electrical cable and installed new fixtures in the house and barn. Rewiring the barn was straightforward, since the wall cavities were open, but wiring in the house was tedious, because the cable had to be fished up from the basement or down from the attic behind the plaster and lathe. Even sober, Papa frequently lost patience, snapping at Harlan, who set his jaw and kept on working. By nightfall they were so filthy that Nana asked them to strip off their work clothes in the barn before coming indoors to shower. Harlan collapsed into bed each night with knees rubbed raw from crawling, hands throbbing from splinters, the joints of his elbows and shoulders burning. Although he took the hardest jobs himself, sparing Papa, he knew the old man must be hurting even worse.

Nana feared they would electrocute themselves, but Harlan assured her that anybody who could read a street map could wire a house—another skill he'd learned from Mr. Winfield. Still, it was slow work, taking twice as long as Harlan had planned. When the last fixture was installed and the circuits were properly grounded and juice from Ohio Edison was flowing into the new service panel, every switch and outlet and appliance worked just as it should. He could sleep better now, knowing the house wouldn't burn down around their ears from a short.

With electricity flowing reliably, Papa ordered a satellite dish, so he could watch Indians games once the new season opened on the last day of March. Nana insisted that the dish be fastened to the barn, instead of being stuck like a carbuncle on the house. Despite her scorn for what she called the idiot box, Nana kept a TV babbling in the kitchen much of the day, as she had in the tavern, switching channels whenever the shows moved toward bloodshed or sex. Romance was fine with her, judging by the

soap operas she favored, and so were the talk shows in which
people divulged shameful secrets. She even watched the televan-
gelists, although she laughed at their fire-and-brimstone ranting.
She would shut off the set, however, when Katarina joined her
for cooking or a cup of tea, proof to Harlan that the squawking
box was only an antidote for loneliness. Papa kept a television going in the shop, tuned to one or another of the sports channels,
usually with the sound off so he could supply his own commen-
tary in place of the announcers' blather. Harlan could bear to be
in the same room with a TV only when it was muted, for then he
could turn his back on the whirl of gaudy images and pretend the
machine did not exist.

*

"You dwell too much in the past," Katarina told Harlan one
night in bed.

"I prefer it back there," he said.

"But you live now."

"What's to keep us from making a little refuge here on the
farm? Grow our food, cut wood for heat, draw water from the
spring. Raise some barefoot kids. Like the pioneers. Let the twenty-first century get along without us."

Katarina lay on her stomach while Harlan rubbed her back,
letting his fingers stray onto her luscious rump, hoping she would
be soothed into accepting his vision. But instead she objected irritably, pointing out that every time he switched on a light or
hopped in his truck or bought a factory product he was partici-
pating in the twenty-first century, whether he liked it or not. The
farm wasn't a bubble, sealed off from climate chaos, from poi-
soned water and air. Nor could it be defended from roving bands
of starving people who would ransack the countryside if trucks
ever stopped delivering food to the cities. And how was all that

food to be grown or processed or shipped once the oil gave out? As she spoke, her voice grew more and more exasperated, as if she held him personally responsible for ruining the planet.

Stung, he demanded, "So you aim to become one of those whispering interpreters at the UN and bring peace and understanding to the world?"

She twitched under his hand and rolled on her side to face him. "You laugh, but that is my hope. What is yours?"

Too angry to reply, he turned away from her without speaking and lay a long while before he could sleep.

★

What did he hope to do with his life? Harlan brooded on Katarina's question as he and Papa worked on their list of chores. For every job they finished, one or two new ones cropped up. They replaced glazing in a window and found the sill had rotted. They jacked up the sagging corner of a shed and discovered termites had riddled the floor joists. They hitched a sickle bar to the tractor, Papa set off to clear a pasture thick with young trees, and on the first round he snagged a roll of barbed wire hidden in the brush; then Harlan had to spend most of the day unsnarling wire from the sickle bar, sharpening the blade, and resetting the teeth, while Papa sat on a stump and cursed the sons of bitches who left trash laying around where a man couldn't see it. Their first batch of mail-order chicks died one chilly night when the bulb in the heat lamp burned out. So they reordered. But the new chicks disappeared one by one, night after night, until Harlan found a black snake feasting on them, caught it, and let it go in the woods on the far side of the river.

He had imagined that restoring a run-down farm and caring for his grandparents and maybe one day raising healthy kids would be enough to hope for. But no part of that vision was coming easily. The land would take years to heal. The old buildings seemed to fall apart as fast as he could mend them. He and Papa argued as much as they agreed, no doubt raising the old man's blood pressure and making Nana fret. And Katarina showed no interest in bearing children any time soon.

Even supposing he could realize his vision, would that be enough of a contribution in a world going to wrack and ruin? Should he do more? And what more could he do, with only two hands and a high school diploma? Since their time together at Black Bear Farm, Katarina had been after him to go to college. Kent State University was half an hour west of the farm and Youngstown State half an hour east. Supposing he could gain admission and figured out how to pay for tuition, what would he study?

On their Sunday visits to the library, Harlan peered over Katarina's shoulder to see what websites she visited, and then he checked them out as well, looking up stories about the wars in Iraq and Afghanistan, AIDS in Africa, the climate crisis, the shortage of freshwater, rising unemployment and home foreclosures, the swelling prison population, the widening gap between rich and poor. He would emerge from an afternoon's research feeling overwhelmed by the profusion and scale of these troubles.

Katarina found her way through this maze by following the thread of her talent for languages. But what talent did he have? He'd never thought of himself as possessing any. He'd earned decent grades in school, but no teacher had ever taken him aside and said, Harlan, you've got something in you the world needs, a real gift. Unlike his classmates, he had no father or mother to brag on him, to tell him he was born to do this or that. Nana had tried to encourage him, and so did Papa, in his rare good moods, but they had usually been too worn out from running the tavern to help him imagine what he might do with his life. True, he had a knack for carpentry and mechanics; he liked working with animals, liked gardening, liked doing almost any kind of outdoor work; but he didn't see how to employ those affections for mending the world.

As he struggled to find a direction, he recalled a story Nana had told him shortly before he ran off in search of Black Bear Mountain. Midway through her studies at art school, a professor advised her that she was wasting her time, for she lacked the talent necessary to become anything more than a decorative painter. Unsure of herself, she took the professor's judgment as final and quit school, explaining to friends that her aging parents needed her at home to look after them. In truth her parents were not yet fifty and could have managed fine without her, but she couldn't bear the prospect of failing at the pursuit she most loved. Even if the professor was right about her lack of talent, she told Harlan, she regretted not having found a way to devote her life to art, perhaps by working in a museum, opening a gallery, or teaching classes in drawing. Nana concluded her story by saying, "Don't ever let anybody turn you aside from what you love."

What Harlan loved most of all, aside from a few people, was nature—the whole of it—rivers and forests, rocks and mountains, wildflowers and butterflies and birds and bears, stars and clouds, thunder and lightning, rain and snow and wind and dirt. If he had to name the quality that all those marvels shared, he would have said wildness—the power that makes things grow, shapes them, fills them with beauty, from amoebas in pond water to galaxies in the depths of space. Here was a thread he might follow. Maybe if he went to college he could study biology, and after graduation he could get work restoring a prairie or cleaning up a river or coaxing some animal back from the edge of extinction.

During their next visit to the library he looked up the Kent State catalog and discovered that the university offered a degree in Conservation Biology, a field he'd never heard of. Just reading the list of courses excited him: Evolution, Ecology, Climatology, Earth Dynamics, Animal Behavior, Biological Diversity, on and on. He wrote down the details, his hand shaking. Unable to stay in his chair, he went pacing about the library, mind awhirl, until Katarina noticed his agitation and gathered her things and said she was ready to go. On their drive back to the farm he told her about his discovery, reciting the names of courses, speculating about what he might learn in each of them, describing the work he might do after graduation.

She listened quietly, her lips curling up, until he paused for breath, and then she said, "I have never seen you so happy."

*

By the middle of May, the last of the plants had been moved from the windowsills to the garden, even the tomatoes, as frost seemed no longer a threat in northeastern Ohio, and in the Upper Peninsula of Michigan, according to the Weather Channel, the last of the snow had melted. Harlan was eager to hit the road. He wondered if the itch he felt for heading north to meet Teresa Two Bears was anything like the impulse felt by cranes and warblers and other migrating birds when they left their winter havens and launched themselves into the chancy air. It was a shaky comparison, he realized, since birds were intent on reproducing their own kind, while he was intent on learning what he could about his father, a motive he suspected was unique to his own inquisitive species.

When he telephoned Mrs. Two Bears to propose a visit, he thought she might have forgotten his earlier call, from back in January, but as soon as she heard his voice she said, "You are the one who claims to be Tommy's son. You may come, but only if you promise you are not from the government." He promised, and they agreed on a date.

Studying the road atlas with Harlan, who had never driven such a distance before, Papa traced a route from Cleveland to Marquette along the turnpike and interstates. But Harlan wanted to avoid highways as much as possible, while passing near lakes and state parks and national forests and any other blue or green spots on the map that promised relief from the usual roadside crap. So, as usual, the two of them argued, their voices rising to shouts.

Later, as Harlan and Katarina took their evening walk to the river, she said, "You and Papa go at one another like hammer and tongues."

"Tongs," Harlan said. "Hammer and tongs."

"Where does that saying come from?"

"Blacksmithing, I guess."

"Ah, I see, the banging. Then why not hammer and anvil?"

"Because, like you say, our language is crazy."

After they walked on a few paces, Katarina asked, "Must you always contradict him?"

"Only when he's wrong."

"Is he always wrong?"

Harlan kicked aside a branch that had fallen on the path. "Not always."

"You make it seem so. As if he has nothing to teach you."

They reached the riverbank, where Harlan bent down to look for flat skipping stones. He gave the best one to Katarina, who flung it sidearm across the water.

"Five skips," she said.

"You've been practicing." He threw a stone that promptly sank, then he threw another and another, his anger rising, as if he meant to punish the river, heaving stone after stone, until Katarina grabbed his arm and begged him to stop.

★

On the day before they were to leave for Marquette, Harlan was sprawled on the kitchen floor with his head and shoulders wedged into the cabinet under the sink, replacing a leaky drain trap, when Nana returned from collecting the mail.

"Bills, ads, and credit card offers," she muttered, easing into a chair at the table. "Not a single letter. I may have to give up and learn to use a computer if I'm ever going to hear from anybody."

Straining with a pipe wrench to loosen a rusted slip nut, Harlan had only breath enough to say, "Katarina could teach you."

"Maybe I'm too old to learn."

"Rubbish. You're not old."

There was a rustling of papers, and then her voice, with a nostalgic tone: "Do you remember when you were little, before you started school, the way you kept watch for the postman?"

Reluctantly, he did remember—how he listened for the rattle of the flap on the mail slot, how he dashed to the door, grabbed the mail, and carried it into the kitchen for Nana, who would search through for a letter that never came. To keep those memories at bay, he let out a roar and pushed on the wrench with all his might. The nut suddenly yielded, the wrench swung free, and his fist slammed into the side of the cabinet, making him roar even louder.

"Oh, dear," Nana cried. "Did you hurt yourself?"

"I'm fine." He could feel the seep of blood on his knuckles.

"We can get a plumber."

"We don't *need* a plumber."

The edge in his voice must have cautioned her, for she kept silent while he removed the old crookneck trap and installed a new one. When he had tightened all the couplings, he asked her to open the faucet. She did so without speaking. As the water sluiced through the drain, he inspected each joint and ran his fingers along the pipes to make sure they remained dry. Satisfied, he slid out from under the sink, gathered his tools, and was already thinking ahead to his next job, when the sight of Nana slumped at the table, her face in her hands, made him stop.

"Look," he said, "I didn't mean to bark at you. I'm just mad at myself for hurrying." When she didn't reply, he asked, "What's the matter?"

She uncovered her face, which was a blotchy red, as if she had been slapped. "All these years. Not a word."

He set down the toolbox, moved to stand behind her chair, wiped his grimy palms on his jeans, hesitated, and then laid his hands on her shoulders, rubbing them gently. "Let her go, Nana."

"I can't."

"Torturing yourself won't bring her back."

"She's part of me. She came out of my body."

"And I came out of *her* body, but she threw me away."

"She *didn't* throw you away. She gave you to *us*."

Under his hands, Nana's shoulders felt fragile, like two birds he might crush if he were careless. "True," he admitted. "I'm grateful to you and Papa."

"I'm not asking for gratitude. I'm asking for understanding."

"Understanding what?"

"She was only a girl when she left. A frightened and hurting girl. She'd been abandoned, too. You need to remember that."

Harlan did not want to hear this, but he could not bring himself to desert his grandmother. So he stared at the back of her head, where more scalp showed through between the gray curls than he had ever noticed before.

Nana began tearing the junk mail into pieces. "I need to tell you something."

"I'm listening," he said, uneasy, the ripping sound like a rasp on his nerves.

Nana scooted the torn paper into a heap on the table, as if collecting her words before she began. "One time, maybe a dozen years after she'd run away, a man came into the bar while you were at school. He showed us a photograph of Aurora, asking if we knew who she was. It had been taken five or six years earlier, when she would have been in her early twenties. She was lying on a grave in that big cemetery they have in Washington, the one for soldiers and sailors."

"Tommy's grave?"

"Yes. You could read his name on the marker."

Against his will, Harlan recalled the snapshots of his mother as a child, and wondered how she might have looked as a woman. "Why didn't you show me the picture?"

"We gave it back to the man. I didn't want to see her in such pain."

"You could have told me about it."

"Papa and I were afraid to raise your hopes, since we had no idea where she was or what had become of her."

"Who was the man?"

"A musician of some kind. I don't remember his name. He was writing a song about Aurora."

"A song? About a woman in a picture?"

"That's what he said."

Harlan let go of Nana's shoulders, lifted the scraped hand to his mouth and licked blood from his knuckles.

*

Nana packed enough food to last a week, which was how long Harlan and Katarina expected to be gone. She spoke of the trip as if they were headed to the North Pole and not merely to the Upper Peninsula of Michigan. Papa spoke of the trip as a fool's errand that would only stir up old miseries.

Undaunted, Harlan and Katarina set out while the dawn chorus of birds near the farmhouse was loud enough to be heard above the rumble of the Ford's engine. Katarina thrust her arm out the window to wave back at Nana and Papa, who were sitting on the front steps, leaning against one another and looking rather forlorn, Harlan thought, as he glanced at them in the rearview mirror. It hadn't occurred to him, back at age sixteen, how much his running away would hurt them; he'd thought only of his own footloose freedom. But now, at twenty, he imagined how unnerving it must be for Nana and Papa to see him driving away in a patched-up old truck with a lover beside him on his way to discovering what he could about the man who'd stolen their daughter.

Thinking about that girl in the photographs as their daughter was a way he had of not thinking about Aurora as his mother. He had vowed early on, around the age when he'd asked Nana to burn those photographs, that he would quit hoping for his mother's return, would erase her from his thoughts as she had erased him. It was a vow more easily made than kept, especially since he'd fallen in love with Katarina. The surge of tenderness she had released in him was wearing through his defenses.

The first day they drove only three hours, stopping near Toledo at Cedar Point, the last place in Ohio where they could camp beside Lake Erie with a view of the sunset across open water. The back of the truck was still filled with light that evening when Katarina laid aside her book and began sobbing. She assured Harlan it was only homesickness, a longing for the Baltic Sea, for the watery country of her childhood, for her mother and brothers. Still weeping, she took off the oversized T-shirt she usually slept in and Harlan took off his shorts and she sat astride him as they made love, her face and breasts ruddy from the sun. The gentle swaying of the truck could have been mistaken for the rocking of a tethered boat.

Harlan was inclined to avoid water views for their second night of camping, so as not to summon up memories of Sweden, but that seemed condescending, and besides he wanted to explore a green spot on the map intriguingly called Wilderness State Park, bordering Lake Michigan near the Straits of Mackinac. They reached the park early enough to walk for a couple of hours, over sand dunes that appeared to be held in place by the green stitchery of marram grass, along beaches littered with water-polished stones, through wet swales and stands of conifers. At dusk they retreated to the camper shell where they cooked spaghetti on their little gas stove. Later, from their joined sleeping bags, which felt good against the evening chill, they watched the sun disappear beyond Sturgeon Bay. Harlan wondered if sturgeon, once plentiful throughout the Great Lakes, were still to be found here, or if the name of the bay was yet another reminder of what had been lost.

Katarina didn't bother to explain her melancholy that night, but stripped to her skin and thrust against him with the same intensity she'd shown in the pond at Black Bear Farm. Since that initiation last August, she had eased him into accepting his desire, which had so befuddled him during his teenage years, when girls had seemed at once enticing and vulnerable. His desire had felt dangerous—not to himself but to the girls, who could be hurt, even ruined, by an act that would give fleeting pleasure to a boy.

Now as Katarina curled against him and her breathing steadied, he recalled with chagrin that he had been unable to decide, on first meeting her a year earlier, whether or not she was pretty. Of course at the time he hadn't been looking for a mate but only for someone who could take over caring for the addled Mrs. Winfield. Yet even if he had been looking for a mate, he wouldn't have known what to make of Katarina, who gazed at him so directly, with enigmatic gray eyes, out of a face as clear as water from the spring. She wore no makeup, unlike the girls he'd known in high school, who used to wear enough paint for a Halloween contest;

and unlike those girls, who had seemed almost strangled by self-awareness, Katarina gave no sign of caring what he thought of her, but merely sized him up, as a cat might do.

Studying her sleeping face in the lantern light, he considered that he still might not call her pretty, for that word suggested to him qualities superficial and transient. Even the word *beauty* had been so cheapened by advertisers and hairdressers and cosmetics manufacturers as to seem inadequate. What drew him to Katarina felt deeper and more durable than anything that could be painted on, a power akin to gravity—or to wildness, it suddenly occurred to him. The arch of her hip might have been the curve of a sand dune, her breathing might have been the lap of waves.

Early the next morning they crossed the dizzying span of Mackinac Bridge, with Lake Huron on the right and Lake Michigan on the left. Katarina gazed serenely down at the freighters and pleasure boats gliding far below while Harlan kept his eyes focused on the pavement directly ahead. Driving from the bridge to Marquette should have taken only four or five hours, even in the sluggish old Ford, but Harlan managed to delay their arrival until nightfall by leading them through a series of green patches on the map. He had never traveled anywhere so clearly ruled by conifers. There were plenty of maples, as in Vermont, along with aspen and birch, but pines and tamaracks overshadowed the hardwoods. The terrain was as flat as the glacial plain in Ohio, and marvelously wet. In Seney National Wildlife Refuge they lingered beside a lake to watch a pair of trumpeter swans elegantly feeding, and at Pictured Rocks National Lakeshore they hiked up trails to soak in the mist of waterfalls. Harlan would have detoured for a look at the Grand Island National Recreation Area, half a mile offshore, but the ferry hadn't begun service for the year.

They finally rolled to a stop in the parking lot of a party store featuring deer jerky and fudge just east of Marquette, where they could scramble down to a stony beach for a look at Lake Superior before sleep. Arms looped around one another's waists, they stood without speaking for several minutes, watching the waves. The lights of ships pricked the darkness here and there all the way to the horizon. Then Katarina said, "Remember the morning when we saw the bears eating blueberries, and I asked you why these are called *great* lakes, and you promised to show me one if I would travel with you?"

"Surely," Harlan said.

"Well, now you have shown me four great lakes in three days."

"Man of my word," he said, or tried to say, as his throat seized up.

She pulled him closer. "You worry about tomorrow."

"I guess so. I keep wondering, what if Mrs. Two Bears takes one look at me and decides I'm no kin of hers and tells me to shove off?"

"Then we will learn about your father some other way."

*

At 9:00 the next morning, a Saturday, the hour and day agreed upon, Harlan and Katarina arrived at the address Teresa Two Bears had provided, a modest, well-kept frame house painted violet in a neighborhood of mostly grander homes near the harbor and just up the street from the Coast Guard Station. A girl of about eight or nine answered the door, wearing pajamas decorated with spaceships. Without saying a word in response to Harlan's greeting, she led them to a room at the back of the house where two other little girls, maybe three and six years old, also in pajamas, were flopped down on pillows watching cartoons. When Harlan and Katarina appeared in the doorway, the TV abruptly went dark, and the girls put up a fuss.

From an unlit corner came a voice, saying, "Go, let the grown-ups talk. Get dressed and play outside. The sun is shining."

As the three girls trooped out, they only glanced at Harlan but they stared at Katarina, and the youngest of them said, "You have princess hair. Like honey."

"Shush, now," said the lilting voice, which Harlan recognized from the telephone.

A lamp snapped on in the corner, revealing a very large woman seated on a recliner, with her legs propped on a hassock and covered to her waist in a brightly-colored blanket. "Come close. My eyes are bad."

"Mrs. Two Bears?" Harlan stepped forward, heart drumming. The woman was old, her face a web of creases, her skin tobacco brown. Her snowy hair was parted in the middle and plaited into two long braids that draped across her chest. She studied him with eyes clouded by cataracts.

Without any further greeting, she asked, "Where were you born?"

"Cleveland."

"What year?"

"1987."

"In the winter?"

"Yes, ma'am. In December, right after Christmas."

"Come closer," she said. "Bend down here where I can touch you."

He leaned close enough to smell liniment and root beer. With a swollen hand she reached up and stroked his hair, rolling strands of it between her fingers, which were as thick as a baby's wrist. Then she traced the shape of his ear, his forehead, his cheek and nose and chin, before letting the arm fall as if exhausted from a great effort.

"So it is true," she declared solemnly. "You are Tommy's son."

Harlan flushed with relief. "Do I look so much like him?"

"You have his face, his hair, the lobe of his ear. On the phone I heard him in your voice. But I had to be sure."

"So you'll tell me about him?"

"Sit," she said, patting the arm of the couch next to her chair. "I will tell you."

Harlan did as she directed. "How do you know him?"

Ignoring his question, the old woman turned her clouded eyes toward Katarina, who had hesitated before sitting down. "You are his sweetheart?"

Katarina laughed. "He tells me so. May I stay? To hear about Tommy?"

"Sit, daughter, sit." Again Mrs. Two Bears patted the couch.

Katarina settled beside Harlan, her knees pressed together and hands folded in her lap like a schoolgirl on her best behavior.

The wrinkled face broke into a smile. "Tell me your name."

"Katarina Swanson."

The smile widened, and laughter bubbled up. "You come from Sweden?"

"My accent is so obvious?"

"You sound like a Swedish logger I knew a long time ago. He was as blond as the midday sun, also tall, and big around as a barrel, which is where Tommy got his size."

A grin stole across Katarina's face. "Ah," she said, "and Tommy got everything else from you?"

The old woman nodded gaily, evidently pleased that Harlan's sweetheart had been first to make the connection.

Harlan looked afresh at the old woman. All he could think to say was, "You're Tommy's mother?"

"Yes." Even as Teresa smiled, tears welled from her eyes and glistened in the creases down her cheeks. She reached over and squeezed the nape of his neck. "And you are my grandson."

★

Teresa Two Bears insisted that Harlan and Katarina call her Nekoma, an Ojibwa word for grandmother. She wouldn't hear of their leaving Marquette before all the relations had arrived to meet them, nor would she let them sleep in the truck. They must move into this house, which belonged to her daughter and son-in-law, and as honored guests they must use the bedroom of her granddaughters, Harlan's cousins, who would share a pallet in an alcove just off the kitchen.

Harlan soon realized that his newly-discovered grandmother was not a woman to negotiate with but rather one to obey. So he and Katarina called her Nekoma, lugged in their few things from the pickup, and settled in for a siege of kinfolk. The three little girls warmed to them quickly, gawking at Katarina and brushing her hair and squirming for a spot in her lap when she read them books, climbing all over Harlan when he lumbered about on his hands and knees pretending to be a horse or a bear.

The son-in-law, Harlan's Uncle Cedar, was the first to come home from work that evening, a wiry man in grease-spotted mechanic's overalls. The girls ignored the grease and flung themselves at him, crying "Daddy! Daddy!" Before he even sat down, Uncle Cedar was kidding Harlan about that rattletrap Ford out front and offering to give it a thorough going-over at the garage the next day. A few minutes later the girls repeated their exuberant welcome for their mother, Harlan's Aunt Rozzie, when she came home from the Legal Aid office where she worked as a lawyer. She was Tommy's only sibling, maybe thirty-five, broad like Teresa, with black hair and a jovial round face. When she spied Harlan she cracked up with laughter, crowing, "You are the spitting image of Tommy."

Photographs of Tommy bore out the resemblance. Harlan studied the pictures with Teresa, who could no longer see them clearly but could remember each image from where it lay in the

album or where it hung on the wall, and she explained the occasion for each one, from Tommy's birth to his departure for
his final Navy cruise. Harlan could see himself unfolding in the
pictures of his father. Never so muscular as Tommy, he was just
as tall, and by his teenage years a couple of inches taller, with
the same stubborn black hair, deep-set eyes, dimpled chin, even
the same lopsided grin before the camera. The resemblance was
clearest in the last pictures, the ones showing Tommy in his Navy
dress uniform, when he would have been nineteen, and his face
revealed a mixture of swagger and wariness that Harlan could
feel in his own gut.

★

Day by day other relatives arrived—from lower Michigan,
from Wisconsin, from Ontario and Quebec, a few of them named
Two Bears, some carrying the Swedish logger's name of Moss-
berg, some with French or Finnish surnames—the whole tribe
a wild blend of Indian and European genes. When introducing
themselves to Harlan and Katarina, those on the Indian side identified their heritage variously as Chippewa, Ojibwa, Oji-Cree, or
Potawatomi, but all of them, according to one of Harlan's great
uncles, belonged to the Anishinabe, whose name he translated as
"the good humans."

"That makes you about one-quarter good," the great uncle
told Harlan amiably. "I can't vouch for the rest of you."

From each of the relatives old enough to have known Tommy,
Harlan gained impressions of his father: the boy who struggled
in school because his eyes read things backwards, who gathered
birchbark and willow withes for Teresa's baskets, who gave her
insulin shots; the teenager who looked after his little sister and
fixed supper while Teresa worked the graveyard shift at the mill,
who killed and butchered a deer for the freezer every winter, who

attracted girls the way a lit candle draws moths; the wrestler who reached the state finals as a sophomore in high school, and who seemed bound to win the championship the following year, but who dropped out of school to work on the lakes when Teresa's diabetes got so bad the mill laid her off and nobody else would hire her; the roughneck who carried more than his load aboard ship and caroused more than his share on land.

The kinfolk proceeded gingerly when they brought up the carousing that led to Harlan's birth. They recalled that Tommy spoke of the Cleveland girl, whose name he never disclosed, with a wistfulness he hadn't shown toward any of his other flames. When they asked Tommy how old she was, this girl he'd gotten pregnant, he replied, "Too young." The elders agreed that he had signed up for the Navy in order to place himself at a safe remove from shotguns and cops. Where they disagreed was about whether eventually he might have returned to claim his Cleveland girl and dandle his baby.

Teresa came down on the side of those who believed that Tommy, had he lived, would have taken responsibility for his child. Her opinion carried the most weight with Harlan. For the first time he let himself think of Tommy Two Bears not as a horny sailor out for a fling but as a father who might have sung to him, told him stories, taught him how to hunt and fish, how to track animals. And if Tommy had lived, if he had come back to the Iron Ore Tavern, if he had proposed marriage, if Aurora had said yes, if Nana and Papa had given their blessing—then Harlan would have had a mother, as well. Even as he traced the possibilities, he tried to stifle thoughts of this lost history.

*

In addition to the parade of kinfolk, numerous friends stopped by to meet this grandson of Teresa Two Bears. Although she couldn't stir from the house much anymore, it was clear to Harlan that many people carried the old woman in their hearts. The visitors included neighbors, a bingo partner, men and women from the mill where she used to work, down-and-out souls from the community kitchen where she used to volunteer, sailors from the Coast Guard station, a librarian with a supply of books-on-CDs, a mailman, and a butcher, as well as three clergymen each of whom seemed to feel that Teresa secretly favored his faith. A few of the older visitors eyed Harlan in a way that made him think they were comparing him with Tommy.

After supper one evening, when Harlan was alone with Teresa, her doctor showed up, an imposing woman named Naomi Rosenthal, who carried a woven shoulder bag rather than the orthodox black leather satchel.

"Should I leave, Nekoma?" Harlan asked.

"Stay, grandson. It is only my faithful Naomi, seeing if I am still alive."

While he watched, the doctor checked Teresa's blood pressure, listened to her lungs and heart, and lightly touched the swollen feet and fingers, asking as she did so, "Can you feel this? How about this? And this?" What struck Harlan as imposing was not Dr. Rosenthal's appearance—that of a slight, attractive, middle-aged woman—but her manner. She laid her hands on Teresa as if caressing rather than examining her, as if nothing else was on her mind, and she spoke with clear affection. Nor did she seem in any hurry to leave, although this house call must have followed a long day at the office.

When the doctor was packing up her instruments, she said, "Well, my dear, you are one tough old nanny goat."

The seams on Teresa's face deepened as she laughed. "Not time for the pine box just yet?"

"Not for a long while, I hope."

"So, Naomi, what do you think of Tommy's son?"

The doctor studied Harlan, who had sat quietly, not wanting to disturb these two. There was a hint of discomfort in her eyes. "We're all so amazed you turned up," she said to him.

"You knew my father?"

"He was a patient of mine."

"You remember him?"

"Vividly." Again there was the uneasiness in her gaze, quite unlike the calm demeanor that showed in her dealings with Teresa. "You're a bit taller, and your skin is a shade or two lighter. Otherwise, you're an uncanny match."

"So folks tell me."

"Your mother must be tall and fair-skinned."

"I guess."

"You guess?"

"I can't say for sure. Last time I laid eyes on her I was four months old."

The doctor's brow furrowed and she seemed about to ask a question, but instead she collected her bag, bent down to kiss Teresa on the forehead, and excused herself, as if, after the leisurely visit, she had suddenly recalled another appointment.

*

In exchange for what the relatives told him about Tommy, Harlan told them what he knew about his mother, beginning with her name.

"Aurora," Teresa repeated musingly, during another rare interlude when she and Harlan were alone in the house, the various kinfolk having departed, Katarina and the granddaughters having gone outside to play hopscotch on the sidewalk. "That is what some people call the northern lights. They say it is magnetism. We say the spirits are dancing. It is a powerful name."

Teresa's great bulk was stretched out on the recliner and Harlan was perched on the hassock rubbing her feet. Swollen, with stubby toes and yellowed nails, her feet had poor circulation and damaged nerves because of the diabetes, and so he pressed carefully, afraid of hurting her. But as they talked, she occasionally murmured "Harder," and he increased the pressure.

"You have never looked for your mother?" she asked him.

"No, ma'am."

"Why not?"

The question nettled him. "Because I don't want to see her any more than she wants to see me."

Teresa sank into one of her prolonged silences. Harlan kept massaging her feet, remembering how Katarina had rubbed the feet of Mrs. Winfield each night after soaking them in a pan of water heated on the woodstove. The memory brought a pang of guilt, for he realized that several weeks had gone by since he'd called the nursing home to check on the old woman. It was so hard to keep in mind even all of those you loved, let alone the world of suffering strangers.

Teresa broke the silence by saying, "No mother can forget her child."

"Well, mine did."

"You are so sure?"

"Why else didn't she come back?"

"You tell me she was sixteen when she ran away. Were you all grown up at sixteen?"

Harlan thought about his own running away, and how oblivious he had been to Nana and Papa's distress. But he'd written letters home, hadn't he? And hadn't he returned? "Yes, Nekoma," he admitted, "I've done fool things. But I've tried making up for them."

"Maybe your mother doesn't know how to make up for what she did." Teresa shifted in the recliner with a groan, reaching for the bag of root beer candies on the table next to her chair. "Anyway, it is something to think about."

Harlan said nothing. As if sensing his disquiet, she offered him one of the candies, but he declined. Only when she muttered, "Harder," did he realize that his hands had grown still, and so, obeying, he tightened his fists around her numb feet.

★

That night, after saying goodbye to Teresa and the relatives who were still in Marquette, and after promising to keep in touch and return soon for another visit, Harlan and Katarina drove an hour east to Sand Point, where they parked the camper in the shelter of red pines and sat on the tailgate looking out over Lake Superior. If the ancient Ford held up, they would make the long haul back to the farm the next day. For tonight, after more than a week in the bustle of Teresa's household, they relished the chance to be alone together, beside big water.

As they talked, Katarina kept lifting one foot and then the other to admire the beaded moccasins Teresa had given her, among the last ones the old woman had made before her eyesight failed. Along with the moccasins, she had given Katarina a gift of language, explaining that the Ojibwa word for beads meant "berries of the Great Spirit."

Teresa had also given Harlan one of her last willow baskets. "For your other grandmother," she instructed, "to thank her for sharing you with me." The gift would come in handy. When he had called Nana to describe his newly-discovered family and to explain the delay in returning to Ohio, she had sounded anxious, as if worried he might be lured away to join this northern tribe.

Katarina spoke mainly of the granddaughters, who had bawled when she said goodbye, and of the many relatives who had trooped through the house; Harlan spoke mainly of Teresa and Tommy. Meanwhile, the sun burnished the water with rose, then ruby, then indigo, before vanishing below the horizon. As the dark came on, Katarina said, "Maybe we'll see the northern lights."

"Wrong time of year," Harlan said.

"Even in May we see them sometimes in Sweden."

He clamped his hands between his knees, to keep from touching Katarina, so as not to sway her answer to the question he needed to ask. "Would you stay on with me another year, until the farm's in shape and I get started at Kent State and Nana and Papa settle in to country life?"

Katarina sighed. "I promised my mother, Harlan."

"But she's not even in Sweden. She's off nursing people in a warzone."

"I have enrolled at the university."

"Couldn't you delay your studies for a year? Then you can go learn about translating and I'll learn about biology over here, and after we graduate we can save the world together. You rescue people and I'll rescue plants and animals."

Katarina tugged his hands from between his knees and placed them in her lap, with her own small hands on top of them. "You always think of me staying. Why do you never think of going to Sweden?"

"For starters, I don't know a word of Swedish."

"I will teach you."

Harlan shifted his weight, making the tailgate creak, and he thought of Teresa in her recliner. "Even if I learned enough to get by, how could I go to college over there?"

"Many Americans study in our country."

"Ones with deeper pockets than I've got. Besides, I can't leave my grandparents in the lurch. You can see the farm is way more than they can handle. And when Papa starts drinking again, how will Nana manage, out there in the boonies?"

"Yes," she replied softly, although he could not tell what she was agreeing to.

"Maybe if Papa stays dry and I get the place in decent shape, I can save my pennies and fly to Sweden when classes let out. You can introduce me to your folks, show me your frozen sea and pine forests and reindeer."

She ran a finger over his knuckles. "I would like that."

The last of the sunlight had drained from the lake, and the first of the stars began to appear. Pulling away from Katarina, Harlan drew the lantern from its cupboard and readied a match. But he paused before lighting the mantles, because the darkness made it easier for him to reveal his other reason for staying: "I figure if I'm ever going to track down my mother, it's likely to be in America."

Katarina sucked in a little breath, as she always did when surprised or agitated. "You're going to look for her?"

"I've been thinking about it."

"At last you wish to meet her?"

"No," he insisted. "I just want to find her, for Nana's sake."

"What if you discover she has died?"

"Then Nana can quit grieving for her."

"And if she is alive?"

"I'll tell Nana and Papa where she is and they can do whatever they want—read her the riot act, throw her a party.

"And you?"

"I don't want anything to do with her."

He lit the lantern, and in the sudden glow he found Katarina giving him one of her cool appraising looks. There were times when the gray of her eyes appeared solid, like granite, and times, such as now, when it appeared like fog that might drift away. Unable to bear the thought of her absence, Harlan turned his gaze toward the lake, which had become an immense obsidian plain.

§ § §

Chapter Ten • February–July 2003

MARTIN

ABOVE THE MARQUEE ON THE CITY'S PERFORMING ARTS CENTER, a border of glowing bulbs framed a sign that spelled INDIANA in white against a scarlet background. Noticing the sign, a remnant from the days when the building served as a vaudeville hall and cinema, Martin Zakar felt a touch of pride for having helped to salvage the old theater. On this frigid evening in February, he was drawn here by the show announced on the marquee: JACK HAYMAKER'S PEACE TOUR. The show had also drawn a throng of demonstrators, who nearly blocked the entrance, waving American flags and denouncing those who streamed in to hear the concert.

As Martin shouldered past the flag-wavers, he was astounded by their zeal, the way they rooted for war, their breath pluming in the chill air. When a demonstrator grabbed his sleeve, Martin jerked his arm free and swung around, suddenly furious, only to find an elderly man staring at him with eyes widened by fear. Wearing a too-tight Army uniform that smelled of mothballs, the man extended a palsied hand, saying, "You dropped your ticket."

With muttered thanks, Martin accepted the ticket, which must have fallen when he was pulling out his wallet. He paused in the lobby to buy Haymaker's new album, *River Blessing*, but he was too distracted even to glance at the CD. The buildup to war had abraded his nerves. When he took his seat in the crowded hall, he still felt a flush of anger. He could easily have lashed out at the old man, a veteran who might have fought the Nazis. Ashamed, Martin closed his eyes and counted his breaths, a trick his mother had taught him in childhood to keep him still during Quaker meeting.

When he opened his eyes a few minutes later, feeling calmer, he gazed around the audience and saw many familiar faces, one of the rewards for having spent most of his thirty-one years here in Bloomington. He waved at friends who were sitting at a distance and called out greetings to those nearby, including a husband and wife whom he had known since they were all toddlers together in a playgroup of faculty brats. Back when the wife was a child, he'd had a crush on her, as he'd had a crush on two other girls who now sat as grown women with their husbands in neighboring rows. Why hadn't he married one of these women, whose faces glowed with pleasure, instead of the woman he did marry, a New Yorker who couldn't imagine settling in a small city tucked away in the hills of southern Indiana?

The regretful drift of Martin's thoughts was cut short by the dimming of the houselights. Silence fell over the crowd, then gave way to applause as Jack Haymaker ambled onstage with his guitar. He was a big man, as tall as Martin and huskier, swelling his white shirt and brown leather vest.

"Hello, Bloomington!" Haymaker roared. "Haven't seen you folks in a while. I've been sticking close to home these past few years, helping my wife raise our daughters. But the warmongers in Washington have forced me back on the road. So here I am to raise a ruckus for peace."

The crowd cheered as he launched into his first song. Although Martin was a Haymaker fan, he had come tonight less for the music than for the crowd, the sense of solidarity with others who were appalled by the push for an invasion of Iraq.

With the hint of a twang, Haymaker sang a mix of his old standbys, about farmers and fishermen and hard luck families, along with songs from the new album, including the title piece about the drowning of his parents. He introduced that song by telling how his parents had been driving to his house in the Cascade Mountains when a rockslide shoved their car into a river swollen with glacial meltwater.

"After they drowned I just locked up," Haymaker said. "I couldn't find a lyric or a tune, and I stayed that way for two years. Then a friend of mine, a Lummi elder, came to help me bless the river. We stood on the bank where my parents went over, we burnt sage and cedar, and we cast our words on the water. Here's what the river gave back."

Martin didn't realize his eyes had filled with tears until the song ended and the lights came up for intermission and he looked around to see others brushing palms or sleeves across their cheeks. To his right, a nattily dressed couple who appeared to be the age of his parents, sixty or so, were openly weeping, the husband patting the wife's hand. On his left, two college students, also holding hands, sat with eyes squeezed shut and the corners of their lips drawn down.

Except for himself, it seemed everyone in the audience was paired with a lover. This was an illusion, Martin realized, yet he stayed in his seat instead of talking with friends during intermission; he didn't want to explain, in answer to questions they would surely ask, that his wife wouldn't be coming back from Los Angeles, and he wouldn't be joining her there, because she had filed for divorce. "No hard feelings," Simone had told him over the phone, "but I have to follow my star, and to do that I need a clean break."

Seeking a distraction from thoughts of Simone, he opened the *River Blessing* album and unfolded the liner notes. Along with lyrics, there were photographs showing the mountains and rivers of Haymaker's home region, his wife at her pottery wheel, his daughters riding horses, and the singer himself working on his farm. One photo seemed to break the pattern, for it showed a woman lying on a grave, her face in her hands and head bowed before a white stone marker, in a cemetery filled with hundreds of identical markers. The unsettling image accompanied lyrics for "Aurora's Child."

This proved to be the final song of the concert. Haymaker introduced it with a call to resist the looming war in Iraq. "We've got to stand up on our hind legs and say, 'No blood for oil!'" he bellowed, and the audience echoed his words: "No blood for oil! No blood for oil!" Martin was swept up in the chanting, his heart pounding. When Haymaker began strumming his guitar, the crowd settled down. Into the stillness he said, "Here's a song about a woman who lost her lover to the war machine. This one goes out to Aurora Eliza Blake, wherever she may be."

The name stirred a memory in Martin, but he couldn't trace it while following the song, which took the form of a duet between Aurora and her lover, who left her pregnant and joined the Navy and died at sea. The story seemed as old as the sea—a woman seduced and abandoned, and her child made fatherless by war. As he listened, Martin felt something break loose inside, like the cracking of river ice in spring.

Amid the cheers following the song, Martin eased his way out, hugging friends, reluctant to speak. In the hubbub, no one asked him about Simone. Outside, where pro-war demonstrators still waved flags and chanted, he paused under the lit-up marquee to study the picture of the woman at the grave. Her face was hidden, but her red hair done up in a bun and her long legs and slender figure could have belonged to a woman he'd known from the Ithaca Friends Meeting during his years at Cornell, a woman whose name, he now felt certain, was Aurora Blake.

She was tall, he remembered, and fair, and rather quiet, even by comparison with the taciturn Quakers. She had worked somewhere downtown as a waitress. Was it at the Seneca Hotel? He couldn't recall for sure, nor could he recall whether she had a child. It wasn't surprising that his impressions were hazy, for in those years he'd been so infatuated with Simone that he scarcely looked at other women. But now, walking home through the chill air, stirred by the concert, Martin couldn't help wondering if that shy woman in Ithaca really was the Aurora of Haymaker's song.

*

When Martin told his parents about the concert over supper at their house the following Sunday, his father, as usual, made no comment, but his mother scolded him for going alone: "You should have taken one of your women friends."

"My women friends are already attached," Martin replied.

"Well, then, find one who's unattached."

"Mother, I'm still married."

"Only because the lawyers haven't finished up the divorce papers. Do you imagine Simone is behaving like a nun while she waits for her big break in LA?"

"Let's not talk about Simone."

Martin had offered to take his parents to hear Jack Haymaker, since they both staunchly opposed the invasion of Iraq. His mother, a birthright Quaker from England, was against all wars. His father, born in an Assyrian village in Iran, felt certain the U.S. would stir up ancient feuds if we meddled further in the Middle East. But they had declined Martin's invitation, for his mother was nursing a cold, and his father, recovering from a stroke, avoided social gatherings because of his slurred speech.

*

During the weeks following the Haymaker concert, Martin was overseeing the restoration of a granary in New Harmony, a round barn in Paoli, a log cabin in Brown County, and a limestone mill in Bloomington. While driving from one jobsite to another, he listened so often to the *River Blessing* CD that he memorized the lyrics. In a way he couldn't explain, the songs expressed the grief he felt over the ending of his marriage and the beginning of war in Iraq.

On March 18th, less than a month after the concert, the U.S. began raining bombs and missiles on Baghdad and other Iraqi cities—an all-out assault designed, in the words of Pentagon spokesmen, to evoke "Shock and Awe" in our enemies. The news called to mind "Aurora's Child." Without consulting the album photo, Martin could imagine the slender woman stretched out on her lover's grave, barefoot, bereft, a lone mourner amid a host of headstones. Her grief, and the grief engendered by those hundreds of graves, and the misery mounting hour by hour in Iraq beneath American bombs, all this made the end of his childless marriage seem like a paltry loss.

Still, he ached while signing the divorce papers. Through six years of marriage, the reason Simone had given him for not wanting children was the fear they would keep her from following her star. The star she was following, the one that drew her from what she called the backwater of Bloomington to the mecca of Los Angeles, was the dream of performing in films. After the divorce was settled and the last of her belongings were shipped to California, Simone sent him a note of thanks in which she listed her recent auditions, mostly for TV commercials. She advised him to find a new woman, as she had found a new man. Above her signature she scrawled, "As always." He wrote back to wish her well, promising to keep an eye out for her name on the silver screen.

*

Although Martin's mother did not much care for folk music, she asked to borrow the *River Blessing* album, since he talked about it so much. On returning it, she said, "You can hear the agony of war in all these songs, especially 'Aurora's Child.'"

"I can't get that one out of my head," Martin replied.

And the picture that goes with that song—the girl at the grave?"

"What about her?"

"Doesn't she look like Yaffa?"

"Really? It hadn't occurred to me." Martin examined the photograph anew, and he could see that the lithe, russet-haired figure at the grave might have been an older version of his sister, who had died during an epileptic seizure the summer after her first year of high school. How long ago? Almost twenty years. Yet she rose in his mind as vividly as if she had just left the room. Yaffa, deserving of her name, which meant "lovely" in Assyrian.

*

Searching the Ithaca directory on-line, Martin discovered several listings for *Blake* but none with the given name *Aurora*. When he called the Seneca Hotel, the manager confirmed that an Aurora Blake had worked there in the café some while ago, but she had since moved on, and the manager couldn't say where. When Martin phoned the Ithaca Friends Meeting and introduced himself, the clerk recalled him from years before and also recalled Ms. Blake, but said that she hadn't attended meeting for worship in recent months.

"It's a pity," the clerk added. "She seemed like a genuine seeker."

Martin decided it was pointless to keep wondering if the woman he had known so casually was the grieving woman memorialized in Haymaker's song. Perhaps it was only her resemblance to

Yaffa in the photograph that had caught his eye to begin with. So he tried putting her out of his mind, as he tried forgetting about the war.

Then one evening, as he was sorting through the mail, he came upon an envelope from Cornell's College of Architecture, Art, and Planning. Inside was a letter from the dean inviting him to speak in July at a conference on preservation architecture. Even in this busy season, with many jobs to supervise, how could he turn down the chance of seeing his former teachers and meeting leaders in the field? And if he allowed himself an extra day to visit old haunts in Ithaca, what would be the harm if he also inquired about Aurora Blake?

*

Leaving home the day before his lecture, he arrived at the Indianapolis airport two hours early, for he had grown accustomed, since the attacks of September 11th, to being tagged as a "traveler of special interest." When he and Simone used to fly together, she, with her ivory skin and blond hair, waltzed through security, while Martin would be taken aside for a pat-down, his luggage would be searched, and occasionally he would be led to a screened-off area for questioning. Simone called it racial profiling, and Martin supposed it was. Had he acquired his mother's English complexion as well as her height, he, too, might have waltzed through security. But instead he had acquired from his father not only an Assyrian surname that sounded Arabic, but also an olive complexion, a prominent nose, and curly black hair and beard. The fusion of Anglo and Middle Eastern features clearly aroused suspicion in those who were charged with protecting America from terrorists.

Sure enough, he was frisked at security in Indianapolis, and his carry-on bag was searched at the gate in Cleveland. But he managed to catch his flights, arrived in Ithaca shortly after noon, and took a cab downtown to the Seneca Hotel. He felt a pang as he entered the lobby, for he had last set foot here on the night of his wedding. Lacking any religious affiliation of her own, Simone had agreed to a plain marriage ceremony at the Friends Meeting House, but she had insisted on holding a lavish reception at the hotel, an extravagance meant to impress her relatives as well as the actors with whom she'd performed at Cornell.

As he checked in, Martin asked the woman at the desk whether she happened to remember a former employee named Aurora Blake.

"Oh, sure," the woman replied. "She used to work in the café. I can't say I know her. She kept to herself pretty much. A real sweet girl, polite as could be, and funny in her quiet way. She was so thin I always wanted to feed her."

"Do you know if she's still in Ithaca?"

"I saw her just the other day. Now where was that?" The woman tapped a lacquered fingernail on the desk. "Ah, yes. At the co-op on Buffalo Street. She was stocking shelves. The place isn't far from here. I could show you on a map."

"I know where it is," he said. "A million thanks."

After stowing his suitcase and calling to let the dean know he had arrived, Martin walked to the Greenstar Cooperative Market, where a nose-ringed cashier consulted a schedule and told him that Aurora was due in at five that afternoon.

With most of the afternoon to fill, Martin walked the mile or so north to the Cornell campus, his calves burning as he climbed the hills, which were even steeper than he'd recalled. He looked into Sibley Hall, where he had studied architecture and where he would be speaking the next day, and into Kiplinger Theatre, where he had first laid eyes on Simone, then a sophomore, who was playing the sultry Maggie in *Cat on a Hot Tin Roof*. He crossed

Fall Creek on the suspension bridge, pausing to stare into the gorge, as he had often done with Simone during their courtship, and then he walked downstream to Ithaca Falls, where he had knelt on the stony bank and proposed to her. As he retraced his path to the hotel, memories of Simone accompanied him every step of the way.

*

Showered, in fresh clothes, unaccountably nervous, Martin returned to the market a few minutes after five. He picked up a shopping basket and wandered the aisles, glancing at every woman he encountered. Twice he thought he recognized a face or a figure, but he couldn't be sure. Then in the bulk foods section he came upon a tall, slim woman who was filling a bin with almonds. She wore the store's green apron over a beige pantsuit, as if she had come here after a day at the office. Her hair, tied back in a ponytail, was the lovely shade of red he remembered, and her pale features, finely carved, were strikingly familiar.

All the lines he had imagined using if he met Aurora seemed nonsensical now, so he cleared his throat and asked her where he might find the trail mix.

"Just to the right there," she said, looking up from her work. He was surprised to see a flicker of recognition in her face. "Oh, hello," she added, smiling. "You used to go to Friends Meeting. It's Martin, isn't it?"

"Why, yes," he answered. "Martin Zakar. I moved away a few years ago."

"You probably don't—"

"I certainly do," he said, interrupting her. "You're Aurora Blake."

Her smile widened and she blushed. "How on earth do you remember my name?"

"How do you remember mine?"

She wiped her hands on the apron. "You sometimes spoke during worship, which I never worked up the nerve to do. Then afterwards, over coffee, I would ask you about what you'd said. Very un-Quakerly of me, but I was so often moved by your words."

"I can't imagine I said anything profound."

"It wasn't *you* speaking, of course. It was the Christ within. So I was complimenting God." There was a wry twist in her voice that might have been irony or apology.

"Yes, well," he said awkwardly. "I know the theory, but I'm not sure I believe it."

"I'm not sure, either. Anyhow, what attracts me to Quakers isn't their theology. It's their kindness."

"For me, it's their opposition to war."

"That, too." Aurora frowned as she replaced the bin of almonds. "How do you feel about what's happening in Iraq?"

"It makes me sick. I wish the politicians who launched the war had to dodge a few bombs."

"Now you're the one who's not being Quakerly."

Certain of the irony this time, Martin said, "I wouldn't want them killed, mind you, only scared. To give them a taste of what they're dishing out."

"Keep talking like that and you'll wind up on the watch list from Homeland Security."

"I already am."

"Seriously?"

"Seriously. It's because I look Middle Eastern."

He could feel her gaze running over his face, a sensation almost as tangible as the brush of a hand. "I suppose you do," she said. "So, what prompts you to brave the airports and return to Ithaca?"

"I'm giving a lecture at Cornell tomorrow."

"Ah, the graduate makes good. Architecture, right? Do you restore old buildings, the way you planned?"

"I do," he said, surprised by how much she recalled of their conversations from years earlier.

As she bent to open a carton of dried apricots, a strand of hair swung loose from the ponytail and curled against her cheek. Suddenly her resemblance to Yaffa was unmistakable. "Did your wife come along for the trip?" she asked.

Again he was startled. "When did you meet Simone? She never attended worship."

"I didn't really meet her. I saw her once, when I served hors d'oeuvres at your wedding reception. That was before I graduated from waitressing to stocking shelves." She laughed. "Actually, I'm a court reporter. I work here four hours a week to get my co-op discount. And is your wife still an actress?"

"She was," Martin began, then corrected himself: "I mean, she's still an actress, but she's no longer my wife. She moved to Los Angeles to pursue a career in film."

"Me and my big mouth."

"No, no. It's old history for me."

"You're lucky if history lets go of you that easily." Aurora gazed at him with no hint of the shyness he recalled from years before. "Well," she added brusquely, "it's lovely to see you, but I'd better get back to work."

"Of course," he said, lifting his empty basket, "and I'll get that trail mix."

Martin didn't want trail mix, but he could think of no other excuse to linger, and so he found the appropriate bin and scooped some into a bag. Meanwhile, he lost track of Aurora, and he berated himself for letting her go without asking about the song. He strode up one aisle and down the next, searching, until he came upon her in the coffee section, where she was cleaning up spills around the grinding machines.

"Hello again," he said.

She nodded at his basket. "I see you got your munchies."

"I like to nibble when I read," he said, and then he added, as if the idea had just occurred to him: "Speaking of nibbling, perhaps you'd join me for supper after you get off work. You could bring me up to date on Ithaca."

Again the color rose in her face. "I don't know—"

"If you need to be with your family—"

"No," she answered, shaking her head. "There's no family."

"Then how about sharing a meal? You'd be doing me a kindness."

She stroked a finger across her chin, leaving a dusting of coffee. "If I tell you about Ithaca, will you tell me about your place?"

*

Over supper at the Moosewood Restaurant, where they sat under a canopy on the patio breathing muggy air, Martin did tell Aurora about Bloomington, about growing up there and going away to study and practice architecture, and then returning after his father's stroke, considering it a temporary move, only to discover that he wished to stay in the hill country of southern Indiana, much to his wife's—his former wife's—dismay. Aurora told him in turn about growing up in Cleveland, living upstairs from her parents' tavern, waiting tables after school and on weekends, putting up with drunks and rowdies until, at sixteen, she bought a bus ticket to the farthest destination she could afford, which turned out to be Ithaca, where she arrived penniless and stayed in a church basement until she landed a job in a café that didn't serve alcohol.

The Moosewood had been Simone's favorite place to eat during their days at Cornell, because she imagined the vegetarian menu would keep her from gaining weight. Martin had assured

her that he liked her curves, but she insisted that film would require a leaner look. "I'll need to be svelte," was the way she put
it. They had sat on this patio often, so it was disorienting for him
to gaze across the table and see this other woman gazing back.
Loosed from the ponytail, Aurora's hair now fell in a cascade over
her shoulders. Her green eyes seemed to measure him.

"Do your parents still own the tavern?" he asked.

"I suppose so." Aurora glanced away, toward the cars passing nearby along Cayuga Street. "That is, I don't really know. I
haven't been in touch since I left."

He took that in, thinking of his own parents, whom he saw
once or twice a week. Of course they sometimes annoyed him,
especially his father, the aloof mathematician with Old World
prejudices, but Martin couldn't imagine cutting himself off from
them. Did this severing from her parents account for the undertone of sadness in Aurora? Or had she suffered other losses? A
lover? A child? No family, she had said. Was she the woman in
Haymaker's song? Hoping to ask her, he had brought the *River
Blessing* CD in the pocket of his sport coat, which the heat had
forced him to take off and fold over the back of his chair.

"I meant to call them after I got settled in Ithaca," Aurora said,
"but I knew they'd be mad so I figured I'd wait. And the longer
I waited, the harder it was to break the silence. By now they've
disowned me."

"Surely they'd want to hear from you, even now," Martin objected.

She stirred a wedge of pita bread in olive oil. "Not after what
I did."

He waited for her to say what she had done, but she kept her
head lowered and her lips closed, making circles in the oil with
the pita. So he asked how she had become a court reporter, and
she seemed relieved to speak of something else. Among her fond-
est memories from the tavern, she told him, was of watching a

courtroom show with her father on the television over the bar, in the afternoons when she returned from school, before most of the regulars arrived. It was quiet then, nobody pawing or puking; with the TV on and her father washing glasses and her mother cooking in the kitchen, the place felt almost like a real home. After moving to Ithaca she had finished her high school degree by correspondence, and then, remembering the courtroom show, she had driven the twisty roads twice a week to Alfred State College for classes that qualified her to record the drone of lawyers and judges and witnesses.

"You must hear some fascinating stories," Martin suggested.

"You can't really follow the stories, or you'll miss words."

Their meals arrived just then—mushroom spinach crepes for Martin and curried sweet potato turnovers for Aurora, dishes that Simone would never have allowed herself because of the starch. He remembered the hotel desk clerk saying she had always wanted to feed Aurora, to fatten her up. True, she was thin, but she wasn't sickly. In fact, Aurora seemed vibrant, radiant, fully at ease in her flesh. In the sunlight that slanted under the canopy he could see her skin wasn't washed out as a sick person's might be, as Yaffa's had been, but was fair and clear, like rich cream. It pleased Martin to watch her eat, the ginger hair tumbling across her forehead as she bent to the plate, her eyes sparkling as she glanced up at him.

Between bites, she said, "It must feel good to preserve things. We throw so much away."

Martin puzzled for a moment before he realized she was talking about his work. "Yes, it does feel good."

"What made you want to become an architect? Not any TV show, I'll bet."

His desire to draw out their time together led him to ramble in his response. He told how his parents had met in the 1960s at Cambridge, where his mother was pursuing a B.A. in classics and his father a Ph.D. in mathematics. After they finished their degrees and married, his father accepted a teaching position in Indiana, a place that seemed to them as remote as Siberia. For his father, the move to the American Midwest was merely another step in what he assumed would be a continuing journey from his native village in Iran to a chair in mathematics at some famous and venerable institution—in Oxford, say, or Budapest.

"He was a good enough mathematician to keep climbing the ladder," Martin said. "But during their first year in Bloomington my mother gave birth to my sister, Yaffa, who had epilepsy, and three years later she gave birth to me. With two young kids to care for, and Yaffa suffering seizures, Mother refused to consider moving, not even when my father received offers from schools willing to double his salary."

"What devotion," Aurora said.

Unnerved to see her eyes glisten, Martin pushed on with the story, even as he felt the sting in his own eyes. He told how his mother shuttled Yaffa to the children's hospital in Indianapolis, as doctors tried various treatments; how she allowed Yaffa to host friends but not to play at anyone else's house, drove her to lessons, rubbed her aching joints, talked with her through sleepless nights, watched over her constantly. All that care, however, couldn't keep Yaffa from dying in the midst of a seizure at fifteen.

"I always knew she was sick," Martin said, "but I didn't believe she could die."

Aurora slid both hands across the table, almost but not quite touching his. Neither spoke while the busboy cleared their plates and the waitress discretely placed the bill at Martin's elbow. At length he sat back and said, "I never told you why I became an architect."

"You told me a lot else."

"I didn't mean to rattle on about Yaffa."

"You needed to."

"I must have." He blinked hard, looked around, and was surprised to see that the patio had emptied and the last light had faded from the sky. "I've kept you out late."

"I'm not the one who's giving a lecture tomorrow."

"It's all on my laptop. Before-and-after photos showing derelict buildings brought back to life."

They stood up, and as he draped the sport coat over his shoulder, a soft clunk against his back reminded him of the album in the pocket. Strolling with Aurora through the humid air to the rooming house where she lived, a few blocks from the hotel, he kept trying to think of a graceful way to ask her about the song. It seemed dishonest not to let her know why he had sought her out.

And then, on the porch of the rooming house, after thanking him for supper, Aurora said, "What a happy accident that we ran into one another at the co-op. I've learned more about you tonight than during all those chats at Friends meeting."

"It wasn't really an accident," he admitted.

She gave an uncertain smile. "You're not saying the stars brought us together?"

"No. I came searching for you."

"Whatever prompted that?"

With a sense of relief he told her about Haymaker's song. When she objected that she'd never met any Jack Haymaker and so the song must have been about someone else, Martin replied, "Maybe so, but there's a photo in the album of a woman who looks remarkably like you."

He drew the CD from his jacket and she accepted it with a doubtful expression. Pulling the liner notes from the case, she leafed through the booklet, tilting the pages to catch the glow from the porch light. When she came to the picture of the woman at the grave, she let out a gasp and squeezed the booklet shut. "Who took this?"

"Then it is you?"

She pressed the album to her chest. "This was private, not for others to see."

The tremor in her voice made him fear he had done something cruel. "I'm sorry," he said. "I didn't mean to upset you. I've just been haunted by the song."

"What does it say? The song—what does it say?"

"It tells a sort of story."

"What story?" She glared at him. "What *story?*"

Martin couldn't bring himself to speak, as the song did, about a deceitful lover, a death at sea, or a fatherless child. "You can listen to it," he said hastily. "Keep the album. Really, I'm sorry. Let me explain."

But Aurora turned away, still clutching the CD, and let herself into the house with a key, pulled the door shut behind her and doused the porch light. Through the glass, Martin could see her rushing up the stairs. Appalled, he tried the knob, hoping to undo whatever it was he had done. But the door was locked.

He swung around blindly and stumbled into a rocking chair, which tipped over with a clatter. He jerked the chair upright and clung to it. After a few breaths he eased himself into the seat, deciding he would stay here on the darkened porch for a while, to gather himself before returning to the hotel. Or why not stay all night, so he could apologize when she came out for work in the morning?

As he rocked, he watched late joggers and dog walkers and cars pass by. Soon, over the creaking of floorboards, he heard music drifting from an upstairs window. He couldn't make out the words, but he recognized the melody of "Aurora's Child." The song played twice, then a third time, and as he listened, sobs welled up in him. Usually he resisted the grief, but now he let it rise, in wave after wave that shook his body and squeezed groans from his throat.

§ § §

Chapter Eleven • May–June 2008

HARLAN

THE NIGHT OF HARLAN AND KATARINA'S RETURN from Marquette, over a supper that included the first snow peas and lettuce from the garden, Papa showed little interest in hearing about the trip but Nana wanted to know all the details, especially anything they could tell her about Teresa Two Bears, whom she referred to as Tommy's mother but never as Harlan's grandmother. Harlan understood why Nana would be jealous of this new claim on his affection, so he was careful not to speak of Teresa as Nekoma, for the name might seem too intimate. Instead he spoke of her as Mrs. Two Bears, and Katarina followed his example. They had agreed not to show off the beaded moccasins or deliver the willow basket to Nana right away, so as not to call undue attention to these gifts.

Nor did Harlan dwell on the three granddaughters, his young cousins, who had filled the Marquette house with a frolicsome energy once they got over their initial shyness; or Uncle Cedar, who had tuned up the truck; or Aunt Rozzie, who had advised Katarina about immigration options. He said little about the tribe of kinfolk who showed up to have a look at him and to recount stories about Tommy. As for what he had learned of his father,

Harlan mentioned only those details that suggested Tommy had been forced to take on adult responsibilities too early, from caring for his little sister while his mother worked to quitting school and supporting the household when Mrs. Two Bears lost her job because of failing health.

"Where was the father?" Nana asked.

"He died in a car wreck when Tommy was a boy," Harlan explained, without noting that Mrs. Two Bears had never married her Swedish logger and was not in fact a Mrs.

"Most likely drunk," Papa remarked. "Indians can't hold their liquor."

"Tommy's father wasn't Indian," Harlan said irritably. "He was as white as you or Nana."

Papa grunted. "Still, I never should have served that boy. Should have taken one look at that fake ID and thrown him out of my bar. Should have broken his neck the first time he made a pass at my daughter."

"It's done, Luther," Nana said. "Besides, if you'd thrown him out, we wouldn't have our Harlan, would we?"

Papa shoved his chair away from the table, got to his feet, and stumped out of the room. In a moment the back door slammed.

Harlan resisted the impulse to chase after him. To hide his agitation he folded his napkin, laid it beside his plate, and smoothed it with his palm. "What's eating him?"

"He lost direction while you were away," Nana said. "He was all right for the first few days. He tried working on the list of jobs you'd left him, but he didn't trust himself to do things, said he didn't know how. And the few things he tried he bungled."

"So he's back on the bottle?"

"We'll talk about that later," Nana said tersely, with a nod of her head toward Katarina, who took the hint and began clearing dishes.

"She knows he drinks."

"Later, honey. Right now I want you to finish telling me what you learned from Mrs. Two Bears."

Harlan rubbed his eyes, sore from too many hours of staring at pavement. He recalled how Teresa's clouded eyes were shut when she ran her swollen fingers over his face and hair. "She thinks Tommy might have wanted to marry Aurora, if he'd lived."

Nana raised her eyebrows. "What do you think?"

"I'd like to believe she's right, because then I could imagine having a father. But I can't be sure." He kept running his palm over the napkin. "I'll never be sure."

"And you, Katarina?"

Pausing beside the table with a serving bowl in each hand, Katarina replied, "Who would know a son's heart better than his mother?"

True in most cases, Harlan thought, but not in mine.

"So he wasn't just a philanderer?" Nana asked.

"Philanderer?" Katarina looked to Harlan for a definition.

"A man who seduces women and dumps them," he explained.

"How odd," Katarina said. "The Greek roots mean the love of men. In ancient Athens, a philanderer would have been gay."

"Oh, my," Nana said, and pressed fingers over her lips.

"Well, in English it means a womanizer," Harlan said. "A rake, a man who chases women recklessly."

"Sounds like my father," Katarina said.

Clearly flustered now, Nana said in a rush, "Well I always imagined Tommy had a girl in every port."

"Maybe he did," Harlan conceded. "But Mrs. Two Bears said the girl in Cleveland was the only one he ever talked about."

All three hushed as the back door opened and footsteps scuffed across the kitchen floor. When Papa slouched into the dining room and reclaimed his chair at the table, the flush on his face confirmed Harlan's suspicion that he'd gone outside to drink, most likely from a bottle hidden under the porch.

"Had to go see a man about a horse," Papa said. "Don't want you to think I'm not glad to have you two back home."

Nana gave him a withering look, but Papa kept his gaze on the blunt, yellowed nail of his right thumb as it drew patterns on the tablecloth.

A spasm of anger prompted Harlan to say what he hadn't counted on saying so soon after their return: "Katarina and I are going to try finding Aurora."

"I figured that's what you'd be up to next," Papa said, without shifting his gaze from the movement of his thumbnail.

"Oh, what a splendid idea!" Nana said.

"It's a stupid idea," Papa grumbled. "The cops looked. Detectives looked. If she was alive, they'd have found her."

"She *is* alive," Nana insisted.

Papa slammed his fist on the table, upsetting a water glass and rattling plates. "She's *gone*, Jenny. Accept it!"

Katarina broke in to say in her unflappable manner, "Let us see what we can discover."

Nana rose to help her finish clearing the table, while Harlan sat watching Papa, who would not return his gaze but merely gouged circle after circle into the white cloth.

*

One morning a few days after the return from Marquette, Harlan accompanied Nana to fetch the mail. Summer had taken hold of the land, heating the soil, drawing leaves from every stem and twig. The smell of honeysuckle sweetened the air. Passing under the branches of oaks and maples, which cast dense shadows onto the lane, Harlan spoke more openly than he had been able to do in front of Papa about the thrill of meeting Tommy's family. Nana listened without apparent jealousy, seeming to welcome whatever made him happy.

In the mailbox, among circulars and catalogs and bills, there was an envelope addressed to Harlan, postmarked from Marquette but without a return address. Assuming it was from Teresa or Aunt Rozzie, he sliced it open with his pocketknife and pulled out a greeting card, which bore a photograph on the front of a hand cupping pebbles that shone like gems. While Nana looked on, he opened the card and found another photograph inside. Before he could examine it properly, Nana let out a gasp and said, "Oh, Harlan! That's the picture I told you about—the one that singer brought to the bar years ago."

And there was the scene she had described—the woman at the grave. He felt a sudden burning in his chest.

"Who sent it?" Nana asked. "Does it say?"

The back of the photo was blank, but inside the card there was a note, which he read aloud: "Dear Harlan: I took this snapshot in April 1995, in Arlington National Cemetery. The grave is your father's. I don't know who the woman is, but Teresa thinks she may be your mother. I thought you might wish to have this. Teresa and her family are overjoyed to know you and your lovely Katarina. Warmly, Naomi Rosenthal."

"Who's Naomi Rosenthal?"

"Mrs. Two Bears's doctor. She stopped by one day while I was there."

"Imagine, a doctor who makes house calls."

"I don't know if she does it with other patients. She lives just down the street and often drops in as if for a chat, but always brings along her instruments. She's clearly fond of Mrs. Two Bears, and worried about her diabetes."

While Nana took the card to read the note herself, Harlan moved the picture into a shaft of sunlight so he could see it more clearly. The grave was his father's, all right, for there was the name on the stone, and the grieving young woman was his mother. Even without Nana's assurance, he would have recognized her as a grown-up version of the girl whose features he had memorized while studying the shoebox of family photos. His mother lay on grass in the foreground, head bowed, hunched in pain, and beyond her, white stone markers stretched away toward the horizon in regimented rows. He gazed at the image as long as he could bear it, and then he looked up between the ranks of trees that crowded the road, and rested his eyes on the blue river of sky.

★

After scanning the photo through a magnifying glass, Katarina pointed out to Harlan the fresh peonies in a vase near Tommy's stone. She also noted the jacket, most likely of linen, folded on the grass beside Aurora, and the careful arrangement of her hair, the stylish cut of the sundress, the leather sandals next to her bare feet. This was no waif, she concluded, but a woman capable of looking after herself.

"That doesn't mean she's alive now," Harlan said.

"No, it only means she was not helpless. You look at her picture and think she is broken. I look at her and think she is strong."

★

Over protests from Papa, Harlan persuaded Nana to dig up the report a detective had written a few months after Aurora's disappearance, but it offered only a jumble of false leads, along with a hefty bill. The missing person report from the Cleveland police was equally sketchy. It disturbed Harlan to read the profile of his mother at sixteen—her height (5'9"), weight (125 pounds), figure (thin), color of eyes (hazel) and hair (red), skin tone (pale), scars (left knee), tattoos (none), other skin markings (freckles on face and shoulders, birthmark on right calf)—laid out drily on the official form as if to identify a corpse rather than a runaway.

Where the form asked for a description of clothing the missing person was last seen wearing, the items listed were blue jeans, black sneakers, and a Cleveland Indians jacket. Although no one had seen her leave, Nana explained, Aurora practically lived in jeans, and the sneakers and jacket went missing along with the girl.

The entries were in Nana's hand, in ink, but where she had written *ginger red* for hair color, someone else had crossed through *ginger* with a pencil stroke. Knowing Nana, Harlan realized she might have come up with color names that would have been even more baffling to the police—*russet, henna, cinnamon, Titian red*—terms he knew from going to the art museum with her as a boy and from studying the oils in her paint box.

The reports left Harlan feeling that he and Katarina were unlikely to succeed where professionals had failed. She refused to be discouraged, however, pointing out that the Internet, with its clever search engines, wasn't yet available when the police and the private detective were hunting for Aurora. Today, she assured him, everybody left a trace in the digital universe, whether they wished to or not.

That Aurora didn't wish to leave a trace was soon evident, however, as they tried, during visits to the library in Ravenna, all of the obvious searches—white pages, social networks, chat rooms, blogs, fee-based people lookups—without finding any reference to her. Or perhaps, like Harlan himself before he'd met Katarina, Aurora wasn't hiding but was merely suspicious of the electronic arena. It felt creepy to wander that vaporous realm, where millions of people seemed intent on calling attention to themselves, like toddlers on the playground shouting "Look at me! Look at me!" His mind clung to the tangible. He could have followed footprints, bread crumbs, bent twigs, or an actual web—like the ones spiders made, with filaments that quivered in the wind and glistened with dew. But he was daunted by this ethereal

Web, which Katarina darted through as blithely as if it were her backyard.

On those Sunday afternoons at the library she would read her new email, write to her mother and brothers and a few friends, browse the *New York Times*, skim two or three Swedish newspapers, and then she would dive back into the search. Before settling down to another computer, Harlan would borrow her phone and go outside to call the nursing home in Boston. When the nurse came on he asked about Mrs. Winfield, identifying himself as the son who lived in Arizona, the golf cart magnate. Week after week the report was the same: frail, failing, refusing to eat. Then he would go back into the library and clunk away at his own email, pecking at the keys, glancing over now and again at Katarina's screen to see where she was zooming next.

Still, after several Sundays of hunting, even her ingenuity, aided by suggestions from librarians, turned up no references to Aurora Eliza Blake. Of course they realized she might have changed her name. But if she had done so through marriage or a court proceeding, the transaction should have left a trace. On the other hand, if she had simply adopted an alias she might really be lost. And that is what Harlan began to suspect must have occurred: his mother must be living—if she *was* living—with a name she had picked up as casually as she had discarded her baby.

*

Meanwhile, the farm claimed nearly all of Harlan's waking hours. The garden teemed with weeds as well as vegetables. The stone foundation of the barn needed tuck-pointing, holes in the the chicken coop needed patching to keep out raccoons and foxes, the uneven stepping stones leading to the front porch needed to be re-laid on beds of sand. The tractor and truck and other antique machines required steady coaxing to keep them running. There were water troughs to rig for the goats they hoped to acquire, fence gates to set right, erosion gullies to stop up with brush and rock.

Katarina and Nana helped him with some chores, especially in the garden, but mostly he worked with Papa, who had remained sober, if testy, since that first night after the return from Marquette. No sober stretch had ever lasted long, so Harlan watched him closely for the telltale signs of drink, leery of the temper that might blaze up at any moment. He wasn't concerned for himself, believing he could hold his own with Papa; nor was he concerned for Katarina, who didn't share the history that kept flaring between his grandparents like an outbreak of malaria. The one he worried about was Nana, who seemed, since moving to the country, even more vulnerable to Papa's surly moods.

Harlan knew it was foolish to think he could fix everything broken, and thereby ease whatever was gnawing at Papa's gut. It would take years to heal the farm, maybe lifetimes. Still, he drove himself. Aside from meals, the only break he took most days was an hour or so, late in the afternoon, when he jogged down to the river, stripped off his sweaty clothes, and dove in. Unless Katarina was engaged in a project with Nana, she would join him, walking rather than jogging to the riverbank, where she hung a blanket and towel on a branch, folded her clothes over a drift log, tied her hair in a knot on top of her head, and then waded into the water, loosing little yelps at the cold. She crossed arms over her breasts, shivering, and lowered herself until the current ran just below her chin, for she didn't like to get the river's silt in her hair.

Her skin smelled of silt when they made love on the sandbar after their swim, the blanket spread beneath them, the patchwork branches of a giant sycamore arching overhead. One time they had tried the grass, which provided a softer cushion, but Katarina came away with chigger bites. They also tried making love in the river, but unlike the pond at Black Bear Farm, here there was a current, which kept tipping them off balance and setting them

adrift, until they gave up the experiment amid laughter and re-
sorted to the firm, chigger-free bank of sand.

The rumble of the tractor approached them one afternoon
just as they were rising from the blanket to retrieve their clothes.
Papa was mowing the path to the river, Harlan guessed. Before
turning around, the old man must have caught sight of them,
because that night, while he and Harlan walked out to make
sure the chickens were buttoned up tight in their coop, Papa remarked that he'd never seen a naked woman in the flesh until he
married Nana, and he'd seen damn few of them since then, and
never without paying a fee. The fee was for looking, he wanted
Harlan to understand, not for touching. He'd never been unfaith-
ful to Nana. Since their honeymoon, he had rarely seen even
Nana without clothes on, for she never undressed with the lights
burning, always emerged after her bath wearing an ankle-length
nightgown, never slept nude, as if marriage made the body no
less shameful. She wouldn't have dreamed of skinny-dipping.
What if neighbors happened by? She'd never live it down. Papa
blamed the Baptists for drumming the shame into her, but he admitted that the Calvinists who'd reared him hadn't exactly sung
the glories of sex. For sex is what it came down to, wasn't it? The
old urge to be fruitful and multiply and populate the earth. What
could be more natural than that? But Nana thought otherwise.
The nature she loved was outdoors, in the landscape, colors and
textures she could paint, not the urges inside a man or a woman.

"So you carry this hunger all your life," Papa said, "you produce one child, and she runs away. What's the sense in that?"

By now they had finished gathering the chickens and were
leaning against the pasture gate, watching the midsummer sun,
two days shy of the solstice, wallow down beyond the river. Harlan was astonished by these revelations from Papa, who had never spoken to him so openly about anything, least of all sex. That
the lifelong hunger had also led to a grandson, who'd run off

but then come back, seemed to count less in Papa's reckoning than the loss of a daughter. When the crimson belly of the sun appeared to slide behind the far treetops, Papa slapped his palms on the gate, as if something were concluded, and turned back toward the house.

They walked in silence. As they neared the kitchen door, where Nana had put on the light for them, Papa gripped Harlan's elbow and drew him to a halt. "You oughtn't to stay here with the old folks. You ought to go to Sweden with your sweetheart."

"It isn't just for you two I'm staying."

"What else holds you?"

"The land."

"You'd choose a few scrubby acres over Katarina?"

Thinking how to answer, Harlan stood watching the sky, where bats were beginning their nightly prowls. A barred owl called, summoning up memories of Black Bear Farm. "I want to have them both—land that can't be taken away from me and a woman to love."

"How you figure on doing that?"

"I'm hoping Katarina will come back here after she finishes her studies."

Papa snorted. "To do what? Raise goats?"

"She might get a job at the Swedish consulate in Cleveland."

"What if she falls for some boy while she's studying over in Stockholm?"

Of course Harlan had thought of that, and so had Katarina; they had made no promises. "She might. But I'm hoping to visit her there, if I can scrape up the airfare, and I'm hoping she'll visit us here next summer. There's not a whole lot to keep her in Sweden. Her parents are divorced. Her mother and brothers are all working in other countries, and she doesn't get along with her father."

"Is he a drunk?"

Hiding his surprise at the question, Harlan said, "He drinks, I guess, but the main thing is what broke up the marriage—a string of mistresses. Young ones. The latest is Katarina's age, according to the brother who lives in London."

Papa nodded but made no further comment until they had entered the house, removed their boots in the mudroom, and stepped into the kitchen, where Nana and Katarina were cutting up rhubarb for canning. There he announced as settled fact what had merely been Harlan's earnest wish: "Jenny, our Swedish girl's going to spend next summer here on the farm. Isn't that grand?"

Katarina shot a vexed look at Harlan.

"Why, that's wonderful," said Nana, her face ruddy from the steam rising off a pan filled with pint jars. She rose on tiptoes to kiss Katarina on the cheek. "Maybe by the time you come back Harlan will have completed his list of jobs and you two can simply enjoy yourselves."

Katarina pushed a damp strand of hair from her face and tucked it behind her ear. "We must see," she said. "Much is uncertain."

*

Again and again, Katarina was the one who refused to give up the search for Aurora. Every time Harlan imagined they had run out of possibilities, Katarina thought of a new angle to investigate. One Sunday evening, following another fruitless session at the library, she asked Nana and Papa if Aurora had ever discussed what she might be when she grew up. Nana recalled that Aurora had occasionally talked about nursing or teaching, once or twice about catering, but never with any conviction.

Katarina made notes, and then raised her eyebrows at Papa. He scratched the bald crown of his head, as if rousting memories from sleep.

"Well," he said, "one thing she used to get excited by was this courtroom drama on TV. It came on every weekday, about the time she got home from school. She'd plop her books on the bar, climb on a stool, and sit there watching almost without blinking. Nana always brought her a snack, and some days Aurora wouldn't even touch it until the show was over."

"I tried getting her to eat healthy things," Nana said, "apples, oranges, crackers with peanut butter or cheese, whole wheat muffins, that sort of thing. But would you believe it, her favorite was white bread slathered in mayonnaise."

Papa loudly cleared his throat. "Like I was saying, she was nuts about this courtroom drama. Usually I'd watch with her, since business was slow that time in the afternoon, and I didn't get many chances to keep her company. The show always ended with a trial where this cagey lawyer proved his client was innocent or the other guy was guilty. Never lost a case. Must have had the best won-lost record in legal history. All the while Aurora was glued to the screen, like she was memorizing the guy's every move. So I'd say to her, 'Kiddo, you like trials so much, you ought to be a lawyer.'"

"And did she agree?" Katarina asked.

"No. She claimed she wasn't smart enough to be a lawyer."

"She was plenty smart," Nana put in.

"Did I say she wasn't?"

"Aurora had a low opinion of herself," Nana said. "Where she got it from I don't know. We praised her to the skies." She glanced accusingly at Papa. "At least I did."

Papa glowered back at her. "Are you going to let me tell this, or not?"

Nana recoiled in a way that pained Harlan.

"As I was saying," Papa resumed, "Aurora would tell me there was no way she could become a lawyer, but maybe she could be one of those secretaries—you know, the ones who write down what's happening in the trial. You see them there tapping keys."

"A court reporter?" Harlan suggested.

"Yeah, that's it."

Nana perked up. "Oh, I hadn't thought of that in ages. She used to catch the bus for school out front of that place there on Euclid—down by Trinity Cathedral—what's it called?—the Court Reporting Academy, I believe. She waited there sometimes half an hour for the bus to come, poor thing, in sun or rain or snow."

"When the weather was real bad I drove her to school, didn't I?" Papa said.

"Yes, dear, yes," Nana conceded. "Anyway, she'd tell me how the girls going in and out of the academy were smartly dressed and the posters in the windows claimed nearly all the graduates found jobs right away, and at good salaries, with health insurance and everything."

"She liked the idea of sitting there listening to all these stories," Papa said, "without having to say a word."

"She was a quiet girl," Nana added. "I could be working in the kitchen, never knowing she was nearby, and I'd look up and there she'd be, watching me like a cat."

"Same in the bar," Papa said. "After the TV show she'd go upstairs to change into her waitress outfit, and a while later I'd hear the broom whisking over the floor. That's the only way I'd know she was there. 'What's new, kiddo?' I'd ask her, and most times all I'd get back was a shrug."

"It came of being an only child, that quietness," Nana remarked.

Papa contorted his face into an expression of mock surprise. "What's this, you're not going to blame it on her living over a goddamn bar?"

Ignoring the question, Nana said, "We wanted more children, but we never got them."

"Maybe we didn't try hard enough," Papa said, and the two exchanged a barbed look.

Afterward, Harlan pushed aside worries about his grandparents, reflecting instead on the new threads he and Katarina could try following through the electronic maze. Nursing and teaching he might have guessed, for they were common ambitions among the girls he'd known in school; and catering made sense from the many hours Aurora had spent helping Nana in the tavern kitchen; but he wouldn't have come up with court reporting.

★

Harlan had never heard Papa call his mother kiddo before, had never heard either of his grandparents refer to her by any nickname. It worried him that his effort to discover Aurora's fate would conjure up in them images of her as a sixteen-year-old schoolgirl. But if she turned up now, she would be a woman in her mid-thirties, filled out, surely weighing more than 125 pounds, her face beginning to crease around the eyes and mouth. Unless she had dyed her hair, it would still be red, for she would be too young for turning gray. She would still be hazel-eyed and fair-skinned, with a birthmark and childhood scars.

Nana would recognize her instantly, Harlan felt certain, even if Papa might not. The shape of Aurora's ear could be evidence enough for Nana, just as the shape of his own ear had convinced Teresa Two Bears that he was Tommy's son. How many hours had each of those mothers studied the convolutions of ears, the shape of eyes, the curvature of lips, while nursing or bathing her baby, changing diapers, spooning food into a rosebud mouth? And what knowledge would go deeper into a mother than the contours and moods of this new life she had brought forth?

Harlan recalled the image of himself as an infant sucking at his mother's breast. Had she really nursed him during those four months before she ran away, or had she merely posed for a photograph? He put the question to Nana, the next time he found himself alone with her. They were in the living room, where she was directing him as he mounted her landscapes on the freshly-painted walls.

"Of course she nursed you," Nana replied. "Every few hours, around the clock. I offered to give the baby—give you, that is—a bottle in the night, to let her get some sleep, but she wouldn't hear of it. She treasured you, the way any mother would."

Harlan thought of several things to say, but held his tongue, and concentrated on tapping the nail for a picture hook into plaster above the fireplace. Nana handed him the painting of a lakeside farm, with red barn and mountains in the background, an autumnal scene that used to hang beside the case of baseball memorabilia in the tavern, one he used to gaze at sometimes until he felt as if he were inside the picture, about to climb into the rowboat or set off on a trail into those mountains. After he suspended the painting from its hook, Nana backed away, squinting, and asked him to touch the frame a bit on the right side, then a bit on the left, until it was level.

As she motioned him to a new spot for the next painting, she said, "I can imagine how her breasts must have hurt after she ran away. The milk would have kept coming in for days. She would have wet through the few shirts she took with her. If she saw any babies while she traveled, or even if she heard one cry, her breasts would have ached and her milk would have let down."

Harlan tried thinking about something else—how the damper above the fireplace needed to be checked, how the mantelpiece ought to be rubbed with tung oil, how the wide pine boards creaking beneath his feet might be quieted with a sprinkling of talc—but he couldn't help envisioning the girl in flight with overflowing breasts, and the baby on the bar wailing for want of what she had.

★

Nana couldn't get over the elegance of the beaded moccasins, which Katarina never wore, not wishing to soil them. Instead they were displayed on the cedar chest in the front hall, where friends from Cleveland and country neighbors who came to visit could admire them. The willow basket was even more of a wonder to Nana. On receiving this gift, she cupped it in her hands delicately, as if it were the nest of a rare bird, with the bird still inside. She turned it around and around, examining the top with its starburst pattern of porcupine quills, the tightly-woven sides, the bottom with its fibers converging in a spiral at the center. She marveled that such a light and sturdy vessel had been fashioned from the shoots of a tree, and by a woman with hands swollen from diabetes.

Immediately Nana set about pondering what gift she could send north with Harlan when he returned to Marquette, as he planned to do in August, after Katarina left for Sweden and before the start of classes at Kent State. His newfound Aunt Rozzie had promised to teach him a few Ojibwa words, and Uncle Cedar had promised to take him fly-fishing, and those seemed likelier ways of consoling himself than by staying on the farm and working himself into the ground.

For days, Nana fretted aloud to anyone within earshot that nothing she had to offer was as exquisitely made as the willow basket. Harlan and Katarina suggested that she give Mrs. Two Bears one of her paintings, but Nana dismissed the idea, saying they were too crude, mere amateur's work. But then Papa told her to quit being so blamed modest. Her paintings were first rate. Hadn't customers at the tavern offered to buy them, and didn't she always say no, they weren't for sale? She ought to just pick one she liked and let Harlan deliver it on his visit up there.

While Harlan and Katarina had failed to sway her, Nana flushed with pleasure at Papa's endorsement. Well, she conceded, maybe one or two of the landscapes had come out reasonably well. She would have to take stock. So the last of her paintings were unpacked and leaned against the walls in the living room, where she could scrutinize them alongside the ones that were already hanging. After soliciting opinions and appraising every canvas, Nana settled on the landscape that Harlan had mounted over the fireplace, the autumn scene with a red barn beside a lake. The lake shimmered with reflections, dun and ocher and rose, picking up the colors of barn and leaves and earth, and a forested ridge arched across the background, a shape that might have been Black Bear Mountain.

Harlan wanted to object that she couldn't give away this picture, his favorite. But as he took it down he realized he had memorized its every detail, as he had memorized Thomas Cole's *View of Schroon Mountain* and a Chinese scroll of pilgrims trekking into a misty valley and any number of other paintings during visits with Nana to the Cleveland Art Museum. Then it occurred to him that the landscapes he'd dreamed of as a boy, the scenes that had set him reading the journals of Lewis and Clark and had sent him on the quest to Black Bear Mountain, were not only the ones he'd studied at the museum but also the ones he'd gazed at day after day on the walls of the Iron Ore Tavern. Maybe that was how he had acquired his longing for wildness—from the countless times when he'd stood transfixed, imagining his way into Nana's paintings.

★

Because Sunday had been devoted to Nana's impromptu art show, Katarina persuaded Harlan to spend Monday afternoon at the library, so they could pursue the new leads. While he sat at one computer catching up on wars and environmental disasters, Katarina sat at the adjacent machine and scoured every database related to nursing. She looked up honor society lists, professional associations, credentialing services, and headhunting agencies, but could find no trace of Aurora. Then she did the same for teaching and catering, with the same result.

Taking a break from the search, they went outside to sit on the library steps as Harlan made his weekly call to the nursing home. After he punched in the number, Katarina pressed her cheek against his to listen in. When a nurse came on the line, he pretended as usual to be the Winfield son from Arizona and asked his usual question. The nurse replied that they had been trying to contact him for two days, to let him know that Mrs. Winfield had passed away, peacefully, on Thursday night. Katarina let out a moan. Harlan squeezed his eyes shut. The nurse went on to say they had called his home to deliver the news, but his wife had told them he was at a sales retreat and mustn't be disturbed. Harlan had the presence of mind to say that he had come home early from the retreat and to ask whether his brother—the stock trader in Boston—had been present for their mother's last moments. No, the nurse answered rather curtly, Mr. Winfield had been unable to break free of other obligations.

After the call ended, Katarina gave him a somber look. "I knew she would die there."

"She would have died on the farm."

"Yes, but on the farm we could have cared for her, and she could have looked out on the mountains and the Mad River. She could have heard frogs croaking in the pond and leaves rattling on the cottonwood. She could have spent her last days in the place she loved, not in some warehouse for old people."

Harlan remembered Katarina rubbing Mrs. Winfield's gnarled feet, remembered her gliding back and forth on the rope swing beneath the great cottonwood, belting out songs, while the old woman sat on the porch laughing, remembered the look of anguish on Katarina's face when the limousine pulled up to cart Mrs. Winfield away.

"We should be going," he said, putting an arm across her shoulders.

But Katarina shook her head. "We must find Aurora."

"We'll come back next week and look some more."

"I need to look now." She stood up, and headed into the library.

"Katarina—"

"Go, if you want," she hissed as they entered the building. "I am not leaving."

A librarian seated at the checkout desk cleared her throat and asked them to please keep their voices down.

Katarina resumed, in a whisper. "Now I have lost three grandmothers, all of them bewildered in their final months. I need to find Aurora while Nana still has her wits. Do you understand?"

Harlan didn't understand, but he knew better than to thwart Katarina now. So he followed her to the computer, pulled his chair up close to hers, and sat watching while she clicked the keys. As websites flashed onto the screen, one after another, he wondered how his own grandparents would end their days. Neither of them had ever touched a computer, so far as he knew, and probably never would. They seemed to have camped out in the 1960s, just as he had tried camping out in the 1800s, until Katarina dragged him closer to his own day.

Soon Katarina turned up a list of agencies representing court reporters, and she began writing down phone numbers. When she had run through the list, they trooped back outside, past the watchful librarian, and sat on the steps. Now Katarina did the dialing and Harlan pressed his cheek against hers in order to listen. On each call she went through the same routine, explaining that she was an assistant at the Swedish consulate in Cleveland, where her superior wished to hire a court reporter to take down depositions, and in particular he wished to secure the services of a Ms. Aurora Blake, who had worked for him in the past with great success but whose contact information he had unfortunately misplaced. Did they by any chance represent Ms. Blake? The first two agencies answered, regretfully, no, but they had other qualified reporters to offer.

A representative from the third agency likewise said no, but then corrected himself. "Wait a moment. Would that be Aurora E. Blake?"

"That is the one," Katarina said calmly.

"Ah, yes, Ms. Blake is indeed in our database, only she has changed her surname to Zakar."

Harlan's heart lurched, while Katarina, unfazed, said, "Very well, then—"

"However," the agent added, "it appears she is not currently accepting assignments."

"Ah, what a pity."

"Could I suggest someone else?"

"My superior was quite intent on hiring Ms. Blake—that is, Ms. Zakar. He recalls that she lived in northeastern Ohio, convenient to Cleveland. Is that still the case?"

"No," the agent replied. "She has relocated to Indiana."

"May I ask where in Indiana?"

"I'm sorry, I can't divulge that information. But we have other eminently qualified reporters in the Cleveland area. Shall I put you in touch with one of them?"

"Not just now, thank you very much. First I must consult my superior."

With that, Katarina broke the connection and flashed a jubilant smile at Harlan. "We've found her."

"But there's millions of people in Indiana."

"Yes, but how many Zakars?"

Back inside, after a few strokes on the keyboard, she answered her own question: "Two households, both in Bloomington. A Solomon Zakar, aged 65 plus, and a Martin Zakar, aged 35-39. And look at the listing for Martin's household."

Struggling to focus his eyes, Harlan made out the name: "Aurora E. Zakar," he read. "My God, there she is."

Katarina leaned over to kiss him. "There she is."

Encircling her waist with his arm, Harlan drew her close, so they could speak in whispers. "It doesn't list any children."

"It wouldn't, unless they're older."

"So maybe she has kids and maybe not?"

"There's the phone number. We can call right now and find out."

"She probably has a child, which is why she's not taking assignments."

"Sweetheart, why don't you just call?"

Panicking, Harlan whispered, "Not yet. We've got to think this over."

Katarina sighed. "You know Nana and Papa will rush to the phone as soon as you tell them."

He shook his head. "We mustn't tell them yet."

"But you've said all along you're doing this for Nana."

"I am, I am. I just have to be sure she won't get hurt."

"Then what do you propose to do?"

He glanced around at the silent readers and mesmerized Web-surfers and vigilant librarians, as if somewhere out there he would glimpse the answer. "I'll go see her."

"You mean just show up on her doorstep?"

"I mean go *look* at her. See where she lives, what she does. See whether she's got any children."

"If she has children, then what?"

"Then...I don't know. I'll figure it out when I get there. For now, promise you won't tell Nana and Papa. Will you?"

Frowning, Katarina nodded, and wrote down the address on Kinsey Avenue in Bloomington, Indiana.

§ § §

Chapter Twelve • August 2004–June 2005

LILLIAN

IT SEEMED CURIOUS TO LILLIAN ZAKAR that her new daughter-in-law gazed so longingly at children everywhere she went, and yet had resolved not to bear any children of her own. Lillian had learned this dismaying news from her son, Martin, soon after the wedding, when she asked him whether she could count on becoming a grandmother while she still had her wits about her.

"You have far too many wits to lose them any time soon," said Martin, always the diplomat. Perched on a stool, he was replacing the incandescent bulbs in the chandelier over her dining room table with fluorescent ones, playing the man of the house as he had done as a boy, only now he had a house of his own and a brand new wife.

"Don't be so certain," Lillian countered. "Consider your father."

"Dad's not demented. He's only had a stroke."

Lillian arched her eyebrows. "Only?"

"His brain still churns away," Martin said. "He has trouble speaking, that's all."

"You're evading the question. Why is Aurora determined not to have children? Tell me it's a medical concern this time, and not another wife obsessed with her career."

Martin screwed in the last of the new bulbs, which were supposed to use only a quarter as much electricity as the old ones, if you could believe it, and then he climbed down from the stool before answering. "Aurora isn't obsessed with a career, Mother. And she's perfectly healthy."

"So the reasons are psychological?"

"They're personal. Can we just leave it at that?"

Lillian patted the coiled braid of silver hair at the back of her head, aware that she was trying his patience, yet she plunged on. "Did you know this before you married her? Or did she spring it on you later, as Simone did?"

Martin closed his eyes, and Lillian knew he was counting slowly to five, as she had taught him to do when he was a boy to dispel his anger. Opening his eyes, which were smoky black, like his father's, he said calmly, "She made it clear early on."

"You didn't raise objections?"

"I said I wanted children, yes."

And yet you agreed to remain childless?"

"I married Aurora for her own sake, not to pass on my genes." Dutiful as always, he gathered up the packaging and the antiquated bulbs, which he would be sure to recycle.

"Well, she isn't at all like Simone, thank our lucky stars," Lillian observed. "So perhaps she'll change her mind."

"I wouldn't get your hopes up, Mother," Martin replied.

*

But Lillian did get her hopes up. How could she avoid doing so, when she saw Aurora gazing fondly at every baby they encountered as the two of them strolled in the park or ran errands around town? How could she keep from hoping that Aurora would change her mind, after the disappointment of Martin's previous marriage, to Simone, whom he had first seen performing the role of a vamp in some play at Cornell, and who had never ceased to perform, it seemed to Lillian, right up until the day she sallied off to Hollywood to seek her fortune in films? Simone had insisted that having children would hold her back, not to mention ruining her figure. It went without saying that marriage to an architect who'd rather restore old houses in Indiana than design mansions in California would also be a hindrance. So when Martin agreed to a divorce, Lillian was neither surprised nor perturbed.

Lillian's hopes for this new wife encompassed more than the prospect of grandchildren. Unlike Simone, Aurora clearly enjoyed living in a midwestern college town. She said Bloomington reminded her of Ithaca, where she had lived previously, working most recently as a court reporter. On moving to Bloomington, she had submitted her resume at the courthouse and at other nearby county seats. While waiting for an opening, she seemed grateful to spend time with Lillian, a gratitude that Simone had never shown.

Simone did not even feign interest in what Lillian might know about life, but Aurora proved eager to learn. As soon as the newlyweds returned from their honeymoon—a week-long architecture tour of Chicago—Aurora sought out Lillian for instruction in cooking, gardening, sewing, decorating, and other domestic arts, which Lillian had learned from her own mother in desolate post-war England, not as quaint pursuits but as economic necessities. Aurora accompanied Lillian to the library and the farmers' market, asking for recommendations about novels or vegetables. She requested Lillian's help in shopping for clothes, wanting to know whether this dress or that blouse suited her. What makeup might she use to lend a touch of color to her cheeks? What could she do with her wayward hair, which looked unkempt when cut short, yet tangled when allowed to grow long? She even asked, shyly, for advice about the safest methods of birth control.

The trust implied by such inquiries was gratifying to Lillian. Yet she wondered how a woman could reach her thirties without having learned these things already. It was as though Aurora had never had a mother of her own.

For that matter, how could such an intelligent and attractive woman not have found a husband before Martin came along? True, Aurora didn't possess the glamorous good looks of Simone, but her lithe figure was graceful and her complexion was as creamy and smooth as the satin of her wedding dress, setting off nicely her russet hair and jade green eyes. What Lillian found appealing in Aurora had less to do with these outward shows, however, than with the curiosity that lit up those eyes, the vigor that animated her long limbs, the playful mind. Surely Martin was not the first man to fall for her.

Perhaps, before Martin, Aurora had taken lovers rather than husbands, the way so many young women did these days, or perhaps some trauma had made her leery of men. Lillian could only speculate. In the time they had spent together since the wedding, she had learned precious little about Aurora's background. Aurora never spoke of her life prior to the years in Ithaca, and whatever Martin may have known he did not share with Lillian— a discretion wholly admirable in a son except when it prompted him to withhold secrets from his mother. The only guests invited to the wedding on behalf of the bride were friends from recent years—no relatives, no chums from childhood. When Lillian had pressed her about inviting family, Aurora answered, in a tone of voice discouraging further inquiry, that she had no brothers or sisters, no aunts or uncles, and she had lost her parents.

*

Before Lillian's own daughter, Yaffa, died of a cerebral hemorrhage at fifteen, they had kept nothing from one another. Or at least so Lillian wished to believe. Yaffa, her firstborn, afflicted

with epilepsy and subject to seizures, had always been frail, quite
the opposite of Martin, who came along three years later. Because Martin was robust, Lillian could focus her attention on her
vulnerable daughter. Not that she didn't love her son; she had
simply counted on Martin to thrive, and he had done so, excelling
in school and sports, working a newspaper route, riding his bicycle rather than begging for lifts, arriving home at the promised
hour, tidying up his room without being chivvied.

Had Martin required more direction, it would not have
come from Lillian's husband, Solomon, who took only a passing interest in all but a few adults, and only a puzzled interest
in children, including his own. Solomon's detachment had been
evident to Lillian from their first meeting, at Cambridge, where
he was dazzling his professors in mathematics and she was ear-
nestly but rather aimlessly pursuing classics. A scholarship had
plucked him from an Iranian village where, she would learn,
Assyrians had been living since the heyday of their empire
2,500 years earlier. She was a scholarship girl from Nottingham,
daughter of a carpenter. They met at a Campaign for Nuclear
Disarmament rally, where the elderly Bertrand Russell spoke,
and afterwards they walked along the River Cam discussing
Aristotle's *Logic* and Euclid's *Elements*. For Lillian, these books
were touchstones of the Greek language, but for Solomon they
were germinal efforts at discerning the order of the universe.
He informed her that mathematics had come first, later giving
rise to the cosmos—to galaxies and pebbles and crickets—as a
material illustration of immaterial laws. While they followed
the river path, bicyclists wheeled by, children dashed in and out
of nearby shrubbery playing tag, yammering babies rolled past
in perambulators, raucous students poled along the stream in
punts, and to all of this commotion Solomon remained oblivious. He was attuned only to ideas.

Smitten by Solomon's husky accent, the leonine angles of his face, the glossy darkness of his deep-set eyes and wavy hair, Lillian persuaded herself that she could bring him down from the clouds. She failed, alas, but this did not keep her from marrying him, or from staying married these nearly forty years. Solomon's accent, strong features, and dusky coloring derived from his Assyrian ancestry, as did his old-fashioned views on the role of wives. A wife, he informed her, was to be first of all a mother; she was not to hold a job, nor to deal with money, aside from the allowance her husband doled out to her; she was not to voice opinions on religion or politics; she was to dress demurely when she left the house, and was to avoid the company of all males except close relatives. Lillian obeyed only those rules that harmonized with her own preferences and Quaker upbringing, such as dressing sensibly and treating faith as a private matter. Less by preference than by necessity, she held no paying job until after Yaffa's death.

The job that lured them from England to America was Solomon's appointment at Indiana University, where he published influential papers on topology and ascended to the rank of distinguished professor in record time. He was barely thirty when he began receiving offers of endowed chairs at some of the fabled centers for mathematics—in Berlin, Budapest, Princeton, even back in Cambridge. By then, however, Lillian had two young children to care for, and she refused to move. She might have uprooted Martin, but not Yaffa, who was under treatment by specialists at the university's medical school in Indianapolis. Each time an offer arrived, Solomon expounded on the many reasons for accepting it, but Lillian would not yield, and he soon drifted back to his study. It worried her that she might be hampering his work. To ease her qualms, she reflected that Solomon did not conduct his work in ordinary three-dimensional space, where children skinned their knees and bills came due and gutters leaked, but in a mental space populated by vectors, lattices, infinite sets, and other arcana, and he could explore that realm as easily in Bloomington as in Boston or Bucharest.

As the years passed, Solomon grew ever more abstracted, and Lillian came to accept his aloofness as the shadow side of his brilliance. He responded to Yaffa and Martin as if they were barbarians with whom he had somehow come to share a house—barbarians not because of their manners, for they were well-behaved children, but because of their obscure habits, boundless energy, and irrationality. He could not imagine what to do with them or say to them, and so he left their upbringing almost entirely to Lillian.

What this meant, in practice, was that Martin looked after himself, because Lillian was busy taking Yaffa to doctors and therapists, monitoring her medicine, making sure she got enough rest, keeping her away from high places lest she tumble in the midst of a seizure, watching over her day and night. When a vessel burst in Yaffa's brain in spite of all these precautions, Martin had just turned twelve. For Lillian, his childhood was mostly a blur. She remembered even less from the months following her daughter's funeral, when she sank into a numbing lethargy that blanked out everything but pain.

Solomon responded to Lillian's turmoil by withdrawing further into his airy cogitations. But Martin did everything he could to rescue her from gloom. At an age when his friends were beginning to rebel against their parents, Martin offered to help her in the garden, to cook with her, walk with her, sing her a song; but she could not accept these gifts. With money from his paper route, he bought her a necklace, a pair of fuzzy slippers, a silk scarf. But she could not bring herself to wear them. She would not open the Greek and Latin volumes he brought her, books she had treasured during her studies at Cambridge. She would not accompany him to Quaker Meeting, leaving him to ride there alone on his bicycle. She would not touch the tapioca or tea he prepared for her. "Mother, you need to eat," he admonished her. "You need to go outdoors, get some sunshine." His voice came to her as if down a lightless tunnel.

Then one day he brought word that a local cabinetmaker was seeking an apprentice. The news stirred a faint yearning in Lillian, for when she was a girl she had loved nothing more than to keep her father company on a jobsite where he was framing a roof or installing cupboards. She remembered the nutlike smell of freshly sawn boards, the arc of her father's arm swinging the hammer, his grunt as he drove a nail. Sensing her interest, Martin kept after her, as if he were fanning a spark in the ashes. At last Lillian agreed to clean herself up, dig out clothes that might look decent on her emaciated frame, and pay a visit to the cabinetmaker. As she entered the shop, the odor of sawdust transported her back into her father's embrace, when he would hug her after coming home from work. For the first time since the funeral, her eyes filled with tears that had nothing to do with Yaffa. After noticing how she stroked a plank of walnut fresh from the planer and then bent down to sniff it, the cabinetmaker agreed to take her on. Month by month, as he taught her about the tools, the wood, the craft, she gradually worked her way back from despair.

When the cabinetmaker retired, his hands grown shaky with age, Lillian took over his business, specializing in bookshelves, desks, and other fittings for libraries and offices, a dependable trade in a university town. Indeed, there was more work than she could manage, especially now that Solomon required so much looking after and Martin was too busy with his architecture practice to lend a hand. Over the years Lillian had hired a succession of apprentices, high school girls who had no ambitions for college, but each of them had married and moved on. What she needed was a partner, someone who would learn the trade and stay. Ideally, she needed Yaffa to be alive and healthy, fascinated by wood, happy to work alongside her mother.

*

"Still no prospects in the courts?" Lillian asked Aurora on one of their Saturday morning jaunts, two months after the wedding.

"Not yet," Aurora answered. "The clerks say there's hardly any turnover. It was that way in Ithaca. No reporter quit the whole time I worked there. I got my position only because a woman took sick leave and then died of ovarian cancer."

"A most unfortunate way to land a job."

"Certainly."

"Do you regret giving up your position to move here with Martin?"

"Oh, no, no."

They had set out later than usual that morning, after dawdling at the farmers' market to select green beans and tomatoes for canning, and already the August sun was beastly hot. They were both perspiring like navvies, and Lillian was panting. At fifty-nine, she had a right to pant, for she was a quarter century older than Aurora, who seemed never to get winded. They kept up a good pace, except when they passed by playgrounds or the swimming pool in Bryan Park, where Aurora slowed up to look at children.

As they paused to drink at a fountain in the park near the kiddy swings, Lillian posed a question she had been turning over for some time. "Until there's an opening in the courts, what would you think of trying your hand at woodworking?"

"In your shop?"

"It's just a notion. If you'd rather not—"

"Oh, I'd love to," Aurora said. "Only I don't know the first thing about it."

"Then let me teach you."

The offer hung there for a moment while Aurora watched a squealing youngster glide back and forth on a swing. Then she turned her shining eyes on Lillian and said, "That would be wonderful."

★

The canning and pickling suffered that fall, because Aurora and Lillian both preferred working in the shop to working in the kitchen. Some afternoons, while gluing up bookshelves or truing the legs on a table, they lost track of time, and Martin brought them supper, after having fed Solomon. As he came in the door, Lillian would glance at the clock, exclaim at the hour, and wonder aloud what sort of wives would leave their poor starving husbands to fend for themselves. Martin would only laugh, give them both kisses, deposit the sacks of Tibetan or Thai or Indian takeout, and slip away to his work.

During the early weeks of her apprenticeship, Aurora vacuumed up sawdust, put away tools, learned to identify the various woods by their grains and smells, and watched Lillian's every move. Gradually she began working with the safest machines, the sanders and drill press, then she graduated to the planer and router, and by winter she was using the band saw, table saw, and lathe. Lillian showed her how to measure with precision, how to use her fingers to judge increments too subtle even for rulers, how to sharpen blades. She taught her the art of finishing with linseed oil, varnish, and beeswax. She demonstrated how to choose a board from the stacks of cherry, walnut, maple, hickory, poplar, oak and other woods that filled one end of the shop.

Aurora agreed to accept a monthly check only because Lillian insisted on paying her. Even if her daughter-in-law had not been so quick to learn, so diligent, so deft, Lillian would gladly have paid for the pleasure of her company. As they worked, they listened to jazz and classical music on the radio, or to reggae, ballads, and blues on CDs. Aurora had taken to wearing her hair coiled in a braid, like Lillian, to keep it out of the machinery, but the wild curls often came undone, and then Lillian brushed them out, lingering more than she needed to, and braided them anew. No matter how busy they were, they stopped work at midmorning and midafternoon to have tea. They laughed a lot. When listening to the news, they second-guessed the reporters, quarreled with the politicians, hooted at the military apologists, scoffed at the celebrities.

One day they were assembling the frame of a desk, squaring the joints and applying clamps, when the president came on the radio. They booed as soon as they heard his snarly voice, and they booed more loudly when he threatened to launch yet another Middle Eastern war, this time in Iran, where most of Solomon's relatives still lived. Lillian knew that taunts would not deter the warmongers in Washington, yet it buoyed her spirits to share this moment of indignation with Aurora. After the news gave way to a Chopin nocturne, Lillian told her about Solomon's rules for wives, including the taboo on talking about politics and religion.

"Really?" Aurora said. "Our sweet Solomon? He seems so mild."

"The stroke has mellowed him, and so has his stubborn wife." Lillian tapped a corner of the desk with a rubber mallet, squinting at the joint with one eye closed. "Have you visited the British Museum?"

"I've never set foot outside the United States."

"Well, I must take you to London one of these days, if only to show you the Assyrian rooms in the British Museum. They feature stone reliefs of a king slaughtering lions, reviewing a parade of captives, and receiving booty from military triumphs—all designed to show what a mighty warrior he is, with his bulging biceps and curly beard. The only women in sight are slaves. Solo-

mon often invoked that tyrant as the male ideal." She gave another tap with the mallet. "He would have been a bullying old
patriarch if I'd knuckled under."

"Martin's not like that at all."

"Thank heavens, no."

"He talks with me about the news, about ideas. He takes me
around to see his projects. He's always asking me what I'm working on, what I'm reading, what I think of this or that. I worry I
don't think enough, or maybe I'm not smart enough."

"You've no shortage of brains," Lillian reassured her. "You just
haven't read as many books as Martin has."

"I've read plenty, but without much rhyme or reason. We
didn't own any books when I was growing up. I got to visit the
library only on Sundays, when my mother would go to collect
an armload of mysteries. The covers of her books were too gory
for me, but I had no idea what else to read. So I'd browse along
the aisles until some title grabbed me—*Lost Lovers, Broken Vows,
In the Dictator's Bunker*—and I'd pull it off the shelf, take it home,
and plow right through, even when I realized it was trash." Aurora paused to concentrate as she tightened a clamp. "There's a
lot I didn't know, or have time to learn. My life was pretty much
school, work, and sleep. The same for my mom, I guess, but without the school. She wanted to be an artist, but she gave that up
when she married my dad. I hardly ever heard her say a word
about politics or books or, really, about anything except what had
to be done next. Not because my dad lorded it over her, I don't
think. She just didn't have any spare breath."

This was the first time Aurora had volunteered information
about her parents, and so Lillian proceeded cautiously. "What
was it like being an only child?"

"Lonely, the way you'd expect. Mom tried for more kids. She
miscarried a few times, but she never could get another baby."

Lillian wiped a spot of glue with a damp rag. "She must have doted on you all the more."

"She might have, if she hadn't been so worn out. She was always in the kitchen."

"Did you help her with cooking?"

"Sometimes, but I was usually waiting tables, or sweeping up the place. And then I had homework to do."

"Your parents ran a restaurant?"

Aurora was slow to respond, skimming her hand over the desktop. And then, as if having made a decision, she said, "They ran a bar. Still do, I suppose. A place called the Iron Ore Tavern." She glanced warily at Lillian. "I never told you, because I was afraid you'd be upset to learn your son had married the daughter of a barkeeper."

"Why should that bother me, as the daughter of a carpenter?"

"Carpentry's a higher calling than my dad's work. The bar was pretty sleazy. Mom tried to spruce it up by hanging her paintings on the walls, but it was like putting lipstick on a pig. I still have nightmares about that place."

Lillian waited a few breaths before asking, "Was this in Ithaca?"

"No. In Cleveland."

"So that's where you grew up?"

"That's where I was a child. I did my growing up after I left."

The drop in Aurora's voice was a sign to Lillian not to ask any more questions just now. So she put on a recording of Scott Joplin ragtime pieces, and the two of them moved around the workshop to a syncopated beat.

*

Heartland Fine Woodworking occupied an old limestone mill that Martin had renovated, one of his first jobs after returning to Bloomington. His return had been precipitated by Solomon's stroke—"You'll be needing help, Mother," he pointed out when she delivered the news over the phone—but Lillian sensed he was glad of an excuse to set up practice in his hometown. Simone was not glad about the move, to say the least. She considered the local theatre companies unworthy of her talents. She never set foot in Lillian's shop, and regarded furniture making as a hobby rather than a craft. But Simone's discontent and eventual departure for Hollywood were old history, easily forgotten now that Lillian had a new daughter-in-law who hummed along with the saw blades and whirling belts.

The shop was on the south side of town, near the high school where Martin had graduated and where Yaffa had completed her one and only year. The mill, which had shipped stone to building sites from coast to coast, was itself constructed of limestone, with walls two feet thick, as solid as a fortress. Designed to house giant machines and handle ten-ton quarry blocks, the space was much larger than Lillian required. The windows were set high in the walls, as in the clerestory of a cathedral. Steel roof trusses arched overhead, stout enough for a railroad trestle. The cavernous space was hard to heat in winter, and in summer, when the windows were opened, pigeons and swallows flew in and out.

Martin offered to fix up a smaller building, or even to design a new one—quite a concession from an architect who believed that existing buildings should be restored and put to good use before any more were constructed. But Lillian preferred to stay in the old mill, with its reminders of skillful work. In carrying out the renovation, Martin had salvaged blueprints from various limestone jobs—a portico for a statehouse, columns for a bank, window tracery for a church, the façade of a museum, an angel for a cemetery—and these he mounted on the walls, alongside graffiti where men had scribbled calculations or jokes. The thresholds in doorways had been worn hollow by the passing of boots. Rusty spots on the floor marked where huge saws and lathes and planers had once stood. Lillian's own machines were small by comparison, and the dust she made from sawing wood smelled sweeter than the dust from stone. Yet she felt a kinship with the old cutters and carvers who had labored here for so many years.

★

In January, Aurora finally received an offer of a court reporter's job, from a neighboring county. When she confessed uncertainty over accepting it, Lillian asked, "Isn't this what you've been waiting for?"

"It's what I've been trained to do."

"Well then?"

They were staining balusters as they talked, quiet work that allowed them to remove their ear protectors. Still, there were long pauses between Lillian's questions and Aurora's replies.

"You know," Aurora said at last, "in all the years I worked in the courts, I never laughed. I barely looked up from the keyboard. I tried to hear only the words, so I could get them right, and tried not to follow the stories, which were always so angry or sad."

"I suppose people usually end up in court because someone's been hurt," Lillian offered.

"That's exactly it." Aurora dipped her brush in the stain, held it poised above the wood. "I sit there all day recording quarrels and betrayals. Cruel things, like teenagers mugging old ladies and people starving their dogs and mothers leaving babies in hot cars with the windows rolled up. Drug dealing, knifing, drunken fights that end with gunfire. Husbands beat their wives and wives cheat on their husbands. People get fired and lose their insurance. People sue one another just to be mean. Drunks plow into kids waiting for the school bus. And I type it all down without knowing who's lying and who's telling the truth."

Lillian said quietly, "That must be terribly wearing."

"It is. It really is."

To fill the silence that followed, Lillian removed the last of the balusters from the lathe and compared it to the original provided by Martin. He had ordered seven of them, to replace those missing from a stairway in a farmhouse he was restoring. Although her hands were occupied, Lillian's mind was on her daughter-in-law, who seemed like a skittish creature—a coyote or a fox—that might run and hide if looked at too directly.

Aurora set down her brush and ran her fingers along the freshly-turned baluster. "As smooth as a baby's bottom," she murmured. Suddenly the corners of her mouth turned down. "My mom used to say that."

"Do you miss her sometimes?"

Aurora shook her head. "I can't talk about her."

"Well then, we won't. It was rude of me to ask." Lillian rubbed the wood with a tack cloth in preparation for staining.

After taking several rapid breaths, Aurora said, "What I really want to do is go on working here with you."

Lillian kept her eyes on the wood and her voice calm. "You do?"

"Could I?"

"Why, of course, dear, of course. But are you sure?"

"I'm sure. That is, if you really need the help."

"Oh, my word, you can see how I need your help. Orders are backing up. And Martin alone keeps me more than busy fabricating parts for his decrepit buildings."

"They are decrepit, aren't they?" Aurora squeezed out a laugh. "They're wrecks, really, when he starts in on them."

"Which makes it all the more stunning how he brings them back to life."

"Yes, I've seen that in photos. Before and after, and all the stages in between."

Now Lillian gazed openly at her daughter-in-law, who seemed less guarded, her face brightened by hope. It was a look Yaffa used to get when some new therapy promised relief from seizures.

The resemblance prompted Lillian to say, "I suppose I deserve some of the blame for Martin's devotion to fixing up wrecks."

"How so?"

"I couldn't bear to stay in the house where Yaffa died. Every room was saturated with memories of her. So I badgered Solomon into moving, and the only place near campus with character and a low enough price was a shambles—an old Victorian that had been carved into apartments for students, who had abused it for years."

"You mean the house you're in now?"

"Yes, that one."

"But it's gorgeous."

"That's because Martin and I restored it, from the foundations to the weathervane. It's what he did on weekends during high school while other kids were playing soccer or cruising the mall. It's why he stayed in Bloomington for college. For me, the work was a way of healing. I couldn't save my daughter, but I could save that battered house. For Martin it began, I suspect, as a way of caring for me. But it clearly got into his blood."

Aurora frowned. "What do you think he'll say if I turn down the reporter's job?"

"He'll want you to do whatever makes you happy."

The effect of Aurora's sudden smile was like a lamp coming on in a window at night. "Being here with you makes me as happy as anything I've ever done."

*

Over the course of that winter and spring, as they worked in the shop or sipped tea or took their morning walks, Aurora disclosed more of her story to Lillian. Her mother grew up in Kentucky, her father in Michigan. They met in Detroit, where her mother went to study art and her father went to sign up for the

Army after getting laid off from the Ford assembly plant. Neither
knew a soul in Cleveland, where the Army discharged her father
after he'd ruined his back, but they stayed there anyway. They
bought the tavern with his disability check. He always wore a
brace, but you'd never have guessed it from the way he broke up
fights and threw drunken louts into the street. Her father served
drinks; her mother cooked; and Aurora, when not in school,
waited tables and mopped floors and cleaned toilets. Once she
was a teenager, she also helped attract customers, according to
her father. Not that she was pretty, by her own estimate; she
was just fresh, like any girl at that age, and men liked having her
around. There were never quite enough customers, which is why
her parents couldn't afford to hire any help.

Aurora got mainly B's in school. She could have done better if she'd had more zip left over for studying. But by the time
she climbed upstairs to the apartment after the bar closed, with
maybe seven hours before she had to get up again for school, she
could barely keep her eyes open. In her early teens, she began
wondering what a girl with no money and a report card full of B's
could ever do for a living. For a long while after moving to Ithaca,
the answer seemed to be waitressing. She had been working at
the court less than a year when Martin showed up.

Lillian already knew from Martin how the Jack Haymaker
song had moved him to seek her out. What she learned now, from
Aurora, was how close their first evening together had come to
being their last. Aurora had thought him firmly married to Simone, and even when she learned that the marriage had ended and
the starlet had decamped for Hollywood, she would not let herself believe that this handsome man, this Cornell graduate, this
architect, could possibly be interested in her. Then over supper he
asked questions about her life, patiently, one after another, really
listening to her answers, and he opened up about his own life,

including his heartbreak over Yaffa's early death. It was the most intimate conversation she'd ever had with a man. Walking back with him to her rooming house, she allowed herself a little flame of hope.

Still, had they simply said goodnight at her door, they might never have seen one another again, Aurora predicted. If Martin had suggested another date, she might have said no. For in spite of the pleasant evening, she couldn't believe he genuinely cared for her. How could he? They scarcely knew one another. Their meeting at the market had seemed to her like a random collision. Then he showed her the album, with its song about her and its disturbing picture from the cemetery. She snatched the album and fled indoors, intending to smash it and tear up the photograph. Who was this Jack Haymaker, who dared violate her privacy? In her room, she tugged the CD from the case, laid it on the floor, grabbed a stone paperweight, and lifted her arm. But there among the titles on the silvery disc was "Aurora's Song," and she had to hear what it revealed about her. So she put it on to play. The first time through, the song merely angered her, the way it pried into her life, getting some things right, others wrong; the second time through she began to hear its tenderness; the third time through she sensed it was a gift. It was as though, after hiding for so long, she had at last been found.

Eventually, she turned off the music and thought of Martin, who would be downcast, certain that he had offended her. But he had only caught her off guard. Now, instead of feeling exposed, she felt unburdened, not because this musician had been moved by her grief, but because Martin had. She wanted to tell him so. But surely by now he would be back in the hotel, dismayed by the way the evening had turned out. Unless—she thought—unless he had stayed on the porch, hoping she might come back down after listening to the song, hoping she might understand he had meant no harm, wishing to make amends. On the slender chance that he was such a man, a man who would wait, she stole quietly down the stairs, opened the front door, and there he was, sitting in a rocker, his head silhouetted against the lit-up street. She knew, then, even before she laid a hand on his shoulder, even before he tilted his face up to her, that here was a man she could trust.

Lillian had her own copy of the *River Blessing* album, and she knew that the Aurora of the song had become pregnant by a sailor who abandoned her and died at sea, leaving the girl to raise the child alone. What portion of the song was taken from life and what was made up, Lillian could not guess. Nor could she guess why the song and picture had inspired Martin to seek out this woman whom he had known only slightly during his graduate school days. Whatever the causes might be, Lillian rejoiced in the outcome.

★

Now and again Aurora would apologize for rattling on about herself, and would invite stories from Lillian, especially ones about Martin and Yaffa as children.

"Do you often think about Yaffa?" she asked one afternoon over tea.

"Nearly every day," Lillian replied.

"Is it always painful?"

"Not always. We had many happy times. She was a spirited girl. A lot like you, really." Lillian stirred honey into her tea. "But there's an underlying sadness that never goes away. A sense of incompleteness."

"Would it be the same if Martin was the one who'd died?"

Lillian pondered the question before saying, "Of course I'd be heartbroken to lose Martin. But, no, it wouldn't be the same.

I can't explain the difference, really. A mother and daughter are close in a way that a mother and son never can be. You do so many things together because you're female, I suppose. You understand one another's bodies. You face the same pressures and fears out there in the world. You're allies, in a way."

One day in June, they were sitting on a bench beside the playground at Harmony School, watching children clamber over the monkey bars. Whenever a child neared the top, Lillian tensed, her body retaining the fear that a seizure might lead to a fall.

"I can't get over their energy," Aurora said. "Just look at them."

"Yes." Lillian smiled to mask her unease. "If we hooked them up to a dynamo, they could light the whole neighborhood."

Aurora watched the children in silence. She and Lillian had eaten mulberries picked from a tree beside the schoolyard, and their hands and lips were stained purple. The color made Aurora's mouth look bruised, which unsettled Lillian.

Without taking her eyes from the children, Aurora asked, "Have you ever done anything unforgivable?"

"Unforgivable?"

"Something you can't undo."

Lillian thought carefully how to answer, for she could hear the tremor in her daughter-in-law's voice. She recalled the Greek word for sin in the New Testament—*hamartia*—which meant "to miss the mark." Who hadn't missed the mark? Not just once but many times? You could only hope that as you matured your aim would improve. How could you fully know, especially as a young person, even what you were aiming at? At length, she said, "I've certainly done things I deeply regret. For example, I neglected Martin terribly when he was a boy, pouring all my care into Yaffa. I've done things I'm ashamed of. But I don't believe I've ever done anything truly unforgivable."

"Suppose you'd hurt somebody so bad that nothing you did could make up for the hurting? You could never be forgiven for that, could you?"

"Maybe the person you hurt won't forgive, but you could still forgive yourself."

"I can't. I've tried." Aurora's eyes glistened. "If I believed in God, maybe God could pardon me. And I tried that, too, all those years in Quaker meeting. I loved those people, so kind and gentle. I loved the silence. But I just couldn't convince myself there's some power we can pray to who'll blot out the cruel things we do."

"If there's no power to blot out our cruelties, maybe there's no power keeping track of them."

"The persons you hurt keep track."

Curling an arm across Aurora's shoulders, Lillian decided to say what she had long suspected. "You had a child, didn't you?"

Aurora looked at her, bit her lip, and looked away. She nodded silently.

So Lillian went on. "And you lost her?"

"Him. It was a boy. No, I didn't lose him." Aurora's voice came out raw and hoarse. "I abandoned him. I left him with my parents." Now the tears were coursing down her cheeks, but she did not wipe them away, nor did she cease to watch the children swarming over the monkey bars as she spoke.

Lillian took a moment to compose herself. "How old were you?"

"Sixteen. My son would be seventeen now, practically grown up, and I don't know a thing about him. I've never had the courage to find out."

Wrapping both arms around her daughter-in-law, Lillian rocked her gently. "Is that why you're afraid to have any more children?"

Aurora yielded to the embrace, turning on the bench and pressing her cheek against Lillian's throat. "I had my chance, and I blew it."

"Who says you get only one chance? You were a girl then. You're grown now, with a husband who adores you, who won't ever leave you. Martin would be a marvelous father. He'd help you in every way."

"I know, I know."

Lillian could feel their two heartbeats in her chest, and could not tell which was her own. "What would it take for you to forgive yourself?"

"I'd have to know my son is happy. That he doesn't hate me." Aurora paused. "I'd have to tell my parents how sorry I am, especially my mother." Again she paused.

"What else?"

Aurora drew in a long, ragged breath. "I'd have to prove I can be a good mother."

"There's only one way of proving that."

"It's scary," Aurora whispered, her face warm and damp against Lillian's throat.

"Yes," Lillian murmured, stroking the unruly hair, which had come loose from its braid, hair so like Yaffa's, so full of life. "Yes, it has always been scary."

§ § §

Chapter Thirteen • June–July 2008

HARLAN

KATARINA MAINTAINED THAT IT WAS CRUEL to keep their knowledge of Aurora's whereabouts a secret from Nana and Papa. Yet Harlan thought it would be crueler to raise hopes of a reunion if it turned out that Aurora wanted nothing to do with them. It was easy to imagine that was the case, for he wanted nothing to do with Aurora. And how else could you interpret her silence? At any time since running away she could have phoned the tavern, could have sent letters, could have walked in the front door, if she'd wished to reconcile with her parents or learn how her son was getting along.

Even now, she could have found them easily enough, since the new owner of the tavern had Nana and Papa's phone number and forwarding address here at the farm. Contrary to Papa's theory, Aurora hadn't died. Whatever she might have struggled through in years past—poverty, depression, drugs, prison—today she was living in a university town, licensed as a court reporter, married to a man listed in the Bloomington Yellow Pages as an architect, and she herself was listed as a partner in a business called Heartland Fine Woodworking. To all appearances she was thriving. What could prevent her from contacting the family she had abandoned, except a determination to be shut of them forever? With a husband, and maybe with children, she had every reason to bury her youth as a barmaid, her teenage fling with Tommy, and her bastard son. All these years she had been creating a new identity for herself, as innocent as pie, like those Nazi war criminals who changed their names and started over in South America.

Grasping for some other explanation, Harlan imagined she might have lost her memory. Such things happened. A concussion, blood clot, or fever might blank out the past. He'd met a park ranger in Vermont who had forgotten his daughter's childhood after contracting Lyme disease from the bite of a tick. But Harlan had no sooner concocted his amnesia theory than he saw through it as a childish fantasy, one that would conclude with his mother opening the front door of her house to find him standing there, this grown son who was the spitting image of Tommy, whereupon the sight of him would suddenly restore her memory and she would rush forward to smother him in kisses. Harlan chose not to share this scenario with Katarina, who would have given him one of her indulgent smiles before waving it aside like a pesky fly.

In the scenario he found far more plausible, she would open the door a crack and peer at him, a gawky stranger on her porch, and when he announced who he was a look of horror would flash across her face and she would slam the door. If he imagined phoning first, she would answer, he would identify himself, and she would abruptly hang up. He could stand being rejected a second time, but he wouldn't let her break Nana's heart again, or Papa's. Better that they not know Aurora had been found. So his plan was to go have a look at her from a distance, careful to remain inconspicuous. He didn't know what he would be looking for, how he could tell whether it was safe to approach her. Against all likelihood, he still hoped to discover some impediment, aside from disdain, that could account for her long absence, some barrier that he alone could remove.

Katarina told him she doubted his amateur sleuthing would yield any such discovery, but she agreed to accompany him to Bloomington, if only to form her own impression of Aurora. What he told Nana and Papa was that he wanted to check out the environmental science program at Indiana University. They asked why he couldn't just go to Kent State and live at home, save the cost of board and room, and help them here on the farm. He assured them that KSU was his first choice, but he couldn't risk putting all his eggs in one basket, so he'd be applying to a few other colleges within a day's drive of home. Katarina played along with his ruse, but afterwards, in private, hardheaded as always, she scolded him for deceiving his grandparents.

★

Although Harlan was itching to go, he delayed long enough to set up a few jobs that Papa could tackle by himself, a strategy for keeping the old man occupied and off the bottle. Papa sniffed out the strategy, of course, since he had a nose for the slightest whiff of bossiness. He often said he'd gotten his fill of taking orders during his years in the Army and his decades behind the bar. Even in the bar, a pushy customer was likely to find himself back on the street sooner than planned. Harlan figured Papa would have walked into a fire if anybody—and especially Nana—had told him to stay out of it. Now, grumbling that he could keep busy without any instructions, Papa nonetheless tucked the list of jobs in the bib of his butterscotch-colored overalls, which he had taken to wearing since moving to the farm, and which made him look even more like a grizzly bear.

As for Nana, Harlan urged her to begin painting landscapes again; for years she had spoken of doing so just as soon as she had the time to spend and the countryside to look at. More than six months after the move, however, the only painting she had done was with roller and brush on the walls of the house. She always had an excuse for neglecting her art. The oils had dried up, she would say, or the easel was broken, or there were no stretchers for her canvas, or the house and garden needed tending. Harlan persuaded her to order fresh paints, which duly arrived by UPS, and he bought turpentine at the hardware store. He made half a dozen stretchers, in sizes she had specified, and he mended her easel. To allay her concern about chores, in the days before their departure he and Katarina weeded the garden and picked everything ripe, from beans to zucchinis, and they cleaned the house from basement to attic.

Lacking excuses, Nana prepared a canvas, set up the easel on the porch, and began sketching a view of the barn, pond, pastures, and hills. She was out there, brush in hand, studying the light, soon after dawn one morning in early July when Harlan began loading the pickup for the trip to Indiana. On seeing him, Nana exclaimed, "Oh my, you'll be wanting breakfast, just let me clean out this brush," but he told her to keep on painting, because Katarina already had omelets cooking and their lunches packed. When the meal was ready Nana said she would wait to eat with Papa but they should go on ahead, so Harlan and Katarina carried their plates to the porch and sat watching dawn flare simultaneously over the farm and over the canvas. Harlan noticed that Nana mixed in with the yellows and reds of her sunrise a range of greens and blues, surprising colors, and yet when he looked up from the canvas there they were in the sky.

"I hope he'll do okay while we're gone," Harlan said.

"Don't you worry about us," Nana replied, without turning away from her painting. "We'll manage fine. You have your own lives to lead."

Just then Papa shuffled onto the porch, a mug of coffee steaming in his fist, one strap of his overalls dangling, a white tuft of chest hair showing above the bib. "Ready to hit the road?"

"Just about," Harlan replied.

"Check the oil?"

"Yep. Oil, radiator, tires, everything."

"Back the day after tomorrow, you say?"

"That's the plan."

Papa took a sip of his coffee and grimaced. "This isn't going to be like that Marquette deal, where you said you'd be gone a few days and you stayed away two weeks?"

"Unless the truck breaks down, we'll be home Friday evening."

"Well, then, I won't run out of things to do." Papa fingered the pocket of his overalls where he had stuffed the list of jobs.

"I'll cut his feed if he loafs," Nana put in.

Papa wheezed out a laugh, a good sign. "See what I have to put up with, Katarina? Now don't you take after her, and go putting a harness on your man. Still, you'd better keep an eye on Harlan. Make sure he doesn't go swerving off the road looking at birds and butterflies."

"I will keep him on the straight and narrow," Katarina promised.

"You do that, honey," Papa said, and his eyes shone with undisguised affection, a look that Harlan himself had rarely inspired in the old man.

★

As soon as the pickup rolled from the gravel drive onto blacktop, Katarina nestled against the passenger door, pressed her cheek against the pillow she had brought along, noted that she had been wakened at an ungodly hour for this journey, and went to sleep. Harlan kept glancing away from the road to gaze at her, a sight more distracting than any bird or butterfly. In a month she'd be gone, and already he felt the ache of her absence. But right now she was here within reach, and it was all he could do to keep from laying a hand on her thigh, bare beneath the hem of her shorts.

He kept his hands on the wheel, following the river road to catch glimpses of the Red Hawk gliding along, its banks marked by the ivory branches of sycamores. Intent on studying the watershed, he followed a series of section-line roads and twisting two-lanes before reluctantly joining the traffic hurtling west on the gray slab of I-76. The day promised to be a scorcher. By the time they escaped from the snarl of Akron, the breeze flowing in through the open windows was already as warm as a sheep's breath. Katarina's forehead glistened, and wisps of hair fluttered around her face like stray thoughts. The Ford dated from an era when pickups were still designed as work vehicles rather than luxury chariots for suburbanites, so it lacked air-conditioning, and the heater, grown temperamental with age, occasionally switched on of its own accord. It did so as they neared Ashland, adding its hot breath to the sultry air. Harlan fiddled with every button and knob, to no avail, and finally shut it off by slamming his fist on the dashboard.

The noise startled Katarina, who jerked upright and looked about in alarm. "Did we hit an animal?"

"No, no. I was just arguing with the heater, and I believe it's come around to my point of view. Sorry to wake you."

She mumbled something, fluffed up the pillow, and drifted back to sleep.

Harlan added the heater to his mental list of things to fix. The truck also needed a ring job, as Uncle Cedar had pointed out while they were up in Marquette, saying he'd do it himself if things weren't so backed up at the garage. The old clunker was burning oil, and got only fifteen or sixteen miles per gallon, which was shameful on a planet warming up from the release of too much carbon dioxide. But even if Harlan had the money to buy a new truck, the smallest model he could rig with a camper shell likely wouldn't get much better mileage. How do you manage in this world without burning fossil fuel? The Amish farmed with horses and rode to town in buggies, and maybe he could learn to do the same. But a horse wouldn't carry you to the neighboring state, let alone to Sweden. So you either gave up traveling or you burned gas and cooked the Earth. Maybe one day he could install solar panels on the roof of the barn and set up a wind turbine and tool around in a biofuel truck. But all of that would have to wait until after he'd graduated from college and landed a job and saved up a pile of money—a pile that was sure to mount slowly on the salary of a conservation biologist. Every trail of thought led him into a briar patch of difficulties.

Meanwhile, Katarina snoozed and the lush terrain of central Ohio slid past in a green haze. He wanted to slow down so he could take in the countryside, but he was barely going fifty and if he went any slower a semi going eighty was liable to flatten them. So he kept the Ford chugging along as fast as he dared push it, well under the speed limit, a pace that should put them in Bloomington by mid-afternoon. He tried to imagine how he'd feel when he first caught sight of Aurora. Would he even recognize her, a woman thirteen years older than the one in Dr. Rosenthal's photograph?

*

Although Harlan had meant to avoid taking side trips, when he spotted a sign near Mansfield marking the exit for Malabar Farm State Park, he debated for only a moment before steering off the interstate. As a boy in the city dreaming about life in the

country, he had read several books about Malabar Farm, a place
he first thought of as imaginary, like Camelot or Narnia, but later
discovered was a patch of Earth you could actually visit. Only
he'd never been able to persuade Papa to drive down here on
one of those leisurely Sundays when the tavern was closed. The
chance of finally seeing the farm today was too good to pass up.

After a few turns they were winding along Pleasant Valley
Road, which lived up to its name, curving past wooded hills,
sloping pastures, sturdy barns, and gussied-up old houses. With
no semis tailgating him, Harlan slowed down to study the land
and listen for birdcalls. He could hear crows hollering from treetops, red-winged blackbirds ringing from the blowsy heads of
cattails, woodpeckers hammering, blue jays fussing, as well as a
few less raucous birds, including song sparrows, a yellowthroat,
and once—unusual for this time of day—a whippoorwill, which
made him laugh.

Wakened by his laughter, Katarina sat up, rubbing her eyes,
and peered out the window. "Are we in Indiana?"

"Not for a good ways yet. We're taking a little detour to look
at a place I read about as a boy. I'd forgotten about it until I saw a
sign back on the highway."

Harlan went on to describe how a writer named Louis Bromfield, who'd made a fortune from his novels and movie contracts,
was living in France in the 1930s, when Europe began to get ugly,
with Hitler and Mussolini spewing hate. So Bromfield decided to
move his family back to America. Instead of buying a mansion in
Manhattan or Beverly Hills or some other ritzy place, he bought a
farm here in Ohio, near where he'd grown up. Actually, he bought
three adjacent properties and combined them into one, which he
called Malabar Farm, and he began experimenting with ways to
improve agriculture. "One of his books is called *Pleasant Valley*,
and that's the name of the road we're driving on right now."

Katarina studied the rolling landscape, with its patchwork of forests and fields. "This could be Sweden."

"You think every pretty place looks like Sweden."

"No, really. This reminds me of Scania, the southern province where my grandparents farmed."

"What all did they grow?"

"Barley, wheat, oats. Hay for their cows. And potatoes, of course. Every Swedish farmer grows potatoes." She stared out the window, and her voice took on a melancholy tinge. "I spent every summer with my grandparents until they grew too old to farm, and then they came to live with us. They could have stayed on the farm, if my parents had let me go look after them. I begged my father to keep the land so I could move there when I finished school, but he sold it even before my grandparents died, saying he wouldn't let me waste my life grubbing in the dirt."

"You wanted to farm?"

"Is it so strange? Because I am a girl?"

"No, I just thought you wanted to be an interpreter and bring about world peace."

Katarina released a peevish huff and crossed arms over her chest and turned away from him.

"Hey," he said, "I was joking."

Without looking at him, she said, "Sometimes you seem too American."

"What's that supposed to mean?"

"You do not know how much pain there is in the world."

Harlan thought of several angry things to say, but he held off, wondering if she could be right, not only about him but also about his country. She often had that effect on him, shining a light on some patch of his ignorance. Never having missed a meal, he hadn't realized that more than a billion human beings were going hungry until she pointed him to a UN report. She was the one who told him that while some three thousand people had been murdered by terrorists in America on September 11th, 2001—certainly an outrage—around the world five times as many children died every day from malnutrition and tainted water. Fifteen thousand children, day after day after day.

They were both silent as they climbed from the truck outside the visitors' center at Malabar Farm. On a pole near the parking lot there was a large nesting box for martins, and the purple-backed birds flitted in and out of their holes, chattering as they fed their chicks. Pausing to watch them, Katarina broke the chilly silence. "Nature's ways are so beautiful."

Human ways can be beautiful, as well, Harlan thought, surveying the carefully tended buildings and fields. He would gladly have spent a day here, or a week, meandering over the nine hundred acres, checking out the sawmill, the sugarbush, the aviary, the old woods, the paddocks and pastures, but he figured they could spare just enough time to see either the main barn or the thirty-two-room Bromfield house. He chose the barn, while Katarina opted for a tour of the mansion.

Afterwards, they compared notes on what they had found most impressive. For Harlan, it was the barn's interior, with post-and-beam construction, the pegged joints creaking in the midday sun, windows admitting slants of light through louvered shutters, and neatly tapered rafters arrayed like ribs beneath the metal roof. He was amused to see plaster owls perched on crossbeams while real swallows and mourning doves, unfazed, perched nearby. Katarina was intrigued that the sprawling house, built in a few months, had been designed to look as though it had accumulated its thirty-two rooms over a couple of centuries. While the Bromfields lived there, she told Harlan, they had often been visited by celebrities, including Lauren Bacall and Humphrey Bogart, who had been married in the big house and had spent their honeymoon on Malabar Farm.

"Wait," Harlan said. "Don't tell me. They're movie stars, right?"

"Very good."

"They did musicals, with lots of dancing?"

Katarina produced a laugh, to signal that she had gotten over their earlier tiff. His ignorance of cinema, as well as television, rock and roll, fashion, electronic gadgets, social networking, and nearly every other aspect of pop culture was a steady source of comedy between them. She often teased him about being a time-traveler from the 19th century.

"You're thinking of Ginger Rogers and Fred Astaire," she pointed out.

"I'm thinking no such thing. I'm thinking it's lucky I don't have a million bucks, or I'd fix up our farm on the Red Hawk River to look as spiffy as this one, and then we'd be overrun with celebrities coming to visit us."

She kissed him, there on the walk out front of the mansion, while other visitors streamed past. Then she hooked her arm through his and said she wanted to show him a spot she had glimpsed from an upstairs window.

"We need to get on the road," he objected.

"Come. It will only take a minute."

They ambled downhill, past a feedlot where a dozen or so Black Angus cattle and a pair of Clydesdale draft horses drowsed in the heat, past a scurry of chickens and a gaggle of goats, past waving blue wands of chicory and white doilies of Queen Anne's lace, on down to a pond filled with wind-rippled images of sapphire sky. Leaning on the railing of a platform that jutted over the water, they watched rings form where fish rose to nab floating insects. Every now and again a bullfrog croaked.

After a spell, Katarina asked, "Do you remember?"

"I sure do," Harlan answered.

Neither one needed to say: the pond at Black Bear Farm.

*

Because of the detour, it was late afternoon when they approached Bloomington through forested hills. Beyond the slew of billboards they rolled past on their way into the city, the roadsides were vibrantly green, and so was the courthouse square, with its lawn weighed down by war memorials, and so was Kinsey Avenue, which tunneled beneath a canopy of branches. At the address on Kinsey where, according to the directory, Aurora lived with her husband, Harlan pulled to the curb before a two-story limestone house, which was tile-roofed, copper-guttered, many-gabled, tricked out with balconies, and set well back from the street. A fanlight arched above the front door, which was flanked by carved stone panels. At one end there was a small greenhouse, brimming with vegetation, and at the other end a patio furnished with sleek wooden tables and chairs. Neatly trimmed hedges framed beds of flowers in the yard, and the yard itself was bounded by an ornate iron fence. In the driveway sat a Volvo station wagon, not the old boxy kind but a sporty new model.

Harlan parked across the street and a few doors down from Aurora's house, a spot offering an unobstructed view of her place as well as shade under the largest pin oak he had ever seen. The tree must have measured nearly four feet in diameter at chest height. If he hadn't been intent on lying low, he would have gone out and stretched a tape measure around the trunk.

"Now what?" Katarina asked.

"Now we keep watch."

"And we are looking for what exactly?"

"I want to see what kind of life she has."

"You think we will discover that from here?"

"Pretend we're on a stakeout." He slid his birding binoculars from the dashboard and handed them to her.

Katarina squinted through the binoculars. "Her car shows that she appreciates the quality of Swedish engineering. Ah, and it is from my father's factory."

"How can you tell?"

"I can see his fingerprints on the hood."

She was trying to lift his mood, but he resisted. "What else do you notice?"

"I see that your mother likes flowers, but she does not like curtains, for her windows are bare. Downstairs, I see an antique lamp resting on a marble table, and upstairs I see a bouquet of zinnias in a lovely glass vase."

"You didn't mention that everything about the place reeks of money."

"True, it is a nice house."

"It's a palace. She's landed in the clover." Realizing that Katarina would require a translation, he added, "She's done all right for herself."

"And you resent that?"

"It burns me up. Think how Nana and Papa have lived all these years, hand to mouth. She could have made things easier for them."

"Well, sizzle away, if you like." Katarina handed him the binoculars. "Here, you play the detective. I will resume my study of your maddening language." From her backpack she took out her textbook on American slang. Instead of reading, however, she fanned herself with the book. "It's beastly hot. In Sweden there are laws against so much heat." She rolled up her T-shirt, baring her stomach.

Harlan ran a hand across her damp midriff. "Why don't you go find someplace with air-conditioning? There's bound to be cafés this close to the university."

"I still say we should just go ring the doorbell."

"We're not going to ring the doorbell. End of story. Now va-moose, find some place to cool off. Meet me here in a couple of hours."

"Vamoose," she repeated. "From the Spanish, meaning to hurry away." She peeled her thighs from the seat with a ripping sound and climbed out of the truck, still clutching her book. "You have the head of a bull," she muttered.

"Bull-headed, is the way to say it."

"Very well, you are bull-headed." She slammed the door and stepped onto the sidewalk.

"Katarina."

She wheeled about. "What?"

"You might not want to show so much of your belly to the college boys."

She yanked the shirt down, tucked it into her shorts, and stalked away.

Harlan watched her go until she disappeared around a corner. Soon he would be watching her disappear down a concourse at the Cleveland airport. The prospect made him squirm in the seat, as he used to toss in bed when the prospect of his own death gripped him in childhood.

He forced his attention back to the street. Students moseyed by on the sidewalk, lugging backpacks, occasionally chatting with one another, more often talking on phones or thumbing messages onto their tiny screens. Wires protruded from their ears, pouring music into their skulls, setting their heads bobbing like windup toys. Didn't they ever long for quiet? Most of the walkers older than college age were pushing strollers or loafing along with dogs. Despite the withering heat, a few joggers loped past. Nobody took much notice of Harlan sitting there in his ancient pickup. Still, he hunched down in the seat, leaving himself a clear bead on the house, then pulled out the book he had saved for this trip, *Crossing to Safety,* a Wallace Stegner novel that was set partly in Vermont. Before he began reading, he glanced at the cemetery photo, which he was using as a bookmark. He took in the image this way in small doses, like sips of venom that could immunize him against sympathy. Thinking of his mother's hurt made it harder for him to hold onto his own. Then he tucked the picture away in the back pages, and Stegner's words conjured up a mountain landscape, blurring his view of the tree-lined street.

Traffic here was thin compared to what he remembered from Cleveland. There were almost as many bicycles as cars. Every few minutes a bus groaned by, and once a police cruiser passed, followed by an ambulance and a fire engine, all with sirens blaring. In the lull that followed, he could hear robins cranking up for their evening serenades.

As the dinner hour approached, screen doors clattered and a few lights came on elsewhere in the block, but nothing stirred around his mother's house. Then a UPS truck stopped out front, flashers blinking, and the deliveryman jogged up the walk with a package, which he placed on the stoop; he rang the doorbell, and without waiting he jogged back to the truck and roared away. Harlan was watching to see if someone would come to the door when a white van, with HEARTLAND FINE WOODWORKING emblazoned on the side, turned into the driveway and parked behind the Volvo. His pulse quickened as the driver's door opened and a woman emerged, tall and slim, dressed in blue jeans and khaki shirt, a cloth cap shading her face. Even through binoculars he couldn't make out her features. She opened the door to the back seat and reached inside; in a moment she stood up and turned around, holding a dark-haired little girl in her arms. The child grabbed the woman's cap and snatched it off, and the woman, laughing, gave a brisk shake of her head, releasing a profusion of red curls that tumbled over her shoulders. The face she turned toward Harlan, happier than in any of his grandparents' pictures, was unmistakable. It was his mother, this laughing woman, hugging her daughter, setting the child down on the stoop and collecting the package, opening the front door of her posh house, vanishing inside to her perfect life.

★

Harlan was all for driving back to Ohio that night, having seen enough to feel certain his mother would be appalled if he showed up on her doorstep. Making no effort to mask her vexation, Katarina persuaded him to stay at least another hour, so they could eat their picnic supper in a park she'd found just a few blocks from Aurora's house. She had come upon the park on her way back from a coffeehouse named Soma, where, in blessedly chilled air, she had read about colorful American slang while young people at nearby tables, dressed mainly in black, conversed in language as drab as their clothing.

When she and Harlan were settled at a table in the park, under a cedar-shingled pavilion between a walking trail and a children's play area, she said with forced cheerfulness, "So you have a sister."

"A half sister," he muttered.

"Why so glum? Shouldn't this make you happy?"

He considered for a moment before saying, "Happy for the girl, yes. I don't have anything against her."

"How old do you think she is?"

"She was little enough to carry in one arm. Like a sack of potatoes." The scene of Aurora's return home replayed itself in Harlan's head. "When do kids start talking?"

"Eighteen months or so."

"Well, it looked like she was talking a blue streak, and when she got down on her feet she scampered off."

"That sounds more like a two-year-old." Katarina took out the cheese sandwiches, apples, sliced carrots, and potato salad she had packed in a cooler that morning. "Your mother must have her hands full, if she's looking after a toddler and a husband, helping to run a business, and keeping a house going."

"Real full, all right." He unwrapped a sandwich, but made no move to eat it. "The last thing she needs is a visit from her bastard son."

"That isn't what I mean," Katarina objected. "I mean you should make allowances—how do you say?—cut her some slack."

"She's had twenty years of slack. Looks like she's made out just fine."

"Do you assume they were easy, those twenty years?"

"I know what they were like for my grandparents and me."

"But what about for Aurora?"

"Why do you take up her side?"

"Because all you feel is your own pain."

"In case you forgot, I didn't abandon her. She abandoned me."

"And you must cling to that?"

They argued more and more heatedly, neither one inclined to eat, lowering their voices only when joggers or walkers passed by on the paved trail. At length Katarina said if he was determined to be miserable she was wasting her breath, and they fell into stony silence.

Squeals arose from the playground, where children were scooting down slides, climbing through labyrinths of brightly colored plastic, careening back and forth on swings. The clank of steel on steel rang from a horseshoe pitch nearby. From down the slope came the shouts of boys racing and leaping on a basketball court, their skin gleaming with sweat. Farther away, a Little League game had begun, the infielders chattering to the pitcher, parents yelling encouragement. Harlan felt cut off from all this exuberance. He pushed his plate away.

"The food will spoil in this heat," Katarina said.

He shrugged, and her lips drew tight. She began putting the food away, her motions shaky with anger. The sight unclamped his mouth. "Look, sweetheart, I'm sorry," he said. "I don't know what I was hoping for, but whatever it was I didn't find it." When she didn't reply, he grasped her elbow and tried pulling her close.

She jerked loose from his grip. "In three weeks I leave, and we do nothing but fight."

"It's not between you and me. It's between me and my past."

"Yes, and the past is devouring you."

The remark banged around in his head while Katarina finished packing away the food. When she slammed the cooler shut, he stood up to grab it from her before she could set off with it toward the truck. Then he quickly sat back down, for at that moment Aurora came walking by the pavilion along the blacktop path, not ten feet away. She was holding the leash of a golden retriever while the little girl trotted alongside, kicking a miniature soccer ball, and a bearded man, who must have been the husband, Martin, followed along pushing an empty stroller.

Harlan squeezed Katarina's knee under the table, hard, and when she glowered at him he nodded in the direction of the passing family. "There she is."

They both watched as Aurora tied the dog by its leash to a post, and then as she accompanied Martin and the toddler through a gate into the playground, where parents and grandparents kept vigil as children frolicked. The little girl, black-haired and olive-skinned like her father, stood shyly just inside the gate, holding her soccer ball. She scanned the play area, as if searching for a friend, then she gave a shout, handed the ball to her father, and ran up to a boy who was digging in the sand with a toy shovel. She plopped down and joined in the digging. Aurora and Martin strolled after her, arms around one another's waists, quietly talking.

As if in sympathy, Katarina's arm looped around Harlan's waist and she leaned her head against his shoulder. "Do you begrudge her this?"

Harlan said nothing, eyes fixed on his mother, who smiled at something Martin had said, or perhaps at her daughter's manifest glee. Aurora would be thirty-six, and although she was still slender, she had matured into a woman's body. Bearing two children would do that, he supposed. In the photograph of her at Tommy's grave, she had looked fragile and distraught, as if she'd never be able to rise. But now she looked fit, perhaps from making furniture or whatever she did at the woodworking firm, perhaps merely from managing a house and lugging a child. And she also looked happy, radiant, her red hair tossing in the breeze, her face animated by pleasure, her lips quickly forming words.

"I don't know what I feel," he said at last.

"Would you prefer that she be miserable?"

He knew what Katarina wanted to hear, so he said, "No." But "Yes" might have been equally true.

"That's a start."

Katarina began humming one of her Swedish melodies. He could feel the vibrations through his chest. So long as she hummed and so long as Aurora stood there in the playground looking blissful, he felt no desire to move. His mother's life couldn't really be perfect; it would have shadows invisible to him. But from what he could glimpse, it was a good life, full to the brim. Like it or not, she would have to find room in it for Nana and Papa, who would barge in as soon as they heard where she was. But she wouldn't need to make space in that life for a son.

By the time he reached this conclusion, Aurora was putting her daughter in the stroller, where the girl protested loudly, reluctant to go home, and Martin was untying the leash of the sad-eyed dog. Aurora placed the soccer ball in her daughter's lap, and the little girl, distracted, began tossing it up and catching it. As the family passed by the picnic shelter, the ball deflected off the child's hands, bounced on the ground, and rolled beneath the table where Harlan and Katarina were sitting. Harlan froze, but Katarina roused herself, picked up the ball, and carried it over to the child, who accepted it while gazing up with large dark eyes.

"What do you say to the nice lady, Olivia?" Aurora prompted.

"Thank you," the child said in a piping voice.

"You're most welcome," Katarina replied, and walked back to the table.

Smiling after her, Aurora glanced at Harlan, locked eyes with him for a moment, and then suddenly the smile gave way to a startled, even stricken look. She abruptly turned away and hurried along the path, so the wheels of the stroller jounced on the uneven blacktop, provoking fresh cries from Olivia, while Martin and the dog were left trailing behind.

*

Not having seen the expression on Aurora's face, Katarina thought Harlan was imagining things. "It is because you fear being shunned."

Harlan would have sworn that his mother's face had been contorted by panic or disgust. But maybe Katarina was right; maybe he had seen only what he had expected to see. So he decided to let the matter drop.

They had driven a few miles north from Bloomington through the gathering dusk to Morgan-Monroe State Forest, where they parked the truck far up a two-track in the shadowy presence of big trees. Because of the heat, they lay on top of their sleeping bags in the camper shell, the sounds of crickets and cicadas buzzing in through the screened windows. Wearing one of his old T-shirts, with its picture of snow-capped mountains spread across her breasts, Katarina tried reading the slang textbook in the beam of her headlamp, but she kept nodding off. Harlan's own headlamp shone on the pages of *Crossing to Safety*. The Vermont scenes in the novel made him ache for Black Bear Farm. He figured condos would be erupting like sores all over the pastures by now, the house would be tarted up as a sales office, and the barn would be crammed with pool tables and video games. No self-respecting bear would venture anywhere near the place.

After a few minutes Katarina's eyes closed and the book slumped onto her stomach. He picked it up gingerly and set it aside, removed her headlamp and shut off the light. She didn't stir. He tucked the photo into his book to mark the page, shut off his own lamp, and by the faint moonlight seeping in he watched her sleep—the slow rise and fall of her chest, the barely discernible pulse in her throat, the darting of her eyes beneath closed lids. We call it life, he thought, or love, but a mystery named is no less mysterious.

He slipped out through the rear door and walked barefoot among the great trees. Wandering from one fat trunk to another, he identified them by feeling their bark—sugar maple, tulip-tree, black walnut, shagbark hickory, beech, various oaks. He recalled how Teresa Two Bears had run her thick fingers over his face, assuring herself that he was Tommy's son. "No mother can forget her child," she had insisted. When Harlan had first glimpsed the image of his mother on Tommy's grave, he had almost welcomed her pain, imagining that if she could grieve for a lost lover she could also grieve for a lost son. Now he knew better.

There was no trace of grief in the picture of Aurora he'd seen today. And that was fine with him. If she had found a pocket of happiness, in this world where happiness was so rare, then let her enjoy it, with her doe-eyed daughter and her bearded husband. When he returned to his grandparents' farm, he would report

everything he'd learned about Aurora's life in Bloomington. She
was their daughter; they deserved to know. What Nana and Papa
chose to do once they heard the news would be up to them. They
might try calling her immediately, might write her a letter, might
hop in the old Pontiac and hustle over here to see her in the flesh.
For his own part, he was ready to let her go.

§ § §

Chapter Fourteen • July 2008

AURORA

NATURALLY, MARTIN HAD NOTICED the attractive young woman who returned the ball to Olivia in the park, but he couldn't recall the young man who had given Aurora such a fright. There were plenty of attractive young women in this college town, and ordinarily Aurora didn't mind that they caught Martin's eye, so long as that was all they caught. In this instance, however, she wished he had been less distracted, for she didn't trust her own recollection of the man at the picnic table.

"He looked for all the world like Tommy," she said.

Martin only growled in response, but it was a friendly growl, giving voice to the rubber dinosaur he was dancing along the edge of the tub as they bathed Olivia. Martin would stand on his head to make Olivia giggle, as she was giggling now. In fact, he *had* stood on his head, with hilarious results, on several occasions since Olivia's birth. Aurora never ceased to be amazed that her sober husband—the architect who resurrected old buildings, who sat on the city's planning board, who spoke soulfully at Quaker meeting, who joined a vigil on the courthouse square every Wednesday to protest the Iraq war—that this utterly serious man had turned into such a goofball on becoming a father.

His antics amused her now as she knelt beside the tub and leaned in to run a washcloth between her daughter's nubbin toes.

"I hadn't thought about Tommy in ages," she went on, "but for a split second, there he was—raven hair, high cheekbones, smoky skin, even the glint in his black eyes. The resemblance was eerie."

"Who is Tommy?" Olivia asked.

"Not someone you know, sweetie," Aurora answered.

Interrupting his dinosaur growls, Martin said, "The way you zoomed off, I knew something had lit your fuse, but I couldn't imagine what."

"It was like I'd seen a ghost."

"Ghost?" Olivia piped up anxiously.

Aurora bit her tongue. Mention anything the least bit scary, and Olivia got the willies.

"Mommy didn't see a ghost," Martin assured her. "There aren't any ghosts."

He propped Olivia into a sitting position so Aurora could shampoo her hair, the stage in their bathing routine that usually provoked howls. But tonight Olivia ignored the sting in her eyes and kept asking about ghosts. Her questions continued as she was dried off, dressed in a nighttime diaper and pajamas, and then snuggled into bed among a herd of stuffed animals. Martin read her three picture books, and after he finished each one she popped up to repeat her question. He gave Aurora a flummoxed look that seemed to say: You got us into this, and only you can get us out. So Aurora bent down to rub Olivia's back while singing lullabies. At last the child grew still, and Aurora stopped singing, whereupon Olivia stirred and sat up, whimpering, "Milky, milky!"

Two years old this month, Olivia had all but weaned herself, asking to nurse only when frightened or distraught, so Aurora had little milk to give. But she knew the sucking itself was a comfort. Hoisting Olivia from the crib, she sat down in the rocker and lay the child across her lap, so long-legged now, growing so fast, but still with the tiniest, prettiest, pink-lipped mouth. She unbuttoned her shirt, which smelled of sawdust, freed a breast, and the urgent mouth found its way unerringly to the nipple. Aurora gently rocked, watching Olivia nurse. Which time would be the last time?

Instead of tiptoeing out of the room to go work in his study, as he did most evenings, Martin cleared a space among the toys and stretched out on the carpet with hands laced together on his chest and eyes closed. Soon his breathing slowed and his legs began to twitch. Finally Olivia, too, gave in to sleep, her mouth relaxing, and she rolled away from the breast onto her back. In the gauzy light filtering in through the curtains, Aurora studied her daughter's face, so smooth, unblemished, and then she studied the face of her husband, this man who had come seeking her, and who would never forsake her.

*

Had she bathed baby Harlan? She must have, but she couldn't remember doing so. She remembered little from those four months between giving birth to him and betraying him. In the early weeks, although frightened and confused, she kept herself going with her mother's help, and with the fervent hope that Tommy would return. A few girls from school, missing her since she'd been forced to drop out, came to ooh and aah over the baby and to ask what it felt like being a mother. There was caution in their voices, but also a shade of envy. A timid, studious boy who'd been her lab partner in biology surprised her by showing up to stammer a few words and give her a copy of *The World's Greatest Poetry*. He had bookmarked a page on which a man in ancient China spoke of missing his dead wife every autumn when the leaves wafted down and the wild geese flew south, a poem that Aurora learned by heart. In those early weeks she still waited tables in the bar during the busiest hours, carrying the baby in a sling across her chest. The regulars tickled Harlan under the chin and doubled her tips. Surely in those days she had bathed him, smiled at him, sung to him. Surely the two of them had enjoyed spells of happiness, as she and Olivia did now.

But the news of Tommy's death plunged her into a stupor, which even the baby's howls could not penetrate. Often her mother would bring the bawling child to her, explaining that he was hungry or dirty or wet, urging her to care for him. Aurora did care for Harlan, in the sense of feeling her heart swell at the sight of his perfect little body, but she couldn't rouse from her lethargy to keep track of his needs. She would forget to wipe his bottom when she changed his diaper, and he'd break out in a rash. Or she would put the diaper on too loosely and he'd wet his clothes. Her milk wouldn't let down when she tried to nurse him, and then it would come gushing out and soak her shirt when he was asleep. For that reason among others, she stopped waiting tables, stopped even going downstairs when the tavern was open. Only on Sundays, when there were no men at the bar, she would sometimes help her mother in the kitchen. Once, she almost fell down the stairs with the baby in her arms, barely catching hold of the banister, and it occurred to her that she might have meant to fall. Another time, coming into the kitchen, she was about to lay Harlan down on the hot grill, when her mother screamed and stopped her.

Worst and most detailed of the memories from those harrowing months was of the blustery April night when she stole away from the bar and carried her sleeping baby to the end of Ninth Street Pier. She had often gone walking with Harlan, especially when he was restless, but always in daylight, when fewer weirdos prowled the streets, and when she could see well enough to avoid tripping on the icy, slushy, or rain-slick pavement. Her mother en-

couraged these daytime outings—stretch your legs, give the baby
some fresh air, away from the reek of booze and ammonia—but
this night, perhaps sensing Aurora's mood, she had tried keeping
them indoors, warning about the darkness, the wind, the cold.

Ignoring her mother's cautions, Aurora tucked Harlan in the
sling, pulled on her baggy Cleveland Indians jacket, and zipped it
up with the baby snug inside. She kissed each of her parents firmly on the mouth, an intimacy she hadn't allowed herself since
early childhood, and then she dodged through the crowd of evening customers and out the door before anyone could stop her.

The walk to the pier took twice as long as in daytime, because
every shadow spooked her. Harlan slept the whole way, even
when a squad car gunned by with siren blaring. She kept crossing the street to avoid the mouths of alleys or the urine stink of
doorways or the sinister sprawl of parks. Once a man followed
her for several blocks, a few steps behind, keeping pace with her,
until she ducked into a ribs joint, where the smell of barbecue
made her mouth water. When she sneaked a look outside, she
could see the man had turned around and was striding away in
the direction from which they had come. After she resumed her
walk, a car drew up beside her, music booming from its open
windows, and an oily voice yelled something indecipherable at
her. She shook her head fiercely no and the car sped on. When
she came to the murky underpass beneath the lakeside highway
she almost turned back, but she nerved herself and rushed on
through.

Reaching the pier at last, she was relieved to see it was well-lit.
She had brought the baby here before, but never at night, never through so much fear. Except for the tang of barbecue and
the warm weight against her chest, she had sensed nothing on
her walk that didn't terrify her. She was unsure where Tommy's
freighter had docked during the week they spent together, but

this was where she had imagined it would be. A ship was berthed here now, tied up by ropes thicker than her arms. Hawsers, the ropes were called—a word Tommy had taught her. Lights outlined the decks and towers, as in the diagram of a ship, and vapor rose from the stacks. From inside that constellation of lights, men's voices sounded faintly, laughing or cursing.

Aurora gazed up at the vast machine, which was like a skyscraper laid on its side and set afloat. Real skyscrapers, modest ones, rose behind her in downtown Cleveland, but she didn't turn around to look. She was drawn step by step along the pier toward the inky lake. The sky was overcast. Not a star shone, not a sliver of moon. A stiff wind blew from the north, bringing a chill from Canada. Whitecaps near shore picked up a glow from streetlamps. Otherwise the water was black. From the tip of the pier, clinging to a metal post, she stared into that lightless expanse and readied herself for what she had come here to do. She had only to let go of the post, hug her baby tight, and climb over the railing. Within a minute or two it would be over, everything would be over. The newspaper would say she had slipped, an accident, no one to blame. She looked back at the lit-up ship, listening, as if someone might call her, but the wind muffled all sounds except the occasional gong of a buoy. The wind loosened the knot in her hair and sliced through her thin jacket.

Perhaps that is what made the baby stir, the wind's cold fingers prodding his ribs, or perhaps he was only hungry. Whether cold or hungry, Harlan awoke and began rooting for her nipple. His motion shook her to the core. She hesitated, glancing at the black water, then turned around so as to shelter the baby, and reached inside her jacket to uncover a breast. He latched on and began to suck. For once her milk let down just as it should. How could she jump while he drank? She nursed him all the way back to the tavern, scarcely looking where she was going, indifferent to dangers.

The crowd had thinned by the time she entered the smoky bar, where her mother, swabbing tables, looked up with evident relief. Aurora kissed her again, this time on the cheek, and kissed her father likewise, and then carried the baby upstairs. She changed his diaper and paced with him for a long while, back and forth across the creaking boards of her bedroom until he fell asleep. She settled him into his wicker basket. Without undressing, she lay down but didn't close her eyes. Eventually her parents came up and went to bed and the whole place fell silent except for her father's snores. She thought of going back to the pier and finishing, alone, what she had begun to do with the baby. But she would have to walk all that way through so many shadows, and the water would be so cold, and if she leapt in, she would never know what became of her son.

Rising from the bed, she quietly gathered as many clothes as would fit in her school backpack, a few toiletries, the book of poetry she'd been given by her lab partner, and an envelope of money she'd saved from tips. She scrawled a note to her parents, telling them she was afraid and had to go, but not telling them what she most feared, which was that she would kill her child. Harlan's blanket was damp when she checked on him, so she changed his diaper again and eased him into fresh pajamas. All of his other blankets must have been in the wash, for there were none in his dresser. Carrying him in his basket, she tiptoed downstairs. Behind the bar she found a clean towel, one bearing the name and logo of some beer, and this she wrapped around him. She nestled him in the basket, laid the note beside him, and set him there on the bar where her mother would find him first thing in the morning. Her breasts ached. Already the milk was seeping. She bent down close enough to feel his tiny puffs of breath but refrained from kissing him, afraid he might wake. Then she slung the pack onto her shoulders and slipped out the front door, heading for the bus station, to ride as far away as her money would carry her.

*

Aurora had never told these darkest details to anyone—not to the blind James Trevor at the waterfall, not to Lillian, not even to Martin. The clear intention of killing her child seemed a sin too shameful for confession. Knowing only that Aurora had abandoned the baby, Lillian talked openly with her about postpartum depression, the way it dazed the mind, cast a pall over the world. Lillian herself had felt euphoric after delivering each of her own children, but a number of women she knew had suffered what, in its milder form, was sometimes called the baby blues. For two of her close friends, the condition had been severe enough to require hospitalization.

"It's a common affliction, even for women who've given birth in ideal circumstances," Lillian said. With characteristic delicacy, she avoided mentioning that the circumstances of Harlan's birth had been far from ideal.

Lillian's own plunge into the paralyzing darkness had occurred following the death rather than the birth of a child. She spoke of the numbing aftermath of Yaffa's death with a candor that made Aurora feel grateful. Lillian admitted having considered and then rejected suicide, for even in her desolation she never ceased loving Solomon and Martin, and that love kept her from leaving the world. She had climbed out of the slough of despond, as she called it, by working alongside the cabinetmaker who reminded her so much of her father.

The subject of depression came up as Lillian and Aurora worked in the shop, surrounded by many of the old cabinetmaker's tools, on the day after the disturbing encounter in the park. They were rubbing the final coat of tung oil onto a Shaker-inspired chest of drawers they had made for a professor at the university. It was the mild sort of work, involving neither loud machines nor toxic fumes, that allowed Aurora to bring Olivia to the shop instead of leaving her at nursery school. Olivia played at their feet, no doubt listening to every word as she plowed her toy bulldozer through a heap of sawdust. So they took care over what they said.

When Aurora described the shock of seeing the young man who looked so much like Tommy, Lillian replied that she'd been fooled in the same way by girls who resembled Yaffa, and even by grown women who looked as she imagined Yaffa might have looked at a later age. Indeed, Aurora was herself one such woman, for Lillian had often compared her to Yaffa, going so far as to say that they could have been sisters. Yet the photographs of Yaffa on display in the Zakars' house suggested to Aurora only a casual similarity—fair skin, long limbs, flyaway hair. Just so, she acknowledged, the man at the picnic table had been transformed into Tommy by the sorcery of longing.

"One's reason admits the death of a loved one," Lillian said, "but the old animal brain goes on scanning the world for a certain gesture, a way of walking, a laugh, and on finding what it seeks it stubbornly proclaims, 'There she is, alive and well!' Hope soars—only to be dashed." She paused, refolding the cheesecloth she was using to apply the tung oil. "One mustn't curse the animal brain, however, because that's what keeps us alive when reason quails."

It was true, Aurora thought. For in the moment of turning her back to the water and baring her breast for Harlan to suck, she hadn't made a conscious decision to live, she had simply responded to the small squirming body.

"Chances are, you'll keep on imagining you glimpse Tommy," Lillian continued, "and keep on having to shake off the illusion. No doubt you'd have been less prone to depression if the actual Tommy had stuck around and helped you raise the baby. But I can't bring myself to wish for such a turn of events, because then you would never have married my son or brought darling Olivia into the world."

Darling Olivia paused in her bulldozing, alert as always to any mention of her name. Hearing nothing further of interest, she revved up her imaginary motor and resumed plowing sawdust.

At midmorning, Lillian washed up and declared it was time for tea.

"Cookies!" Olivia crowed.

"We'll have to see what's in the biscuit tin, won't we?" Lillian tousled Olivia's hair, which was finer than Martin's, but just as black and lustrous. "You're making some grand roads, young lady. Now come to Grammy and let's wash your paws."

Olivia climbed onto a stool at the sink and thrust her hands under the faucet, suffered them to be scrubbed and dried, and then she climbed back down and repeated her call for cookies.

"What do you say?" Aurora reminded her.

Olivia's dutiful "please" came out sounding like "peas," the letter *l* still baffling her tongue. They all sat down at the scarred oak table reserved for tea. With her usual ceremony, Lillian placed a ginger snap on the saucer she had turned from a piece of bird's-eye maple for just such occasions, and presented it to Olivia, who murmured thank you without being prompted.

Lillian beamed at her. "I'm sufficiently old-fashioned to think a daughter should grow up at her mother's side, absorbing everything, the way this one does."

The kettle began to whistle, and Olivia gave a breathy whistle in response.

"But I thought you preferred spending time with your father, watching him do carpentry," Aurora said.

"True enough. There are exceptions to every rule." Lillian poured steaming water into the pot, releasing the fragrance of bergamot from the Earl Grey tea she ordered from England. "Indeed, sometimes I fear that I kept Yaffa too close to me, because of her epilepsy. Not that she would have lived a day longer had I given her a freer rein. But she might have spread her wings a bit more in the time she had."

"I'm sure she treasured every hour with you."

"Not as much as I treasured them. But that's the way of parents. Even more so of grandparents." Again Lillian cast a smile at Olivia. "We're constantly watching the children, as if gazing back along the path we've already traveled, while they're looking forward, beyond us. Which is only as it should be." She lifted the teapot and filled Aurora's cup, then her own. "But tell me, dear, how did you and your mother get on?"

Aurora usually avoided thinking about the time at home before Harlan's birth. But now, in response to Lillian's question, she allowed herself to go there. "Well enough, I suppose. We never fought, if that's what you mean. My friends told me about quarreling with their mothers over makeup, miniskirts, boyfriends, homework, anything and everything. But I knew my mother had all the stress she could handle, without me adding any more."

"Fighting is bad," Olivia said.

"Yes it is, sweetheart." Aurora wiped Olivia's nose with a tissue. "My mother didn't keep very close tabs on me because she was nearly always working. If the tavern was open, she was cooking. If it was closed, she was cleaning up or keeping the books, ordering supplies or doing laundry. The paintings on the walls were all from her art student days. I never saw her pick up a brush. She took me to the museum several times a year, on Sunday afternoons, and she took me to the library nearly every week, until I was old enough to go by myself." Aurora paused. "It was a hard life, for my father and mother both. They did their best. I just couldn't see it at the time."

"How could you have seen? You were a child."

"Well, I stopped being a child a long while ago, and I haven't made their life any easier." Aurora stared into her cup, unwilling to meet Lillian's eyes. "You must think I'm terrible for having cut myself off from them."

"I don't make a practice of judging other people, my dear."

"You couldn't think any worse of me than I do myself." What pained Aurora most deeply was the fact that when she had stood at the end of the pier, ready to jump, she hadn't even considered what that act would do to her parents, the heartbreak they would feel, the guilt. Now, as a mother herself, the horror of such a loss was all too apparent.

Frowning at her, Olivia said, "Don't be sad, Mommy."

"I'm not sad, sweetie." Aurora forced a smile and reached across the table to stroke her daughter's cheek.

As if sensing her advantage, Olivia asked, "More cookie?"

"One more."

"Here you are, love," Lillian said, offering the open biscuit tin to Olivia, who perused the ginger snaps, all identical, before choosing one.

Now that memories from the buried past were flowing, Aurora could not staunch them. "My mother used to give me little jobs in the kitchen, simple things a child could do, like spreading mayonnaise on buns for the endless stream of hamburgers or forking dill pickles onto plates or spooning out coleslaw. Bar food, Mother called it. When she and my father first bought the tavern, she tried making soups and stir-fry and casseroles, but the customers wanted burgers, brats, fries, onion rings, that sort of thing."

"Pub food is just as dull," Lillian put in.

"Sometimes she told me about more refined dishes she used to make, early in her marriage, recipes from countries where my father was stationed in the Army—quiche, eggplant Parmesan, sauerbraten, tempura—but as long as I lived at home, we ate the same food she fed the customers. Even on Sundays she stuck with meatloaf or stews. She didn't have the energy to make anything fancier."

"You still think of the tavern as home?"

Of course Lillian would notice the word, which Aurora had let slip without thinking. "It was home back then," she replied. "Now home is wherever Martin and Olivia are."

Hearing her name once more, Olivia stopped chewing the cookie, which she had been nibbling slowly, making it last. She flicked her gaze from Aurora to Lillian and back again, intently listening.

Aurora lifted her cup, and then set it down without drinking. "I hope you don't think I love Martin any the less because Tommy is still lurking in my old animal brain."

"Of course not, dear," Lillian said. "It's clear you cherish Martin."

"Martin is Daddy," Olivia chimed in.

"Yes, sweetheart," Aurora said. "Grammy and I call him Martin, but you call him Daddy."

"Your name is Ro-rah."

"Yes, I'm Aurora and Grammy is Lillian, but you call us Mommy and Grammy."

Lillian picked up the thread of their talk. "That first boy leaves an indelible mark."

"Solomon wasn't your first?"

"Oh, hardly." Lillian patted the silver braids meticulously coiled at the back of her head and gave a wistful smile. "There was quite a parade of beaus before Solomon, I confess. But he was the first one whose mind captivated me."

There had been no parade of beaus for Aurora, either before Tommy or after. The only boy who showed her more than passing interest during high school was the shy lab partner, who slipped notes to her bearing poems, which she later discovered had been cribbed from *The World's Greatest Poetry*. After she ran away, and overcame the worst of her own shyness, a number of men treated her with flattering courtesy, and she supposed a few of them might have pursued her if she'd given them any encouragement. Laughing now, she said, "I wish I could claim it was Tommy's mind that captivated me."

With a tremor in her voice, Olivia said, "Tommy is a ghost."

"Oh, bosh," Lillian said.

"Mommy seed a ghost," Olivia insisted, suddenly on the verge of tears.

Not knowing the source of this outburst, Lillian shot a perplexed look at Aurora, who shook her head, signaling to let it drop. But Lillian wasn't one to ignore a child's fears. "Nobody has seen a ghost, young lady. Surely you mean a *goat*. Mommy saw a goat." Lillian waggled her index fingers, one poking out from each side of her forehead, to illustrate horns. "Now, is that anything to be afraid of?"

Olivia smiled uncertainly. "Goat?"

"What else could it be?"

Relief washed over her round face. "Mommy seed a goat!"

"Right you are, my cherub!"

And just like that, the ghost had been exorcised—from Olivia if not from Aurora.

★

On the Sunday following her glimpse of Tommy's lookalike in the park, Aurora sank into the silence at Friends Meeting under the weight of remorse. Instead of easing the weight, her conversation with Lillian had only increased it, by summoning up all those memories. In her tactful manner, laying a trail of questions, Lillian had coaxed Aurora into seeing that she hadn't been irreparably torn from her parents and son; she had banished herself, and only she could undo the banishment.

Aurora missed having her mother-in-law's tranquil presence beside her on the bench this morning. Lillian had stayed home with Solomon, who could no longer be left alone and yet couldn't be persuaded to attend worship, for his dementia had not yet advanced far enough to overcome his resolute atheism. In former days, when he could still speak, his mildest denunciation of religion was to call it poppycock, and his most severe was to call it genocidal superstition. Since many of his fellow Assyrians had been slaughtered by Turks on religious grounds, and his remote ancestors had done their own share of slaughtering, his misgivings were understandable.

Before closing her eyes, Aurora glanced around the meeting room, which was a plain white box illuminated by sunshine pouring in through windows of unstained glass. No crucifix, no pulpit, no altar, no symbols at all, just wooden benches arranged in a square and facing toward the center. The benches were occupied this morning by some forty or fifty worshippers, a typical turnout for a summer Sunday—or First Day, as traditional Quakers deemed it, since the old name harkened back to pagan worship. The scruple seemed an odd one to Aurora, for the sun had been shedding its body and radiating energy without pause for billions of years, a miracle of generosity that seemed worthy of reverence.

After shepherding Olivia to the children's room, Martin took a seat beside Aurora and patted her thigh. Then he clasped his hands in his lap and settled into stillness, which he was capable of maintaining for the full hour of worship, without fidgeting, without so much as clearing his throat. He would straighten his long legs and rise, of course, if he felt called to speak. She hoped he'd be called this morning, even though she knew it wasn't supposed to matter who spoke. Truth could emerge from any mouth. Even from hers, according to the teachings. And yet in all her years of worshipping with Quakers, first in Ithaca and now in Bloomington, and in spite of numerous inward promptings that might have been the spirit moving within her, Aurora had never spoken. Several times she had become agitated enough to stand, even to open her mouth and form a first word, but a pressure on her throat had always kept her from making a sound.

Fans whirred softly in the corners of the meeting room, stirring the humid air. Now and again someone coughed, a noise as abrupt as gunfire. The voices of children, Olivia's no doubt among them, sounded faintly from the Sunday school rooms, like distant music. To quiet her mind, which seethed with memories and fears, Aurora began following her breath. Time and again she failed to count as high as ten before the frets returned. As a birthright Quaker, Lillian would have counseled her to wait for the Inner Light. To Aurora it felt more like hunkering down in a storm, waiting for the wind and rain to let up so she could see the way ahead. She would have been thrilled to receive "the true light that enlightens every man," as promised in the Gospel of John. She was too skeptical a Quaker, however, and too convinced of her unworthiness, to expect lucid guidance from God, so she merely opened herself to whatever hint might come.

At one point, Martin's breathing quickened enough for her to notice it, and she thought he might stand up to speak. But he held his place. She stole a glance at him, delighting in his rugged face, the broad forehead and angular cheekbones, the dense ebony curls of his hair and beard, the firm set of his lips. She loved him utterly, as she loved Olivia. For years, ever since the night when she'd almost drowned her son, she had thought herself incapable of such love. Martin had taught her otherwise, beginning when he waited for her on the roominghouse porch instead of stalking away. Overcome with gratitude on discovering him there, she had kissed his wet cheeks, then his lips. They were slow in saying goodnight. The next morning, she had gone to hear his lecture on preservation architecture, the official reason for his visit to Ithaca. He showed slides of leaning churches, collapsing barns,

roofless mills, and dilapidated houses, and then he showed slides
of the same structures fully restored. She noticed how often, in
describing his work, he used the words *heal* and *salvage* and *rescue.*
At first it disturbed her to think she might be just another of his
reclamation projects. But gradually, as he spoke about one neglected building after another, she realized it wasn't their broken-
ness that drew him but their underlying integrity. In a shambles
he could see wholeness. After that first visit, it took months of
calls and letters and further visits for Martin to convince her not
only that he saw such potential in her but that she actually possessed it—the potential of a broken creature to be made whole.
Once persuaded, she could finally agree to marry.

A slight commotion drew Aurora's attention back to the meeting room. Since the allotted hour was nearing its end without anyone having spoken, she imagined that one of the elders on the facing bench must be rising to offer a few words before the end of
meeting. But when the expected throat-clearing didn't occur, she
allowed herself a look. Standing on the far side of the room, backlit
from a window, was a girl named Carrie, whom Aurora knew from
taking turns working with the children in Sunday school. Carrie
must have been twelve or thirteen by now; she had only recently
begun sitting among the adults instead of remaining with the children. Her mother and father sat on either side of the empty space
on the bench from which she had risen, and it seemed to Aurora
they were making an effort not to gaze up at their daughter. The
girl stood for a minute or more, swaying slightly, eyes closed, without making a sound, and then, instead of speaking, she sang. What
came out of her was a sound as pure and sweet and buoyant as the
trilling of a bird. It sent shivers through Aurora. She kept her eyes
closed, listening, registering neither words nor melody but only
the ecstasy in the child's voice.

After the girl sat down, several minutes of silence followed.
Eventually an elder marked the end of meeting by grasping the

hand of the person next to him, and then handshakes and greetings were exchanged around the room. Aurora heard others shuffling from their seats, but still she did not move, did not open her
eyes. Martin slipped away quietly. Soon he returned with Olivia,
who climbed into Aurora's lap, smelling of face paint and begging
her to look, Mommy, look! Aurora looked, and saw a butterfly
painted on one of her daughter's cheeks, a dolphin on the other,
and a beatific smile in between. She kissed Olivia on the forehead,
careful not to muss the art, saying, "You are magnificent!"

Martin sensed that she didn't want to shatter her mood with
talk, so he suggested they skip the coffee hour and bicycle home
straightaway. Without a further word, he carried Olivia outside
and strapped her into the child's seat on his bike, buckled on their
two helmets, and rode on ahead. Aurora followed, scarcely aware
of the gathering heat. Every now and again Olivia would swivel
her head in its pink helmet to look back, making sure Mommy
was there, and Aurora would give a reassuring nod. She was
there. As long as she breathed, she would be there, if not always
within sight then always within the reach of love.

The house when they entered was suffused with the aroma of
lentil soup bubbling in the crockpot. Olivia scampered off, most
likely to inform her stuffed animals about what she'd been up to
all morning. Martin embraced Aurora in the hall, drawing her
face against his chest. "What is it?" he murmured.

"I'm going to call my mother."

"That's good," he said, stroking her head. "That's wonderful."

§ § §

Chapter Fifteen • July 2008

HARLAN

Since Nana and Papa weren't expecting them back at the farm until Friday evening, Harlan figured he and Katarina might as well stick around another day to check out his mother's town, even if he wanted no part of her life. Early on Thursday they drove from the state forest to Bloomington and parked on the courthouse square, across the sidewalk from a World War II memorial, which consisted of a bronze GI with his arm cocked as if about to lob a grenade into the street. Nearby was a Civil War monument, its lettering blurred by a century and a half of rain. From a spot behind the monument a vintage cannon, relic of some later war, tilted its barrel at the sky. There must have been a ready supply of limestone nearby, for the courthouse was built of it, and so were most of the storefronts on the square, and so were the church towers rising beyond.

While Katarina browsed in a few shops, Harlan waited outside, watching the flow of people and vehicles. The only reason he could see for entering a store was if he needed some particular thing—a ¾" wood bit, say, a pair of work boots, or a loaf of bread—and then he would get in and buy it and get out as fast as he could. Katarina wasn't much of a shopper either, he had

learned, unless she was looking for gifts, as she was doing today. After she had found small presents for Nana and Papa, her
mother, and her two brothers, she declared herself shopped out.

So they moved on from the courthouse square to sample
the exhibits in a local history museum, which was housed in a
former Carnegie Library; they poked their noses into a science
museum, which rang with the hubbub of children; and they
looked around inside an old cinema, which had been fixed up as
a community theatre and still had a marquee out front reading
INDIANA. By then, Harlan's stomach was growling. Instead of
making sandwiches in the truck, they splurged by eating lunch at
a place called the Uptown Café, two doors down from the theatre. Voices around them spoke in a babel of languages, some of
which even Katarina didn't recognize. She had to advise Harlan
how much of a tip to leave, since on the rare occasions when he
had eaten in restaurants his grandfather had always paid. After
their meal, they walked the few blocks to the university, where
they strolled among more limestone buildings and old trees and
crowds of summer students.

When they returned to the square, they made a tour of the
courthouse lawn, because Harlan wanted to see if anything was
commemorated there aside from war. He was pleased to discover, among the memorials to seven wars, a monument for peace—
the statue of a robed woman with arm uplifted and a dove poised
in her hand. Judging by a crack at the wrist, the hand must have
been broken off and cemented back on, which could be taken
as either a bad sign or a good one, depending on whether you
focused on the damage or the repair. Carved into the base of the
statue was an open book bearing the inscription: "Blessed are the
Peacemakers, for they shall be called Children of God."

"That's a verse you don't hear quoted much these days," Harlan said. "It's right up there with 'Love your enemies' and 'Turn

the other cheek' among the ten most ignored passages in the gospels." Katarina didn't respond, only gazed up at the statue as if she expected the dove to fly. "Do you know," he went on, "the U.S. once had a nuclear-tipped missile called the Peacemaker?"

"I am not surprised," she said, her voice barely audible.

Her subdued manner should have warned him to clam up, but instead he blustered on. "They stole the name from Colt Firearms, which used to make a six-shooter called the Peacemaker. There's frontier logic behind it. If somebody gets uppity—Indians, cattle rustlers, foreigners—kill them. Nothing's more peaceful than a corpse."

To that she did not reply.

★

Late in the afternoon, they drove south of town to the address for Heartland Fine Woodworking, and discovered that it was in an old limestone mill, which had clearly been refurbished since the stonecutting days. Harlan slowed down as they passed the building, but the view from outside told him nothing about what his mother might do inside those massive walls. As if summoned by his thoughts, Aurora emerged from the mill just then, climbed into the Volvo, and headed toward the courthouse square. So Harlan turned the Ford around and followed her downtown until they came to a Methodist Church, where she entered at a door near a children's play area. Daycare, he thought. He parked across the street in front of the low-slung post office. Sure enough, in a few minutes, Aurora came back out leading her little girl by the hand, the two of them all jolly smiles and chatter. Harlan had no desire to revisit the classy house where his mother and Olivia were most likely headed, so he decided to call it a day. Katarina seemed relieved. Something was bothering her, but he couldn't tell what.

They returned to the forest grove where they'd camped the previous night, and heated stew for supper. Sitting on the rear bumper of the pickup, cradling the bowls of stew in their laps, they watched fireflies blinking in the dusk. On other midsummer nights, Katarina had marveled at the dancing lights and reminisced about the glowworms on her grandparents' farm. But this evening she made no comment. Nor did she say a word during the washing-up. Forgoing her usual bedtime reading, she gave him a glancing kiss and then curled on top of her sleeping bag with her back to him, signaling she had no interest in talking, let alone in making love. So he contented himself with brushing a hand over her hip, and then he lay atop his own sleeping bag, wide awake. As he replayed their day, he realized how little thought he'd given to Katarina's departure, only three weeks away, while she might have been thinking of little else. Instead, he'd been brooding on his mother, testing his decision to let her go, the way he might probe a scar to make sure an old wound had healed.

★

The next morning they set out early for Ohio, the eastern sky just beginning to pale. The Ford groaned as Harlan nudged it up near highway speed. He felt more at ease than he had in a long while, as if he had shrugged off a heavy load. Only after giving up hope of reuniting with his mother did he realize how thoroughly that longing had possessed him these last few weeks. It had nearly squeezed from his mind the hope of a continuing life with Katarina. She must have sensed his neglect, and this could account for her moodiness. Now, glancing at her from time to time as they drove, he saw her afresh, with the full force of his desire. Here was the one person in the world he could not give up. He could live apart from her for a season, even for the duration of their studies, if need be, but not forever.

She would be leaving on the last day of July. Once their classes began at the end of August, his at Kent State and hers at Stockholm University, how much time would they find to write or call one another? No power on Earth could make him forget about her, but would the demands of her studies and the attentions of Swedish boys and the sounds of her mother tongue make her forget him? Even now she seemed to be withdrawing, for she was pressed against the far door, her face turned to the open window.

"Why don't you scoot over here within reach?" he urged.

"I am thinking."

"You've been doing a lot of that lately. I can see the little gray cloud over your head." He patted the seat next to him. "Come over here and we'll cogitate together."

"It is too hot."

"Not as hot as it's going to be."

She made no reply, so he left her alone with her thoughts. He didn't complain about the roadside trash, as he would have done ordinarily. He didn't bemoan the rash of burger joints and gas oases and RV lots and fireworks warehouses. He didn't ask her to read the map or remind him of route numbers. For the next two hours or so, they exchanged no more words.

Then as they neared the Ohio border, they passed a billboard that proclaimed in towering letters:

AVOID HELL

TRUST JESUS

"They *make* hell," Katarina muttered, suddenly breaking the silence.

Her words caught Harlan by surprise. "What's that?"

"All of them use the same trick—preachers, generals, politicians. They stir up fear, and then they say: Bow down to us, and we will protect you."

"Whoa! Don't let Homeland Security hear you talking like that, you Swedish firebrand." Even before she turned her reddened eyes on him, he realized he had struck the wrong note. "What?"

She shook her head. "Nothing."

"Tell me."

"It will only upset you."

"Sweetheart, *tell* me."

Edging closer to him, she sat without speaking for a minute, gathering herself. Finally, she said, "When I was out walking yesterday, I stopped at the library downtown to check my mail. There was a message from my mother, the first one in a month."

A needle of alarm pierced Harlan. "Is she all right?"

"She is safe."

"Then why are you down in the dumps? That's great news."

"She is not in danger," Katarina went on, "but she is plunged in horrors. She has moved to a hospital in Amman, where they do repairs—how do you say?—they do reconstructive surgery on wounded Iraqis, who risk their lives to reach Jordan. She works in the operating room twelve hours a day, and falls into bed at night exhausted. That is why she did not write me for so long. Then this week she assisted on surgeries for five children, all of them maimed or blinded by American bombs. One boy, not yet old enough for school, was having his fourth operation. His face had been shattered, his eyes and tongue burnt away. She had to tell someone, so she told me."

Through all of this, Harlan had kept watching the road. When she fell silent, he sensed that she was looking at him, as if he could explain why his nation was at war in the Middle East. When he glanced over to check, she was indeed looking expectantly at him.

"It's that frontier credo," he said. "God, guts, and guns. Especially guns."

She glared at him, her chin quivering. "Your president says God told him to invade Iraq, and now more than a hundred thousand civilians have been killed. A few broken children are rescued and smuggled into Jordan, where my mother helps piece them back together. It is madness."

"I agree, it's appalling," Harlan replied, "but he's not my president. Those aren't my wars."

Katarina slid away from him and squeezed against the passenger door. The incoming air stirred her ponytail. He could barely hear her say, "There, I have upset you."

"You haven't upset me. You've stumped me. I don't know how to civilize my bloody country."

She retreated into silence. He set his gaze resolutely ahead, along the black spear of pavement aimed due east into the glare of sun. After a spell the Ford began to shudder, and he realized he was pressing it to go faster than it could safely go, so he let up on the accelerator. He shrugged to loosen his shoulders and neck, which had begun to cramp, and he relaxed his grip on the steering wheel.

When the traffic thinned, he looked over the fields on either side of the highway, as if he might discover out there an answer to Katarina's challenge. The terrain was flat here, leveled by glaciers; as far as he could see it was planted in corn and soybeans. The farmsteads, each one a cluster of white or barn-red buildings, lay scattered like islands in a sea of green. It was a subjugated landscape. He knew that almost every acre within sight had been covered with hardwood forest when the first white settlers arrived, yet now the only scraps of forest remaining were spindly woodlots here and there. Across Ohio, Indiana, and Illinois, there were millions of such acres once covered with great trees, nearly all of them cleared in a few decades with hand tools and muscle power. And cleared not only of trees. Passenger pigeons, Carolina parakeets, wolves, bison, bears, panthers, and lynx were all driven from this part of the country or hunted to extinction, along with the Shawnee, Miami, Piankeshaw, and other native tribes. Once we had exploited the continent from sea to sea, we began sending our soldiers anywhere on Earth that possessed something we wanted. This bullying was an old habit, ingrained in us over three centuries, since the Pilgrims arrived in the New World with their muskets and their writ of ownership from God and king.

How could he explain to Katarina this view of his nation, which he had arrived at slowly, reluctantly, through reading and reflection, and which ran so contrary to what he'd been taught in school, where the subduing of land, Indians, and beasts had been portrayed as the triumph of civilization over wilderness, where every U.S. military venture had been justified as a crusade by the powers of light against the powers of darkness?

Out of this muddle, one thing had become clear. "Hey, sweetheart," he said.

"Hmm?" she murmured, without turning from the window.

"I've been thinking how your mother can't stop the slaughter any more than I can, but she can help patch up broken kids. Well, that's why I want to learn how to patch up the land—restore prairies and swamps, bring back whooping cranes and wolves, clean up rivers. It's not much, I realize, but it's what I can do." He glanced at her. "Does that make sense?"

Katarina returned his look, her eyes still red. "Yes, I see. It is a kind of mending." The line of her lips softened in a way that could have been a smile or a tilt back toward crying. "And I am sorry. I do not mean to blame you. I just do not know if I could bear to live in such a country."

★

They reached the farm in late afternoon, wrung out from the long sweltering drive. The trees arching over the lane, lush with

high summer, offered a stretch of shade, and then the truck rolled
into the farmyard where the view opened out to embrace the
house and barn and sheds, the garden and orchard, the pasture
sloping down to the river, and the forested ridges beyond. The
vista was humbler than the one at Black Bear Farm, but it had
begun to lay its claim on Harlan. Everywhere he looked he saw
the need for work, as well as the fruits of work already done. Although he felt apprehensive about delivering the news of Aurora
to his grandparents, he was eager to set his feet once more on
this ground.

When they climbed from the truck, he was surprised to see a
small black-and-white dog come bounding up to meet them. He
recognized it as a border collie, like ones he'd watched herding
sheep in Vermont. The dog approached to within a few feet and
then crouched down, studying them, loosing tentative yips as if
uncertain whether to bark or keep quiet. Nana and Papa bustled
out of the house. Harlan was relieved to see the old man looked
steady on his feet.

"It's all right, Buddy," Papa called, without any slurring.
"They're family."

"Your grandpa's finally got himself a dog," Nana cried gaily,
rushing up to give hugs, first to Katarina and then to Harlan.

"He's only a pup, a couple of months old," Papa said. "I got
him at the pound. Only fifty bucks, with all the shots. Can you
believe it?"

Katarina knelt before the dog and slowly reached out a hand.
"Hello, Buddy," she murmured. He licked her fingers, and then
her chin. She looked up at Nana and Papa with the happiest expression Harlan had seen on her face in days. "My grandparents
had such a dog. Her name was Bridget. When I stayed with them
she slept at my feet."

"If you want to sleep with Buddy, you'll have to do it on the
porch," Papa said, "because Nana won't have him in the house."

Nana rolled her eyes. "Dogs belong outside, but you all belong inside. Come on, let's get out of the sun. We're dying to hear about your trip."

Harlan promised to give a full account over supper, but first he wanted to cool off in the river with Katarina, whose Swedish blood was about to boil away in this Midwestern heat. Katarina said it was true, she had never felt so hot outside of a sauna. As they unloaded the truck, the dog shadowed them, head low to the ground, watchful, making sure none of them strayed.

Taking a change of clothes from their bedroom, Harlan and Katarina set off for the river, following a rutted track along the pasture's edge and down through the woods. As they walked, he noted spots where he ought to build water bars before the fall rains, to curb erosion, and other spots where a tree fallen across the track needed cutting or a section of fence needed tightening. He was musing on this work when Katarina suddenly took off running and yelled, "Last one in is a spoiled egg!"

"Not a spoiled egg," he called. "A rotten egg!"

Then he raced after her down the slope. By the time he reached the riverbank she had already peeled off her damp T-shirt and was slipping out of her shorts. He kicked off his shoes, and hopped first on one leg and then the other while pulling off his jeans, but she was already splashing into the stream, hooting triumphantly. He paused in his undressing to watch her. The view caused him to speculate, not for the first time, that the shape of a valentine heart must have been inspired by the sweet retreating prospect of a woman's rump.

On reaching waist-deep water, Katarina stopped and turned around grinning. "Slow poke!" she cried. Then the familiar quizzical look came over her face. "Why do you say the last one in is a rotten egg?"

"You got me," Harlan answered.

"Why do you say slow poke?"

"You got me again."

He shucked the last of his clothes and waded in. Though tepid, the water was cooler than the air, and he shivered as he approached her. Her nipples had tightened into kissable pink buds, so he obligingly bent down to kiss them, making her shiver in turn. Then he cupped a hand over each of her breasts and gently squeezed. They were small and firm, like the rest of her, and, like the rest of her, they seemed to him perfect. Although his experience of naked women was limited to Katarina, he couldn't imagine any way of improving on her—dressed or undressed. He reached around to the small of her back and drew her close. "Hey, you know that pond at Malabar Farm?"

"The one I had to drag you to see?"

"True enough," he admitted. "Well, it set me remembering the pond at Black Bear Farm, which set me figuring how to make love in moving water."

She cocked an eyebrow at him. "How so?"

Bending slightly, he locked his hands together under her buttocks and lifted, and as she rose she opened her legs and clenched them around his waist and wrapped her arms about his neck. He shifted his footing to brace himself against the current, and then he let her slowly down until their bodies joined. Again Katarina shivered, and they started moving in the rhythm he imagined was as old as the flowing of rivers. She moaned, a satisfying sound, and presently she laughed, a more ambiguous sound, and then from behind him came an excited yapping. Harlan shut his eyes, silently damning all nosy dogs. Audience or no audience, he was too far gone to stop, and Katarina seemed happy to continue, but she did crane her neck to gain a better view of the barking pup.

★

Nana and Papa were so stunned by what Harlan told them about Aurora that they didn't chastise him for having kept his knowledge of her whereabouts secret from them for a month. Instead they made him repeat every detail, first over supper and then again after the meal while they all sat on the back porch, as if only the repetition would persuade them that their daughter had truly been found. Harlan and Katarina shared the porch swing, while Nana and Papa occupied two bentwood rockers. Nana kept wiping her eyes with a dishtowel and Papa kept opening and clenching his fists.

"Did she look crazy?" Papa asked.

Nana glanced up anxiously, as if she had been wondering the same thing.

"No," Harlan said.

"Didn't look broken somehow?"

"She looked right as rain."

"I still can't believe it," Nana said. "How could you keep from running up and throwing your arms around her?"

"I was afraid she'd scream if I did," Harlan said, provoking a scowl from Katarina.

"Well I don't give a damn—" Papa began, but his voice cracked and he had to start over: "I don't give a damn what kind of swanky life she's got. I don't care if she's the Queen of Sheba. I'm going to call her and ask what the hell she's been doing all these years."

Nana laid a hand on his thick forearm. "There's no use fuming, Luther. Nothing's going to bring back those years." It was as if her touch had breached a dam in him, and he began to sob, his breath rasping, his great bulk shuddering.

Harlan looked on, dismayed, for he had never seen his grandfather cry. No one spoke for several minutes. There was enough of a breeze to keep the mosquitoes at bay. The sun dipping beyond the farthest ridge cast a rosy light onto the porch. Frogs trilled and cicadas buzzed and in the rare intervals of quiet the splashing of water could just be heard from the springhouse.

The air smelled of damp soil and rank vegetation. Except for the breach that yawned in their midst, the irredeemable loss of time, it was a beautiful evening.

At length Nana said, "We must call her. I need to hear her voice."

"Go right ahead," Harlan said. "But don't be surprised if she hangs up on you."

This provoked another scowl from Katarina, and a vigorous shake of the head from Nana, who said, "I won't give her a chance to hang up. I'll tell her straight off I never stopped loving her, not for a minute."

"You do the calling, honey," Papa said, his voice back under control.

Nana stroked his forearm. "I will. But not tonight. She'll be putting her daughter to bed. We'll wait until tomorrow, when everybody's rested and we've had a chance to absorb all of this."

★

But the next day Nana kept finding excuses to postpone the call. Because it was a Saturday, the little girl would be home from daycare, and who knew when she might be taking her nap? Young as she was, maybe Olivia still napped in the morning as well as the afternoon, and a ringing phone might wake her. Aurora might be running errands, and it would be awkward if the husband answered. What could one say to him? This is your mother-in-law calling?

Harlan heard these excuses when he came indoors for meals. Otherwise, he stayed outdoors, and Papa stayed outside with him, the two of them working together steadily from sunup to sundown, with only occasional friction. They had no end of jobs to do, for sure, yet Harlan sensed that Papa avoided the house for the same reason he himself did—not wanting to be within earshot of Nana when she dialed the number, in case she finally reached Aurora only to be spurned.

By nightfall, Nana had decided to hold off yet another day, until the quiet of Sunday. She asked Harlan if he thought Aurora and her family seemed like the sort who would go to church, and he answered that they just might. So Nana declared she would wait until early afternoon, say two P.M., and no more shilly-shallying.

★

Following the Sabbath practice he'd learned from Mr. Winfield, Harlan planned no work for Sunday, but he did plan to be well out of earshot whenever Nana made her call. All morning he walked the fields and woods and riverbank alone, having left the house before Katarina awoke. He knew that Nana would fuss if he stayed away through the noon hour, so he went indoors to join the others at the kitchen table long enough to eat a few bites, and then he excused himself, saying he needed to go look at the stand of maples he counted on tapping for syrup next spring. Suspecting his true reason for hurrying back outdoors, Katarina followed him to the mudroom, where he sat on a bench to put on his boots.

"What if your mother wants to talk with you?" she asked in a low voice.

Harlan tugged one set of laces tight and tied them. "That would be the first time she's wanted to talk with me in twenty years."

"You don't know that. You don't know what she has wanted."

"There you go taking up for her again."

"It's because we have no idea what she has gone through."

"I don't give a damn what she's gone through."

"Why are you determined to see her as a monster?"

He was lacing up the other boot, thinking how to reply, when the phone rang in the kitchen. Not so rare a sound as it used to be, since Nana and Papa had begun to form a circle of friends out here in the country, still, a ringing phone was unusual enough to cause Harlan to hush, wondering who it might be, and Katarina hushed along with him. He could hear Nana offer a cheery hello, and then she loosed a sharp cry, followed by shouts: "Aurora? Is this really you? Oh, my stars in heaven! Papa, it's our girl!"

Harlan stood up hurriedly from the bench and headed for the back door, but Katarina grabbed his arm. "Wait, sweetheart."

He tensed, ready to tear loose from her grip. "Let go," he warned.

But she didn't let go. "Think a minute. Your mother is the one who called, not Nana."

He hesitated, confused. It was true. How could Aurora be calling? He swung around and Katarina turned with him, keeping hold on his arm. Together they stood in the doorway between mudroom and kitchen, listening. Papa sat across the table from Nana with hands covering his face, while she rattled on and then fell silent, rattled on and fell silent. Harlan was too dazed at first to pick up more than the general tone of the conversation, which, on Nana's end, in spite of her initial excitement, was guarded and stiff. As he calmed down he could hear her briefly describing the move from tavern to farm, the state of her health and Papa's, and their new life in the country, as if responding to a string of questions. When she took her own turn at posing questions, she gave no hint that she knew anything about Aurora's life. She professed surprise at news of the husband, the daughter, the woodworking business, the home in Indiana. This puzzled Harlan, and it puzzled him even more that Nana made no mention of him. He glanced down at Katarina, wondering if she had noticed the omission.

Then he heard Nana remark, "Yes, he's quite grown up now, and following his own path."

He swayed in the doorway, and Katarina tightened her grip. His mother was asking about him. And she must have kept on asking about him, for after answering yes or no a few times, Nana declared abruptly, "No, he's not available. But you can talk with your father." Across the table, Papa lifted a hand from his face and waved the notion aside. "Ah, he's overcome, just as I am. We don't know what to think, this is such a shock." After a pause, Nana said, "Why, certainly you're welcome to visit." There was another pause, and then: "August 2nd would be fine. The days are all the same to us here. No, no, not a motel. You must stay with us. We'll show your daughter the farm." She glanced at Harlan as she said, "Well, he might be here or he might not. I can't say for sure. He's his own man now. But I'll let him know you're coming."

After Nana hung up, Papa uncovered his face and the two of them exchanged a look that seemed to Harlan less joyful than bewildered.

He stepped toward them from the doorway, forgetting that he wore his dusty boots, barely conscious of Katarina at his side. "She asked to talk with me."

"Yes," Nana conceded.

"Why did you say I wasn't available?"

"I thought you wouldn't want to talk."

"You could have given me that choice."

"Harlan, that's not fair," Katarina broke in. "You've been avoiding the phone for the past two days as if it were a bomb. What was Nana to think?"

"Okay," he said, chastened, softening toward his grandmother. "But why did you pretend we hadn't told you about her?"

Nana shook out a napkin and refolded it. "I was being cautious."

"We don't know what she's after," Papa said. "That's why, isn't it, honey? We don't know what sort of person she's become."

Nana pressed the napkin flat with her palm. "It's a terrible thing to say about one's own daughter, but I don't know if I can trust her." She looked up then, distraught. "Papa and I have been hurt by her as much as we ever can be, Harlan. But I couldn't just hand you over without being certain she won't hurt you."

"Besides," Papa said, "isn't it suspicious that she'd phone us on the very day we were fixing to call her? Like she has our place wired or something."

"It does seem strange," Nana said.

"I have an idea why she called," Katarina said. Drawing on what Harlan had told her, she described Aurora's startled response on seeing him in the park a couple of days earlier. "She mistook him for Tommy, just for a second, and that set her wondering about her son. Finally she worked up the courage to do what she had been meaning to do for a long time."

Remembering the photographs of Tommy he'd seen at Teresa's home in Marquette, Harlan admitted that Katarina could be right. He also admitted that if Nana had offered him the phone when Aurora was on the line he would have shied away.

*

The four of them had worked hard since the move to the farm, but never so hard as in the weeks following Aurora's call. Harlan knew his grandparents wanted the place to look as good as possible when Aurora and her family arrived, and so did he. Living on Social Security, veteran's benefits, and meager savings, they might have been poor, as the world measured such things, but they didn't feel poor, and didn't want to appear so.

With Harlan driving the pickup and doing the heavy lifting, Nana and Katarina bought enough furniture from thrift shops and yard sales to fit out the two empty bedrooms, the dining room, and the parlor. It was a motley assortment, yet each item was appealing to the eye, reflecting Nana's flair for design, and all the furnishings looked presentable after some scrubbing and stitching and gluing. Katarina pitched in, as usual, with a strength and endurance that seemed too great for her size. She waxed floors. She scoured the copper-bottomed kitchen pots until they shone. While Buddy circled her as if keeping watch against wolves, she weeded the garden and flowerbeds, swept cobwebs from the springhouse, hung throw rugs on the clothesline and beat them with a broom until the dust quit flying. She and Nana sewed the rest of the curtains, which added strokes of color to the white walls, and they cleaned the house from top to bottom.

Meanwhile, taking care as always to spare Papa's back, Harlan enlisted his help to prune the shrubs, whitewash the porch railings, and level the flagstone path leading to the front steps. They tore out the worn kitchen linoleum, exposing a floor of wide maple boards, which they sanded and sealed, all the while puzzling over why anybody would hide such handsome wood. They refinished the last of the walnut trim in the upstairs rooms and the cherry trim downstairs. They put a fresh coat of black on the woodstove. They framed and hung more of Nana's paintings, from what she jokingly called her art school period, plus two luminous landscapes she had made since taking up her brush again at the farm, and the house began to look like a gallery. Through it all, miracle of miracles, Papa stayed sober.

Harlan was glad of the work, because it kept his mind off Katarina's departure, which was scheduled two days before Aurora's visit. They had talked about postponing her flight, but changing the ticket would cost several hundred dollars, and her mother had arranged a brief visit to Sweden just to see her. As the leave-taking neared, Katarina also seemed glad to keep busy, for she never slacked, no matter how hot the weather. Only in the late afternoons, when the heat was most intense, would she agree to lay down whatever she was doing and go with Harlan to the river.

Not wanting the dog to tag along, Harlan made sure to tether him before they set out. If they were too tired for making love, they still took off their sweaty clothes and waded into the cool water and held one another, limbs entwined, hands gliding over slippery skin. Harlan would lose track of where his body stopped and Katarina's began, lose track of the boundary between flesh and river, between river and air. In that rapture, which lasted a few seconds or a few minutes, he sensed a vast communion that made his ordinary sense of self appear illusory.

After supper, when the sun relented, they ambled over the farm, planning how to make a home on this place, without specifying how they might manage to live here together. Katarina picked out the location for a sauna, below the spring house and next to a pool in the year-round creek that fed into the Red Hawk. In summer they could emerge from the sauna and leap into the stream, and in winter they could roll in the snow. Harlan showed her the stand of maples he meant to groom into a sugarbush and the spot where he would build a shed for boiling sap. He explained how he would thin the woods here and there to release the larger trees, how he would re-lay the tumbled stone walls. They figured out where they could put in a vineyard, where they could build a greenhouse, where they would pen goats and hogs. They spoke of how to move sheep around using portable fences, as they had learned to do from Mr. Winfield, to keep the grass fresh.

Where the highest pasture met the woods, a spot that re-minded them both of the upper pasture at Black Bear Farm, they paced out the boundaries for a snug house, placing stones at the corners. Built of timbers harvested from the woods, it would be just large enough for the two of them and a couple of children. Inside the boundaries of their imagined house, they traced the walls of kitchen, bedrooms, and family room, situating each so as to catch the light of sunrise or sunset or the midday warmth.

Living up here, they could leave the big house for Nana and Papa, and they could enjoy a view down the rolling green hillside to the river. The hill was much smaller than Black Bear Mountain, but the Red Hawk, bordered by creamy sycamores and elegant willows, could hold its own for beauty in comparison with the Mad River.

Harlan knew they were risking even deeper sorrow by investing the landscape with their dreams. But in the face of Katarina's departure, he felt compelled to envision her return. He hoped that the sheer abundance of what they imagined together would overcome her misgivings about America. She seemed equally intent on summoning up a shared future, here on the farm if possible, and if not here then someplace else where they could live close to the land and within reach of his family. With her grandparents gone, her parents divorced, and her mother and brothers working abroad, all that remained of her own family in Sweden was her father, whom she loved, but who, in their occasional phone calls, expressed concern about how his new mistress would react to Katarina. During the last few days before her flight, she spoke often of her affection for Nana and Papa, of her wish to visit Teresa and Rozzie and the granddaughters up in Marquette, of her desire to know Aurora and Martin and Olivia.

Nana and Papa's affection for Katarina had been evident from the moment they met her, but now it was even more obvious, in the way Nana consulted her on everything from yard sale purchases to supper menus, the way Papa asked her views on American politics and the Mideast wars, the way both of them made little offerings to her—a glass of lemonade, a fallen bird's nest, an oatmeal cookie, an arrowhead found in the garden. When Harlan and Katarina returned to the house from an evening ramble, Nana and Papa greeted her with hugs and a flurry of questions, as if she had just returned from a lengthy journey. Only the devoted Buddy, straining at his rope and leaping up to lick her face, showed his feelings more openly.

★

The 31st of July dawned clear and bright, a good day for flying, Harlan imagined. Never having flown, and not knowing how many security hoops Katarina would have to jump through before boarding the plane, he decided they should leave for the airport soon after breakfast even though her flight was scheduled for late morning. He was just as glad of the security hoops, because every day, to judge by the news, the U.S. was goading more and more people into hating America. Fortunately, only the first leg of Katarina's journey, from Cleveland to Chicago, was aboard a U.S. carrier. The rest of the way she would ride on Scandinavian Airlines. He couldn't imagine anybody hating Sweden or the other Scandinavian countries, at least not since the Vikings had quit marauding.

After long hugs on the front porch, Nana and Papa urged Katarina to call when she arrived in Sweden, to write letters, to come back next summer. For once, Buddy was subdued, head lowered, pressing against Katarina's legs, licking her ankles. Harlan observed this parting ceremony as he hoisted her suitcases into the truck. He knew from watching Katarina pack that the only items she had acquired during her sixteen months in America were a few gifts for family and friends, several books, and a clutch of small stones gathered from places where she and Harlan had lived or traveled. She had told him early on that she didn't care to buy things unless she truly needed them, a sentiment he regarded as yet one more reason she was the right woman for him.

Nana and Papa finally let her go, waving as she joined Harlan in the truck. They kept on waving, he could see in the rearview mirror, as the truck rolled down the lane. Katarina sighed, watching the trees and fields slip away behind. He swallowed, but didn't speak, and neither did she, as if the pressure of having too much to say kept them from saying a word. As they had laid out stones to mark the corners of their imagined house, so they had laid plans for the coming year. Having checked airfares, he realized he couldn't afford to visit her in Sweden over Christmas, but one way or another she would return to the farm next summer. She might land an internship at the Swedish consulate or at some nonprofit in Cleveland. If no internship came through, she and Harlan would expand the garden and sell produce at the farmers' market in Kent.

Navigating the dense traffic near the airport, Harlan made three wrong turns before he found his way into the parking garage. He estimated the Ford was two decades older than the next oldest vehicle they walked past on their way into the terminal. The number of luxury sedans and bulbous SUVs astounded him; he didn't know a soul who could buy any of these cars. Katarina insisted on carrying one of her bags, but she let him grab the other, which was one more than she had allowed him to carry when she arrived at Black Bear Farm.

The tumult of people, carts, hucksters, and loudspeaker gabble inside the terminal made Harlan wonder how anyone could bear to work here every day, or bear to work any job that required frequent flying. He'd rather dig postholes. He shuffled alongside Katarina through a sequence of lines, as she disposed of her bags, checked in for her flights, and wound through a maze of roped-off aisles. Eventually they came to a sign forbidding all but ticketed passengers from proceeding any farther, and there they stopped, causing people behind them to grumble about the delay.

Katarina reached up and pulled his face toward hers until their foreheads touched. "I love you," she whispered.

"I love you," he whispered back.

As they kissed, people began shouldering past them.

She pulled away, wiped her cheeks with her palms, and fixed him with her mist-gray eyes. "You should make peace with your mother."

"I don't know if I can."

"She is reaching out. You reach back."

He nodded, biting his lower lip.

More people shouldered past, and a guard approached, looking stern.

"I must go," Katarina said. "Do you say skedaddle?"

"You might, if you're a Swedish girl who's swallowed an American dictionary." He squeezed her tight and planted one more kiss on her smiling lips, and then they drew apart, turned away from one another, and opened an unbearable space that widened with every step.

§ § §

Chapter Sixteen • August 2008

AURORA & HARLAN

WHAT AURORA HAD SET IN MOTION by phoning her parents frightened her more than she was willing to admit, even to Martin. She told him after the call that her mother had sounded conciliatory but wary, offering only a single vague remark about Harlan, divulging nothing of where he was or what he was doing. And her father would not talk on the phone—because he was "overcome," her mother had said, without specifying whether he was overcome by happiness or by fury. Martin pointed out, in his reasonable way, that it must have been disconcerting for her parents to hear from their daughter out of the blue after all these years, so there was no point in reading too much into this brief conversation.

The conversation had not felt brief while Aurora was immersed in it, perhaps because she had built up such a store of questions to ask and news to impart. Yet it had lasted only a few minutes, from the moment when Olivia trotted upstairs for her nap, trailed by Martin, to when he came back down after singing the mandatory three naptime songs. Aurora knew that her parents had moved, for she had been given their number by a gruff man who answered when she dialed the Iron Ore Tavern—now, implausibly, a sushi bar—but she did not know where they had moved, or why. After dialing their new number, hands trembling, she had almost hung up, but her mother answered on the first ring, and the sound of her voice, so familiar, so warm, had constricted Aurora's throat, making words come hard. Most of what she had stored up to say went unsaid.

She hadn't intended to propose a visit but only to establish contact and begin an exchange that might lead, after many tiny steps, to reconciliation. She had imagined their phoning back and forth once a week or so for a while, swapping photographs and stories, gradually knitting together the threads she had unraveled by her leaving. But her father's silence worried her, and her mother's reticence about Harlan worried her even more. It was easy to assume the worst—that her father was drunk or fuming, that Harlan was in trouble or filled with bitterness. Desperate to learn more, she had impulsively suggested a visit, an idea her mother had embraced before Aurora could withdraw it.

At least she had managed to delay the visit until the first Saturday in August—a date, she realized afterwards, that Martin had kept clear of appointments in order to join a group of Quakers and Unitarians in framing a Habitat for Humanity house. This crew amused him, because the Quakers hardly said a word and the Unitarians hardly shut up. Well, they could swing their hammers without him, he had replied amiably when Aurora proposed the trip, but she knew he coveted these rare chances to wield tools himself, instead of merely overseeing the craftsmen who restored his derelict buildings. Never one to pry or push, he had nonetheless welcomed her efforts to reunite with her parents and son. A different husband might have preferred that she ditch Harlan, this offspring of another man. But not Martin. He was a grownup version of the boy who'd rescued Lillian from depression after Yaffa's death and helped Lillian turn a shabby Victorian roominghouse into the showplace where the Zakars now lived. The impulse to mend broken things ran deep in him.

★

On his way back from the airport, Harlan pushed the old Ford harder than he should have, wanting to reach home by the time Katarina landed in Chicago, because she had promised to call during her layover there before the flight to Stockholm. Each time he downshifted for a turn, the transmission grated with the sound of a spoon scraping a pot, and when he swerved onto the river road, only three or four miles from the farm, there was a sudden loud clatter, as if a whole drawer's worth of silverware had been heaved into a steel sink. The engine revved, but the gears were shot, and the truck began to coast. Harlan steered as far onto the shoulder as he could go without running into the ditch, leaving two tires on the blacktop when he rolled to a stop. He cut the ignition, set the brake, lowered his forehead onto the steering wheel and loosed a string of curses, aimed at the fool driver rather than the ancient machine.

Then he set off walking. There was no reason to hurry, especially in this heat, for now he was sure to miss the call from Katarina, who would have taken off again before he reached the farm. Nana would get to hear her voice, and maybe Papa would, too, since he'd invited her to place the call collect. Coming from Papa, such an invitation was as clear a sign of affection as the bouquet of wildflowers Nana had presented to Katarina at breakfast that morning. Every time Harlan imagined he had taken the measure of his grandparents, they surprised him, sometimes with small gestures, such as those flowers, sometimes with grand ones, such as moving to the farm so he could try out his dream of living in the country. It was as though, freed at last from serving customers in the tavern, they were only just now revealing their true capacities. Still, he wondered if the arrival of their long-lost daughter and a cute little granddaughter the day after tomorrow would leave enough space in their hearts for Katarina. He was prepared to like Olivia, and why not Martin, as well, for neither of them had done him any harm; but he didn't know how he should feel about his mother.

He caught himself thinking he would talk it over with Katarina, who had guided him through so many emotional thickets. Her absence threw him off balance, as if half his limbs no longer worked. For a year, now, ever since the dawn last August when she had climbed to the high pasture and lay down beside him and they watched bears feasting on blueberries, he had been unwilling to imagine a life separate from hers.

As though aggravated by his thoughts, his right leg cramped, and he paused to shake it loose. Tar bubbled on the road, releasing its pungent smell, which mixed with the tang of creosote from telephone poles. Through the trees he could see the Red Hawk sliding along, the water glinting like tarnished silver. For a moment he thought of shucking his clothes and taking a dip to cool off, but then a breeze kicked up, swaying the Queen Anne's lace and black-eyed Susans and oxeye daisies along the roadside. There now, even the flowers of the field reminded him of Katarina, for he could see her picking these high-summer blossoms and arranging them in a vase on the kitchen table at Black Bear Farm.

He lifted his cap to let the breeze wash over his simmering brain, ran fingers through his sweaty hair, lowered the cap, and resumed walking. As he neared the farm's gravel drive, he noticed a box turtle starting to cross the pavement, a risky venture even on this little-traveled road. So he picked it up, causing the head and legs to pull in, and carried it to the berm on the far side. Setting it down well away from the blacktop, he studied the swirling orange-and-black pattern of the shell, wondering, as he often did, why so many of nature's productions were gorgeous. If survival were the only goal, surely an ugly shell would do. He watched until the head and legs eased back out and the turtle clambered away through the weeds. Then he ducked into the shade of the lane and passed under the arcade of branches.

★

On the eve of their visit to her parents, Aurora gave Martin a series of reasons for postponing the trip. Olivia had the sniffles. It was a shame for him to miss the chance of working on the Habitat house. Lillian needed help in caring for Solomon. Orders were backing up at the shop. The Volvo was due for an oil change. The weather was too hot.

Martin listened patiently to each excuse, and then he set it aside, all the while continuing to pack his suitcase. Aurora's suitcase, still empty, rested beside his on their four-poster bed. She had already packed up Olivia's things, and all of the food except what needed to stay in the refrigerator overnight. Finally, unable to come up with any convincing reason for delay, she opened her closet and surveyed her clothes, debating whether bright colors or muted ones would best fit the occasion. Should she appear celebratory or penitent? Youthful or mature? The first garment she selected was the fawn-colored pantsuit she had been wearing the day Martin tracked her down in the Greenstar co-op. Maybe it would bring her luck again. Imagining she might be able to help with jobs in her parents' new place, she packed a work shirt and jeans, and then, as a concession to the heat, she added a pair of shorts and a cobalt blue summer dress.

That night, after Martin had fallen asleep, she kept imagining scenarios for the next day, most of them gloomy. How could her parents forgive her? How could Harlan? Would he even be there? Her mother had sent a terse note, confirming the date and giving directions to the farm, but making no mention of Harlan. Aurora couldn't help feeling a sense of foreboding.

A lesser worry about the trip was the prospect of spending six hours in the car with Olivia, who grew restless when strapped into her padded seat even on the hour-long drive to Indianapolis for a visit to the children's museum or zoo. Lillian, who was a wizard at entertaining Olivia, used to go along on those expeditions before Solomon's dementia worsened. Martin had offered to hire a helper to stay with his father during the day, but Lillian wouldn't hear of it, and she refused to consider moving into an assisted living apartment. For now, she coped by taking Solomon along when she ran errands, and by leaving him at an eldercare center when she needed to put in a few hours at the woodshop.

When Lillian and Aurora left the shop in the afternoon, they would often go together to collect Solomon from his daycare and Olivia from hers. The contrast between the old man's lethargy and the child's vitality could not have been more dramatic. Week by week, Aurora could see her father-in-law losing the very powers her daughter was gaining—mobility, balance, bowel control, speech. Now he was the one who wore a diaper and a bib, the one who needed his food cut up into small bites, the one who couldn't form a sentence. This accomplished mathematician, whose name appeared in textbooks, could no longer count to ten, while Olivia could rattle off the numbers, if erratically, and could sing the letters of the alphabet. Even before his precipitous decline, Solomon hadn't known what to do with Olivia. When she crawled into his lap and lifted her face for a smooch, he would pat the top of her head and stare at her as if she were an inscrutable problem. Now, he showed no sign of noticing her, as she played nearby with modeling clay or wooden blocks or stuffed animals. Nor did he appear to recognize Aurora or Martin when they came to visit. Only when he heard Lillian's voice or felt her hand on his face did he perk up, as if she were his one remaining link to the person he used to be.

Growing drowsy, Aurora tried to picture herself as an old woman, bereft of memory, everything familiar having fallen away. Whom would she recognize last of all? Would it be Olivia, grown up by then and perhaps with children of her own? Would it be Martin, assuming he kept his wits after she had lost hers? Or could it even be Harlan? Not likely, she admitted, not likely at all.

*

Harlan steered the Ford while Papa towed it with the Pontiac, snaking along slowly, the chain grinding at the turns, all the way into the farmyard and up onto the repair ramps. The bolts on the transmission housing were seized up, so it took Harlan much of the afternoon and every ounce of his strength to loosen them. There were quite a few places he would rather have spent the afternoon than underneath the truck, but he liked the smell of dirt and grease and the feel of a stubborn bolt finally yielding. He found satisfaction in removing the old transmission, cleaning out the metal shards, and swabbing the housing with a gasoline-soaked rag. Still, he told Papa, who had pulled up a stool to observe the proceedings, it was high time one of them owned a vehicle manufactured in the twenty-first century. Papa remarked that he had never bought a new car, never had enough of the green stuff. He went on to reminisce about the succession of used cars he had owned, and how they had eventually failed. In the trunk of each jalopy in turn he always carried jumper cables, to goose it when it refused to start, and also carried woolen Army blankets, in case it gave up the ghost in winter.

Harlan punctuated Papa's monologue with an occasional grunt, as he strained against the socket wrench or caught a drip of penetrating oil in his eye. The talk never touched on Aurora, which suited Harlan fine. Thinking about her set his mind in a whirl. When Papa exhausted his catalog of delinquent cars, he began to speculate about how far out over the Atlantic Katarina might be by now. When she had called from O'Hare, Nana was the one who answered and did most of the talking, leaving Papa only a minute to say a quick hello and goodbye. He had groused a bit afterwards when he learned that Katarina hadn't called collect, whereupon Nana reminded him that Katarina's cell phone made such a favor unnecessary. Now he grumped to Harlan that young people were getting to be so independent you could hardly do a thing to help them.

"Who's helping me pay tuition?" Harlan muttered from beneath the truck.

"Well, that's mostly what you sent from your wages at the farm. We just put that in a savings account and never touched a dime."

"Still, I wouldn't have enough for tuition without your loan."

"I keep telling you it's not a loan. It's an investment, so you can become a big shot scientist and take care of us in our old age."

"Well, then, who's giving me a place to live? Who's feeding me? Who's raised me up to be the fine young man I am today?"

Papa chuckled. "Humble, too."

Harlan scooted into the daylight and wiped his hands on the rag. "Admit it, now, you and Nana should have given up on me when I was a kid, the way I kept running off."

"Damn right, you scoundrel," Papa said. "You worried us sick. But you came back. That's what counts."

Neither one mentioned Aurora's impending return, but Harlan sensed it looming there between them, like a haze too thick to see through.

★

While Martin was getting Olivia dressed and fed on Saturday morning, Aurora went to the farmers' market to buy corn and peaches, enough to deliver some to Lillian and Solomon, and some to her parents. How odd it was to think of doing something for her parents. Ordinarily, she would have brought Olivia and would have lingered for an hour or more, talking with growers and friends, listening to music, admiring the bounty. But today she hurried from booth to booth, filling her cloth bags not only with peaches and corn but with tomatoes and zucchini, as well, unable to resist their plump, shining forms. She also picked up a honey stick for Olivia, to mollify her for having missed the trip to the market. When Aurora returned home, Olivia accepted the treat with a pout, clinging to her disappointment, but gradually the honey sweetened her temper, and by the time the car was packed she was bouncing with eagerness to go.

Aurora had hoped to dash in at Lillian and Solomon's just long enough to drop off the produce, but Olivia insisted on saying hello to Grammy and Pappy. So all three of them trooped up the front walk, Aurora carrying the bag of veggies and fruit, Martin carrying Olivia. When Lillian failed to answer the doorbell, he pulled out his keys, for now the house was kept locked, day and night, to prevent Solomon from wandering. Martin pushed the door open and called to his mother, but she wouldn't have been able to hear, because the vacuum was roaring upstairs and the television was blaring downstairs.

Olivia slithered to the floor and scampered off toward the TV, which was in the den at the back of the house, and Martin climbed the stairs to let his mother know they had stopped by. Aurora paused at the spinet desk in the hall to tidy up a heap of unopened mail that seemed about to topple. No telling what bills and letters and checks were buried in that mound. There were signs of neglect everywhere—dust bunnies along the baseboards, dried-up zinnias in a vase, a basket of unsorted laundry at the foot of the stairs. She put the zucchini and peaches in the nearly empty refrigerator and cleared a space on the kitchen table for the corn and tomatoes. The table was sticky and so was the floor; the sink was piled high with dishes.

In the den, she found Solomon slumped in his easy chair with Olivia in his lap, both of them watching cartoons. Or at least Olivia was watching, her alert eyes jerking in response to images on the screen, while Solomon's rheumy eyes appeared fixed in their deep sockets. The volume was painfully loud, and seemed even louder when the vacuum suddenly quit. Aurora found the remote control and lowered the sound just as Lillian and Martin entered the room.

"Kindly turn it off," Lillian said, her face drawn, her usually kempt hair in disarray.

Aurora thumbed the remote, wincing at her mother-in-law's obvious discomfort. Olivia fussed when the screen went blank, but Martin swiftly picked her up and shushed her. Solomon began to fidget, whether because the child was gone from his lap or because the colorful shapes had quit dancing, Aurora couldn't tell.

"It's terrible, I know," Lillian said, tucking strands of hair behind each ear, "but it's the only way I've found to keep him in his chair while I do housework. If he roves about, he's liable to hurt himself."

"There's nothing to be ashamed of, Mother," Martin said.

"It *is* shameful. Your father, watching cartoons."

"If you'd let me hire someone to help—"

"When I need help I'll ask for it," she said firmly.

"At least let us give you a hand with the cleaning," Aurora said.

"No, my dear. You have a long trip ahead of you. Run along now. We'll be fine."

"Go drive," Olivia said.

"Yes, honey bear," Lillian said. "You're going to meet your mommy's mommy and daddy. They'll be ever so happy to meet you."

Just then Solomon struggled from his chair and went blundering off toward the kitchen, his scant gray hair jutting out in all directions from his scalp.

"He's hungry," Lillian said. "I'll go feed him. Now shoo. Drive safely. And Aurora, dearest, chin up. Whatever the awkwardness at first, surely your parents will rejoice to see you. I hope your son will be there, too."

*

Harlan set the alarm for two A.M., the hour when Katarina was scheduled to land in Stockholm, but he need not have done so, for in spite of his exhaustion from working on the truck, he lay awake, waiting for her to call. Katarina's father had made it clear that he didn't approve of her having an American boyfriend, so she would try to phone as soon as she got off the plane, before meeting her father outside the security gate.

Glancing at the clock every few minutes, Harlan saw the lighted numerals tick past two, two-thirty, and three. He finally gave in to sleep sometime after three-thirty.

The sun was already up on Friday morning when Papa rousted him from bed and led him, groggy and stumbling, downstairs to the kitchen, where Nana was talking into the phone. "Here he is," she said, handing the receiver to Harlan, who pressed it to his ear and prepared a grin.

"Oh, sweetheart!" Katarina whispered, her voice ragged.

His grin faded. "Where are you?"

"In my father's house."

"What's the matter? You sound scared."

"I do not want him to hear me. When I landed, my phone was dead, and he would not let me use his to call you. No talking with Yankee boys, he said. He blames every American for the war in Iraq and your cowboy president. He would not let Mama come along to the airport. Since she arrived two days ago they have been fighting, and she has moved to a hotel. She is flying back to Jordan on Monday."

A burst of static erased several of her words.

"I missed some of that," Harlan whispered, caught up in her panic.

"I said things got worse when I reached the house. His new mistress is only two years older than I am. She was a class ahead of me in school. She treats me like an intruder. Mama wants me to stay with my brother in London until the term begins."

"You should come here," Harlan said urgently. "Stay with us."

"Sweetheart, don't. I have my studies. You have your studies. It is all arranged."

"But you're miserable."

"It is only a few weeks, and then I will be in a flat in Stockholm, beyond reach of him and his girlfriend. Wait," she whispered, "here he comes. I must go. I love you. Bye."

The dial tone buzzed in Harlan's ear. After setting the receiver in its cradle, he lowered himself to the floor and leaned against the wall. His grandparents were sitting at the table, eyeing him, each with a mug of coffee and a worried expression. He conveyed the gist of what Katarina had told him.

"How despicable," Nana said. "Imagine, a schoolmate of Katarina's!"

"The man needs to keep his pants zipped," Papa said.

"Could alcohol have made him foolish?" Nana wondered. "Those Scandinavians are terrible drinkers."

"Why drag in booze?" Papa countered.

"Because it impairs judgment."

"What's that supposed to mean?"

Leaving them to their spat, Harlan escaped to the back porch, where Buddy stood waiting, eager for a walk. In no mood for company, he clipped the puppy's collar to a leash that was tied to the porch railing. "Not this morning, Buddy boy," he said. Then he stepped down into the yard, barefoot and wearing only what he had slept in, a pair of orange boxer shorts decorated with pictures of endangered frogs, a gift from Katarina. He stood looking down toward the river, the early sun at his back, the dirt warm beneath his feet. Nothing had ever hurt so much as her absence. If she were happy, if she were certain to come back, it would be easier to bear.

A piercing cry shivered down from the sky, scattering his gloom. Stepping gingerly along the flagstone path, he hurried to make sure the chickens were safe in their coop. Canny birds, with fear of hawks coiled in their genes, they were hunkered down in the nesting boxes he had built for them. He went in among them and spoke soothingly, stroking a feathered back here and there. They quivered under his hand.

"Easy, easy," he murmured. "I won't let any redtail get you."

Hoping his grandparents had settled their tiff by now, he turned back toward the kitchen, suddenly hungry. No different from the hawk in that respect, he thought. As he passed the springhouse, he stopped to breathe in the smell of moss and damp stone and to hear the faithful splashing, which did not let up even in this dry season.

★

For the first hour of their drive—Martin at the wheel, as usual, and Aurora in the back seat with Olivia—they refrained from talking about his parents, hoping Olivia would take a morning nap, as she still did some days. They played Jack Haymaker's album of children's songs, which usually quieted her. But Olivia was too keyed up about the trip to close her eyes. She kept chattering away, singing along with the music, rummaging through her bag of books and toys and snacks, making up rhymes, laughing uproariously for no apparent reason except that the world itself struck her as funny. Cheerfulness was her default mood, although on occasion, especially when she was short on sleep, she could see the world as a vale of tears.

Aurora had not said anything to her about Harlan, not knowing how to explain who he was, and so she half expected that Olivia would ask about the son Lillian had mentioned. But apparently the reference had slipped right by her tiny, lovely, seashell ears, for she did not bring it up.

Finally abandoning hopes of a morning nap, Aurora leaned toward the front seat so she could keep her voice low. "What should I tell her about him?"

"About Dad?" Martin replied, turning off the CD.

"No, about Harlan."

"More music!" Olivia cried.

"Not now, sweetie. Daddy and I are trying to talk."

Martin's eyes peered at Aurora from the rearview mirror. "We've been working on different puzzles, Sherlock."

"Yes. Let's start with your father, then."

And so, against the backdrop of Olivia's happy palaver, they discussed Solomon's decline, Lillian's reluctance to accept help, and various strategies for providing care. Although Martin laid out the options with his usual precision, the way he might describe to a client the strategies for restoring a barn, Aurora could hear in his voice an undertone of bafflement, as if here at last was a breakdown he could not undo. This rare note of uncertainty moved her. Studying his profile as he turned to cast words over his shoulder—the curly beard, forthright nose, high forehead, vigorous black hair—she realized how much she had relied on his strength these past several years, as she had slowly gathered strength of her own. At the beginning of their marriage, he had taken the lead in everything, from making love to choosing a car to planning suppers with friends, not because he was domineering but because she mistrusted her own judgment. Having made grievous mistakes in her early years, she dreaded making more. If Martin had not taken the initiative, they would have drifted, like two people in a canoe and neither one paddling. In retrospect, she could see that he had coaxed her along, consulting her, praising her, deferring more and more to her judgment, until she had come to feel an equal partner in their marriage.

Now, in a quandary over how to care for his parents, Martin asked if she would work her magic on Lillian.

"My magic?"

"You've been able to persuade her of things over a cup of tea that I've spent ages trying and failing to get her to do. Like arranging a neurological exam for Dad or charging more for her cabinetry or putting in central air."

The tribute made Aurora smile. "I'll do my best."

Taking advantage of a lull in the grown-up talk to launch into a game, Olivia shouted, "I spy something *blue!*"

Aurora played along, guessing half a dozen things inside and outside the car before she said the obvious: "The sky?"

Olivia squealed with glee. "Yes!"

They took turns, then, spying and guessing, until Olivia decided it was time for a snack. While she ate a handful of raisins, chewing them singly and thoroughly, as if each were a separate treat, Aurora gazed across the flat land. It appeared lonely to her, this expanse of green spread out beneath a cloudless sky, the houses dotted far apart, the clumps of trees. Presently, she noticed a sign for Richmond, which she knew had once been a major stop on the Underground Railroad, but which billboards now identified as the RV capitol of the world. Quite a comedown, in her view. After a few miles they entered Ohio, passing under an arch that spanned the highway. With such a grand portal, you would expect a customs post or a military band, but the only sign of government here was a truck weigh station, which was closed.

Since running away, she had returned to her native state only once before, back when she and Martin, newly married, drove across the northern counties and right through Cleveland on I-90, on their way from Ithaca to Chicago for their honeymoon. She smiled, remembering how excited Martin had been to show her houses designed by Frank Lloyd Wright, towers designed by Louis Sullivan, and other architectural treasures of the Windy City. She hadn't been the most attentive listener, for she was luxuriously drowsy from morning and evening bouts in bed at their suite in the Drake Hotel, and from meal after meal of fancy food.

Martin broke into her reverie by saying, "How old is he?"

Aurora calculated for a moment. "Sixty-four, I believe."

Martin laughed. "Not Dad. Harlan."

Now she laughed. "Oh, he'll be twenty-one in December."

"Have you always kept track of his age?"

"Always. I've probably spooked quite a few boys over the years, staring at them, thinking they were about the age Harlan would be just then."

Hearing the name a third time must have tickled Olivia's curiosity bone, because she suddenly asked, "Who is Harlan?"

Again Martin returned Aurora's gaze in the rearview mirror. He lifted his eyebrows. He must have read in her face a plea for help, because he paused only briefly before announcing, "Harlan is your big brother."

"Brother?" Olivia repeated.

"Yes, Livy bird. Maybe you'll get to meet him this afternoon. Wouldn't that be super?"

It was just like Martin, Aurora thought, to cut through the tangled history surrounding Harlan by stating the essential truth—that Olivia had a grown-up brother. Never mind, for now, how she had acquired one.

★

All night Harlan breathed in Katarina's smell, from the Mount Denali T-shirt that she'd dug from his dresser to use as a summer nightgown and that he'd rooted from the laundry hamper to use as a pillowcase. The mingled fragrance of soap, shampoo, and skin was overpowered, as he awoke on Saturday morning, by the smell of baking—something sweet and fruity, maybe pies or applesauce cake. His mouth watered, and he rolled over to nuzzle Katarina. Not finding her beside him, he imagined she must be in the kitchen with Nana. Then he came full awake, and felt anew the pang of her absence. With the next breath came a spike of anxiety. His mother was coming today.

Sore from having worked until nearly midnight installing a rebuilt transmission in the pickup, he hobbled downstairs and made his way to the kitchen, where he found Nana kneading dough at the counter and Papa at the sink washing green beans in a colander.

"Decided to put in a showing before noon, did you?" Papa said, his voice clear as a bell, as if he'd never touched booze or cigarettes in his life. The spectacle of him at work in the kitchen was about as likely as the sighting of a unicorn grazing on the porch.

Harlan squinted at the clock over the archway into the dining room. "It's a hair past seven."

"Sun's been up for an hour, and hardworking folks have been up longer than that."

"Harlan, don't pay him any mind," Nana said. "He's got no idea how long the sun's been up. He just lumbered in here himself, and only because I bribed him with a promise of cinnamon rolls."

Papa turned from the sink, his big mitts dripping water. "Who's scrubbing these beans, I want to know? Did you ever see cleaner beans in your life?"

"Yes, and who picked them?" Nana countered.

"Well, you've got the limber back and I've got the busted one, which just goes to show who's carried the heavier load around here."

It was the sort of wisecrack that might have gotten Nana's dander up on any other day, but today she laughed.

Harlan could not remember ever seeing them so playful together. But why not, with their daughter on her way? Yawning, he raked a hand along his jaw, the bristles reminding him he needed to shave. "What's that fruity smell?"

"Apple pies. But they're for supper. So is this bread." Nana huffed as she punched the dough.

"You see where we rate, partner?" Papa dumped the beans onto a cutting board and began slicing off the stems. "Everything I try to eat, Nana says, 'That's for Aurora and her family.' A man could just wither away."

"Does he look like he's missed any meals?" Nana reached over and swatted Papa's ample belly, leaving the floury imprint of her hand on the tan swell of his overalls.

"When we do get a few crumbs," Papa said, "we can eat them right off the floor, this place is so clean. The mice are wearing socks so they won't leave tracks and the spiders are waving white flags."

Their gaiety lifted Harlan's spirits. He knew there was a shadow side to their happiness, a residue of grief that would never go away. But this morning only the happiness showed.

"I can help deal with some of those cinnamon rolls," he offered.

"No grub around here unless you work," Papa said.

"They'll be done in five minutes," Nana said, "and you can
have all you want. Scramble some eggs while you're waiting. You
need to eat hearty, because I've got a long list of things for you
to do."

The list was indeed long, from sweeping the front walk and
wiping down the porch railings to hanging one of Nana's latest
paintings in the guest bedroom and turning all the jars on the
canning shelves so their labels showed. He skipped over the instruction to gather eggs, wanting to save them for Olivia. Buddy
kept him company on the outside chores, and flopped down on
the front or back porch with a woebegone look whenever Harlan
went inside. The final item on Nana's list was to haul down from
the attic a cardboard box marked TOYS. He poked around in it
just enough to catch a dose of nostalgia, as he recognized the
scuffed matchbox cars, Lincoln logs, puppets and puzzles, chem-
istry set and baseball glove. He would leave to Nana the task of
deciding which of these playthings might be suitable for a two-
year-old.

By noon, Nana had run out of instructions, except she wanted
him to change into something more presentable than the thread-
bare Levis and oil-stained T-shirt he was wearing. After a shower
and shave, he put on his newest jeans, the denim still dark blue
and stiff, and a yellow button-down shirt Katarina had picked up
at the Goodwill in Ravenna. He rolled the sleeves to his elbows
and scraped grease from under his fingernails. He parted his
thatch of hair in the middle and combed it straight back, feeling the damp ends brush his neck. He had let it grow because
Katarina liked it that way, but if it got any longer he would have
to tie it in a ponytail, the way he'd worn it when he showed up at

Black Bear Farm, and the way Tommy wore his Indian hair in the
photos taken before the Navy scalped him.

Enough of this lollygagging, Harlan thought, frowning at his
reflection in the mirror. If he hurried, he might have just enough
time to finish making a little present for Olivia.

Buddy followed him to the barn, tongue lolling, feet kicking up dust. Bent over the scarred workbench, Harlan set about
fashioning a miniature tool belt from an old harness strap and
leftover pieces of Nana's canvas. While going to fetch the rebuilt
transmission from Youngstown the previous day, he had passed a
toy store, and on the way back he had stopped there and bought
a set of wooden carpenter's tools—kid-size hammer, pliers,
screwdriver, folding ruler, and saw. Now he cut up the canvas to
form loops and pockets, pierced holes in the leather with an awl,
and stitched it all together with a stout needle and upholstery
thread. He had to guess how big around the waist of a two-year-
old might be. Katarina could have told him, he felt certain. He
glanced at Buddy, considering, then ran a tape measure around
the dog's chest, just behind the forelegs.

"Humph. Under all that fluff you're a scrawny pooch. We'll
have to double your chow." Buddy tilted up at him a longsuffer-
ing gaze. "Let's say twenty inches, just to be on the safe side. I can
always punch another hole if it's too big."

When the belt was finished, before fitting each tool into its
pocket or loop, he ran his fingers over the wood, sanding any spot
that felt the least bit rough. As he worked, careful not to smudge
his canary-yellow shirt or sea-blue jeans, he kept listening for the
crunch of tires on gravel.

★

Back in high school, when Aurora's classmates wanted to describe a place as so far out in the sticks that even the word *boon-*

docks failed to convey its remoteness, they would say it was "way to hell and gone." Evidently her parents had moved that deep into the country. As she read aloud her mother's directions, which led them onto ever smaller and bumpier roads, past lunging dogs and rusting trailers and ravines full of junked appliances, Martin finally asked, "Are you sure?"

"That's what it says here." Aurora waved her mother's note, which included an artfully drawn map showing landmarks such as a covered bridge, a barn advertising Mail Pouch Tobacco, a river complete with minuscule fish, and, at the end of the trail, like the treasure on a pirate's map, a tiny house. Aurora feared that the place might be a dump, that her parents had gone broke or lost their health, or both, and had taken refuge in a tarpaper shack in the woods.

Olivia was mercifully asleep at this point, having held out until they reached the Columbus bypass, where she finally succumbed, oblivious to the giant trucks crowding the Volvo like so many boxy elephants. The nap was a blessing, for she might have grown queasy from the twisty roads.

At last they turned onto a narrow blacktop that was supposed to be River Road, according to the map, and there was a bent sign confirming the name. The buckled pavement had been patched here and there, giving it a dappled look, black against gray, like the fur of the snow leopards Aurora had taken Olivia to see when two of those majestic animals were on loan to the Indianapolis Zoo. The recollection made the road seem less desolate. No matter how grim her parents' new abode might be, at least it wouldn't be frequented by drunks—with the exception of her father, unless he had mended his ways. Almost any place would be an improvement on the Iron Ore Tavern.

"Slow down, now," Aurora told Martin. "There should be a driveway up here on the left in a whipstitch."

"A whipstitch?"

"You know—a short distance."

"I never heard that expression."

"Well, you've led a sheltered life." Aurora studied the road ahead. "There'll be a sign."

"A sign saying what, exactly?"

The crabby note was rare for Martin, but she guessed he had earned the right to crabbiness after six hours of driving. Naturally, he had refused to let her take the wheel, even while Olivia was asleep. "It says Blake," she replied.

"As I should have guessed."

Just then the signpost came in view, and sure enough, there was her maiden name incised in gold letters onto a slab of wood that had been jigsawed into the shape of an oak leaf and painted green. Below the leaf dangled another board, this one a rust-colored silhouette of a soaring bird with the words, also incised in gold, RED HAWK FARM. Whether store-bought or homemade, it wasn't a sign you would expect to see out front of a tarpaper shack. Somebody is handy with a router, Aurora thought, and it's unlikely to be Daddy. She caught herself, for she had decided to think of her father as Luther and her mother as Jenny, not as Daddy and Mama. Using their names would provide a buffer, should the reunion turn ugly.

Martin steered onto the gravel drive, which proved to be surprisingly smooth. Still, the change in motion or sound, or maybe just the end of naptime dreams, awakened Olivia, who blinked her eyes open and looked out the window. "Nunnel," she said.

"Yes," Aurora said. "The trees make a tunnel."

After a stretch of shade, the car emerged into full sunlight, ran along between mowed fields, and pulled up before a substantial brick house, two stories high—three, if you counted the dormers—with an inviting porch across the front and a slate roof. Aurora burst out laughing, from surprise and relief. Olivia laughed along with her.

"American foursquare," Martin said, giving the place a once-over through the windshield. "1880s, most likely. The ring-and-diamond pattern on the roof shows a Pennsylvania-German influence. Sandstone lintels and sills. The shutters appear to be original, and also the gingerbread on the porch. Fresh paint on all the trim. From the outside, it looks in remarkably good shape."

"Doggy!" Olivia cried, pointing.

A nimble, black-and-white dog zipped around one side of the house, crouching lower and lower as it approached the car, until its belly nearly scraped the ground. When Martin climbed out, the dog—a puppy, really—flopped onto its back at his feet, begging for a scratch. Martin obliged. Aurora unbuckled Olivia and eased her out of the car on the side opposite the puppy, just in case it took a notion to bite.

The screen door clattered shut. Aurora turned, holding her daughter like a shield, like an offering. There were her parents, noticeably older but unmistakable, hovering on the porch, as if deciding whether to come forward or retreat into the house. Her heart pounded. What if they had invited her here only to reject her? To give her a taste of her own medicine? She very nearly told Martin this was all a mistake, they needed to climb back in the car and go home, but instead she took a few steps toward the house.

The movement seemed to break a spell, for her mother came forward then, crossing the porch and hurrying across the grass, white hair aflutter. Aurora barely had time to balance Olivia on a hip before Jenny seized them both in a bear hug. Small though she was, Jenny rocked the three of them side to side, chanting, "Oh, my girl! Oh, my girl!" Aurora squeezed her eyes shut and gave herself to the embrace.

When Olivia loosed a scared little squeal, Jenny relaxed her hold and stood back, saying, "Luther, will you look at this grown woman! And this darling granddaughter! Can you believe your eyes?"

Blinking hard to clear her vision, Aurora squinted over Jenny's shoulder at her father, now entirely bald except for a gray fringe. As he shuffled closer, she instinctively read his eyes, and was relieved to see they were not inflamed. In fact they were tender, whether on her account or Olivia's, she couldn't tell. Either way, his expression made her intensely happy. Hunched over, he teetered there on his stout legs, the ogre of her childhood now turned into this burly old man in bib overalls.

"Well, for Pete's sake, give them a hug," Jenny said.

Luther obeyed, enveloping Aurora and Olivia in his arms, which felt heavy and soft. He didn't say a word, and neither did Aurora, but Olivia, sandwiched between them, called out, "Where's doggy?"

Luther let them go and stepped back, resting one of his beefy arms across Jenny's shoulders. The hunger in their gaze made Aurora look away, searching for Martin. Just then he came up to shake their hands, and the puppy trotted along beside him. Olivia squirmed to get down, but Aurora set her on the ground only after Luther said, "It's all right. Buddy won't bite anything that's not in his food dish."

"Buddy, Buddy," Olivia echoed, squatting beside the puppy, which once again rolled onto its back to invite a belly scratch.

Jenny asked Martin about the drive, and while he was answering, Aurora looked toward the house, hoping that a face might be peering from one of the windows. Seeing no one there, she turned slowly in a circle, as if she were merely taking note of the barn and outbuildings, the garden and orchard, the flower-bordered yard. About to give up, she heard a scuffing sound, and swung around to see a figure striding from the doorway of the barn, a tall, husky young man in a bright yellow shirt with crow-black hair down over his collar and a chiseled face the color of oiled oak. She felt the skin prickle on her arms and the back of her neck.

The puppy suddenly rolled onto its legs and scooted off toward the young man, and Olivia scooted after.

"Well, there you are, Harlan," Jenny scolded. "Whatever's been keeping you?"

My son, Aurora thought, lapping up the look of him as he bent to lay a hand on the puppy and to grin at Olivia, who had stopped a few feet away from him. My son, my son. Was it possible, this man? Aurora noticed he was holding something in his other hand, a belt of some kind, and then she saw the little wooden tools.

"Harlan?" Olivia said, with a boldness that surprised Aurora.

"That's right."

Olivia took a step closer. "My big brother."

"Well, now." Harlan set the tool belt on the ground and stretched out his brown arm, ropy with muscle below the rolled-up sleeve. "Let me have that paw of yours, to see if we match."

Again, to Aurora's surprise, her daughter walked right up to him and rested her tiny hand in his broad palm.

Jenny, Luther, and Martin watched in silence, as if, like Aurora, they feared that a word from them might interrupt this encounter.

Harlan ran a finger lightly across Olivia's palm. "See that line there?"

Olivia bent close to look, until her black topknot brushed against his. "Yes."

"And see this line on my hand?" When she nodded, he said, "Now don't they look the same to you?"

Olivia beamed up at him. "Yes!"

"That clinches it. I must be your brother—which makes you my sister."

Olivia paused to absorb this. Then she asked, "Why are you big?"

"Because I'm older than you, and I eat my vegetables."

She blinked up at him. "I eat vegetables."

"Good. We've got a whole garden full."

"We bringed corn."

"That's good, too," Harlan said. "You can never have too much corn."

Noticing the tool belt, Olivia drew close to study it. "What is this?"

"A little present for you."

Touching each wooden tool, she recited, "Hammer, saw, ruler, screwdriver, squeezer."

"Some folks say pliers, but squeezer works just as well. Who taught you all those names?"

"Mommy," Olivia said.

Harlan tilted his face and looked squarely at Aurora for the first time, and the shock of his dark gaze felt like a blow to her stomach. She could read nothing there. After a moment, he turned his attention back to Olivia. "I can see this belt's way too big," he said. "But we can fix that. And while we're up near the barn, we can gather some eggs. Did you ever go looking for hen's eggs?"

"We get eggs at market," Olivia said pertly.

"Well, we get ours in the chicken coop. You want to come help?" He stood up, holding the tool belt in one hand and reaching the other hand toward Olivia. She grasped it, and off they went, Buddy scurrying along behind.

Aurora watched them go, dumbfounded. Olivia had never taken so eagerly to anyone on first meeting, least of all a man. And that's what Harlan was. The baby left asleep on the bar had metamorphosed into a man, who spoke in a deep voice and carried himself with confidence and moved with the grace of a snow leopard.

§§§

Chapter Seventeen • August 2008

AURORA & HARLAN

ALL THAT AFTERNOON, EVERY TIME THEY CAME within talking distance, Harlan and Aurora swerved away from one another, as if they were elementary particles carrying the same charge. He avoided the car unloading and the house tour by taking Olivia to the chicken coop. When he and Olivia trooped into the kitchen with their basket of eggs, Aurora left the room by the other door, and when she came downstairs from organizing suitcases, portable crib, and toys in the guest bedroom, Harlan ducked back outside, saying he needed to deal with slugs in the garden. Observing this coming and going from the sink, where she was scrubbing eggs, Jenny urged Aurora to go have a look at the garden and get Harlan to explain about the old-timey tomatoes he was growing, but Aurora decided she needed to brush the chicken feathers out of Olivia's hair. And so it went, right on through supper, when Harlan and Aurora sat at opposite ends of the long harvest table, as far apart as they could get without leaving the dining room entirely. He still wore the stiff denim jeans and yellow shirt, now damp and rumpled from the heat, but she had changed from her traveling clothes into a dark blue summer dress.

During the meal, Aurora busied herself with Olivia, cutting up beans, buttering bread, slicing corn off the cob, spearing morsels of chicken on a fork. Used to feeding herself, Olivia balked at these attentions, wriggling atop the pile of catalogs that served as a booster seat on her chair. Meanwhile, Jenny and Luther asked leading questions of Harlan, but he answered only in monosyllables. He finally perked up when Martin ran a hand across the rich, chocolaty grain of the tabletop and murmured, "Prime chestnut."

"Did you ever see a prettier wood?" Harlan asked. "It was covered up by five coats of paint."

Jenny said cheerily, "Harlan's girlfriend spied this table at a yard sale. She has quite an eye for beauty."

At the mention of a girlfriend, Aurora paused in her feeding of Olivia and looked up just as Harlan bent down to study the worm holes that scrawled across the wood. Before anything more could be said about a girlfriend, Harlan asked Martin if he knew of the research aimed at breeding a blight-resistant variety of chestnut. Martin knew enough to give a thorough answer, root and branch and twigs, for he had visited not only the American Chestnut Foundation farms in Virginia, where such work was going on, but also the Elm Research Institute in New Hampshire, where efforts were underway to rescue another great American tree.

"I thought you restored buildings, not trees," Harlan said.

"I do," Martin replied. "But restoration includes replacing wooden parts that have decayed or burned—banisters, moldings, cabinets, flooring, and so on—and the hardest replacement woods to come by are chestnut and elm."

"When you do find the right material, how do you get the new woodwork to match the old?"

"I give a measured drawing or a sample of the original to my mother, and then she and your mother turn out a replica in their shop. They're marvelous craftsmen—or craftswomen, I should say."

Now it was Aurora's turn to look down just as Harlan looked up. Everyone fell silent, even Olivia, as if they all felt the pressure that was shoving these two apart.

At length, Jenny broke the silence by announcing, "Save room for apple pie."

Luther slapped his belly. "It's about time. I've suffered all day, waiting for that pie. Haven't you, Harlan?"

"I'll eat mine later." Harlan scooted his chair and stood up. "I need to make sure the chickens are tucked in tight."

"I can see to that," Papa offered.

"I said I'll do it."

Martin folded his napkin. "I'll go along, if you don't mind. I'd like to take a look at the barn before we run out of daylight."

"If you want, sure. You can advise me what to do about some squirrely joinery."

"I better go hear this," Luther said. "It sounds like there's more barn repairs in my future." As he rose heavily from the table, pushing upright with his arms as well as his legs, he added, "Now, Olivia, don't you go eating all that pie while we're gone."

"I go, too." Olivia tugged off her bib and scrambled down before Aurora could stop her, and ran to join the three men. The pile of catalogs tumbled to the floor in her wake.

From the dining room windows, the expedition could be seen moving toward the barn, Olivia skipping along between Martin and Harlan, holding each of them by the hand, and Luther limping behind, while the puppy raced in circles around them.

"You go on," Jenny said to Aurora. "I'll clean up here."

"I'd rather stay and help. We haven't had a chance to talk."

Standing there with a stack of dirty plates, Jenny drew in a deep breath. "There seems almost too much to talk about."

"Well, at least we can make a start."

They made a start while doing the dishes. Without discussing who should do what, they quickly fell into a rhythm of work, Jenny putting away the leftovers, Aurora scraping the corncobs and other leavings into the compost bucket, Jenny washing, Aurora drying. By the time the last dish was back in the cupboard, they had touched on most of the high points and a few of the low points in their lives from recent years, but they ventured nowhere close to the moment when Aurora had run away.

"Here," Jenny said, offering Aurora a bottle of lotion. "Rub some of this on your hands, to keep them soft for that baby of yours."

Aurora squirted a dollop into her palm, releasing the fragrance of lilac, and Jenny did the same. Rubbing their hands—"like a pair of raccoons at the creek," Jenny remarked—they moved to the back porch, where they sat on the swing, a few inches apart, idly rocking, their faces toward the lowering sun. The day's heat had broken, but the air was still muggy. Jenny picked up a magazine from the seat to fan herself, and Aurora fluttered the hem of her dress.

"I hope you all don't roast upstairs in that bedroom," Jenny said.

"It's fine, really."

"We hope to put in air-conditioning before next summer. But right now we're tapped out."

"If you need money—"

"No, no. We're fine. We just have to space out our big purchases."

"I didn't mean to imply—"

"That's all right, dear. We're managing."

For a few minutes, the land did all the talking, in the voices of crickets, crows, and splashing water. Then Aurora said, "Your paintings are wonderful."

"Oh, they're just a duffer's attempts."

"No, really. The new ones, from here on the farm, are so full of light. But I've got a soft spot for the pictures that used to hang in the tavern. Sometimes, when nobody was around, I'd study them, imagining I could walk right into those landscapes."

"Now there's a surprise. I never thought you noticed them."

"Oh, yes. When I was little, I'd stand on a chair to get a close-up view of the rivers and mountains. They were about my favorite things in the tavern. Aside from you and—" Aurora hesitated.

"Daddy?" Jenny suggested.

"You and Daddy." The swing rocked a few times, and then Aurora asked, "Has he quit drinking?"

"It's in remission, you might say. Dormant, but not defeated. That's largely Harlan's doing. He keeps your daddy on the straight and narrow, working night and day to fix up this place. I worry what's going to happen when classes begin."

"Harlan's in college?"

"He's starting at Kent State the end of this month."

"Does he know what he wants to study?"

"Biology. He's been curious about nature since he was a boy."

"Starting college," Aurora mused. "It's hard to believe."

"Life goes by like a rocket."

Aurora gave a push to the swing with the toe of her sandal. Her bare legs gleamed as she rocked them slowly, back and forth, as if she was building up energy to say what came out next: "Daddy used to scare me."

"I know it," Jenny said, looking off into the distance.

"He seemed like a giant, when I was a girl. And when he was drinking, the least thing would set him off, and he'd go rampaging around. I used to hide in the linen closet. Do you remember?"

"I remember. I'd leave snacks in there for you to nibble on."

Aurora was silent for a moment. "You did, didn't you? Crackers and raisins and boxes of juice. I hadn't thought of that in ages."

"You were always skin and bones. I tried getting food in you any way I could." Jenny reached over to pat Aurora's thigh, and left her hand resting there. "I'm glad to see you've filled out some. Having a child will do that."

"Having two children."

"Yes, of course. Two children."

Aurora laid her hand on top of Jenny's. Far down the slope, the river, just visible through the trees, appeared to be laminated with copper from the late rays of sunlight. A breeze kicked up, bringing the scent of honeysuckle.

"Do you remember Tommy?" Aurora asked.

"Of course."

"What he looked like, I mean."

"Yes, pretty well."

"Don't you think Harlan looks like him?"

"That's what Tommy's family says."

Aurora pressed her foot to the floor and stopped the swing, staring at Jenny. "How do you know anything about Tommy's family?"

"Harlan hunted them up and went to see them. He knows a lot about you, as well."

"About when I was a girl, you mean?"

"No, no. Right up to a few weeks ago."

"How could he?"

Jenny paused, returning Aurora's stare. "I'd better let him tell you."

Aurora set the swing back in motion, the chain rasping on its hooks in the ceiling. "I don't see much chance of that. He hasn't said boo to me since we arrived."

"And you haven't said boo to him," Jenny pointed out.

"Well, it's hard." Aurora stroked the back of Jenny's hand, releasing a fresh whiff of lilac. "I don't know what to say. I'm sure he hates me."

"He doesn't hate you."

"He has every reason to."

"He doesn't. Believe me. He's not a hating sort of person."

"Mama," Aurora said softly. The word made Jenny loose a puff of air, but she did not speak. "Mama, I need to tell you something. Only you, though. I'm not ready for anybody else to know, especially Harlan."

Jenny quit fanning herself and set the magazine down. "I'm listening."

Aurora continued stroking Jenny's hand. "Remember the night before I ran away?"

"Like it was yesterday."

"Remember how I went for a walk with the baby?"

"Lord, yes. I didn't want you going out there after dark, with every kind of pervert and hoodlum roaming the streets. I begged you to stay in."

In a pinched voice, rushing her words as if to keep them from jamming in her throat, Aurora confessed, "Well, I went down to the lakefront aiming to jump in and drown us both. I would have, too, but right at the end of the pier Harlan woke up and started rooting for milk and my body just turned away from the water and gave him what he wanted. If he'd slept a minute longer he would have slept forever. I came that close."

Jenny had squeezed her eyes shut as she listened. Now she opened them and studied Aurora. "That's why you ran away? To keep from killing your baby?"

"That's why. I was afraid I'd go through with it the next time."

Tears brimmed in Jenny's eyes. "I've always thought you were running away from us because we'd been such rotten parents— from us and that stinking tavern."

"No, no, no." Aurora shuddered. "I loathed the tavern, true enough, but I loved you and Daddy. Look how I trusted you to care for Harlan. You're what kept me alive those next few months—the thought of seeing you again. When I got over wanting to kill myself, I kept meaning to come back. A couple of times I even bought a bus ticket. But then I'd be paralyzed by shame. I couldn't imagine telling you I'd come within a heartbeat of murdering my child." Aurora withdrew her hand from Jenny's and folded her arms across her chest, shivering despite the heat. "Today, when I saw him all grown up, healthy and strong, I could still feel him as a baby, pawing at my breast, intent on staying alive."

Jenny took off her glasses and rubbed the back of a wrist across her eyes. "Why are you finally able to tell me this?"

"For a host of reasons—getting an education, marrying Martin, coming to know his mother. But mainly it's from having Olivia."

"Proving you can take care of her?"

Aurora nodded, biting her lip. "And before I could think of having another baby, I had to get over my fear of men, which ran deep after Tommy. That's why it's taken me so long."

"I can see that," Jenny said. "I suppose raising Harlan was my way of proving I could be a good mother, after I'd failed with you. When he ran away, I thought I'd messed up again, but then he wrote letters, and he came back."

"Don't say you failed with me."

They rocked a while, the swing creaking. Cicadas and katydids joined the crickets to fill the dusk with an amorous buzz, and fireflies began their dance of lights.

Jenny picked up the magazine again and resumed fanning herself. "Martin seems like a gentle soul."

"He is," Aurora said. "I didn't believe men could be that way, trustworthy and kind, until I got to know him. I wish he didn't work so hard. I wish he were less moody. I wish he didn't worry so much about horrors in the world he can't do anything about. But he's a keeper, for sure."

"He must have good parents," Jenny said. "I want to hear all about them."

"You will. You'll hear about everything, in time. And I want to hear about this girlfriend of Harlan's."

"That's another thing I'd better let him tell you. Let me just say he's wild about her, and no wonder."

"It's strange to think of him in love."

"Well, that's where he is, head over heels."

The insect chorus grew louder as darkness gathered. The river had lost its sheen. The soil released a fecund smell, a mixture of decaying vegetation and rank new growth.

Jenny said, "Are you going to tell Harlan what you told me, about that night?"

"Eventually," Aurora answered, "when I get to know him better. When I think there's a chance he'll forgive me. It's hard enough to believe you and Daddy can forgive me."

Turning, Jenny kissed Aurora on the cheek. "Could you imagine Olivia doing anything that would make you give up on her?"

Aurora shook her head emphatically. "No. Never."

"Then you understand why I'll never give up on you."

The sound of voices approached them through the dusk—the expedition returning from the barn. Their shapes were just visible against the paling sky, and there astride the highest set of shoulders, which would have been Harlan's, sat Olivia, arms waving, her voice the loudest, crowing with discoveries.

★

Before dawn on Sunday, so early that nobody else was up, Harlan sat by the kitchen table drinking coffee and eating his way through a quarter of an apple pie. He wore his usual work togs of battered jeans and patch pocket shirt. His chair was pushed back and one of his legs was cocked under him, as if to allow a getaway if the wrong set of footsteps came down the stairs before he finished his breakfast. The steps that did come down barely made a sound, and into the kitchen padded Olivia, dressed in leopard-print pajamas, holding up the tool belt at her waist with one hand and rubbing her eyes with the other.

"Looks like we need another hole in that belt," Harlan whispered to her. "You're a challenge, you know, not having any hips."

Without saying a word, Olivia crawled into his lap, the hammer and saw and other tools clacking softly against one another.

"Lucky me," Harlan said. "I never had hold of a leopard before." He pushed the coffee away, laid down the spoon, and encircled her with his arms. "You don't bite, do you?"

She giggled. "No, silly."

"You still got sand in your eyes?"

She twisted around to look at him. "Sand?"

"The way you're rubbing your eyes."

"Oh." She lowered her hands and pressed the palms against his chest. "Is it morning time?"

"It's getting there."

"Mommy and Daddy sleeping."

"Sawing logs, are they?"

Once more she giggled, setting her tools a-clatter. "Daddy snores. Not Mommy."

"So she can hear you if you wake up in the dark?"

"Yes."

"That must be a comfort." Harlan tried smoothing Olivia's downy hair, which stood out in all directions, charged with static electricity, but it clung to his hand and would not settle. "Do you cry at night sometimes?"

"Sometimes." She toyed with the buttons on his shirt. "Do you cry?"

"Sometimes."

Olivia scrutinized his face, as if she found this hard to believe. Having come to some decision, she reached into his shirt pocket, wiggled her hand around, and then pulled it out with a bit of fluff pinched between finger and thumb. "You have fuzz."

"I store that up for winter, to keep me warm."

She tucked the fluff back into his pocket. "Go see chickens?"

"They're still asleep."

"See Buddy?"

"He's snoozing, too. Out there on the porch, with his legs twitching. Means he's chasing rabbits in his dreams."

"Go see."

Before Olivia could slip down from his lap, Harlan said, "How about some pie?"

"Okay," she said.

With a spoon from the sugar bowl, he scooped up a small bite of syrupy apple and lifted it to her mouth, which opened wide like the beak of a begging chick. "Down the booby hatch," he said, as she swallowed.

"Booby hatch!"

Her laughter masked the sound of approaching footsteps, and Aurora entered the kitchen wearing a green bathrobe, feet bare, hair tousled from sleep. Harlan was pinned to his chair, caught in the midst of hoisting another spoonful to Olivia's lips.

"There you are, munchkin," Aurora said drowsily.

"Mommy!" Olivia called, turning toward her eagerly. "Eating pie."

"So I see. Now don't talk with your mouth full, please." Her cheeks flushed, Aurora said to Harlan, "I hope she didn't wake you," the first words either of them had spoken directly to the other, aside from the pleasantries of hello and good night.

"Oh, no. I've been up. She's just keeping me company."

"Mommy, Buddy chases rabbits."

"In the dark?"

"In dreams. Harlan says."

"Well, then, I'm sure that must be right." Aurora ran both hands through her rebellious hair, combing it with her fingers, but it sprang right back and stood out from her head like a flaming corona. "Is there more of that coffee?"

"Sure," Harlan said. "Help yourself. It's on the stove. Cream's in the fridge. You'll need to get a spoon if you want sugar."

"I take mine black." Aurora brought the pot and a mug to the table. Before pouring her own coffee, she asked Harlan, "Heat yours up?"

He lifted his mug and nodded thanks. "You sound like you've waited tables."

Aurora let herself down on a chair across from him. "Starting at age ten."

"Right. At the good old Iron Ore."

"And a long while after that. If I totaled up my hours, I'd qualify for a Ph.D. in waitressing." Aurora sat looking at him, holding the hot mug in both hands.

Harlan kept his eyes on Olivia, who reached up and rubbed a finger along his jaw. "You're stickery," she said.

"That's because I haven't scraped my whiskers yet this morning."

"Daddy has a beard."

"I noticed that. He looks like an Assyrian king."

"However did you know?" Aurora asked with surprise.

"Know what?"

"That Martin is Assyrian. Or half, anyway. From his father."

"I had no idea," Harlan said. "He just reminds me of those curly-bearded figures in the Assyrian panels at the Cleveland Museum."

"Oh, yes." A smile spread over Aurora's face. "I remember those. Mama used to take me there."

"On Sundays?"

"Only on Sundays."

In a bid to regain Harlan's attention, Olivia toyed with a lock of hair that slipped down over his ear. "You have black hair."

"Same color as yours," Harlan said. "But mine's like straw and yours is like silk."

"Don't pester him, sweetheart," Aurora said.

"She's not pestering me. But if you've had all the pie you want, kiddo, I've got to go do some chores."

"Okay." Olivia slid to the floor, holding onto the tool belt, and ran around the table to climb into Aurora's lap.

"Harlan, it's pitch dark outside. How can you do chores?"

"There's lights in the barn." He stood up and moved to the door of the mudroom.

"Harlan—"

He swung around. "What?"

"Can we talk?"

"What have we just been doing?"

"I mean a real talk."

He filled the doorway, the angles of his face cast into shadows by the overhead light. "Maybe when we don't have an audience."

Aurora cuddled Olivia close. "Little pitchers have big ears, don't they, munchkin?"

"I have *little* ears," Olivia protested.

"You certainly do," Aurora said, kissing one of them. When she looked up again, the doorway was empty.

★

It was full daylight when Harlan returned from the barn, sawdust clinging to the hair on his forearms, the bill of his lumberyard cap tugged low over his eyes. Jenny and Aurora were on the front porch, studying a photo album.

"There's batter left if you want to make yourself some pancakes," Jenny said.

"I filled up on pie," Harlan said.

"So I hear." Jenny turned a page in the album. "We're just looking at pictures of you from when you were a boy."

"Cute little devil, wasn't I?" he said, his tone implying the opposite.

"You were," Aurora insisted.

Harlan sat on the front steps, facing away from them. "Where's Olivia? I need help picking cucumbers."

"She's gone down the lane with Papa and Martin and the puppy, after the newspaper," Jenny said. "They're dawdling, I'm sure. Why don't you show your mother the land? Take her to the woods. Let her see the river."

He stared away down the lane. "Maybe I'll go meet them on their way back."

"No, Harlan," Jenny said forcefully. "Those cucumbers will keep. You take your mother for a walk."

Turning to face them, he pushed up the bill of his cap. "If she wants to go."

"I'd love to," Aurora said.

He studied her briefly. "If you brought any shoes besides those sandals, maybe you ought to put them on. Long pants would be a good idea, too."

"Of course. I'll just be a minute." Aurora stood up and hurried into the house.

As soon as the screen door closed, Jenny fairly hissed at him. "Harlan, you've got to quit being so standoffish. You seem bound and determined to drive her away. You're trying to punish her."

"Maybe," he conceded.

"No maybe about it. You're punishing her. And I want you to stop."

He shifted on the step, and the sandstone gritted beneath his tail bones. "I just don't know how to act. I never had a mother before."

"You've had *me*," she said indignantly, the rims of her spectacles flashing silver in the early light. "Treat her the way you'd treat me."

He watched a swirl of crows settle high in treetops beyond the pasture, their raucous hullabaloo carrying all the way to the porch. Swallows darted in and out of the barn, feeding their second brood of the summer. Far off, a dog was barking, the pitch too low to be Buddy's. "I'll try, Nana," he said.

"Don't just try. Put your heart into it. I didn't raise you to be cruel."

Presently, Aurora emerged from the house wearing running shoes, jeans, and a khaki shirt, with long sleeves rolled up to the elbows. It was similar to Harlan's outfit, except instead of running shoes he wore leather boots, and she didn't wear a cap. Her hair was pulled back and snared in a wooden clasp, from which it had begun to escape.

Harlan slapped his thighs and stood up. "You ready?"

"Let's go," Aurora said. "Oh, and Mama, please ask Martin to keep Livy here at the house until we get back. She'll just monopolize Harlan if she comes after us, and I won't get a word in edgewise."

"She is a little chatterbox, isn't she?" Jenny smiled at them, and then turned the photo album to a new page.

As Harlan and Aurora set off along the path toward the upper pasture, she asked him, "How did you learn to be so good with children?"

"Am I?"

"Judging by how you get along with Olivia, yes. She's always shy around people she doesn't know, but she cottoned on to you right away."

He plucked a stalk of timothy grass from beside the track. "Well, I guess I just remember being a kid myself, what it felt like, what made me happy."

They walked a few paces before she asked, "Were you happy?"

He chewed on the grass stem, and then flung it aside. "Enough. Sure."

A pair of bluejays zoomed across in front of them, one chasing the other, making a ruckus. Harlan stopped to watch, and Aurora stopped to watch him.

"You've been cutting black cherry," she said.

He looked surprised, and then he chuckled, brushing sawdust from his forearms. "You've got a nose for wood."

"Nothing else smells like cherry. What are you making?"

"A fold-up stool for Nana to use when she goes outdoors for painting."

"I'd like to see it."

"Oh, I'd be embarrassed to show you."

"Did you make that sign out by the road?"

"Yes."

"Well, then, I doubt you'd have any reason to be embarrassed."

In the upper pasture, he showed her the stones marking the corners of a house he meant to build there one day. Aurora kept looking at him rather than at the stones or the river valley down below or the green ridges beyond. She watched him closely as he paced out the walls and described where the various rooms would go, and when he had finished, she said, "It's strange, I could have sworn I saw you a few weeks ago in Bloomington, at the park just down the street from our house."

He glanced sideways at her. "You did."

"Really?" She put her hands on her hips. "What on earth were you doing there?"

"Looking for you."

"For me?"

"I was curious. I wondered what you looked like, what your life was like."

She took a moment to absorb this. "But if you knew where I was, why didn't you call me or write me or come to my house?"

"I did go to your house. I parked across the street and saw you pull up in the van from your woodworking business, and watched you and Olivia go indoors."

"You were right *there,* and you didn't let me know?"

"I figured if you wanted me in your life you'd have claimed me long ago."

Aurora's legs seemed to give way, and she sank onto a cornerstone of his imagined house. She stared at the ground. "Harlan, I've wanted you in my life every second from the moment I learned I was carrying a baby."

"You've had a funny way of showing it."

She flinched as if he had struck her, and then she flared up. "All right. I don't expect you to believe me. I can't undo what's been done. But I've come here now, haven't I? Do you want me to turn around and leave?"

He lowered himself onto the grass, maybe to keep from looming over her as he spoke, maybe to atone for the harshness of what he had said. "No, I don't want you to leave."

"I was hoping we could start over, and once we got to know one another, we could work back through all those old hurts."

"I'd like that," he said, looking squarely at her for a moment.

She studied his eyes. "You mean it?"

"That's why I went looking for you. I kept imagining how we'd have this grand reunion, like a mother and son who'd been separated by earthquake or war or some other disaster they wanted to put behind them." Now he turned from her gaze, plucked a pebble from the grass and tossed it downhill. "But when I got there, you looked so happy, I figured I'd just spoil things if I nosed my way in."

"I *am* happy. I love Martin and Olivia, and Martin's parents. I love my work and friends. But in the midst of that good life, there's an emptiness where you should be. I've ached from it all these years. It's like I'm missing a limb, or a whole side of my body."

He straightened his legs and scuffed at the dirt with the heel of one boot. "I know how that feels, like you've been sawed in half." He spread his arms, gesturing at the array of stone markers. "This house I'm planning to build? It's meant for me and a woman I love, and right now she's on the far side of the ocean."

"The woman I saw you with in the park?"

He nodded. "Katarina," he said, and the name loosed a spate of words. "She's the one who discovered where you lived, and where Tommy came from. She went with me to meet his family up in Michigan. She wanted me to call you the minute we found your number, and when we drove to Bloomington, she nearly pushed me out of the truck to go talk with you." He went on to describe the stages of their romance, from Katarina's arrival on the farm in Vermont to her departure for Sweden. He told how she had coaxed him out of his shell; how she spoke four or five languages and knew about as much American slang as he did; how she woke him up to things going on in the world, like wars in the Middle East and climate chaos; how she treated Nana and Papa as if they were her own grandparents; how she pitched in to help bring the farm back to life; how she'd become a part of every plan he had for the future.

"When is she coming back?"

"Next summer, we're hoping. Maybe sooner, if things get real bad with her father, and if she can find the right place over here to study languages." He tipped his head back and groaned. "But I've got to stop talking about her, or I'll tie myself in knots." He stood up then and reached a hand to Aurora. She grasped it and he pulled her up. "You've got some pretty good calluses," he said.

"Not as thick as yours."

"That's because I'm wrestling stone and fence posts and you're doing fine woodworking. Tell me what all you do."

As they walked down the pasture slope and in among the trees, she told him about her woodworking, how she was learning the craft from Lillian but still had much to learn, and she went on to tell about Martin's parents, about her friends, the Quaker meeting, the Farmers' Market, the community chorus she sang in, the volunteer work she did for Middle Way House and Community Kitchen, and about a host of other things. Harlan in turn described his worries about Papa's drinking, his delight over Nana's painting, his plans for studying biology, his hopes of learning how to restore endangered species and damaged land.

She asked him what he'd learned about Tommy's family, and he described Teresa Two Bears, Aunt Rozzie and Uncle Cedar, the three little cousins, and the host of relatives who had come to meet him and Katarina. They were a wild mix of Great Lakes tribes, he said, mainly Ojibwa, with French and Swedish and Lord only knew what else thrown in. They wanted him to go back up there in October for the rice harvest. But he'd be in school by then. Instead, he was going up before classes began, to visit Teresa, who was ailing, and to deliver a painting from Nana as thanks for Teresa's basket, and maybe while he was there he'd get a lesson in fly-fishing from Uncle Cedar.

As he finished telling all of this, they came into the stand of old maples, which prompted him to explain how he meant to create a sugarbush here. He recalled learning from Teresa that the Ojibwa name for sugar maple meant "people tree," because it served the needs of humans in so many ways, not the least of them by providing sweetness. Once he had begun telling Aurora about his visions for the farm, he went on to say where he'd like to put a wind turbine and a bank of solar panels, where he'd build a sauna and dam up a pond, and then he listed everything he hoped to raise on this land, from wine grapes to sheep, a list that ended with children. "Two, maybe," he said.

"Lucky children, to grow up here," Aurora said.

"Katarina would like a girl and a boy, but I'll welcome whatever comes."

When they emerged from the woods onto the riverbank, they scared up a great blue heron, which took off from the shallows with a flailing of its long wings and twiggy legs, like an umbrella turned inside out by a gust of wind. Aurora flapped her arms crazily and laughed, which made Harlan flap and laugh. When he lowered his arms, he draped one of them across her shoulders, and she curled an arm about his waist. They stood that way a long while, watching the current sliding by with a blue ribbon of sky stretched along its back, and then they drew apart and headed up the path toward the house. As they climbed the hill, Harlan kept pulling ahead and Aurora kept falling behind, until he shortened his stride and she lengthened hers and they found a pace that allowed them to walk side by side, and then they eased into talk, the murmur of their voices sounding less like human speech than like tumbling water.

§ § §

Author's Note

"One of the penalties of an ecological education," Aldo Leopold wrote, "is that one lives alone in a world of wounds." A person need not bear this knowledge alone if he has been blessed, as I have, with friends who care deeply about the fate of Earth as a home for life, human and nonhuman. They have helped me to see not only the wounds but also the ways of healing. I am especially grateful to Wendell Berry, Alison Deming, Elizabeth Dodd, John Elder, Robert Finch, Peter Forbes, Buddy Huffaker, Wes Jackson, Hank Lentfer, Barry Lopez, Bill McKibben, Christopher Merrill, Kathleen Dean Moore, Carrie Newcomer, Robert Michael Pyle, James Alexander Thom, Dan Shilling, Helen Whybrow, and Terry Tempest Williams.

I am also grateful to the editors of journals in which earlier versions of chapters from *Divine Animal* first appeared: Gregory Wolfe at *Image*, David Lynn at *The Kenyon Review*, Christian Knoeller at *Midwest Miscellany*, Laurence Goldstein at *The Michigan Quarterly Review*, and David Shields at *Seattle Review*. My recent essays related to themes in *Divine Animal* were welcomed by H. Emerson Blake and Jennifer Sahn at *Orion*, Stephen Corey and Douglas Carlson at *The Georgia Review*, Kerry Temple at *Notre Dame Magazine*, Denis Donoghue at *Daedalus*, and Janet Rabinowitch at Indiana University Press. To these editors and their staffs I give thanks. Among those who read this book while it was in draft form, I wish to thank in particular Patrick Thomas at Milkweed Editions and my agent, John Wright, both of whom offered illuminating insights that proved fruitful as I revised.

My first book appeared in 1973, my most recent one in 2012. During those four decades, I published altogether nineteen books for adults, eight books for children, and one edited anthology. Some of these works appeared from commercial houses—Viking; Morrow; Simon & Schuster; Tor; Franklin Watts; Farrar, Straus & Giroux—some from university presses—Indiana, Illinois, Georgia—some from independent or nonprofit publishers—Beacon, Milkweed, Capra, National Geographic, Wooster Books. Why so many publishers? Partly because I've worked in several different genres, but mainly because editors moved, retired, or were fired; budgets were cut; divisions were shut down; contracts were cancelled; books that still enjoyed steady sales were allowed to go out of print; smaller publishers were bought up by larger ones, which were bought up by international conglomerates, which rarely had any interest in books except as a source of (unlikely) profits in their vast portfolios. My experiences have been typical. These trends affect all authors to a greater or lesser extent.

After starting over from scratch time and again in the search for a publisher, I decided to produce this book myself, a decision made easier by the advent of digital technology. Within the span of my writing life the book as a physical artifact made of ink on paper has been gradually supplanted—some would say, doomed to extinction—by the book as a digital file readable on various electronic devices. While I love books printed on paper, and will continue reading them by preference as long as I live, before publishing *Divine Animal* in this traditional form, I wanted to experiment first with an e-book version that I would be able to give away.

Why give it away? The practical reason is that I earn my living by teaching, not by selling books. In writing *Divine Animal,* I did not set out to produce a commodity for sale; I set out to tell a story, to inhabit the lives of characters who had captured my imagination, to reflect on how things fall apart and how they might be mended. Of course it is perfectly honorable to earn one's living by writing. But that was never my ambition, nor would it have been a realistic one, given my subjects and concerns and style. A deeper reason for giving away the e-book version is to make a small return to the cultural commons, that indispensable source for all creative work, including my own—the commons of language, literature, libraries, schools and colleges, the arts and sciences and all forms of knowledge, as well as countless conversations with fellow seekers and makers.

Producing this ink-and-paper version of *Divine Animal* would not have been possible without the expert eye and generous help of David Wiesenberg, publisher of The Wooster Book Company. For this gift of friendship, I offer thanks.

Whether or not a divine animal carries us through the world, friends and loved ones certainly do. I have named a few of my essential guides in the paragraphs above. My nearest and dearest guide is Ruth Sanders, my wife of more than four decades. Without her company, without her voice, I would long since have wandered lost. When I began work on *Divine Animal,* Ruth and I had one grandchild; when I finished, we had five. They were born into a world less wild, less resilient, and less beautiful than the one into which I was born. They were much in my thoughts as I wrote. For their sake, and for the sake of children everywhere and children yet unborn, I tried in these pages to imagine how we might restore at least some of that wildness, resilience, and beauty.

Scott Russell Sanders was born in Memphis, Tennessee, in 1945. His father came from a family of cotton farmers in Mississippi, his mother from an immigrant doctor's family in Chicago. He spent his early childhood in Tennessee and his school years in Ohio. He studied physics and English at Brown University, graduating in 1967. With the aid of a Marshall Scholarship, he pursued graduate work at Cambridge University, where he completed his Ph.D. in English in 1971. From 1971 until his retirement in 2009, he taught at Indiana University, from 1995 onward as Distinguished Professor of English.

Among his more than twenty books are novels, collections of stories, and works of personal nonfiction, including *Staying Put, Writing from the Center,* and *Hunting for Hope.* His most recent books are *A Private History of Awe,* a coming-of-age memoir, love story, and spiritual testament, and *A Conservationist Manifesto,* his vision of a shift from a culture of consumption to a culture of caretaking. The best of his essays from the past thirty years, plus nine new essays, are collected in *Earth Works,* published in 2012 by Indiana University Press.

Sanders has received the Lannan Literary Award, the Associated Writing Programs Award in Creative Nonfiction, the Great Lakes Book Award, the Kenyon Review Literary Award, the John Burroughs Essay Award, and the Indiana Humanities Award, among other honors. He has received support for his writing from the Lilly Endowment, the Indiana Arts Commission, the

National Endowment for the Arts, and the Guggenheim Foundation. The Society for the Study of Midwestern Literature named him the 2009 winner of the Mark Twain Award; in 2010 he was named the National Winner of the Glick Indiana Authors Award; in 2011 the Fellowship of Southern Writers presented him with the Cecil Woods, Jr. Award in Nonfiction; and in 2012 he was elected to the American Academy of Arts & Sciences.

He is currently at work on a play, a collection of short stories, and a book about the meaning of wealth. His writing examines the human place in nature, the pursuit of social justice, the relation between culture and geography, and the search for a spiritual path. He and his wife, Ruth, a biochemist and musician, have reared two children in their hometown of Bloomington, in the hardwood hill country of Indiana's White River Valley.